ADRIAN

By

PATRICK J. SCHNERCH

This book is a work of fiction. Places, events, and situations in this story are purely fictional. Any resemblance to actual persons, living or dead, is coincidental.

© 2003 by Patrick J. Schnerch. All rights reserved.

No part of this book may be reproduced, stored in a retrieval system, or transmitted by any means, electronic, mechanical, photocopying, recording, or otherwise, without written permission from the author.

ISBN: 1-4107-6362-5 (e-book)
ISBN: 1-4107-6363-3 (Paperback)
ISBN: 1-4107-6364-1 (Dust Jacket)

This book is printed on acid free paper.

1stBooks - rev. 09/30/03

Part One

PATRICK J. SCHNERCH

Chapter One

It was still pretty warm for the first week of September, 2002. Everyone was hustling to work, trying to miss the rush hour traffic. The streets were severely congested in the morning commute. It tended to be a normal Monday morning, even for Matt Ruzo.

"Matt!! Get up; you'll be late for work again!!" Marilyn bellowed from her tiny lungs, trying to wake her slumbering husband.

The 250-pound lump lay in the middle of the bed, not paying attention to his wife of fourteen years.

"Matt!! Get up! It's seven-thirty and Mike will be here any minute!"

Marilyn looked out the south kitchen window and saw Mike pull into the driveway. In a panic she summoned her daughter. "Sweetheart, go wake your father. Mike is here."

Emily raced up the stairs on her mother's command to her parents' bedroom and jumped on the bed where her father was still snoozing.

"Daddy get up. Mike is here!" She giggled and stripped the blankets off this hulk of a man.

He shrivelled up like a penis in forty below weather and said, "O.K. sweetheart, I'm up! I'm up!" Matt dragged his sorry ass into the bathroom for his morning rituals.

Emily raced back down the stairs and bumped into Mike who was standing in the doorway. "I'm sorry Mr. Parsons; I didn't mean to bump into you," she mumbled and lowered her head in a playful pout.

Mike smiled and said," That's o.k. little munchkin; don't worry about it." He then took his right hand and messed up her hair in a friendly manner.

Marilyn warned, "Sweetheart, you should be more careful. Someone can get hurt."

Shamefully Emily said, "Yes mom, I'll be more careful. Oh yeah, Dad's taking a shower. He should be down in a while."

Marilyn asked, "Mike would you like a cup of coffee? Matt will be in there for awhile."

Mike replied, "Yes, Mrs. Ruzo. I would love one. I presume that I will have more than enough time before Matt is ready."

Marilyn said. "Oh Mike. You don't have to call me Mrs. Ruzo; my name is Marilyn. It's been almost a month.

I think it's about time to drop the formalities." She put out her hand in friendship.

Meanwhile, Matt exited the steam-filled bathroom like a shadowy figure in jolly ole England. His wardrobe of the day was piled on the floor at the foot of the bed. He turned to his nightstand and turned on his mobile radio.

He was dressing when he heard the call.

"1L1, 5124, code 10-35 at the Lincoln Apartments at the corner of Davis and East 61st."

As commanded by the distant dispatcher, Matt grabbed the radio and said, "1L1, 10-4, out."

All of a sudden, Matt lit up and moved into high gear. He quickly finished dressing and grabbed his service revolver from the drawer.

At the same time, Mike quickly put down his coffee and thanked Marilyn. He yelled upstairs, "Let's get a move on! We don't want the show to start without us!"

Huffing and puffing Matt replied, "Yeah...I know! I'm ready, let's go!"

Matt raced down the stairs and quickly kissed his wife on the way out. He bellowed. "See you tonight. I love you!"

The two detectives sprinted to the car. Mike did not waste any time. He squealed the tires and raced towards Davis Ave.

Matt hurriedly put the bubble on the roof. From beyond the smoke of the tires and the blaring siren, the two detectives emerged as the city's heroes.

> *This transcript is my gift to God. As strange as the events are that took place in my life, God has it all planned out for me. The forces of good and evil have both been in my heart at one time or another. My eyes were closed, unable to see the evils or the good. My occasional desire for the darkness has broadened my perception on life.*
>
> *I invited God into my heart and he gave me the freedom of choice. He does not use the tricks or traps like Satan does.*

ADRIAN

Have you ever stopped to smell the flowers? Did you ever consider what the phrase really means? Our society doesn't even care about the global genocide of humanity.

We ignore the rape and pillage of nearly every species and natural resource on the planet. We don't have to worry about it now. You can thank yourself and your neighbours for fucking ourselves up the ass!

Another phrase to ponder is," Money is the root of all evil." Duh...that should not be too hard to fathom. Our greed and selfishness are the sole reason for our demise.

Nature takes what it needs to survive and nothing more. Unlike us, we take what we need and exploit the shit of it. We do this in order to make truck loads of money.

The wealthy did not get rich by making moral decisions. The hunger for money and power will be the basis of world destruction. We have to learn to share our resources without greed, so there won't be any evils plaguing our society.

If we could just learn to live within what nature has intended. We would all be rich within our hearts. Use what you need for yourself and your family to survive on in our society. Include the necessities such as food, shelter, and clothing to survive on. Nothing more is needed.

Mix the necessities with love and morality and you will have a rich and happy family who will cherish the good life.

Perhaps, joy will be in their hearts when nature takes back what rightfully belongs to it.

Walk in Central Park and smell the fresh air. Admire the beauty of Long Island and become part of nature. You will be rewarded with the beauty and the astonishment the world offers you.

In other words, "We made our beds, now we have to sleep in them." Nature has no other choice. The only hope there is for nature is to destroy the evils. Humanity will be wiped out of existence. We are the evil. Armageddon is at our doorstep.

We really fucked up, eh? Money and greed is the recipe to fuck ourselves up the ass. Congratulations.

Einstein was at least thinking of the world when he discovered the theory of relativity. Einstein," Every action has an equal and opposite reaction." That relates to everything we do.

There is a consequence for every action we take or ignore. Nurture a flower with love and care and it will bloom with beautiful colour and fragrance. All of this will happen during the cycle that nature allows.

There is the other side of the coin to consider. After driving around in your poorly maintained vehicle, you figure if you do an oil change it will prolong the beater's life by a week or two. Since it's cheaper to do it yourself, you proceed. After a job well done, you are left with a disgusting sludge. You could not have this stuff lying around the house. The kids or the dog could get into it.

Neglecting the proper method of disposal, you look up and down the street to see if anyone is watching.

As you are pouring this shit down the drain system, you feel a slight quiver of guilt.

You quickly shrug off your conscience and become more concerned about getting caught rather than anything else.

Job well done! Now you go in the house and grab a coffee, cigarette and a newspaper. You go to your recliner to relax and catch up on the news. Upon reading the newspaper, you are dumbfounded at the state of the world.

The ocean life is dieing off rapidly from unknown causes. The governments are going to pay millions of dollars for environmental studies. You are disgusted at the paper. You crush your cigarette and take a nap. That's progress! You dumb fuck!

Journal
September 8th, 2000
MADMAN

There were swarms of police cars blocking the streets around the Lincoln Apartments as the detectives pulled up. Matt barked, "Where is it, Paul?"

The uniformed officer replied, "It's upstairs on the second floor, third door on the left, apartment 207."

"I hate these crime scenes; every uniform in New York is up there destroying evidence!" Matt grumbled as he strained to climb the stairs.

"What do we have, Captain?" Matt uttered as he tripped over another uniformed officer.

"We have a female Caucasian, eighteen years old. She has been brutally raped and her head was beaten to a bloody pulp. We are still trying to find out her identity. Hey...Matt. Why is the Special Task Force involved in a routine murder case?"

"It doesn't look routine to me. I think there's a link between this murder and another one that I investigated a couple of years back. This isn't your case anymore. It's mine!"

Matt turned to Mike and said, "Now get these fuck'n clowns out of here and give me a perimeter of four blocks! I want the whole area cordoned off, and run over with a fine tooth coomb! I want all of the notes and evidence in my hands before you leave this apartment! Now go!!!" He sneered as he fired out his orders like a drill sergeant. The uniforms were finally leaving the apartment and the detectives behind.

Mike took a step back, quite surprised by his partner's confidence.

"Hey...I could learn a lot from this guy," he thought to himself. He quickly caught up to his partner's pace.

Matt demanded, "Rookie, come here. I want a state computer search for crime scenes with the same M.O. I want a print team from our department ASAP.

Don't let the coroner touch the body until I take a look first. I want the whole place photographed, and count the rats too! You got it?"

Mike replied, "Got it."

Matt moved to the bedroom where he saw the body. By looking around he could tell there wasn't a struggle. It seemed as if she was cooperating with her killer to avoid getting him angry. Nothing was out of place or disturbed.

Her eighteenth birthday cards on the nightstand were splattered with blood. There were about ten to fifteen splatter marks on the ceiling.

Her face was unrecognizable; her was skull crushed. The body was stripped from the waist down. He saw the groceries by the front door.

The killer must have been waiting for her to open the door before he surprised her. There were no drag marks or upset furniture. However, there was no wallet or ID.

It seemed that the perpetrator had been watching her for awhile, since he knew where the apartment was. This was obviously premeditated and not a random rape. It was carefully planned.

Matt uttered, "You know what, Mike?"

Mike turned around with a puzzled look on his face.

"I bet we don't find a single print or witness on this case."

Mike twisted up his face and said, "Why is that?"

Matt replied, "I saw this before. I just can't place it. There is something that I am missing."

Matt nervously stomped around the body, scratching his head. All of a sudden he blurted out, "That's it! The body! She was fuck'n praying! Look at the fuck'n body! She is in the foetal position. Now, what position would she be in if she were on her knees?"

Mike said, "Probably giving him a blow job."

Matt shook his head and said, "No, I bet the coroner and forensics prove you wrong. Look at her hands. They are clasped together so tight that her knuckles are bruised. Her hands were clasped together when he struck the first blow to the head."

Feeling content, Matt headed to the door and said, "We're finished here. Let everyone else do their job and we will take it from there."

Mike put away his notebook and took one last look around the place. He pondered for a second and said, "Matt, what about the weapon? What was it?"

Matt turned his head back and said, "I already know that. It was a baseball bat."

Mike was really confused now and said, "How the hell do you know it is a baseball bat?"

ADRIAN

Matt grabbed the stairway railing and said, "I already told you. I saw this before."

"Survival of the fittest." We believe that phrase only belongs to the animal kingdom. The belief is that nature is sometimes cruel. It weeds out the weak and ill. It does that so the strong and healthy will mate and continue the species for generations to come.

This eliminates the chance that a species will kill itself out of existence. Only the best will live; all others will die.

Would it be so wrong if human nature would also follow the same path? What if we only allowed the strongest to survive? It used to be that way at one time. Those must have been glorious days. Of course medical science is amazing, but it is also the exploitation of nature.

Greed is the source of this problem. Large drug companies gain billions of dollars in grants for scientific research. At the same time, they line their pockets with silk.

Once a cure or a drug is developed to calm the symptoms of an illness, they soak the governments and the public for billions of dollars more.

This is to feed the greed and is not for a necessity. The CEO'S all agree this is necessary to continue public service. These million dollars a year salary Good Samaritans started off with a good idea. They just don't have to exploit the shit out of us.

When our pets reach the end of their lives, we believe it to be humane to put them to sleep. I believe when done humanely and smothered with love, this can be a very moving experience. Medical treatment would be affordable if we allowed nature to take its course. This would allow the chosen to die in dignity when called.

Eliminate the pain and allow the body and soul to experience the final chapter of life. Medicine would go a lot further with preventative measures against diseases, than change the course of nature. When illness is upon us, nature can be cruel. Death must be accepted as a part of life.

If nature was allowed to continue on its own course, there would be a decrease in our social problems.

Poverty, overcrowded jails, mental illness and most other problems in the world would be easier to handle.

Survival of the fittest would ensure only the strong would survive and mate to strengthen the human race. Governments, industry, and technology all started off as good ideas; it was the greed and money that distracted the ideas from actually helping humanity. Food would be plentiful for everyone, not only the people in developed countries.

The economy would be stable around the world. Everyone in the world would be able to buy a loaf of bread. All people would be rich within their hearts and not in their wallets.

Were we born assholes or did we have to work at it? The time for nature's major correction is upon us. Every evil that we have committed will blow up in our faces. You should have noticed the word "nature" has been frequently used in this journal. Think about what you are reading and replace the word with "God."

Can you see the relationship between the two? This journal was written to help society understand what our actions have done to the world at large.

All you can do now is reflect on the past. This will allow our past sins to surface and allow you to recognize your wrongs. Understand where and when you went wrong in your life.

You must feel the sorrow that you caused to others and God.

When your heart and mind weeps with real tears of guilt, only then can you ask God for forgiveness. You must allow him to replace your sorrow with love.

Journal
September 9th, 2000
MADMAN

Chapter Two

In the waiting room of Belleview sat an unshaven scruffy-looking forty year old. His hygiene was not up to standard - he could be smelled quite readily. He seemed to be the nervous type. He was fidgeting with his hands, unable to sit comfortably in his chair.

His wardrobe was old and tired looking. The man was avoiding visual contact with anyone; his head was basically between his knees staring at the floor. He nervously checked his watch every two minutes as he waited for his appointment.

"Adrian. Hi, my name is Doctor Ken Stuart," the tall clean-shaven man said. "Come this way and we will have a little talk."

Adrian scuffled slowly behind the doctor with his hands in his pockets, staring at the floor. He slumped into the spare chair by the doctor's desk.

Stuart closed the door and took a seat in a large swivel chair. He opened a new file and said. "Well Adrian, I understand your last doctor gave you a diagnosis of manic depression. I like to make my own diagnosis on the first visit, so I will hear from you first. Ok?"

Adrian replied in a low voice, "Ok."

The doctor turned in his chair. "Tell me what is happening right now that have brought you to my office."

Adrian sat up and blurted out rapidly, "These thoughts are spinning around in my head. I can't get them to stop. I can't sleep; the thoughts are racing and spinning out of control. It's like a nightmare, but I am awake.

I can't focus on a single thought; there are multiple thoughts all at once. My head feels cloudy and I'm unable to focus or concentrate.

As you can tell, I am speaking at a hundred words per minute. Things are happening so quickly."

Adrian was running out of breath when he blurted out, "I can't calm down or relax. I am extremely agitated. I've started writing this journal and I just can't stop writing. I've never had this happen before. The words are just pouring out of me without any thought and I write them down."

Adrian pulled out a thick binder and handed it to the doctor. Stuart started thumbing through the journal as Adrian continued. "I could write forever. I never get tired.

I am excited about the journal and I can write for days without stopping. The thoughts just keep coming. I have to keep on writing."

Adrian was closely watching for the doctor's reaction to his masterpiece. Without a blink of an eye, Dr. Stuart handed the binder back to Adrian.

Adrian continued. "I had another episode this week. It usually starts off two or three days prior. I get very agitated.

I feel like I am on pins and needles. This feeling continues until I can't stand it any longer.

I feel so hyper that I have to calm down or I will explode with emotion. Late at night, when my wife was sleeping, I took off towards the nearest bar. From the point that I take the first sip of beer, I know that the episode will continue for the next ten hours or so."

Adrian's recollection continued at a fast pace. "The beer automatically slows down my heart rate, and calms me down a little.

I'm still hyper, but not as bad. At that time, I am no longer in control. I only act on reactions from my current environment."

He took a breath and said, "I feel dead inside, and I continue the evening as if I was a zombie."

Adrian's eyes glared when he said, "Whatever is happening in my surroundings will dictate what my actions will be. When I am in the bars, I like sitting alone. I don't try to mingle with the other patrons. I sit quietly in my corner and watch people."

As the recollection continued, Adrian became more and more hyper. He said, "I can drink all night and not get drunk; I have a very high tolerance to alcohol and medication. I usually drink ten mugs of draft or more and still walk out on my own steam.

I am quite unapproachable when I am in an episode. It does not take much for me to fly into a rage. I will attack anyone who makes the slightest intension of aggression. Once I start, I cannot stop."

ADRIAN

The doctor was carefully listening to Adrian and noticed some familiar signs of mental illness. Adrian stared directly into the doctor's eyes and continued. "After all the bars close, I start to walk the streets and alleys.

I share the same night time air as the druggies, pimps and prostitutes. It is a dangerous thing to do, but I have no fear.

I like the shadows and the darkness that engulfs my soul. I sometimes have the desire for the dark side.

This always happens during an episode. I don't know why I walk the streets till early morning when the rest of the city is awakening from a restful sleep."

Adrian seems to be a little more relaxed now that he was near concluding his story.

He said, "After about ten or so hours of this, I go home and hit the bed. It takes me about three days to recover. I used to cut my body when I had an episode before, but I stopped doing that a couple of years ago. I sometimes become very suicidal."

The doctor had heard enough to make a diagnosis. He said, "Well Adrian, you do have manic depression. However, you are mainly plagued by a character defect which is not treatable by me. You have to do that on your own.

I can treat the manic depression and make life a little easier to handle. But to treat the disassociation problem, you will have to learn how to recognize its onset prior to losing control.

You can take several deep breaths and allow more oxygen into your brain to help clear your mind. Character defects take many years to change. Perhaps the changes will never come. I don't know.

You could have had a tragedy in your life that has triggered this type of problem. That's a whole can of worms, and it is not worth your time to open old wounds."

Dr. Stuart also said, "By looking at your journal, I can tell you suffer from psychotic episodes as well. I can treat that with medication. There are a number of issues that we have to work on in the future. I will give you this prescription and we will make an appointment for next week."

He looked at the calendar and said, "How's next Friday at four?"

Adrian looked at the doctor and replied, "That will be just fine."

The doctor said, "Ok. Adrian, we will see you on the 15th of September at four. It was nice to meet you." Stuart extended his hand to Adrian.

Adrian didn't pay any attention to the intended handshake and shuffled out the door. He was confused and did not know what to make of the doctor's diagnosis.

His thoughts were racing and he was highly agitated. He was so hyper; he knew he had to calm down. He boarded the bus and went off to the red light district. He had to have a drink and he thought he would catch a strip show while he was at it.

He got off the bus at E 79th St. and Davis. He then went towards Foxy Ladies in the middle of the block. He opened the door to the darkened pit where the ladies had their stage. Adrian preferred the upper seats away from the stage and the crowd. There he sat in the shadows, barely in the sight of anyone. The first mug of draft arrived and he impatiently took several large gulps. This immoral place and the nectar seem to calm him down.

The sweating and the shaking hands subsided. The beer tasted so good he just melted into his chair.

The shadows made him comfortable and he ordered another mug of draft. He now turned his attention to the stripper on the stage. He had this emotionless stare that penetrated right through her. She caught his eyes staring and they shared visual contact.

She became startled by the icy stare and quickly turned around to the other patrons of the bar. Without any movement or gestures, Adrian continued to stare at her as she finished her act and left the stage.

Her head made a quick snap back and caught his eyes following her every step to the dressing room. In a panic she quickened her step and entered the room out of sight of Adrian's wild stare. He still sat there, emotionless, slowly sipping his beer.

Without his own knowledge, Adrian slipped into a disassociate state. Not only were his emotions gone, so were his thoughts, morals and soul. He stared at each and every woman who appeared on stage, not taking his eyes off of them for a second.

Beer after beer, the afternoon crowd left and the evening patrons filed in. Adrian still sat in his darkened shadow.

He was still in full sobriety, not being affected by the large amounts of alcohol that he had consumed. This was a manic episode and there was no way of stopping it. He was now out of control. The empty shell of the man just stared, there was no stimulation. He gave off an eerie aura about him. The staff were aware of him, but could not do anything because he did nothing wrong. He just sat there, drinking his beer and staring emotionlessly.

The night continued to the early morning hours and the star performer was about to take to the stage.

Adrian was transfixed on this woman; she was so beautiful. This was the first time that he had some type of emotion in him that day.

He was truly taken back by her show; he was left speechless. She finished her act and moved to the autograph table. Adrian got off his chair and stood in line with a twenty dollar bill.

When he approached the table, Adrian asked, "Will you write anything I want on this napkin for twenty bucks?"

The busty woman replied, "Yes, but I'll give you a poster instead."

Feeling disappointed in her response he said. "Keep the money." Then he turned and moved to his darkened corner.

Last call for drinks was being served, and Adrian was nurturing his beer.

He continuously stared at the beautiful woman by whom he had become enchanted. It was a quarter after two in the morning and the bar lights were turned on so the patrons were aware of the upcoming closing time.

Adrian wasn't going to move until he finished his last beer. The woman whom he adored came and sat down next to him. She asked, "Are you sure you don't want a poster or something?"

Adrian remained emotionless and somewhat unapproachable when he said, "No thanks, you keep the money." He then turned away from her and ignored her.

He was not going to let on that he was weakened by her presence. She then left the table and proceeded to her dressing room.

Adrian was still feeling hyper and full of energy when he finished his beer and left the bar.

Upon entering the streets he noticed that the hookers were out in full strength that night. He walked by them, carefully scanning their sexy bodies.

He was sexually aroused and started to play with himself as he walked the darkened streets. This was not readily noticed by anyone for Adrian had a large hole in his pocket, allowing access to his stiff penis. He gently stroked it as he watched the hookers.

Adrian was now deep within his darkest thoughts, fantasizing about raw and passionate sex.

As he walked, he was propositioned for business several times. Somehow within the darkness, he was still able to make a moral decision and say. "No thanks."

The streets were endless. Soon, the city would awake from its slumber.

As Adrian took a piss in a darkened alley, he noticed a black limousine pull up half a block back. He then turned out of the shadows and sat against the wall on the sidewalk.

He could see from the distance the silhouette of a gorgeous woman getting out of the car. The lights behind her illuminated the voluptuous figure. She then approached him, and Adrian offered her a smoke. To his surprise, it was the same woman with the poster.

She has been following him all night. He did not start a conversation or try to make the woman feel welcome. He just sat there with his cigarette and his icy stare. Not knowing if she was a cop or not, he kept to himself. She finished her cigarette and went back to the limo. The car then pulled away.

Sexual thoughts were eating at his soul; he did not know what to do.

The confusion, hypertension and sexual desires were too much to handle.

He noticed a very pretty young woman on the street corner. He walked up to her and grabbed her hand, sticking it down his pants. She grabbed him. With an explosion of pent up pleasures, he ejaculated all over her petite hand. He turned to her and said, "Thank-you." He then handed her a twenty dollar bill and walked away.

The episode was now over. The sexual release delivered him from his disassociation and Adrian had now joined the living. The episode had depleted all of his energy and he grabbed the next taxi home. There, he would remain in bed for two to three days until he recovered from his ordeal.

The two detectives were approaching the car when Mike asked. "Where did you see that before?"

Matt opened the passenger door and said, "I don't remember. I want to go to the station house and check the records. I want to look at clippings, files or anything that may give us a clue."

Mike popped into the driver's seat, turned to Matt and said, "Don't you ever change your clothes? You wore those same clothes for the last four days."

Being disturbed by the comment, Matt scoured back and said, "It's a clean shirt!

Besides, I'm a cop, not a fashion model like you with your expensive suit and custom Italian shoes! You college brats, all you think about are fashion. You hit the runways and I'll catch the bad guys, thank-you very much!"

Mike sneered and then started the car and moved out towards the station house.

Matt blurted. "Hey...rookie, since we're getting personal. Didn't you just get your detective shield last month?"

Mike was not the least happy about that comment and said, "So what if I did? You have to start somewhere. Even slobs like you were a rookie at one time!"

Matt's eyes peeled back like headlights on high beam; he couldn't believe a rookie would talk like that to a senior officer.

In a sombre voice, he warned Mike. "Be fuck'n careful of what you call me. You could find yourself in a hell of a lot of shit for a comment like that."

Mike now realized how far he could push Matt. Matt wasn't the type to be degraded by a rookie or anyone else for that matter. For the rest of the trip, the two detectives remained silent until they reached the station house.

As they approached the steps to the station, Matt said, "Mike you check out the records and I'll check out the newspapers. That way, we can cover more ground if we split up."

Mike went to records. There he received three stacks of files of suspects that might lead to the closure of this case. Knowing that this would take some time, he grabbed a large black coffee from the vending machine. He then sat down and started reviewing the files.

Meanwhile, Matt was at the micro-fiche, checking out newspaper clips from five years back. He started at January 1997. It was gnawing at him; he knew that MO. It just had to be here! Suddenly, something popped up that Matt recognized. He stood up and yelled. "Mike! I think I got it!"

Mike ran from the records room and took a look at the fiche. The date read, "September 8th, 2000." The headline read, "YOUNG WOMAN BRUTILIZED TO DEATH IN ALLEY."

Matt said, "This is the one. I remember it now. The alley is off Davis Ave. Bob and I were on foot patrol on September 8th when we came across the body.

Her hands were clasped and her knuckles were bruised. We didn't get any prints, but we did manage to get a DNA out of the semen. There was no match to anyone in North America.

Her body was hidden in the shadows and her head was crushed in. The MO is exactly the same as what we found today. The foetal position and everything is the same, including the rape."

Mike scratched his head and said, "Are you sure about this?"

Matt turned around in amazement not believing his ears that someone has questioned him about his job. He snapped, "Sure, I'm fuck'n sure! I wasn't a rookie you know!"

Mike moved back quickly as Matt spun around waiting for another remark. They stood eye to eye for a moment when Mike said, "Maybe we should call it a night. What do you think boss?"

Matt stood back from his aggressive pose and said, "You're right. It's been a long day. Besides, we now know that this guy has killed before. We uncovered enough dirt for one night. Let's pack it in."

Because he was the rookie, Mike shut down the microfiche and put the files away before they left.

He was thinking that he had better watch his step.

Besides, the lieutenant was assessing him on the case so that he could confirm his promotion to detective. If he pushed the old man too far, he might find himself in a uniform so fast it would make his head spin.

This was a special case for the lieutenant. He never did catch the perpetrator back in 2000. It had been a cold case file for two years and now it was starting to warm up. The old man would desperately want to clear this case up.

The two detectives pulled into Matt's driveway and said their farewells. Matt could see Marilyn peeking through the drapes. He waved hello, Marilyn then waved back. After a long day, he shuffled his feet to his front door and opened it.

Cheerfully Marilyn said, "Hi sweetheart. How was your day?"

Matt grabbed a cold beer from the fridge and said. "It was a long day, hon. I do think we are onto something though. Do you remember the cold case file I had a couple of years back?"

Marilyn faced her husband with her hands over her mouth in shock and said, "I sure do. I never saw you so worked up on a case before. You didn't sleep for weeks. Why?"

Matt sat down in his recliner and started taking off his shoes when he explained. "He's back. He struck again on Davis Ave."

Marilyn looked at him with a terrified look on her face and said, "Please Matt! Don't let this happen again. You know what happened two years ago."

Matt put on his slippers and lay back in his chair with his head hung in shame. He mumbled, "I remember."

Marilyn quickly dropped the issue and continued putting the finishing touches on dinner.

Emily pranced up to her father and gave him a kiss on the cheek. "Hi Daddy."

"Hi pumpkin. How was your day?"

Emily explained. "We beat Hoboken in the semi-finals today. The finals are Saturday here in town. Can you come and watch me play?"

Matt smiled and said, "I'll come; I wouldn't miss it for the world."

Emily skipped off to help her mother set the table and replied, "Thanks Daddy. I love you."

Matt smiled and eased back in his chair.

Chapter Three

The design of this journal was mastered to trap the immoral to discover who they really are. If you are reading my journal, be prepared to be brutalized. It is obvious that you never discovered the teachings of your Bible. After reading this, may I suggest that you pick up your Bible and do something for yourself? Learn about yourself and God. Welcome the end of the human race and evil with glory in your hearts.

At birth you were of God's design. Your soul was pure, innocent of any wrongs that surrounded you. Quite likely you were a cute child, since we know God can create miracles. That one could've been one of his finest. This is the purest innocence of your life. From this point on, your choices and the direction you take is yours alone.

At this time, God is in your soul. Your cries are only for the necessities of life. You do not have greed or hatred in your heart. Waa...Mommy, I shit myself. Waa...Mommy, I'm hungry. Waa...Mommy, I need your love. This is basically all you wanted when you were a baby. I honestly hope all of your needs were fulfilled as a child.

This is the time corruption and the wills of man take over the will of God. Actually, the most formative time of your life is between conception and the age of five. During this time you will have the foundation of what you will be like when you become an adult.

Your fears, hates, and love have all been established. You will carry these characteristics with you till the day you die. This can be established by your parents, family, and friends or the surroundings that you are subject to.

You could be an angel or the devil himself. This all depends if there was love, morality, and a family plan. Did your family have faith in God?

These are also the necessities of life. They are just as important as food and water. Without this stability in life.

You may be in the same circle as the dictators and mass murderers of our time. These are the monsters whose table manners were not corrected at the dinner table. Physically you can survive on food and water. To become a real person, you need the whole package.

Even when you were in your mother's womb, you were subject to the evils of this world. Did your mother smoke, drink alcohol or take non-prescription drugs? Did she eat properly, sleep properly and exercise?

Was your mother under stress in her environment? Was your father supporting your mother mentally, emotionally and financially? Did your parents even plan for your birth?

All of these factors have a powerful outcome, depending on what choices your parents made, good or bad. They did have a severe impact on you. The most important factor of all, was there love? Chances are the deck was stacked against you even at the time of conception.

Now that you are already born, new evils enter your world. Permanent conditions already scar you small body. At a hefty four pounds, the doctors race to intensive care with your limp body. They place you in an incubator. Your mother's lifestyle caused you to be born four months early.

Nature knew that your parents didn't deserve a newborn. You also didn't need to enter world without having a decent chance at survival.

You have suffered mild brain damage due to Foetal Alcohol Syndrome. The extent of the damage is not known until you start to develop.

You have lung problems which will plague you for the rest of your life. You barely had a chance to develop properly. Your early birth was caused by a bitter fight between your parents. This happened while both of them were in a drunken stupor mixed with a cocktail of drugs. Tempers flared and your father kicked the shit out of her.

Her body just could not possibly handle the full term. Her body rejected you. After four months of treatment, they released you to your mother's care. Death was at your door several times. However, medical science stepped in and allowed you to live.

Now at home you start to develop new evils. These evils will become your character make up. What will happen to you now, will become you? Your thoughts, emotions and actions for the future have already been planned for you. All of this shit happened in ten months. You're fucked!

This cute innocent little toddler will now learn the standard of living. You won't be exposed to anything else for the next five years.

You will soon accept the mannerisms and character of your parents. The environment will have a severe impact on you.

This could be a healthy, loving environment where you will be taught the best things that life has to offer. The other side could be chaotic, abusive, and selfish. It can actually be a dangerous place to live in.

This could be carried on to your children depending on what path you choose. It is an easy concept. The environment to which you expose your children will have a severe impact on them.

Now we will go back to that ten month old baby. The surroundings around this toddler are not to his best interest. Remember the baby's past? It will have an impact on how this child views the happenings that surround him.

Shortly after arriving home with her new bundle of joy, Karen already notices that something is wrong. The baby is not acknowledging that she is his mother. He seems distant and not responsive to her voice or gestures.

Puzzled at her son's behaviour, she lights her self a cigarette and pours herself a whiskey. She studies the boy who is in the playpen.

From a distance she notices he has limited interest in his surroundings. He has this blank stare that leaves a shiver down her spine. Now, Karen is really rattled and nervously butts out her cigarette. She lights a joint and pours herself another drink. Shaken by her son's icy stare, she screams, "What the fuck is wrong with you, you little shit?"

He doesn't even twitch to Karen's scream. Not a cry or slightest response. This time while pouring her drink, her hands are shaking so much that she spills her sacred nectar. Karen screams a second time. "Fuck off and die!"

She plops down on the couch like a bag of shit, not even realizing that she has a son. Soon the glass is replaced by the bottle. Karen's world is now peaceful as she lies down and quietly passes out.

The same thing happens every day. The house is an absolute mess. Pizza boxes with the stench of rot and a layer of maggots litter the entire house. House cleaning has never entered her mind.

Day after day she shuffles her feet, stirring the garbage enough just so that she doesn't injure herself. Liquor bottles are strewn where ever there was room.

The stench of urine is unmistakeable. Karen has a little problem with her bladder when she is in a drunken state.

This is intensified by another problem of hers, the inability to wash herself or her clothes. Oh yes. The little boy is still alive, but barely. His condition is worsening. He has lost way too much weight. A horrible cough interrupts his gasps for air. A yellow shade to his skin tends to clash with his sunken eyes. One more time, nature is calling for him.

Through the graces of God, he will survive. This was due to a complaint by a neighbour who vomited uncontrollably when she passed Karen's residence. The police, child services and a team of doctors were scrambling to save the little boy's life.

ADRIAN

Journal
September 10th, 2000
MADMAN

The next morning, Mike pulled into Matt's driveway. He was expecting to be late for work like usual.

He knocked on the door and opened it. There is Matt sitting at the kitchen table with a new suit on. He surprisingly looked pretty good.

It was a bit of a shock to see Matt actually sitting up at 7:00 am.

"Good morning Matt."

Matt turned his head toward Mike and said, "Good morning. Grab yourself a cup of coffee and have a seat."

Mike grabbed a coffee and pulled up a chair. "What's on the agenda today?"

Matt replied, "It's going to be a big day today. We have to go back to the station house and finish checking out those records.

I'll start off with reviewing the evidence from back in 2000 and compare it to what we found yesterday.

Then we'll start talking to the neighbours of the deceased and see if anyone heard or seen anything unusual. We will also check the family members to see if she was dating anyone and stuff like that."

Mike nodded his head in agreement and took a sip of his coffee. Emily entered the kitchen with an armload of books and her soccer uniform. "Good morning Mr Parsons." Emily smiled.

Mike smiled back and said, "Good morning munchkin."

Emily turned to her dad and said, "Don't forget about what you promised. You said you would be at the game on Saturday."

Matt smiled and said, "I won't forget, pumpkin."

Marilyn entered the kitchen and said, "Emily, sit at the table and I will get you your breakfast." Emily sat down across from Mike and smiled.

Marilyn turned to Mike and asked, "Would you like another cup of coffee?" Mike looked at Matt with his cup held up, waiting for permission from his boss. Matt shook his head in a negative manner. Mike quickly replied, "No thank-you Mrs. Ruzo."

Matt remarked, "We have to get to the station house a little early this morning. We can grab a coffee when we get there."

Mike got up from his chair and handed the cup to Marilyn and said, "Thank-you for the coffee. I'll see you both tomorrow."

Matt got up and kissed his family good-bye and said, "I'll see you tonight."

The duo then left through the back door and headed off to the station.

As the detectives entered the station house, Mike headed straight for the records department. There he would start from where he had finished last night.

Matt went to his office to check for messages. On his desk was a stack of notes from yesterday's murder, detailing what was discovered at the scene.

There was a preliminary coroner's report and the photos of the apartment on the desk under the heap of messages. Right on top was a report from the print lab. As suspected, no unidentified prints were found in the apartment. Matt headed to the coffee machine for a large black coffee.

He then went to records to check on Mike. Behind these stacks of files a head could be seen bobbing up and down once in a while.

Matt said, "How is it going?"

Looking very discouraged, Mike replied, "I haven't found anything that could give us a break in the case."

Somewhat disgusted at how the case was going so far. Matt replied, "Well, keep it up. Something has to turn up. There are no such things as ghosts." Matt then returned to his own pile.

He pulled out a report form so that he could decipher this mess and have something on the Captain's desk tonight. It had to look all official and shit like that. Matt took a sip of coffee and started jotting notes on a scrap piece of paper. He started off with the evidence they found.

It basically had everything in it except the autopsy report. However, he did have the preliminary report. One thing that he had missed was a semen-stained twenty dollar bill that was under the body.

ADRIAN

Forensics would conduct a much deeper analysis including DNA testing. That won't be ready for about six weeks.

Matt continued writing down the evidence. There was no weapon found, but a preliminary report documented that a blunt object was used to crush the head and face inwards.

The object that police should be looking for was a baseball bat. There were nineteen blows to the head and face of the victim. The rape was vicious and there were tears to the vagina that were excessive. Tears and bruising determined that a rape actually took place. Semen was found and was sent to the lab for DNA Analysis.

Stains were found on the panties and smears on the skirt.

There were bruises on her knuckles from the force of her hands being clasped together while the blows to the head took place.

There was no skin under the fingernails, so it didn't look like much of a struggle took place. The blood splatter patterns showed where the perpetrator was standing at the time of the murder.

It was determined that the man they were looking for was approximately six feet in height and very strong. The apartment was intact with the exception of the missing wallet and ID.

To Matt, this was old news, the exception being the 20 dollar bill which perked his ears a little. It seemed very familiar to him, like he had seen it before. This puzzled him. He decided to go to the evidence room where the evidence of the 2000 murder was already bagged and tagged.

Matt demanded of the clerk, "Give me the stuff on Allison Rachael Chambers."

The clerk said, "Give me a few minutes, Lieutenant. It's near the top shelf."

Matt waited impatiently.

The clerk came back and said, "Here it is Lieutenant. Sign here and you can use that table over there."

Matt took the evidence to the table and spread out the items. Instantly, he found what he was looking for. He found another semen-stained twenty dollar bill. The stain had already been typed by forensics. All they had to do is wait for the DNA on the twenty that they found yesterday. Then they would be able to pin two murders on him. One thing was strange, however. The sample that was taken from the twenty did not match the sample from the rape kit.

She was a hooker; she could've been swimming in the shit. It would be hard to determine if the rapist had left a sample or not; it could've been a customer. Matt blurted out, "Damn!"

The clerk looked up and asked, "Is everything alright, Lieutenant?"

Matt shook his head and said, "Yeah...I'm alright. I hate loose ends!" He put the evidence back into the box and returned it back to the clerk and said, "Thanks."

Matt returned to his cluttered desk. He was disgusted that he had to wait six weeks for the DNA. He needed the answers now. He went through the remainder of the notes and reports and transferred the information to his report for the Captain.

Matt went to the Captain's office and knocked on the door. He heard the Captain say, "Come in." He walked up to the desk.

"Here is the report on yesterday's murder on Davis Ave. sir." He started to turn and move towards the door.

The Captain blurted out, "Not so fast! I want to talk to you. Close the door." Somewhat curious, Matt closed the door.

The Captain thumbed through the report and said, "I understand that yesterday's murder is linked to the Chamber's murder a couple of years ago."

Matt nodded his head in agreement and said, "Yes sir."

"Have a seat, Matt. To tell you the truth, I don't think you can handle a second round with this guy! You do remember what happened last time."

Matt's head hung low for a second and he replied, "Yes, sir. I remember. I can handle this guy!"

The Captain warned, "I'm watching you, Matt. If you can't, I'm going to take you off the case. Do you understand?"

Matt straightened up in his chair and barked, "Yes sir!"

The Captain then pointed to the door and Matt understood the gesture. He closed the door behind him and leaned back against the wall. He was sweating profusely and his hands were shaking.

He was obviously taken back by what had just happened. He had to catch this guy and fast. He decided to speed up the case and flush this guy out.

Chapter Four

It had been twenty-four hours after the episode and Adrian was slowly awakening from an erotic dream. He was sweating and agitated. He took a peek under the sheets and saw that he was extremely aroused.

His fantasy woman was imagined as he slowly comforted himself. The pleasures were erotic, the heat intensified as he awakened and found himself with a mounting pleasure inside of him.

His eyes widened and his body stiffened. It was unbearable and deeply satisfying. He fantasized about the stripper he had met at the bar. Suddenly an explosion of desire soaked the sheets.

Adrian was exhausted by his hyper libido. He lay back to gather his strength. Slowly the energy came back to him and his breathing recovered. This had been going on for a long time. Several times a day, he had to release the uncontrollable pressures of a sexual overdrive.

If he did not control it himself, there was no doubt that a poor unsuspecting woman would find herself in a lot of trouble. It was uncontrollable; this was the only way to stop things before they got out of control.

The episode had tired him for the time being, but he knew that it was still not over. The agitation and the sexual drive were still intact. His strength was regaining faster than normal. Adrian was basically recovered in only two days.

This was something he had never told anyone before, not even a doctor. He was too embarrassed to reveal his deep dark secrets.

Any woman he saw was a potential target, horrifically, even the young ones. This was getting way out of control. Basically, anything with an orifice was not safe when Adrian was at full strength and vigour.

Adrian got out of bed and put on the exact same clothes he had been wearing for the past several days. He went upstairs and found that his wife had left a full pot of coffee on for him before she went to work.

The strain on the relationship had been near breaking point several times already. His outrageous temper kept a distant boundary between the couple.

She was too scared to approach him for she feared that his actions were unpredictable. They had kept this distance from each other for years.

There hadn't been any sexual relationship for the past fifteen years. They didn't even sleep on the same floor.

The love was there. However, the love had an extremely hard time to reach the heart. The trust was questionable; the secrets and the unknown built up those fears. She never questioned his actions or whereabouts. They were both free to do as they will. There was a trust, but a concerned one.

They were two separate entities in the same household. Adrian's self esteem had plummeted to the depths of hell. He was a shell of a man and his love for his wife had been long extinguished. The self destruction had always plagued him. He would likely die a young man.

The risks that he took were tremendous and foolish. He felt that he had already died, and all he had to do was wait for the body to catch up.

A flash of a thought raced into Adrian's mind. He knew what he had to do. He put down his coffee and raced downstairs. He went to the bedside table and scrambled through the drawer. In a panic, he dumped the drawer on to the bed.

To his relief, he found what he was looking for. It was his dad's army pocket knife from World War II. Adrian let out a big sigh and bonded with the knife.

He slowly climbed the stairs. He had desire in his eyes. He then went to the kitchen junk drawer and pulled out a sharpening stone.

With stone and knife in hand, he slowly proceeded to sharpen the knife to its finest edge. This took hours to accomplish. As he was slowly edging the blade, he fell into a disassociated state. He had lost all sense of reality and had deepened into his own little world.

The child has been put in the care of an aunt and uncle. They will ensure that the little boy will receive the best attention available. It is unlikely Karen will see the child any time soon.

Just less than twelve months of age, his ambition and happiness as a baby are absent. He is not progressing at the same speed that an average child his age usually does. He never attempted to stand, he never smiles, and he doesn't even cry. All he ever does is stare into space for hours at a time.

This emotionless child is a great concern to others who are trying to help him. The aunt and uncle have attempted several methods of stimulation, but all has failed. A bond cannot be established, and no one can enter his world.

What do you think will happen to him in another four years and then another five? How could a twelve month old baby be so badly scarred?

At his young age, he doesn't show a will to live. Babies don't think like that. He is too small to feel the effects of his past. Maybe nature should have taken its course. If nature did this, the little guy would avoid all the shit that is yet to happen.

Nature did not intend this to happen to the innocent - we did! Our black hearts interfered when God was going to take him to a better place. Now that he lives, what do you think are his chances to grow and become a respectable member of society? God knows a lot more about him than we do. We still repeat our mistakes hundreds of times each day.

Yeah...I know you don't believe in God. Is God just a belief that artificially feeds morals and love into our hearts? If so, why not believe? People believe so they can enrich themselves and become better people.

Even artificial belief is better than thinking that we are superior. If those writings are not to be believed word for word, then read between the lines and believe in the teachings.

The laws of nature are basically what the Bible is all about and nothing more. They are interesting short *stories that reflect the consequences that occur due to our greed and selfishness. They illustrate very cleverly to respect and love everyone and everything, including our selves.*

That shouldn't be that difficult for you to grasp. So, why can't you believe? It seems that if we did, it would do us a lot more good than harm. It doesn't matter who wrote the scriptures or if the stories are fictional. It doesn't matter.

What is important is if a man rapes and murders a woman.

We can't tolerate shit like that any more. The best way to accomplish better behaviour is through education. The text is your Bible.

*Journal
September 11th, 2000
MADMAN*

Matt took a couple of deep breaths to regain his composure and went to the record room to see Mike. Matt asked, "Have you found anything yet?"

From behind the mountains of files a muffled voice said, "Nope, nothing yet."

Looking depressed, Matt said, "Put that stuff away; we have to try a new approach. We have to step up the investigation and make things happen. We are wasting our time here."

Looking satisfied with the order, Mike quickly put the files back in their proper place. Matt went back to his office while Mike finished putting the files away. He knew he had a first name on a piece of paper somewhere. He hurried through the pile and found the paper.

"Not bad," Matt mumbled to himself. The note had the full name of the deceased. It looked like the uniforms did a pretty good job. Sara Jessica Parker; she was also a prostitute. Well, at least the detectives had something to go on when they checked the neighbourhood.

Mike knocked on the open door and said, "Ready?"

Matt looked up and said, "Yeah...Let's hit her apartment building first."

So off they went, back to the Lincoln Apartments. As they were driving along Davis Ave., they came across a police barricade. They parked the car on the other side of the street and proceeded to the cordoned-off area.

Matt went around the corner into the alley and saw that another woman had been murdered. Same MO. He was furious and yelled, "Why wasn't I told about this? This is my fuck'n case!!"

Matt took a closer look at the body and saw a twenty dollar bill lying beside her.

He continued screaming. "Where is your fuck'n supervisor? I don't see a God damn supervisor! Let me tell all of you guys, heads are going to fuck'n roll on this one!

You are tramping all over evidence without any direction from a superior officer! I am the superior officer of this case. I want a list of names of every officer on this scene. You will all be severely reprimanded!"

Matt was clearing his throat when he said, "Mike, get all the names and stories of every officer here. I want to know why I wasn't notified!"

Now that the officers were supremely reprimanded, they were cautious that they wouldn't set the old man off again.

Matt then went to examine the body more closely. Everything was exactly the same. There was no wallet or ID.

The head was basically missing; the bruises on the knuckles were visible. Things were so similar! This was the exact spot he had found the first victim two years ago.

Matt ordered, "Mike, make sure forensics, the photographer and the coroner were called. I don't want any more screw-ups!"

Mike was busily reviewing the officers and followed the other demands.

Matt ordered, "Hey...you! I want to see yellow tape in a four-block area of this site. You and your men will conduct a full scale ground search of every square inch of this place. Don't forget to check all of the neighbours in case they heard or saw something."

The officer snapped his heels and blurted out, "Yes sir!" He then ran off to gather the other officers.

Finally, the Calvary arrived. The experts were here to do their job. Straggling in behind was the Lieutenant who should have been on the scene.

Matt didn't miss a beat. He caught the officer right dead in his tracks. "Get the fuck over here, Lieutenant!! I don't give a shit where you were. I'll get the details later, when I recommend that you get busted down to sergeant. This is your last duty as an officer! Now, I want you to take over here. I have already set everything up for you. All you have to do now is stand there and look pretty."

The oncoming officer knew he was going to get shit. He had no idea that God was going to pay him a visit.

Mike finished up with the details and met up with Matt. Mike stated, "I got the information you wanted, sir. It seems to be they were covering the Lieutenant's ass because he tied on a heavy one last night."

Matt said, "Thanks. You can call that asshole sergeant from now on. We're finished here. Let's get back to the car."

They crossed the street and got in the car.

Matt gets on the radio. "All units, this is 1L1.

I want all the Johns picked up and processed between E 61st and E 95th St. I want prints, the whole works, and you can let them go when you are finished with them. You will do this until I give the order to stop. Double the patrols in the area, I'll be watching. Out."

Matt put the transmitter back in the cradle and said, "Now that everything is taken care of here, we'll go to the apartment. When we get there, you take the third floor and I'll take the second. Use standard procedure and all that rot."

Mike nodded his head and said, "Ok."

Mike could sense the urgency of catching this guy. Matt looked a bit up tight about something.

Mike could see that Matt was still visibly shaken. They pulled up to the apartments and Mike asked. "Is everything alright?"

"Fine, everything is fine."

They both got out of the car and moved towards the apartment door.

Mike opened the door for Matt and went to the stairwell. "What kind of guy would do such a thing?" he asked.

Matt gasped and said, "I don't know yet, but I'm going to find out."

Mike proceeded to the third floor, where Matt stopped to catch his breath on the second. The questioning of the neighbours took all afternoon till early evening. No one had heard a scream or a disturbance of any sort. The two finished up at the apartment and went back to the station, disappointed.

Matt went to his office and found an envelope with his rank and name on it. There was no stamp or postage marks on it, so that meant it was hand-delivered. Matt opened the note and his eyes widened.

> Dear Matt Ruzo,
> I watched the news today, and it said that you are on the Lincoln Apartment case. It's been two long years. I missed you, Matt. How are Marilyn and your sweetheart, Emily? I understand that Emily has a soccer final on Saturday. Will I see you there?
> I guess you are at a dead end again, eh Matt. You might as well give it up before you start. You don't have the guts it will take to get me. You are too soft, Matt. Maybe I'll meet your protégé. Mike Parsons is a little inexperienced to handle this case, don't you think? Anyway Matt, I have a date tonight. I'll talk to you soon.
>
> See you at the game!
> MADMAN

"Mike!! Get the fuck in here!!"

Mike came running into the office and said, "Matt!! What the fuck is wrong with you?"

Matt replied anxiously, "The murderer wrote me a fuck'n note!! There is going to be another murder tonight. You and I are working overtime; we are hitting the streets ourselves.

We are going to hit every bar, every dump we can find. We are not going to let this bastard get away from us this time.

I want so many cops on the street, that it will match the hooker population one to one! Don't just stand there! Get the fuck'n word out!"

Mike stood to attention and barked, "Yes sir!"

Matt nervously picked up the telephone receiver and dialled home. "Hi sweetie, can you call your Mom to the phone?"

He could hear Emily yell in the background, "Mom!! Dad's on the phone!!"

Matt waited a few minutes. "Hello," Marilyn answered. Matt said anxiously. "Hi hon. I'm putting two cars at the house tonight and two officers inside."

Marilyn replied, "Oh...Matt. It's happening again, isn't it?"

Matt replied sombrely, "I don't know. I'm just not taking any chances. Mike and I are working late tonight. I don't know when I will be home."

Somewhat shaken, Marilyn assured Matt that they will be alright. Marilyn spoke softly into the receiver. "Please be careful, hon. I love you."

Matt acknowledged. "I love you too. I'll be careful. Good night."

Matt got on the radio and dispatched two cars and extra officers to his home address. He then bagged and tagged the note and envelope for evidence. He then went down to the Desk Sergeant and asked, "Who dropped off this note?"

The Sergeant replied, "Some little kid. I couldn't get a name out of him. He just took off."

Matt mumbled, "Messenger."

Mike came back and reported to Matt, "All the troops are out in full force, Lieutenant."

Matt replied, "Thanks Mike. We will grab a bite to eat first then we'll hit the streets."

Mike said, "That sounds good to me. I'm starved. What do you feel like having?"

Matt's stomach was grumbling and he said, "I don't know. Maybe we should try Chinese."

Mike looked excited as he opened the station door and said, "It sounds good to me."

Adrian got off the bus at E 95th St. and Davis. He crossed the street and started walking down the strip. He didn't get any further than fifteen steps before he was stopped by a couple of foot patrol officers.

Officer Hammond asked, "Sir, where are you off to tonight?"

ADRIAN

Adrian looked very nervous and started to sweat when he said, "I'm just off to the bars for a few drinks and I'm not driving."

Officer Hammond noticed how tense this man was and asked, "Sir, can I see you're ID?"

Adrian fumbled for his wallet and it fell out of his back pocket. The two officers stared Adrian down as he bent over to pick up his wallet.

"Why are you so nervous? Do you know something that we should know about?"

Stuttering and spitting Adrian blurted, "No...No...I didn't do anything wrong. I just want a couple of beers."

Adrian finally got his ID out and handed it to the officer. Hammond wrote down Adrian's name, address and phone number. The officer warned Adrian, "You better keep cool tonight Mr Eisner. I better not see too much of you tonight."

Adrian took back his ID and fumbled trying to get the card back into the wallet. "No sir, I'll be good. I promise."

Officer Hammond tipped his hat and said, "Ok sir, you can leave now."

Adrian quickly spun around and hit the next bar he saw. It was the "Golden Goose," a fairly rough type of bar. Adrian went to the self serve and ordered a jug of draft and one mug. He looked over the haze of smoke to find a dark little corner. He found a perfect spot in the back by the exit doors.

Trembling, Adrian poured himself a beer and lit a cigarette. With a deep inhale and a large sip of beer, he eased into the chair. Almost instantly, he felt much more at ease. This was the atmosphere that made him comfortable.

Taking a couple more sips, he started to scan the bar to see if he could find anything interesting. He could see the whole bar from where he was sitting. He started to watch the other patrons.

Slowly he scanned the bar. He didn't see anything of interest at the time. He just stared down at his burning cigarette and fell into a disassociate state. Reality was behind him now. The bar looked much different now.

He could see a couple of beauties in halter tops playing pool. He stared at their breasts as they bent over to take a shot. He carefully scanned their tight asses as they bent over.

He fantasized about spreading them out on the pool table and giving it to them.

Adrian was in his world where dreams come true. He sat in his darkened corner, motionless. He stared them down as if they were his prey.

He was so focused on them that nothing else really mattered. It had been some time now and Adrian ordered his second jug of draft. The women had left the bar an hour ago.

From across the bar, Adrian could see the two officers who had stopped him before at the entrance.

They stood there for a few moments and the female officer pointed to Adrian's table. They then started to come his way.

Adrian had had enough of their shit.

He got up and left through the back door into the alley. From there, he stayed in the shadows.

He waited a few minutes and then he went to the next bar. Adrian thought to himself, "G-Spot, that's a good name!" So in he went. To his surprise, it was a three-stage strip bar. He was shaken out of his disassociate state by fleeing the police. Certain things awakened him. Adrenalin was one of those things.

Again, he went into the darkened corner by the back door. He could basically remain out of sight in here. He ordered a mug of draft and lit a cigarette. He liked this bar much better anyway. Hoping for a quiet evening, his beer arrived and he left a healthy tip.

The lights were dim with the exception of the spot lights on the stages. Here in the shadows was his comfort zone. He stared upon the first stage, which was closest to him. He sipped his beer and leaned back into the chair.

Slowly the reality drained out of Adrian and his world was now present. The women were beautiful and his dreams were erotic. His icy stare made contact with the woman on the stage and she smiled. Emotionless, he stared back.

Beer after beer, Adrian pierces every stripper's soul. Some of them could feel his presence and avoided all visual contact. His soul was cold and dark, and no one could penetrate him now.

Strutting from the dressing room was a long-legged beauty. It didn't take long before he recognized her. It was the same stripper he saw a couple of nights ago.

ADRIAN

As she walked by to enter the stage, she turned her head to Adrian and winked. She stood on stage waiting for her cue. The music rang out and she exploded into motion. She danced with vigour and passion.

She was extremely exotic and pleasing to the eyes and groin. Her every movement was beautifully choreographed and precise.

The blonde highlights in her hair were very seducing. Adrian was now transformed into her world. Her movements had put him under her control. The act ended with a clash of excitement. However, Adrian still did not show any emotion.

She walked off the stage and walked toward the dressing room when she flashed Adrian. She then turned her head and smiled. He was impressed.

She didn't know how dangerous it was to make contact with him. The shows continued and Adrian kept on drinking.

From the corner of his eye he could see the same two officers and two plain clothes detectives at the entrance. Suddenly, some one grabbed his hand and raced to the sound room.

"Stay quiet, you'll be safe here," the mysterious woman said.

Even though the room was darkened, he knew who this woman was. It was the stripper he had just finished watching. Adrian was puzzled and said, "I've got two questions for you. Who the fuck are you? Why are you helping me?"

The stripper replied, "I'll tell you when the time is right. As for now, I have to get rid of some cops." She left the room and walked towards the detectives.

"Hello officer, my name is Trixie. How may I entertain you?"

Matt said, "Your waitress said a scruffy person, about five feet ten inches, wearing a baseball hat was in here."

Trixie replied, "He was here, alright. He had a bit of a stench to him. We asked him to leave."

Mike asked, "Did he do anything wrong?"

Trixie said, "Hell no, he just stank. It's bad for business, you know."

The detectives agreed and thanked her for the help. Matt called the officers back to the entrance and they left.

Trixie went back to the sound room and summoned Adrian to come out. She grabbed him by his hand and led him back to his own table.

"Have a seat. I'll grab you another beer, on the house."

Adrian sat down and lit a cigarette. Trixie came back with a mug of draft for him and a gin and tonic for herself.

Victoriously, Trixie raised her glass for a toast and said, "Here you go sport, cheers."

Adrian actually smiled and said, "Thanks."

She sat down across from him and said, "They call me Trixie. What do they call you?"

"My name is Adrian."

"Well Adrian, I think you should stay here for the night."

Startled, Adrian said, "I can't do that! I have to go home to my wife!"

Trixie calmed him down and said, "Relax; you can call her from here. Let her know that you are alright, and that you have a couple of things to settle."

Adrian had a worried look on his face.

Trixie said, "Trust me, you'll be alright."

She got up from the table and said, "Stay here; the drinks are on the house. I've got to get ready for my act. I'll talk to you later."

This was very strange to Adrian and he wasn't sure what he should do.

For the time being, he ordered a jug of draft and sat back. As Adrian watched the show, he deepened into a disassociate state. He lit a cigarette, stared at it and butted it out onto the temple area of his head. He was trying to ground himself from falling deeper into his trance. Perhaps, he could shock himself out of it.

He lit another cigarette and went to the men's room. He entered a stall and closed the door. He pulled the knife out of his pocket and opened it. Without any thought, his shirt was lifted up. With a quick vicious flash of the blade, Adrian crumpled over with satisfaction. He recovered from the deep wound. Again, there was another flash of the blade. Blood was now running uncontrollably, spilling onto the floor. Feeling relieved, he tucked in his shirt and did up his coat so that no one would notice that he was bleeding.

ADRIAN

Before leaving the washroom, he stuffed several paper towels down his shirt. This was to prevent the blood from spilling onto the floor or on the table in the bar.

Temporarily relieved from the disassociate state, Adrian went back to his table. He rejoined his beer and lit a cigarette. The relief was overwhelming; there was never any pain at all. The pleasure was immeasurable. Adrian sat in his corner, fully satisfied.

The night was still early and the detectives were still checking out the bars for possible suspects in the murders.

Matt put out a full scale drag net tonight; he wasn't going to let this bastard do it again and get away.

As they left another bar, Mike pointed his finger and said, "Isn't that Frank Azario's limo in front of the G-Spot? I wonder what he is up to tonight."

Matt turned back to look and replied, "That's his limo, alright. He owns every building and hooker on this street. Why shouldn't he be here? He must be checking out the business."

Mike looked puzzled and asked, "Aren't we going to check this guy out?"

Matt replied, "Nah, he's a business man. He's not our killer. He has too much money invested in this. He won't throw it all away."

Something was bugging Mike and he said, "I think I'll check it out."

The two detectives turned around and went back to the G-Spot. Mike walked in with Matt close behind. They slowly start scanning the bar for Azario.

Mike yelled to Matt over the loud music, "I can't see Azario anywhere."

Matt yelled back, "Keep looking."

Adrian caught a glimpse of the two detectives and slowly turned away from them and moved toward the rear exit. Trying not to raise suspicion, he left the bar unnoticed.

Mike and Matt walked to the corner where Adrian was sitting not more than thirty seconds ago. Matt stopped the waitress and asked, "Did you see Azario tonight?"

The waitress shook her head and said, "No."

"Well, are you satisfied?" Matt asked.

Looking disappointed Mike said, "Yeah...Let's go."

In the alleys and the shadows, Adrian remained out of sight of the main drag. He decided he needed some more beer.

There was a convenience store just up the street a bit. Adrian headed over to the store in the cover of the night.

He carefully checked Davis Ave. for cops and then proceeded to the store. He bought two packs of cigarettes and three six packs of beer. Again, he checked the street before leaving the store and entered the night once again.

He headed away from the busy streets and found a quiet school yard. He entered the property with beer in tow and found a nice, dark, secluded place. No one would bother him here.

He popped a beer and lit a cigarette, and soon slipped from reality. The morals and good judgement disappeared. He took a sip of beer and stared out into the darkness.

Chapter Five

When you get to understand the evils on earth, that's when you can learn to reject it. When you become aware of your surroundings, only then can you save yourself. You must realize that this is wrong. Cheating, murder, and rape are all wrong!

The simple language in this transcript should make the immoral to stop and think about themselves and their neighbours.

The Devil uses one more powerful tool. Think of what fills our prison system. Think of our down town streets. Think of the mental hospitals. "Mental Illness." That's what we call it today. The mind and soul are replaced by evil. This is a serious infliction that society has not bothered to understand. We consider these people to be bad asses. They don't deserve the time of day.

Have you ever heard some one say, "How could a person in his right mind do such a horrific crime?" Duh...obviously, they were not in the right frame of mind. We failed them by not recognizing the other realm of nature.

This is the Devil's infliction on humans to capture their souls. He does so without their desire to do so. Mental illness could be described as a condition that causes a person to commit an act that they would normally not do.

Today, there is medical science that can help those who briefly recognize that they need help. We failed these poor people. We do not recognize their absurd behaviour. We think that they are just going through a phase, and that they will get over it.

Even when inflicted with such a disease, they still try to fight back and regain their true character. It is a constant fight. It is a struggle that leaves them exhausted and physically ill.

Rather than committing acts onto others, the little bit of sanity they have directs the evils towards themselves.

Harming themselves or committing suicide is a desperate attempt to sacrifice themselves rather than others.

Some of them really don't have an explanation for their actions. They usually don't know why. Support, understanding and love mixed with a mood stabilizer will usually do the trick. The big problem is that no one wants to help. We are selfish and we cannot spare our time to help a neighbour.

Have you ever wondered why some of the loony tunes down town will scream their religious beliefs at everyone they pass? Even with this infliction, they were able to find God and save their souls. They are constantly fighting a tough disease.

To be able to destroy the evil in their hearts is extremely exciting and gratifying.

They are so excited about their victory, they are trying to tell you to change and accept God. He was truly saved. We should be happy for that poor soul. Instead of pushing him and swearing at him, warning him to leave us alone. Give him a nod and smile. A quiet thank-you for his concern and you will be on your way.

This is the Devil's infliction within his realm of nature. Some will win, while others will lose their battle. God is willing to help those who are willing to help themselves. It may be that we are to blame for the overcrowding in our jails and hospitals.

Our attitude may be the cause for some of the poor disturbed people wandering our streets. Instead of being selfish, we should extend our hand to those who need help. Possibly, we can make a difference in someone's life. A little love can go a long way.

Journal
September 12th, 2000
MADMAN

The two detectives continued on their search of the bars and streets. Nothing showed up. The only thing they wanted was to talk to that guy with the baseball cap. They hadn't

ADRIAN

found Azario either. Matt was wondering if they were on a wild goose chase. Matt turned to Mike and said, "We've been at it for hours. How about stopping for a cup of coffee?"

Mike couldn't argue with that logic and said, "Sure, let's go." They crossed the street and went to an all night diner.

Back at the school yard, Adrian finished his first six pack. He decided that he was a little lonely, so he thought he might go and find some company. He took his beer and hid it behind the dumpster, then moved toward Davis Ave.

He would like to be inside of one of the strip bars, but the cops were everywhere. He slowly edged up to the main drag when he spotted a young beauty standing on the corner.

Adrian yelled from a distance. "I'll pay you for your time if you will have a couple of beers with me."

The girl turned around and shrugged her shoulders. "Ok."

"What's your name?"

"My name is Pam."

They both moved back into the shadows and entered the school yard property. Adrian went behind the dumpster and retrieved his beer. They sat in the darkness of the night, secluded from everyone.

Adrian pulled out his wallet and handed Pam one hundred dollars and said, "That should do it."

She smiled and put the money away. Adrian started to drift away and his emotions disappeared as he stared at Pam. She was a young, beautiful woman: he wouldn't mind giving her the bone. However, he still had some morals left to resist the temptation.

But even his morals were sliding as he looked up her skirt. He could see that she was not wearing any panties and that she was shaven clean.

They drank their beers and sat motionless. Adrian's stare was very obvious to her. She took her right hand index finger and placed it up her skirt. Adrian grew uncontrollably weak when he saw that Pam was highly aroused.

He withstood it no longer and exposed himself. Pam lustfully lunged at Adrian's centrepiece. For the next few minutes, Adrian was in heaven. His pleasures exploded in a firestorm. He was extremely relieved, the pent up pressures having been released.

Adrian smiled and handed the girl a twenty dollar bill. "Thank-you."

Pam smiled and said, "My pleasure." She then cleaned herself up.

They both gathered themselves together and each grabbed a beer and a cigarette. Adrian's fantasy had come true. However his morals were now catching up with him. He was now feeling tremendous guilt.

This was the first time that he could not resist temptation. There was a large hole in his heart where trust once resided.

He had slipped out of his disassociate state, and the tribulations of reality were upon him.

Quietly, the two drank their beers and allowed the morning hours to pass. Adrian started to become nervous and decided to call it a day.

He gave Pam the rest of the beer and headed back to the convenience store to call a cab. His night was over and he managed to slip by the police dragnet. He went home. The bars were all closed and the detectives were strolling up and down Davis Ave. It was a good night. They had picked up sixty-five Johns. Once they were processed, Matt would go through the list and weed out the possible suspects.

Even the hookers were calling it a day. The street was basically occupied by police officers, except for two of them. Matt asked, "Where is Hammond and Quenelle?"

Mike scanned the street up and down and said, "I don't know. I don't see them."

Matt fired out orders. "Mike, I want a search conducted for those two officers. If you see them, tell them that I am going to have their heads in a basket for leaving their post!"

Mike snapped back. "Yes sir." He had the officers dispersed to conduct a grid search of the whole area. The search included alleys, dumpsters, and shadows.

About forty minutes into the search, Matt heard a yell from the back alley of the G-Spot. "Lieutenant!!" A uniformed officer yelled.

Matt huffed and puffed his way into the alley. There were the two officers in foetal positions, side by side. They had their heads bashed in.

Matt looked in astonishment and said, "How the fuck did two officers get wasted by one man?"

ADRIAN

Matt was surly taken back by what he had just seen and said, "I want a ten-block search of this entire fuck'n place!"

Mike caught up to Matt and gasped. "Holy shit!"

The uniformed officer went back to the troops and a detailed ground search was on the way. Matt looked at the bodies. The guns were in the holsters and again it didn't look like a struggle took place.

Their hands were clasped together as if they were in prayer. It seemed to match the other three murders perfectly.

Mike took a closer look and noticed that Officer Hammond's note book was missing. The motive now had a twist.

"Matt, Hammond's note book is missing," Mike said.

Matt looked disgusted and said, "Shit! The name of that guy we want to talk to is in that book. I didn't get the name off of Hammond!"

Suddenly, a uniformed officer ran up to Matt and said, "Lieutenant, you better come and see this!" The threesome took to the alley and entered the school yard.

"We found her like this," the uniformed officer said.

Matt went hysterical. "Three fuck'n murders right under my fuck'n nose! Shit! I can't fuck'n believe it!! Who the fuck are you?"

Mike grabbed Matt and tried to control him and prevent him from losing his control. He took him to the side and said, "Don't blow it now; the situation is bad enough with out you going fuck'n loony on me."

Matt replied, "You're right, Mike. Thanks."

They went back to examine the body. She had obviously been raped and the MO was exactly the same as the other murders.

Matt said, "I want forensics, photographer, and coroner here and about a million cops to gather every piece of evidence they can dig up. I want both areas cordoned off: no one gets in or out! I want all the evidence on my desk by noon tomorrow. Make sure the word gets around, Mike."

Mike nodded and said, "Yes sir."

Matt turned around to see the Captain approaching. "Oh shit. Am I ever going to get it!" he mumbled to himself.

The Captain was stomping so hard, the ground shook. "Ruzo!! You're off the God damn case as of right now!

I want you to go to the station and put your gun and badge on my desk.

You are on suspension until the next blue moon! Don't say a fuck'n word! There is no excuse why three people including two police officers get murdered on your dragnet! No excuse! I am taking over the case until I find a replacement. Now, go home!"

Matt grabbed Mike. "You got to drive me to the station, I'm suspended," he whispered.

Mike looked at his boss and quietly said, "Sure."

They went back through the alley to Davis Ave. and back to the car. It was a very quiet ride to the station house. When the detectives arrive at the station house, Matt took out his gun and badge and placed it on the Captain's desk.

As he was heading to the door, he heard the phone ring in his office. He wasn't going to answer it, but it might be Marilyn.

He picked up the receiver and said, "Special Task Force, Lieutenant Ruzo speaking."

An electronically-altered voice said, "Good morning, Matt. I see you had a bit of a tough night."

Matt hurriedly signalled Mike to answer the other phone in the office. Mike picked up the receiver and listened in.

The voice on the phone said, "I told you, Matt. You don't have the guts to take me down. I hope you will like the little vacation the Captain gave you tonight; that was quite moving. Too bad you're off the case. I have a few more things planned for you. See you Saturday."

The phone was hung up and Matt felt ill to his stomach. He raced to the men's room in a panic.

Mike waited in the office for about twenty minutes, and then went to check the men's room. He saw Matt was washing his face and getting cleaned up.

Matt blurted out, "That son of a bitch was watching our every move and he slipped through our fingers! Now it sounds like he is after me and my family. What do I do Mike?"

Mike shrugged his shoulders and said, "I guess the best thing to do is write a detailed report and give it to the Captain. Let him handle it. You can't do anything; your hands are tied."

Not happy with the answer Matt said, "That's not good enough! Mike, we are talking about Marilyn and Emily! They are my whole being. I can't just sit on my thumb and rotate. I have to act!"

Alarmed with that response Mike said, "Matt, remember you are suspended! You legally cannot do anything.

The Captain put you on ice so you can cool off. He will take care of it, trust me. I'll drive you home and you can get some sleep."

It was a quarter after four in the morning when they pulled up to Matt's house. Matt could see that the porch light had been left on for him. Matt waved good-bye to Mike as the car pulled out of the drive way.

Matt saw the two patrol cars on the street in front of his house as ordered. He walked up the porch steps and was greeted by an officer.

"Good morning, sir."

Matt waved in acknowledgement. He entered the house and saw Marilyn sleeping on the couch.

Two officers on the inside met Matt at the door. One of them said, "Hello, Lieutenant. All is clear, sir."

Matt replied, "Good morning gentlemen. I presume you stay on watch until the Captain takes you off."

The senior officer snapped, "Yes sir."

Matt took off his shoes and went to the fridge for a beer. Marilyn woke up from her restless sleep. "Hi honey," she whispered so as not to wake up Emily.

Matt whispered back, "It was a terrible night. I got suspended."

Marilyn moved over on the couch and patted the cushion indicating for Matt to have a seat beside her. Matt put on his slippers and sat down on the couch.

Looking concerned Marilyn asked, "What happened out there?"

Matt responded, "That bastard killed two of my officers and a civilian on my watch. I was there the whole time, and he slipped in and out.

He has indicated that this is going to become personal, and he has targeted our family."

Marilyn gasped. "What are we going to do about it?"

"The first thing we are going to do is not let Emily play in that game on Saturday."

Marilyn was shocked by the response. "We can't stop her from doing that! She has been waiting all year for this championship. It will crush her if she can't play!"

Matt was standing quite firm when he said, "It's a lot better than being raped or murdered, don't you think? She cannot play this week-end! Don't you understand? We are all targets!"

Matt finished that beer and got up to get another one. "We can't take any chances, honey. This guy is extremely clever. He slipped through a dragnet and managed to kill three people!" He popped the lid on the fresh beer.

He came back into the living room and sat down beside Marilyn. "I'm very sorry honey, but it has to be this way."

With tears in her eyes, Marilyn wrapped her arms around him. "I'm scared, Matt."

"I know honey. So am I." They embraced each other without another word spoken.

Adrian was home. He couldn't seem to shake off the mania. He was wide awake and full of energy even though he had gone through a very stressful night. It was five-forty five a.m., and he was sucking back a 40 oz. bottle of rye.

His wife would get up in fifteen minutes so that she could get ready for work. Adrian put the dog out to do his business and brought him back in.

He grabbed the dog's dishes and filled them with fresh water and food. He then placed the dishes on the dog's mat.

What he could remember of the night before was quite sketchy. Adrian could only recall bits and pieces. That was the reason he had started a journal. He had done that so he could remember past events that normally slipped away from his memory. His memory had not failed him when he met Pam. He remembered her very well and the guilt was eating at his soul.

But there was something that he did not remember; he had blood all over his shirt. He lifted his shirt and saw two large gashes stretching across his belly. They were very deep and still bleeding slightly.

He quickly went down-stairs to change his clothes so that his wife didn't notice anything. He emptied the pockets from his pants and jacket and put them in the washer.

Adrian would do the laundry when Carol left the house. Now looking respectable, he was ready to see Carol. He could hear that she was awake for he could hear the shower running.

Adrian went upstairs, grabbed another rye and cola and sat down at the kitchen table. He had a few sips of his whiskey when his wife came out of the washroom.

Carol proceeded to get dressed and didn't utter a word to her husband. Adrian waited for about fifteen minutes and started to make tea for his wife.

He took a last sip of whiskey and poured another one. He just couldn't seem to calm down. He was usually exhausted after an episode. This meant that it was still not over.

The tea was ready. Adrian put some milk in it, and placed it at Carol's place setting. Carol came in and had a seat.

She could very well tell that he had been drinking, but ignored the fact and talked about how her work was going. Adrian didn't know if Carol knew that he had been out all night again. She never mentioned it to him. She figured he had had an episode and would crash for a few days. Then he would totally recover. This had not happened lately.

Carol finished her tea and put her cup into the sink. She then went to put on her jacket and knapsack. She opened the door and the two exchanged kisses. The dog also came to say good-bye and Carol gave him a healthy pat on the head. They said their good-byes and she left the house.

Adrian went downstairs to do the laundry. He came upstairs and grabbed his drink. He was sitting back and lit a cigarette; he stared at the smoke swirling and drifted away.

> *Our immoral acts are always countered by consequence. Smoking tobacco causes many diseases as well as cancers. Not only does it harm the smoker, it does the same to everyone else around that person. It is a trick against nature. It's a lure to cause your greed and selfishness to flourish without any thought or concern of the real dangers.*
>
> *Alcohol is a wonderful elixir that the Devil uses to cloud the mind. Besides the physical ailments that occur from prolonged use, it will also destroy other people's lives as well. Alcoholism in the family destroys relationships, promotes violence and disaster. Car crashes that cause*

death or injury to the innocent scar all the loved ones of who were all involved.

With the mind and soul absent, evil will have its way with you. It will rape you of everything you ever loved or cared for. The evils of alcohol are endless and disastrous.

Drugs are really cool. Greed, violence, and murder are a necessity to keep the Devil in high ranking with the world today. They destroy lives by the scores. They make the evil dealers and suppliers wealthy and powerful. The mind and soul are replaced by evil.

The court system is busting at the seams with drug pushers and addicts. Physical damage from these substances is deadly. The selfishness to feel good or high removes any concept of danger.

The sex trade damages society to the depths of hell. Souls of the immoral are captured by the thousands. Exploitation of themselves and others is the price they pay for greed and money. Their minds are consumed by dollar signs.

The almighty dollar gives them the courage to murder thousands with deadly diseases such as Aids.

There really isn't much difference between spreading the disease to your loved ones, or gunning them down with a machine gun. If you choose to murder any way, shooting them is much more humane.

Such illnesses are the outcome for the immoral acts that you have committed. This infliction of the Devil is directed at the immoral. The self pleasure and greed is satisfied by horrible acts of sex. God allowed us this pleasure so that we can raise children with our spouse.

He did not intend us to waste his gift. Any act of sex that does not involve your spouse is against what nature has intended for humans to survive.

Those who do not respect God are rewarded the Devil's infliction.

Money is the source of all evil. It is the exploitation of society as a whole. They sell for profit immoral behaviours. Publishers, TV, producers and editors are selling entertainment of no moral value.

ADRIAN

Most of the evils discussed so far is shown and promoted in theatres, television, and literature. Violence and sex is the daily abuse aimed at the public for entertainment. These ideas are being accepted as being normal. This has a severe impact on our society.

This also has no benefit to our survival. The money is good. All of those involved in the higher ranks are rich and powerful. They will continue to destroy what is really important for profit.

Governments throughout the world allow this behaviour to continue. Not only that, they put a sin tax or fee on to operate. Election promises are put in place by those organizations who can afford them. Money is traded off for continued success to both parties.

This is known as good business, not extortion. Some governments even own such business enterprises for their own gain.

These governments do not represent the people for the sake of improving life, but to gain power and wealth for themselves. The evils are countless throughout the world. They are everywhere. They have been all accepted into our minds and souls.

Most of humanity has accepted the Devil as their master. There is no thought other than greed and selfishness. There is no longer love in the family home. There is no longer any peace, understanding or morality. Poverty, starvation and disease could have all been avoided if greed and selfishness were not more important than God.

The choices were made from our own free will. We destroyed humanity and nearly every species on this planet due to our free will, our conscience and temptation were the only two things we had deal with. We made the wrong choice.

Journal
September 13th, 2000
MADMAN

Chapter Six

It had only been two hours since Matt had gone to bed and he was already up and awake at six a.m. He couldn't sleep very well because of the nightmare they call life. He put on his house coat and went down stairs to the kitchen to put the coffee on.

As the coffee brewed, Matt quickly went to the washroom and returned to the kitchen table. He got up and went to the back door to pick up the newspaper that was left on the steps. The coffee finished brewing and Matt poured himself a cup and sat down with the paper.

The headlines read: "Dragnet unable to prevent three murders." No details were given in the paper because of the on-going investigation. Not even the names were released yet.

Matt was reading the article when he heard a knock at the door. He turned his head and saw Mike through the window. Matt signalled him to come in.

Mike came in and said, "I didn't think you would be sleeping, so I came for a coffee before I go to work."

"Didn't the Captain give you the morning off because you worked a double shift yesterday?"

"No, the Captain wants every available officer to work on this case and catch this guy by dinner time tonight."

Matt shook his head in disbelief and said, "What makes the Captain think he can do that, when I couldn't?"

Mike grabbed a coffee and sat down in his regular chair. "I don't know.

Maybe he thinks he has enough evidence to pick him up."

Matt's eyes lit up. "Mike, when you are finished work tonight, bring me all the notes and evidence you can find on this case so far, ok?"

Mike didn't like the sound of that. "I can't do that. The Captain would have me kicked off the force!"

Matt gave Mike an evil stare. "I need those files! My family's lives are at stake here! You have to understand, Mike. I don't have any other choice!"

Mike took a sip of coffee and replied, "I'll see what I can do, but I'm not promising anything." The panic seemed to flush

ADRIAN

away from Matt's face. "Thanks Mike, I understand that you are taking a big risk."

As they were enjoying their coffees, they could hear thumping sounds coming from the stairwell.

Emily raced down and gave her Dad a kiss on the cheek. "Good morning Daddy. Good morning Mr. Parsons." She went to the cupboard, got a bowl and some cereal and sat down across from Mike.

Somewhat lost for words Matt said, "Pumpkin, I have some bad news. There is a man out there who wants to hurt us. That's why the uniformed officers are here. They are here to protect us from this guy.

Until he is caught, we all have to stay together in the house where it is safe. I'm sorry honey, but that also means you cannot play in the championships on Saturday."

Emily's heart sank and tears welled up in her eyes. "Daddy!! I have to play Saturday! I just have to!"

"I'm sorry, pumpkin. That's the way it's going to be."

Emily jumped from her chair and stood eye to eye with her father and screamed, "I hate you, Daddy! I hate you!" She then ran to her room in tears.

Matt was deeply hurt by what has just transpired, but he felt he had to do it for safety's sake.

Mike looked at Matt and said, "I'm glad I'm not in your shoes." He then grabbed the pot and filled the two cups. Putting the pot back on the burner, he sat down.

About twenty minutes later, Marilyn came down the stairs and said, "Matt, did you really have to?"

Matt looked back at her astonished. "Yes, I had to. This guy is a psycho; he will kill any one of us if he has the opportunity. I'm not going to give him one!"

Marilyn looked disappointed and poured herself a cup of coffee. She sat down and said, "Can't we have police protection for the game or something like that?"

Matt was getting a little angry. "No, she would be way out in the open. It's too risky. Besides, no one would approve a request like that. We have to stay in the house until the whole thing blows over."

Mike took a look at his watch and said, "Well folks, thanks for the coffee. I'll check back later with you, Matt."

Matt looked back and said, "Yeah...see you later, Mike."

Mike left through the back door and drove away.

Later that afternoon, Adrian was getting very irritable; his nerves were on edge. The stiff drinks had not done a thing. He finished the bottle and still needed something to help calm him down.

Not being able to handle it any longer, he went to the clothes dryer and pulled out his shirt and coat. He went upstairs and put the dog out for a minute.

He then left the house and hopped on the bus heading towards the strip. As he approached Davis Ave., he noticed that there were more cops than yesterday. He got off the bus two stops prior to Davis. He used the back alleys to get to the back door of the G-Spot. He knocked on the back door and the bouncer answered.

Adrian explained. "Trixie knows me." The bouncer nodded and let him in.

The bouncer went into the dressing room. A few minutes later, Trixie came out. "Adrian, what are you doing here? The cops are all over the place!"

"I need a place to relax. That's all!"

Trixie agreed. "Well, since you are here anyway. You might as well stay." She ordered a beer and a gin and tonic. "We'll sit you at your regular seat; it's a little more out of sight." They sat down.

The drinks arrived and Trixie said to the waitress, "Remember this face; this guy is never to buy a drink in here again. They are all on the house." The waitress nodded and left.

"Trixie. Why are you being so nice to me? I didn't do anything for you."

She smiled and said, "I like you Adrian, and it looks like you could use a friend."

Adrian raised his mug and said, "You're right, I do need a friend." They touched glasses to celebrate friendship.

They chatted for a while, when Trixie said, "I'm sorry Adrian, but I have to get ready for my act."

Adrian nodded and Trixie finished her drink. She then got up and went to the dressing rooms.

Adrian lit a cigarette and took a sip of beer. He sat back and watched the show and relaxed. A few shows went by and then it was Trixie's act.

ADRIAN

She came on stage wearing an elaborate night-gown and high heels. She waited for the music for the act to begin. She was so sensuous and desirable that the whole bar stopped and stared at her. Her movements were precise and very well executed.

Adrian stared at her sensuous body, fantasizing about having passionate sex with her. Adrian's pants quickly got tight around the crotch as he entered his dream world. Oblivious to anything else, Trixie was deep into his dreams. Her movements were hypnotizing and sumptuous.

Her show ended and Adrian was left in a daze; he couldn't even move. Trixie came up to Adrian and said, "How did you like my act?"

Adrian was unaware that she had even approached him. She gave him a shake and asked, "Are you alright?"

Adrian quickly snapped out of his trance and replied, "Oh...fine...really."

She repeated herself. "What did you think of my act?"

Adrian looked into her eyes and said, "I think that is a dangerous thing you do up there."

She smiled and went to the dressing room. Adrian sat back into his chair and ordered another mug of draft. He lit a cigarette and watched the women on stage. He closely watched the entrance to make sure that no cops came into the bar.

He felt safe in there; Trixie had everything in control. He couldn't believe that this episode was running into its second day in a row. He was still wired. He still hadn't come down from his high and the alcohol was not bringing him down. He had an episode like this a couple of years ago that had lasted a long time.

Meanwhile, outside on Davis Ave., the Captain had his men doing detailed searches on every bar, alley and any other hiding spot.

The whole area was cordoned off. There was nothing happening without a cop knowing about it. The bars were being individually searched by a team of uniformed officers. They were looking for a man of Adrian's description. Trixie got word that the on-going searches were closing in on her establishment.

Trixie grabbed Adrian and moved to the service elevator. She hit the top floor button and said, "The cops are on their way. You will be safe here. The cops have no idea that this place actually exists."

The door opened into a cluttered hallway, in need of repair. They went around a bunch of debris and found a door.

Trixie took out a key and opened it. To Adrian's amazement, he saw a luxurious apartment all decked out in Italian furniture and décor. Adrian's mouth hung open as he stared at the elaborate art that littered the entire place.

There were no outside windows, so no one even knew that there was a floor up there.

Adrian asked, "Why are you doing this? You must have a better reason than just liking me."

Trixie smiled and said, "Don't worry about it; you are not going to get harmed or anything like that.

You could help yourself to drinks at the bar in the living room. There is a keg of draft in there, too. There is a big screen TV and stereo. If you are hungry, there is food in the fridge."

Adrian couldn't believe how nicely he was being treated, but was very concerned about why. Nobody does things for anyone without getting something in return.

Trixie turned to him and said, "The walls are soundproof, so you can turn up the stereo as high as you like. I have to go back and run a business.

Your bedroom is the last door on the right down the hallway. See you later." She opened the door and turned to smile. She gave a little wave and left.

Adrian headed straight for the bar and poured himself a mug of draft. He looked around the apartment-it was just beautiful. He went down the hallway and checked out the rest of the place.

He was more impressed than ever. It was a four bedroom, three bathroom unit. The room that Trixie said was his was actually the master bedroom with its own private bathroom and walk-in closet. The bedroom itself was huge, with its own TV and stereo. It was so large that it had a living room suite off to the side. The room even had its own bar fridge and coffee pot.

Adrian thought to himself, "Who did she have to blow to get this? It's truly incredible!"

After it started to sink in that this was real, he went and turned on the TV. The six o'clock news was on.

Adrian lit a cigarette and watched the headline story. It looked very familiar, but it didn't seem real.

They were talking about him! He was wanted for questioning relating to the six murders in the immediate area! He remembered all the people alright, but he didn't remember raping or killing anyone.

That's why Trixie had been concerned and helped hide him. She must know something about the murders or him. Adrian's heart sank into his stomach. He couldn't believe what he was watching. They had a full scale search on for him, right then.

Adrian saw the cell phone on the kitchen counter and called Carol. "Hello, is that you Adrian?" an unidentified man said.

Adrian quickly turned off the phone. He yelled. "Damn bitch!!" Carol had called the cops on him. Now they knew his name and where he lived.

As Adrian drank his beer nervously, he heard the locks on the door open.

Trixie walked in and saw that Adrian was watching the news. Sadly she said, "Oh...Adrian. I was only trying to protect you."

"From what? What if I didn't do those murders? I don't remember doing them, but I do remember the victims sort of. It's all bits and pieces; maybe I did do them. I don't know."

Adrian was in a panic; he went to the bar and poured himself a whiskey straight up. He downed that in one gulp, and he quickly poured himself another drink. Looking concerned, Trixie said, "Take it easy on the juice, Adrian."

A rattled Adrian said, "My wife called the cops on me! Now, what am I supposed to do?"

Trixie smiled and said, "Just relax; you can stay here as long as you want. The cops were already here and gone. They will never find you here. You can't go home! This is your home now." She then handed him the keys to the apartment.

In disbelief Adrian asked, "Are you giving me the apartment?"

Trixie nodded and said, "Yes."

In amazement, Adrian sat down on the couch and said, "You sure are going through a lot of trouble and money keeping me safe. How come?"

Trixie poured herself a gin and tonic and said, "You're in a little trouble and I am in the position to help."

Adrian replied, "I understand that, but not by giving away furnished apartments."

There was something very strange going on around here, and Adrian didn't know what to make of it.

Trixie said, "Your home computer and journal are safe; I will have them brought over tomorrow morning."

Adrian turned angrily and said, "Who are you? How the hell did you break into my house and take my computer?"

She explained. "If I didn't take it that would mean the cops would have it. Then you would be in jail."

"How did you know I had a journal?"

"I make it my business to know things."

Feeling very uncomfortable, Adrian was not sure if he could trust her.

She was a very mysterious woman with a lot of secrets. He went to the bar for a mug of draft.

He was thinking, "What if I turn myself in? The police can't do anything. They don't have any proof that I killed those people. It might be safer than staying here."

Adrian was very confused and was finally coming down from his high. He was very tired. It was still early evening, but he could hardly keep his eyes open. The shock of being a murder suspect had exhausted him. He dozed off.

Matt and the family were relaxing in their living room watching TV when the officer in the kitchen alerted Matt.

"Sir, Mr Parsons is here to see you."

Matt yelled from the living room. "Thanks let him in."

Mike walked in and said, "Hi everyone. How is everybody tonight?"

Matt sighed. "We feel a little cooped up being prisoners of our own house."

Mike signalled to Matt. "Can I talk to you in private for a moment?"

Matt replied, "Sure, we can go down in the basement."

He got up from his recliner and led Mike into the basement.

Mike said, "Our suspect is Adrian Eisner, forty-two, of Queens. His wife phoned in a tip today saying that the description on the news matches her husband. The home computer was missing when she came home from work today. Apparently, Mr Eisner is writing a journal."

Matt questioned Mike, "Where is this Mr. Eisner now?"

Mike replied, "I don't know. It seems that he has just disappeared. He used to hang out at the bars along the strip."

"Was there anything different about the murders last night that might give us a clue?"

"There sure was. They found a semen-stained twenty dollar bill on the Jane Doe in the school yard, and her knuckles were bruised. Mr. Eisner's prints matched the beer cans at the school yard with the prints that they found at his home. It at least proves that he was at the murder scene."

"What can you tell me about the officers?"

"That's a little different. They didn't have bruises on their knuckles. It looks like the first blow to the head was executed while they were standing up.

They were then dragged into position, and were beaten to bloody pulps.

They were placed into the foetal position as symbols. Their hands were clasped. It looks mainly like a robbery. Officer Hammond's notebook is missing."

Matt scratched his head and said, "Is there anything else?"

Mike blurted out, "The Captain has put a priority on the DNA evidence of the last four female murders. The report should be in by Monday morning. The task force has also been lifted on Davis Ave."

Matt paced up and down and said, "There are six murders and still no trace of the guy. Somebody must be holding him up somewhere. Why are they doing this? He is a murder suspect! Now that we have a suspect, I want you to do a background check on him.

Check out the works, his friends and his history. We should find out what kind of guy he is. I want you to especially check out his wife. She would have the most information we need."

Mike nodded and said, "Is that it?"

"Yeah, that's it; let's go upstairs for a beer."

The two detectives went upstairs for a few beers before calling it a night.

September 15th, 2002. Adrian was at Bellevue, waiting for his appointment with Stuart. It was almost four o'clock and Adrian was getting anxious. He was not sure what he was going to allow the doctor to hear. Adrian was thinking that he had to say a lot more than he had.

Peeking around the corner was Doctor Stuart. "Adrian, please come with me."

Slowly Adrian shuffled behind the doctor. Stuart then signalled to Adrian to have a seat.

Stuart closed the door and asked, "Well, how is it going this week?"

With his eyes staring at the ground, Adrian said, "I'm still on this terrible high. I just can't seem to calm down. I have another problem that I never told anyone. I am sexually hyper. My sexual desires are at an ultimate high. It is a very dangerous situation. I even thought about rape."

Stuart said, "That is very common among people like you. Some people have that feeling all the time. That kind of behaviour usually gets the patient into a lot of trouble. Don't worry, I can fix that."

Adrian looked a little more at ease when he said, "I can't help myself. I want sex with basically anyone. It's awful!"

Dr. Stuart said, "I will give you a prescription that will calm that down. However, it will affect your sex life with your wife."

Adrian blurted out, "I don't care! Just as long as it's under control and no one gets hurt."

Stuart replied, "I'll give you a good dose of an anti-psychotic. That should cure the problem for you."

Adrian wasn't quite as anxious when he said, "Good! I'm very afraid that I am going to hurt someone. What about this manic high that I can't come down from?"

Stuart said, "It's going to take some time for the medications to kick in at full strength. We just have to be patient. It's only been a week."

"I still have all the other symptoms like racing thoughts, and I am still writing the journal."

"It will take a little time for the symptoms to calm down, but please be patient."

ADRIAN

Somewhat discouraged at what was happening, Adrian said, "I hope so. I can't take much more of this. I am at the end of my rope."

Stuart signalled to Adrian that the time was up. He wrote him a prescription and made him an appointment for the 22nd of September, 2002. Adrian then shuffled out with prescription in hand.

This is something of interest. You cannot hear, smell, or see it. However, it is there. Sometimes you may recognize it as being a little off the wall, or absolutely mad. It is a gift from the Devil himself to all of humanity.

The medical systems in more developed parts of the world are still not able to treat it. It may not be an illness at all. Maybe it's a character defect. Of course, that must be it.

There had to be a reason for an eight year old to cook up his favourite dish of road kill. His character is just a little off. Massacres at high schools, murder and bloodshed are just good old character building.

The manly thing to do is to have pistols and rifles in every room of the house. The stack of mercenary magazines and a Magnum in the baby's nursery are good building tools. Finally, a tender moment, little junior kills and dissects a neighbourhood pet.

These are treasured moments in today's society. You fuck'n assholes!! You think that was funny or creative writing. There is nothing funny about Junior stalking the family with a commando knife, while the family is sleeping.

Thanks to all of those mercenary publications, he was able to sneak up to each of the family members' bedrooms, and cut their throats.

Even his ten month old cousin is now forever in peace. It was like killing the neighbour's cat. There is no remorse or sadness.

Now, that the morning was upon him, he didn't want to be late for school. With his aunt's and uncle's dried blood on his hands, he buttered his toast and made up a bowl of cereal.

With breakfast in hand, he wandered into his aunt and uncle's bedroom. He slid up between the two bloodied corpses, and ate his cereal. He sat back and watched his favourite cartoon. Upon leaving the bedroom after breakfast, he wished his aunt and uncle a nice day.

He stopped at his baby cousin's bedroom. He went in and kissed her on the cheek, and put her favourite pink teddy bear under her lifeless arm. As he came up to his older cousin's door, he just pissed on it and went downstairs.

Thank goodness, it was only a character defect. It might have been worse. He was a good boy.

There was never any problem over there. They were a little quiet though. The adults worked at good respectable jobs. They loved the children and provided everything for them.

They have two cars, a boat, and a nice house. We just don't understand. How can such a horrible thing happen right next door, without us noticing that something is wrong?

This is the most common conception of other people. Their eyes were closed. The signs were there everyday, and no one noticed. The parents were responsible for the family's demise. Only they are accountable for this happening.

There were a million different signs. Did they notice the signs at all, or did they just shrug it off as being not important. This was bound to happen. It had to happen.

The lives were bombarded with negativity. There was nothing positive being taught or demonstrated by the parents. The children were not a part of their lives. Their lives were both separate and belonged to their jobs.

There was never time to spend with them, love them or teach them. The money was available and the most obvious things were provided. This was in the form of material things.

ADRIAN

The most important factor that led them into misery was that the parents did not have a bond between each other, or the children. Without a bond being established, there could never be love. It was every person for himself.

The parent's lives never evolved around the children. They were always left out. The children had no choice but to strive for attention that was not provided at home. They found it elsewhere.

There never was any teaching of good morals or good behaviour.

God or the Bible was never a topic or a belief. There was never time to correct a problem with words. The belt did that.

Violence was the quickest and most effective method of discipline. Understanding the feelings of other members was never discussed.

Love never existed between the parents. They never held hands, kissed or showed any affection towards each other at all. The children never saw or felt love either.

Since there was no love, there was also no trust. They were empty souls living under one roof.

The children witnessed infidelity of their mother and father on several occasions. Dad had a real affection for guns and booze. Mercenary magazines, girly magazines, and beer were the common products littering the house.

They never sat down for a family meal. They fed themselves when they were hungry. Auntie was never home. She was very involved with work and the other workers. Sometimes, she wouldn't come home for two or three days. No one ever questioned her on where she was nor did anyone care.

Special events like Birthdays or Christmas were never celebrated or even thought of. The gifts were always there, but never in the heart.

Once in a while it would look like there was love in the family. That was just a show for the neighbours to watch.

PATRICK J. SCHNERCH

Besides, how do you know what your neighbour is doing behind closed drapes? Since you cannot see through locked doors and closed curtains, you cannot see the incest, drug and alcohol abuse or physical violence. You don't see the fear in the eyes of the children.

Journal
September 13th, 2000
MADMAN

Chapter Seven

Matt came downstairs from a restful night's sleep and went to the kitchen to make coffee. He then went to the back door and retrieved the paper from the back steps. The date read, "September 16, 2002."

There was a huge picture of Adrian Eisner on the front page. Matt took a long look at the picture and thought to himself, "So, this is the bastard that is terrorizing my family." He walked up to the coffee pot and sneaked a cup before it was finished brewing.

He sat down in his normal spot and started reading the paper. Suddenly the phone rang and Matt got started. He got up and went to pick up the phone.

"Hello."

The electronically modified voice said, "Good morning, Matt. How are you today? Did you get a good night's rest?"

Matt blurted out angrily "Adrian! I know it's you. Give it up and turn yourself in!"

The mysterious voice said, "Sorry, Matt. I can't do that. I have a lot of unfinished business to take care of."

Matt's temper flared and he said, "You're finished with these fuck'n games Adrian! Finished! Do you hear me?"

Laughingly the voice said, "You're very funny Matt. I'll see you tomorrow at the game." The phone then clicked off.

Matt then went back to the kitchen table and sat down. He stared at the picture in the newspaper and said out loud, "I'm going to kill you, you son of a bitch!"

The on-duty officer turned around and said, "What did you say, sir?"

Matt just waved off the comment.

The officer alerted Matt, "Mr Parsons is coming up the driveway, sir."

Matt replied, "Thanks. Let him in."

Mike gave a quick rap on the door before entering. "Good morning, Matt." He didn't wait to be asked. He went straight to the cupboard and pulled out a cup. He then poured himself a cup of coffee and sat down.

Matt quickly blurted out, "Mr. Eisner decided to phone me this morning. It looks like we are going to have a meet and greet tomorrow."

"Are you sure it is him? It seems to me that you already have this guy tried, convicted and executed before we get the DNA results back."

"It has to be him!! Who else can it be?"

Mike warned him, "Don't do anything stupid! The first thing you need to do is report the call to the Captain. Then, he will put a trace on the call to see where it is coming from."

"I know this is our guy!"

"No, you don't. There hasn't been any real proof that he killed anyone! You have to wait for the evidence to come in."

Angrily Matt said, "Whose side are you on anyway? My family is in danger!"

"I take the side of justice. Until I see the proof, I'm not going to execute someone!"

Matt stood up and pointed at the door. "Get the fuck out of my house you traitor! I will get the bastard myself!" He opened the door and pushed Mike out onto the back step. He then slammed the door shut.

He then went into the basement. In a rusty tool box under the work bench, he retrieved a 9 mm. He said to himself, "If it's a showdown he wants, it will be a showdown he gets!"

The next morning, the family was sound asleep as Emily awakened to the alarm clock that she had set. Quietly, she got dressed in her soccer uniform. She tied her hair back and was now ready to become a champion.

She knew she couldn't go downstairs. Both entrances were watched by on duty officers. She opened the window and climbed onto the roof. In the dead of night, she quietly walked along the roof until she reached the large oak tree. She looked over the edge and saw an officer outside by the entrance.

She watched him closely as she descended down the large tree. The officer turned her way. Emily's heart was racing with adrenalin; she tucked out of view behind the other side of the tree. She patiently waited for the officer to turn the other way.

As he looked away, Emily finished her descent down to the ground, and quickly hides around the corner of the house. She quietly tiptoed her way along side the house to pick up her bike.

ADRIAN

Avoiding the front and back yards, she quietly hoisted her bike over the side of the fence and into the neighbour's backyard. She climbed the fence and walked along the back of the neighbour's house. She came along the other side, and climbed another fence into the back alley. She quietly sat down and allowed her heart to slow down. The game was much too important to miss.

She had this deep guilt that she had disobeyed her father, but she had to play. No matter what the consequences were, they were going to win the trophy today!

Unable to sleep, Matt looked at the clock and it was only five in the morning.

He woke up and went downstairs to start a whole new day. The uniformed officer said, "Good morning, sir. All is quiet, Lieutenant."

Matt mumbled, "Good morning."

He stumbled around, scratching his ass, and got the coffee brewing. He then got the newspaper as usual and sat down, waiting for his coffee to brew.

He was amazed that nothing had come out in the wash. This Adrian guy was still out there, and nobody knew where he was. He had committed six murders in total and he had not left enough evidence to make a case. Even if they caught him, they couldn't prove anything except that he was at the scene of that Jane Doe.

The phone suddenly rang and Matt almost shit himself. Angrily he said, "Who the fuck is phoning at this time of the morning?" He got up and went to the phone. He picked up the receiver and grumbled, "Hello."

The electronically modified voice said, "Now...Now, Matt. Is that any way to answer the phone?"

Matt's eyes widened with rage and he yelled, "What the fuck do you want?"

The voice answered back, "Listen very closely, you fat son of a bitch."

Over the crackling phone he could hear sobbing and desperate cries. "Daddy! Daddy, please help me!"

Matt's eyes welled up with tears, and he started to shake. His knees were getting weak: they just couldn't support his large frame. He sat down on the carpet trembling. His voice crumbled and he said, "If you hurt her, I will kill you!"

The officer in the kitchen overheard the conversation and quickly radioed the station.

He then ran upstairs to Matt's bedroom phone, and picked up the receiver. Marilyn woke up in an instant, wondering what was going on. The officer put his index finger to his lips to signal to Marilyn to be quiet.

The voice grumbled, "I told you it was game day. I think it is your turn to move, Matt."

Matt started to cry uncontrollably as he heard the screams for her Daddy. His little pumpkin was screaming for her life.

He could not do anything about it, except listen to the torture. His heart and soul were drowned over by her cries.

The voice grunted, "You raised a mighty fine whore, Matt." Matt said in a broken voice, "Leave her alone!! She is only a child!! Take me instead!"

There was a sigh of relief and he said, "Sorry Matt, you just wouldn't do. I have something planned especially for you; you'll just have to wait.

Have a nice day. I'll keep in touch." The phone went dead, and then there was a dial tone.

However, Matt's heart was silenced. Marilyn ran down the stairs towards the cowering shell of a man. She wrapped her arms around him and sobbed. They sat in the middle of the living room floor with their lives shattered. It was unknown what the future had in store for their baby.

Adrian had been awake for awhile. He had started his second pot of coffee to kick start the old body. He heard a knock at the door. He went closer and nervously asked, "Who's there?"

The voice from the other side of the door said, "It's me. Trixie."

He unlocked the door and let her in. Trixie said, "How did you sleep last night?"

Adrian replied, "It was one of the best sleeps I ever had. Did you want a coffee?"

Trixie shook her head and said, "No thanks, I never touch the stuff."

She opened a couple of bags she had brought and said, "I bought you some new clothes. We are going to change your style of wardrobe, so that you are not so recognizable."

ADRIAN

Adrian looked at the clothes. He would never buy that stuff for himself. "It looks too preppy for my liking."

Trixie snapped back, "I don't care if you like it or not! It's going to change the way you look. It will make it much harder for the police to find you. You don't want to stay cooped up in here forever, do you?"

"No, of course not."

Trixie then smiled and said, "That's settled then. Go take a shower, and put your new clothes on."

Somewhat reluctant to doing either of those demands, he did what he was told. Trixie waited in the living room and watched the morning news. She saw Adrian's face take up the whole TV screen. She thought to herself, "I have to change the way he looks; the whole world knows what he looks like now!"

After about twenty minutes, Adrian stepped out of the bathroom wearing his new clothes. "I look like a forty year old college brat."

Trixie looked him up and down and said, "Perfect! We changed your image already. Now, we have to change the way your face looks.

Before we go out today, you have to be unrecognizable from the picture in the newspaper. I have a barber kit at the bar.

I'll go get it and in the meantime, you can go and shave your moustache off. I'll be back in five minutes. See ya."

Adrian went to the bathroom and proceeded to shave off his moustache and old growth. His appearance changed suddenly, and he was no longer Adrian Eisner.

Trixie went behind the bar and got the kit. She rummaged through the lost and found box and found a pair of stylish sunglasses. She then raced back upstairs and knocked on the door. Half shaven, Adrian unlocked the door and let her in.

Adrian said, "I'm just going to finish up and I'll be out in a few minutes."

Trixie prepared the razor, got a chair and a towel and hollered, "I think we will give you a buzz cut to put you in fashion."

Adrian yelled back, "Fine that will be just fine."

He stepped out of the bathroom and Trixie was taken by surprise. She exclaimed, "Wow!! That did the trick, alright! Now, let's get you into the chair."

Adrian sat down, and Trixie set the razor to its lowest setting. The hair quickly came off.

When she placed the sunglasses onto his face, she said, "No one will recognize you at first glance!"

Adrian stood up and went to the washroom mirror to take a look. To his amazement, he even looked good. There was no way he could be identified easily.

Back at the Ruzo residence, police cars littered the entire neighbourhood.

Matt and Marilyn were in the house with shock on their faces. The situation seems so unreal. The Captain directed an officer to tap and monitor the phone.

The Captain said, "Matt every conversation will be tapped and monitored. We will try to put a trace on him when he phones back. Don't worry, we'll get this bastard!"

The Captain put out a kidnapping alert for twelve year old Emily Ruzo. The entire city was looking for her and the main suspect, Adrian Eisner. Time was something they didn't have a lot of; they had to find her quickly.

The Captain put his hand on Matt's shoulder and said, "Do you have any idea who is targeting you?"

Matt strained to say, "I'm a cop; I made a lot of enemies in my life time. It could be anyone, but I don't remember crossing paths with Adrian."

The kitchen door flew open and in raced Mike. "Matt, I just heard the APB on the radio! Are you guys ok?"

Marilyn got up, hung on to Mike and whispered, "My baby is gone."

Mike patted her on the back and said, "Don't worry Marilyn; I'll bring her home personally. I promise."

Marilyn was then led to a chair by Mike, and sat down. He went to the coffee pot and poured three coffees. He put them on one of Marilyn's silver trays, carried them to the table and said, "Here you go, have a coffee. Maybe it will help if you have something hot."

Matt turned to Mike and said, "Thanks Mike, but I think we need something a little stronger.

How about going to that cabinet over there, and getting the forty ouncer of dark rum?"

Mike looked to the Captain who nodded his head in agreement and said, "Take the rest of the day off Mike, and stay with the family."

Mike replied back, "Thank-you, sir."

He then poured a little rum into each coffee and passed out the cups. He said, "Maybe, these will help calm your nerves a little." Then he sat down and looked at the empty chair across from him. He could feel a tear welling up in his eye; he then took a sip of coffee.

He couldn't believe that his little munchkin was in the hands of a monster. He just hoped that she was still alive, and not left for the dogs like the other poor victims.

The Captain asked Matt into the living room. He said, "Matt, I know this is a very difficult time for you and Marilyn. I think you need some professional help to get you through this. I don't think you can do it on your own."

Still shaken, Matt said, "Are you sending me to Ken Stuart?"

The Captain replied, "No, he doesn't practice anymore. I'm sending you to Dr. Jason Freemont, an old associate of his. I can make an appointment for Marilyn, too, if you like."

Matt said, "Sure, make one for her too. This is too much to handle."

The Captain said, "Don't worry; I'll take care of everything. I just want you to try to relax and stay home today."

Matt then went back to the kitchen table and sat down. He took a couple of big gulps of coffee and rum, and slid into his chair.

Marilyn smiled and said, "She'll be alright, honey." Marilyn still had tears streaking down her cheeks. She couldn't believe that someone would do this to a twelve year old.

The whole mess was too unbelievable to be true. The three of them sat in silence with their sorrow.

Meanwhile, Trixie turned to Adrian and said, "Oh...I almost forgot. Your computer is downstairs in the bar. Come downstairs with me and help me lug it up here."

Adrian looked very anxious and couldn't wait to start writing again. He opened the door for Trixie and they used the service elevator to the bar. Finally, there it was behind the bar. This was his most prized possession.

They packed it up and took it upstairs. Adrian immediately started setting it up.

Trixie asked, "Why are you so excited about writing?"

Adrian replied, "I don't know. I think it is because of the mania I am going through. It has become an obsession to write. I have so much to say."

Trixie looked confused and said, "Oh well, its up and running. You can write anytime you want."

Adrian was very appreciative of her help and thanked her. Almost oblivious to Trixie's presence, he began to write. Trixie felt that she was in the way, and quietly opened the door and sneaked out.

Was this a character defect? Could the negative influences in his life have an impact on this child's life? Just because he liked Punk Music or watched bizarre cartoons on television doesn't make him a killer.

Although his preference for music and television didn't do it alone, but together with the rest of the negativity he was exposed to, it all had a severe impact on his morality.

It is the environment that we expose our children to will have a major impact on them. As parents, we are responsible for a positive environment for our children.

The impact on your children should be love, respect and positive. If you are not ready for children in your lives, use precautions. If your career needs to be established first, just wait. Family planning usually never happens; it should always be planned and not a mistake.

You need a good solid plan of what the priorities will be once the child is born.

The child's life prior to conception to the time of their death should all be considered. What values do you want them to posses through out their lives? Do you want this child to be successful with a planned solid goal in their life? Honesty and compassion is a characteristic you would be proud of.

ADRIAN

After exposing your child to different things in life, your child may choose one of these elements for their own life. Exposure to positive elements will drive your child with excitement.

They will learn to better themselves with the enthusiastic will to do well. Music, different cultures, and sports are positive elements which can promote a child's well being. They will learn to accept the treasures in life and not the negatives.

The benefits to their mental and physical development are totally dependant on your own judgement and direction.

You must keep your child consumed by positive building blocks. Your endless love and support for all of their accomplishments wouldn't leave any time wasted on the evils of life.

Time and love will be your greatest gift to them. They will keep those memories in their hearts forever. The values that they have learned will be passed on to their children and so on. We are all responsible for the future generations. The family bond will be powerful. It will be able to survive any evils that cross its path.

This is a very simple idea to prevent a character defect from ever happening. As parents, coaches and teachers, we are all responsible for the outcome of the future.

The children learn from us. They copy our lifestyle and our values. We must show them how to love and be compassionate to others. We must open our eyes and recognize the evils that are affecting our children. This must be questioned by all of us. Our demise could have been avoided if we allowed God into our hearts.

Instead of teaching our children at all, we decided it was better to fulfil our personal greed and pleasures. These pleasures do not benefit anyone or anything.

The evils have been passed on from one generation to the next. This is what we taught our babies. The aunt and uncle were totally responsible for all the events that happened in that household, including their own demise.

PATRICK J. SCHNERCH

They can also be held responsible for the nineteen deaths at Gregory James High School.

*Journal
September 14th, 2000
MADMAN*

Chapter Eight

The masked man who terrorized Emily had been gone for hours. Emily's naked body lay stretched over an old office desk, in an abandoned office building near ground zero. Her cold body was tied from each appendage to each corner of the desk.

Gagged with her own underwear, she was unable to scream for help. She was terrified that he would come back and kill her. She could see from the corner of her eye a blood-stained baseball bat leaning up in the corner.

She almost wished to die, rather than go through that torture again and be left in the cold building. She could hear sirens outside, but was unable to alert anyone. She thought of how things would have been so different, if she had only listened to her father.

As she shivered uncontrollably, she shed tears of guilt and remorse. She could vision her parents in deep sorrow, wandering if she was alive or not. Emily could not believe that she thought that she was smarter than her Dad, and that he didn't know anything.

Emily knew a lot better now. If she came out of this alive, she would never disobey her father again! She then cried as her sunken heart ached. In fear, she patiently awaited her saviour. It was her deepest hope that her father would be at the top of the stairs to take her home.

However, when she looked at those stairs, she saw the shadowy figure of her captor. She cried uncontrollably, wondering if this was the end of her misery.

Back at the house, Marilyn and Matt were calming their nerves with rum and coffee.

The Captain was in the living room, collecting reports from the division of officers he had on the streets looking for Emily. Mike sat quietly, thinking that there must be something that he should be doing.

All of a sudden, the phone rang. The Captain signalled Matt to pick up the receiver, while the Captain put the call on speaker phone.

Matt picked up the receiver and said, "Hello."

The electronically-modified voice said, "Hello Matt, you sound a little better this time around. Don't you have the stomach for our little game?"

Matt said, "You are not going to get away from this, I promise you."

The voice said, "Your little girl didn't look all that happy to see me. I wonder if it was something I said. What do you think her problem was?"

Mike went to grab Marilyn to leave the room, but she swept his arm away and whispered, "I'm staying for this!"

The gag had been removed from Emily's mouth. Matt could her sobbing in the background. Matt's little girl is in the hands of a murderer and he is totally helpless.

His heart aches so deeply, he only wishes that he can do something. The modified voice said, "What do you think, Matt? Should we wrap up this game?"

Matt choked and said, "I will never give in to you, the games not over yet! As a matter a fact, it has just started you son of a bitch!!"

Emily's voice cried out, "Daddy, help me! He is hurting me, Daddy!"

The voice strained and said, "Do you think Emily is ready to concede to her fate?"

Matt said, "She is a fighter!! She will never give in to the likes of you, Adrian!!"

There was a terrifying screech that could be overheard on the phone. It was almost too painful to listen to.

Without any thought of the consequences, Emily screamed, "I'm at ground zero, Daddy! Ground zero!"

The voice was caught off guard and yelled, "Bitch!!"

The phone line then went to a dial tone.

The Captain instantly had all available officers converge at ground zero to search every room in the abandoned buildings, which had once surrounded the World Trade Centre.

Mike ran out of the door and squealed out of the driveway. No one was going to do this to his munchkin, and ever walk again. The adrenalin surged through Mike's veins as he moved closer to the business centre.

The whole city was racing to Emily's hopeful rescue. Within a short time, the whole area was cordoned off and the searches began.

Matt and Marilyn went quietly into the living room holding hands, and knelt down for prayers. There was a glimmer of hope, but there was also the fear that they would never see their little girl again. They looked up at Emily's picture sitting on the mantle. They were praying for their little girl to come home.

Mike arrived at the scene and took a close look at the buildings, looking for evidence of entry. He scanned the buildings carefully and found a door ajar on the North West building next to ground zero.

Mike pulled out his service revolver and carefully looked over every square inch.

Cautiously he found his way to the stairwell. Each floor was examined and turned upside down.

Every broom closet and cranny was examined personally, until he heard moaning coming from upstairs.

Mike cautiously climbed the steps and followed the sounds. He scanned the area for any sudden movement, because the bastard might still be in there. He could see where there were footprints where they disturbed the dust. The moaning was getting louder, but Mike didn't want to become over anxious and careless.

Slowly following the footprints, he glanced up and saw Emily stretched over the desk. She had been badly beaten, but she was alive. Mike untied the ropes and set her free.

She was shivering from shock and Mike took off his coat and wrapped her up. He put her over his strong shoulders. He radioed in and proceeded downstairs to the awaiting ambulance.

Meeting him at the building entrance was the Captain and the ambulance attendants. Mike carefully handed the little girl to the attendant and said, "Don't take off without me."

The attendant said, "Ok, but hurry. She needs care right away!"

Mike turned to the Captain and said, "Where are Matt and Marilyn?"

The Captain said, "They will meet you at the hospital. Now go!"

Mike yelled to the attendant, "Ok, let me go with her." The ambulance then drove off.

The Captain sent up a forensics team to gather the evidence at the building where Emily was found.

He then had the building taped off, and the search for the assailant was heightened. The Captain had suspicions that this guy had already left the area. The uniformed officers were questioning everyone to see if they saw someone entering the building. The investigation was far from over.

There had been six murders and one attempted murder. The killer had to make a mistake sometime. Matt and Marilyn waited at the emergency entrance, hoping to catch a glimpse of their miracle child. They could see the ambulance backing in now. Their hearts heightened with anxiety.

The ambulance doors opened and their little girl was carried out in a gurney.

Her face was badly bruised and cut; she was shivering uncontrollably. Mike followed in behind and Marilyn pounced into Mike's arms and whispered, "Thank-you, Mike."

After a big hug for her knight in shining armour, she followed the gurney to the emergency room.

Matt patted Mike on the shoulder and said, "Thank-you. God answered our prayers and he sent you."

Mike lowered his head gracefully and said, "You are welcome."

They all followed in behind of Emily and were stopped at the emergency lobby.

A nurse said, "I'm sorry folks, but you have to wait here. In the meantime, you can fill out these insurance papers."

Matt took the papers and sat down. He carefully filled out the forms and signed the documents. The nurse said, "It's going to take awhile.

Why don't you folks go to the cafeteria for lunch, and I will page you if I hear anything."

Matt nodded his head and said, "Thank-you."

He got the thumbs up for lunch, so they headed off to the cafeteria.

Matt asked, "Did Emily say anything about her assailant?"

Mike said, "No, she was semi-conscience the whole time; she never said a word."

Matt angrily said, "Damn, another dead end."

"Wait until she wakes up. She may be able to tell us more."

ADRIAN

They arrived at the cafeteria and were picking through the menu. They filled their trays and went to the cashier. Matt took out his wallet and paid for the meals.

Mike turned to the couple and said, "Thank-you for buying the lunch."

Marilyn said, "Don't mention it! It is the least we can do for you. She is alive!"

They found a clean table and sat down. Marilyn was all smiles that her precious daughter was alive. Her brave daughter had survived against this monster. Everyone was in better spirits than they had been, but have concern for the child's injuries and trauma etched their faces.

They heard a page over the PA. "Will Mr. Matt Ruzo come to the front desk; there is a phone call for you."

Matt said, "Excuse me, I'll be right back."

Mike then said, "Sorry to leave you all by yourself Marilyn, but I think I should go too."

Marilyn smiled and said, "Ok, I'll be fine."

The two hurriedly went to the front desk. Mike then raced ahead. He flashed his badge and said, "Excuse me! Can I have two phones for this line?"

The head nurse said, "Sure, you can use these two phones."

Matt and Mike simultaneously pick up the receivers and Matt said, "Hello."

The mysterious voice shouted, "You son of a bitch! You think you can do this to me?" That little whore ruined my plan!! Ruzo!! I am not finished with you!"

Matt shouted back, "You blew it! You made a mistake! You can't believe you fucked up!"

The electronic voice said, "I don't make mistakes! You're not going to get off so easy next time, Matt! I promise." The phone then went to a dial tone.

Matt asked, "Did you get that, Mike?"

"I got every word. Boy!! Is he ever pissed?"

Matt explained, "That's what psychos do. They think they are invincible and smarter than you. Then they will rub your nose in it. They tease and taunt you. They know how to manipulate you into submission. This guy is a classic case of psychopathic behaviour. I think we should run Adrian's name through all the psychiatrists in the city, and see what we come up with."

Mike looked very happy with the possibilities of this and said, "Matt, I think you discovered the first major break in the case."

They then proudly walked back to the cafeteria to join Marilyn. Marilyn looked up and saw the two detectives coming back to the table.

She said, "I hope your lunch isn't too cold. The meatloaf is delicious."

The two men sat down and Matt said, "It will be fine, honey. I think we just discovered a major break in the case."

Marilyn's eyes showed hope and she said, "That's wonderful!"

Mike then said, "You can thank your huggy bear. He came up with the idea."

She turned to her husband and gave him a kiss on the cheek.

Matt said, "Mike, don't you ever call me huggy bear again!"

They all laughed.

Meanwhile, Adrian was enjoying his new found identity while walking past police officers on Davis Ave.

He came up to the G-Spot and walked in. He saw that Trixie was talking to a waitress and waved. Trixie waved back, and Adrian went to his normal seat and took off his long coat. He then ordered a mug of draft and sat down. Adrian lit a cigarette and sat back.

Trixie came to the table and said, "Well honey, what do you think of your new-found freedom?"

Adrian replied, "It's great! I walked past a dozen cops and not one recognized me."

Trixie warned, "Don't get too cocky. You should still try to avoid all police contact as much as you can. You still can get caught."

Adrian said, "I feel really good today. I guess I really needed that sleep after all."

"Did you go out last night?"

"No...why?"

"There was a kidnapping and attempted murder last night on a cop's daughter."

ADRIAN

Adrian sat back in his chair with shock on his face and said, "I didn't do that! Honest, I wouldn't hurt anyone!"

Trixie said, "Adrian, I know that you are a very ill man. Is it possible that you don't remember?"

Adrian replied, "That is possible, but I usually remember bits and pieces of things. I really don't know! I honestly don't know!"

Trixie calmed him down and said, "Relax, you are safe in here. We will just keep our ears to the ground and see what happens.

Don't worry. Nothing is going to happen to you, I've got a plan. First of all, I have to go back to work. See ya."

The beer finally came to the table, and Adrian nervously took a couple of sips. He thought to himself, "I don't think I saw a little girl, never mind hurt one. I don't remember nothing at all, not even bits and pieces of it. I usually remember something."

He took another sip of beer and became consumed with swirling thoughts. They were racing through his mind like a whirlwind. His mind was so consumed that it became filled with thoughts of no design. It was just absent thoughts swirling in his mind.

Nothing was clear and he was confused. Adrian had no idea where he was, or what was going on.

All he knew was that he had a beer in front of him and a pack of cigarettes in his pocket. He put out one cigarette and lit another one.

He was dazed in his environment; he didn't even hear the music blaring. He drank his beer and another one was put on the table by an observant waitress. Adrian suddenly recognized something that he may have seen before.

A tall sensuous woman came out of the dressing room wearing a tux, top hat and cane. Her long legs were covered in black silk. Her bosom burst out of her black long tails.

She seductively walked past the table and to the stage. The stage lights were dimmed and the house was quiet.

In a burst of energy the woman, lights, and music came to life. She was adorable; her movements were captivating and fluent. Adrian's groin was swelling with interest.

His mind was visualizing the fondest of all pleasures.

His libido was growing to maximum heights and he could barely refrain from raping the woman. His mood was turning to darkness. His soul was black. He stared at the woman with lusting desires. He had never seen anything so beautiful before.

As quickly as it had started, it also stopped in the same manner. The house blew the roof with applause.

She disappeared into the darkness. In a short moment, she appeared at the table, across from Adrian. He stared at her naked flesh with uncontrollable desire.

The woman said, "What did you think of my show, Adrian?"

Adrian was surprised that she knew his name. He questioned, "How did you know my name?"

The beautiful woman stood straight up in shock and said, "Adrian, it's me! Trixie! Don't you recognize me?" Knowing that this could be trouble, she grabbed him by the hand and headed upstairs to the suite.

Adrian followed behind quite readily. He said, "My goodness you are a beautiful one!"

Trixie looked him right in the eyes and said, "Oh shut up, Adrian!" They arrived upstairs and Trixie hurriedly opened the door.

Adrian then turned around and pushed her up against the door, pressing his groin to hers. He then kissed her. Trixie's towel dropped to the floor.

She suddenly pushed him backwards, and slapped him as hard as she could across his face.

Adrian fell back and yelled, "Trixie!! What the hell did you do that for?"

She yelled back, "You son of a bitch! You were going to rape me!"

Adrian looked shocked and said, "No. I wasn't. I wouldn't do that!"

"What the hell do you think you were doing?"

Adrian was confused from the very beginning and said, "I didn't do anything to you!"

Trixie leaned against the door and calmly said, "You don't remember anything that you just did, do you?"

ADRIAN

Adrian looked around the apartment and said, "I don't remember coming up here. I remember waving to you in the bar when I came in."

Sadly Trixie said, "Oh Adrian, a lot has happened since then." Crying, she put her arms around him and hugged him.

Confused, Adrian said, "What's wrong?" He gently held her and said, "Please Trixie, tell me what's wrong?"

Trixie then buried her head into his shoulder and sobbed.

After a few minutes, Trixie took his hand, took him to the couch and sat him down. She then went to the bar and poured a draft and a gin and tonic. She came and sat down beside him and asked, "Could I have a cigarette? I obviously don't have pockets." She covered herself with the towel.

Adrian pulled out two cigarettes and gave her one. He pulled out his lighter and gave her a light and then he lit his own.

Trixie said, "Oh Adrian, you just tried to rape me. The worst thing about it is that you don't remember!"

Adrian quietly said, "I trust you with all my heart. I know you wouldn't lie to me. Trixie, I just don't remember. I don't remember this kind of thing happening to me before. At least, not like this. I think I'm getting worse. I think I need to go to the hospital."

Trixie explained, "I want to help you, but I'm afraid we can't risk having you in hospital. They will throw you in jail, and that's not where you belong."

Adrian started to cry. "Does that mean I hurt that little girl?"

With tears in her eyes Trixie said, "I don't know. You might have really done it."

Adrian couldn't stand it any longer. He cried, "My good God, what is happening to me?"

He placed his face into his hands and sobbed heavily.

Trixie placed her arms around him and said, "I don't know, honey. I really don't know."

They both sat and cried together.

Trixie grabbed Adrian by the hand and said, "I have to tell you something really important. I promised my father that I would never tell you, but I have to. Adrian, you could never have me."

Adrian asked, "Why not? I would be very gentle with you."

Trixie said, "I know you would make a wonderful lover. My real name is Donna Azario, and your name is Marcus Adam Azario. Your real father is Frank Azario. You are my step brother. That is why I am trying to protect you. You are my flesh and blood.

You have two brothers. Your older brother is Jonathan, and you had a younger brother Frank Jr.

Adrian asked, "What happened to Jr.?"

Trixie explained, "He was shot and killed by a police officer. I don't know much of the details of the shooting."

Adrian sat back in astonishment and said, "You mean I have been having wet dreams about my own sister?"

Trixie laughed and said, "Yes, dear brother, you have. Don't worry; I like you that way too."

They smiled and hugged each other. Adrian couldn't believe it! He wanted to desperately fuck his own sister!

Trixie warned him, "Father must never find out that I told you. He would have me killed."

Back at the hospital, the trio sit patiently in the emergency waiting room. Marilyn asked, "What time is it, honey?"

Matt looked at his watch and said, "It's almost four-thirty. They've been in there for a long time. I wonder what is taking them so long."

Just as Matt finished speaking, a doctor came to them and said, "Mr. and Mrs. Ruzo?"

"Yes, that's us."

"My name is Doctor Sanchez, I have been treating Emily. You will be happy to know that she will totally recover from her injuries. However, they will take some time to heal. The rape kit determined that she was raped viciously twice, leaving severe tears, which had to be fixed by surgery. She had haemorrhaging in that area, and we had to stop the bleeding.

She has a broken bone in the pelvis area, and we had to put a cast on her from the waist down. She has a broken jaw that we had to wire shut until the bone heals.

We have treated her for shock and hypothermia which is no longer a threat. We got her body temp back to normal. She has contusions and lacerations some of which had to be stitched up.

She is a very lucky girl that this animal didn't use a weapon on her. I am looking forward to total rehabilitation for her in about three or four months."

The couple looked relieved and asked, "When can we see her?"

The doctor said, "I'll take you to see her right now. I don't want you to stay too long. She really needs some rest."

Marilyn said, "Thank-you."

The doctor led them to the room. They gathered around their little angel.

Emily smiled through the bruises and picked up a pencil and paper and wrote, "I'm sorry, Daddy."

Matt smiled at her and said, "I know pumpkin, I know. It isn't your fault." He leaned over and gave her a gentle kiss on the forehead.

Emily glanced at Mike and smiled. Her eyes were gleaming and she wrote, "Thank-you, Mike. I love you!"

Mike stood proud and said, "She remembered me from the building! I love you too, munchkin."

Marilyn patiently waited her turn, and then grabbed Emily's hand. They looked each other in the eyes and shared a moment that only mother and daughter can understand.

They smiled and Marilyn kissed her on the forehead and said, "I love you, sweetheart."

Emily wrote on the pad, "I love you too, Mom."

The doctor came in and said, "I'm sorry folks; I have to ask you to leave. Emily needs her rest. She had a very traumatic experience and she needs some time to herself."

The trio filed out of the room and Matt asked, "How will this affect her mentally?"

The doctor said, "Good question; Emily is a mentally stable girl. However, it is unknown at this time what effect this has taken on her. I have assigned a rape councillor to treat her in the meantime. Hopefully, we can lessen the effect with counselling."

Matt asked, "Did you say that no weapon was used?"

The doctor repeated, "Yes, that's what I said."

"Thank-you for everything, doctor."

"You're welcome." The doctor then waved his hand and went down the corridor.

Chapter Nine

At the G-Spot, after their unusual relationship had been explained, Trixie and Adrian both decided to go downstairs.

Trixie had to go and get changed anyway and Adrian wanted a drink.

Upon arrival, he sat at his favourite spot and ordered a mug of draft. Trixie waved good-bye and went to the change room. Adrian lit a cigarette and sat back. He was totally floored by what Trixie had just finished telling him. That sure was a mood killer!

The beer arrived and Adrian took a sip. It was also possible that he had hurt that little girl without his own knowledge. It seemed that his condition had worsened, and he had become out of control and dangerous.

What else could happen to make things worse? He was losing control more often and remembering less every time he had an episode. He needed a doctor, but was unable to get to one because of the manhunt for him.

Trixie then came back and sat down across from him. She ordered a gin and tonic.

Adrian questioned, "So, what am I supposed to call you now?"

In a whisper, Trixie said, "Always call me Trixie. Never call me by my real name, or ever let anyone know that we are related. No one should know about our little secret. You do understand, don't you?"

Adrian took out his cigarettes, took one and gave Trixie one. He nodded favourably and said, "Sure, I understand."

He took out his lighter and lit the two cigarettes. "I'm still not sure why it is such a big deal."

Trixie replied, "It is a very big deal, and Daddy wants his plan to go off without a hitch. It took him many years to get this far. He has plans for you, but I'm forbidden to speak a word. He is a very powerful man who is very capable of getting rid of obstacles."

Adrian said, "Even you?"

She nodded. "Yes, even me. We have to put the conversations that we had behind us, and never speak of them again. You have to promise me!"

ADRIAN

Adrian looked at her soft brown eyes and said, "I promise."

Trixie's drink arrived and they touched glasses to seal the secret forever.

She stated, "I have a plan that will give you more freedom and access. You will even be able to see a doctor for treatment."

"How are you going to do that?"

"I know a few people that owe me favours. I'm going to get you a whole new identity. That will include a new Social Security Card, birth certificate, and the works."

Adrian looked surprised and said, "You mean you can actually get that kind of stuff"

Trixie shrugged and said, "Sure, it's simple. All we need is a picture of you. My friend is coming down a little later tonight to take your picture. It's that easy."

Adrian was excited. He could start a fresh life all over again. He looked at Trixie and said, "I really want to thank-you for everything that you have done for me. You are giving a life back to a broken soul that had no hope. You mean the world to me!"

She smiled back. "You are very welcome. How about another beer?" She turned around and signalled the bar for another round. This was the first time in many years that Adrian had felt so good about life. He was really sponging up this lifestyle.

Meanwhile, back at the hospital, Matt was saying, "We just about had him! He didn't have enough time to use the bat!"

The Captain came in and met them. "Hi folks, I overheard your comment, Matt. Talking about bats, the suspect left his calling card. We found the murder weapon. It was a baseball bat. It was leaning up in the corner where Emily was found. He was going to use it. We also found a blood-soaked paper towel, which we believe was used as a bandage by the suspect.

We will know more after forensics do their testing. That is a brave girl you two have. She took a big chance risking her life. It was her quick thinking that has kept her alive."

Matt replied, "Thank-you, sir."

The Captain asked. "Could I take a peek on her? I promise not to disturb her."

Marilyn said, "Yes Captain, you could see her for a moment."

He then left the trio to themselves. The three of them proceeded to leave the hospital.

Now that we know that a character defect can be avoided with love, how about mental illness? There is another infliction the Devil has bestowed upon us. Mental illness is very common.

It is not recognized as a real illness. Most of the time, you cannot see any physical inflictions of the illness.

Sometimes, we don't see any disability at all. It is a quiet, personal disease. It is an infliction of one's mind, heart, and soul. Those who are inflicted battle everyday to stay sane. They have to mask themselves so that the general public cannot recognize a disability.

This is a secret which they try to guard against detection. They don't want other people to know they have a disability.

Fighting the ailment leaves them exhausted. The constant fighting within themselves drains them of their life. They are semi-conscious of their surroundings. They are crying for help through their actions, because they are unable to do so for themselves. These actions are automatic responses to their own mental pain.

There is no thought or planning. Their mind is no longer in their control. They can usually remember their actions. However, they are not in control of them.

They usually cannot explain the actions that they committed, because they really do not know for themselves. We must remember, there is no decision making process. The actions happen automatically.

Characteristically, the ill are very calm and quiet in nature and tend to be very reclusive. They prefer to be loners. They don't tend to get too close other people for the fear of letting their secret out.

Generally, they are very meek, although they are usually very intelligent, sly and deceptive. They wore a mask all their lives, and they know exactly which face to put on for a certain type of environment.

ADRIAN

They are very clever with deception, and usually are not detected. Even with medical aid, some compulsions are difficult to treat. A lot of the mentally ill are substance abusers.

They try to clear or remove their anguish with any means available. The most common substances in order are: coffee, cigarettes, booze and drugs.

Unfortunately, these substances greatly interfere with a solid treatment program. This makes treatment to be much more difficult to achieve.

The battle continues within, hidden from the eyes of the outside world. God helps relieve the pain and suffering, and gives them the strength to battle such powerful forces. Only then, do they have a chance to survive.

During the short periods between episodes, they have to find God and allow him into their hearts. Not many have been able to obtain God's strength to fight Satan's infliction. Peace and quiet are all they want.

They are too exhausted to fight the evils. Still, with enough will, they will direct the evils towards themselves rather than others. Suicide to the sufferer is considered to be the peace that they were yearning for.

Of course, the mind and soul are empty and Satan takes them to his realm, and peace never comes.

The cry for peace and the will for death are constantly in their thoughts and dreams. They are not afraid of it; they welcome death with open arms. They pray for the end.

This is what affects the physical aspects of the illness: loss of sleep, poor appetite, confusion, mood swings and others. When these effects batter down the mind and soul, Satan pops into the driver's seat. The human is now out of control and unable to resist.

There may be times when they don't remember their own actions or location. All that drives the body is greed and personal satisfaction.

This power over the body becomes a compulsion. The greed and satisfaction has to be fed at regular intervals. Some people cannot resist the compulsions. Some people may be able to direct the force to positive outcomes rather than the negative. However, they can flip from a positive to a negative in a second's notice. Some of the compulsions may seem a little weird. With help from God, they just may seem strange rather than dangerous.

Without God in the heart of these people, their souls are lost forever. The negative compulsions are too powerful to resist. A call from the wild or instinct is triggered. The powerful greed has to be satisfied to calm the hunger. Once the hunger is satisfied, a cooling off period usually occurs to allow the human to regain its strength.

This happens before the next hunger pain strikes. This hunger lives in the hearts of serial murders, serial rapists and child molesters. They have no thought about their actions or consequences. They don't feel any pain or remorse for their actions.

The person that once owned this body, no longer exists. This is pure evil. It is Satan himself. Satan only rears his ugly head when there are no witnesses. Only the victim sees the evil, and rarely survives his personal touch.

Journal
September 15th, 2000
MADMAN

Adrian lit a cigarette and signalled for another beer. The guy with the camera had already been there and gone. Now, Adrian had the rest of the night to himself. The prospects of having a new life excited Adrian.

Adrian started to watch the stage intensely. The women were beautiful tonight.

Trixie booked some real class acts today. Adrian watched as the naked flesh flashed under the bright lights. The lights illuminated the woman as if she was a goddess.

ADRIAN

The seductive movements were very inviting indeed. Adrian got drawn into the world of ecstasy. His mind swirled with ultimate pleasures.

The woman on stage was very exciting to Adrian, and his groin started to swell. Adrian had thoughts of intimacy and erotica in his mind. He was well into his own private world.

The beer came to his table and Adrian took a sip. Without taking his eyes off the stage, he sat motionless. All that was between this woman and Adrian was an icy stare.

The show ended and Adrian was transfixed on this young lady. She passed by his table, smiled and waved as she went to the dressing room. Trixie had noticed how Adrian was acting and went up to his table.

"Adrian! Adrian! Do you hear me?"

Adrian broke out of his trance and said, "What?"

"She's off limits to you, Adrian. In fact, all the women that work here are off limits!"

Confused, Adrian said, "Why?"

Trixie replied, "I don't want pleasure to be mixed with business. These women have a job to do, and I can't have you chasing them like a dog in heat. Do you understand?"

Looking disgusted, Adrian said, "Alright, I got it!"

Trixie then sat down and said, "Don't take it the wrong way, Adrian. I need her to be focused on her job."

Adrian looked at Trixie and said, "Maybe, you are worried that she might be the next victim of mine."

"To tell you the truth, it has crossed my mind. I am just taking a precaution, that's all."

"Even you think that I am the killer!"

"The evidence is sure stacking up against you. I don't know what to think anymore."

Adrian got a little pissed off and said, "I'm going for a walk. It's getting a little stuffy in here."

He grabbed his coat and went to the bar to buy a twelve of beer. He then went onto the street.

The street was busy with the regular nightlife. This was more like it. This was Adrian's old turf, mingling in with the crowds of hookers, pimps, and drug dealers. This was where he felt safe, and at ease with himself.

He decided to go back to the school yard and have a few beers. Upon arrival, he could see the chalk marks of the last victim. The concrete was still stained with blood. He thought they would have cleaned up this mess by now.

He went to the other side of the school and sat down. He popped open a can of beer, lit a cigarette and pondered the possibility that he might be the real killer. It sounded feasible to Adrian that it really may be true.

Trixie was right. The evidence was stacking up against him. It still seemed strange. He met the victims and talked to them, but he didn't remember hurting them. However, he also didn't remember trying to rape Trixie.

While deep in thought, Adrian didn't notice that someone had approached him.

Adrian suddenly got a fright and said, "Don't fuck'n do that! You'll give me a fuck'n heart attack!"

The shadowed figure came closer and said, "I'm sorry; I didn't mean to startle you."

Adrian looked up and saw the same woman of who had transfixed him while she was on stage. He asked, "What are you doing here? Didn't you know a young woman was just killed here a few days ago?"

The beautiful woman said, "I know."

Adrian was mystified and said, "Aren't you afraid to be out here alone with me?"

She smiled and said, "No...should I be?"

Adrian shrugged his shoulders. "I don't know."

"Where is your hospitality? Aren't you going to ask if I want a beer?" She asked.

Surprised, Adrian said, "I'm sorry. How rude of me! Would you like a beer?"

The woman took a beer and a cigarette, and then she sat down. Adrian stared at her beauty. Her long blonde hair whisked across her face as the wind gently blew. Her body was beautifully proportioned with nice legs and large breasts. She was a dream girl come true.

"What is your name?"

"My name is Christine; what's yours?"

"I'm Adrian; it's nice to meet you, Christine."

They shook hands in salutation.

"Trixie told me to stay away from you."

Christine blurted, "That bitch! She can't control what I do in my off time! She has no right telling you who you are allowed to see or not see!"

"Relax Christine; she doesn't know that we are together."

"How are we doing on the beer?"

Adrian looked into the case and said, "We have six left."

Christine said, "It's getting cold out here. Do you mind hiding that stuff, and we'll go to another bar?"

Adrian picked up the beer and placed it behind the dumpster, right beside the chalk marks. The two of them then walked back to Davis Ave. and to "Wet Dreams." Adrian took a look at the bar and was impressed. It had a large stage, good music, and lots of beautiful women.

The two of them found a table near the back, exactly the type of area Adrian liked. Adrian ordered a mug of draft and Christine ordered a Caesar. They took off their coats and lit a couple of smokes. The drinks arrived and Adrian paid for them, leaving a bit of a tip.

The two mingled into small talk and they started to become friendly with each other. The drinks kept on coming one after another, till the morning hours.

The couple were getting intimate and Adrian's groin was swelling. Christine had her hand on his lap and slowly moved it upward. When she realized the situation, she whispered in his ear, "Do you want to get out of here?"

Adrian nodded his head and said, "Yes."

They finished up their drinks and put on their coats. They went outside to brave the cool wind.

"Would you like to come to my place for a drink?" Christine asked.

"Sure, but first I want to stop by the store and buy some beer and cigarettes."

Christine agreed and they went to the convenience store on Davis Ave. They went inside and Adrian paid for his goods.

The couple then went a couple of blocks to E 72nd St. to the Sherwood Apartments on the corner.

Christine said, "Well, this is it. Home, sweet, home." She opened the lobby door with her security card. They took the elevator to the fifth floor. The couple went to suite 507, and she opened the door. She turned on the lights and the place came to life.

Adrian looked around and said, "You have a nice place, Christine."

She replied, "Thanks, I like it too." She then went to the kitchen to mix herself a drink. Adrian pulled a beer out of the case and put the rest in the refrigerator.

Christine went to the stereo and put some soft music on. She sat on the couch, and signalled to Adrian to come and join her.

He popped his beer and sat down beside her. "I've got something to tell you."

Christine looked puzzled and asked, "What?"

"If this is going to end up the way I think it is, I have to tell you, I would rather keep my shirt and sweater on."

Christine laughed so hysterically, she almost peed herself.

This pissed Adrian off, and he lifted his shirt and sweater to reveal two large open wounds still oozing with blood and infection.

Christine suddenly stopped laughing and looked at the deep wounds with horror on her face. "What the fuck happened to you?" she said.

"It doesn't matter how it happened! I think it's time for me to go now."

Christine grabbed him by the arm and said, "You're not going anywhere until we get those gashes cleaned up."

She went to the closet and brought out a first aid kit. "Now, take off you shirt and sweater and lie back on the couch."

Adrian did what he was told and laid back.

Christine cleaned his wounds with rubbing alcohol and cotton swabs. She then placed two large gauzes across the gaping cuts. "That should heal now, but you really should have had stitches. I'm going to wash your clothes and try to get the blood out. You relax right there, and I'll get you another beer."

Adrian thought that not only was she beautiful, she was also compassionate and kind.

He could hear the washer fill up with water. Christine came back and grabbed another beer from the fridge. "There you go."

ADRIAN

Adrian sat up and said, "Thanks." He looked Christine into her deep blue eyes. "Thank-you for everything you have done for me."

She grabbed Adrian by the hand. "Don't mention it. However, there is a way you can pay me back." She got up and pulled Adrian by the arm, and led him into the master bedroom.

She went down on her knees and undid his buckle and pants, dropping all the clothing down to his ankles.

Adrian's eyes rolled to the back of his head. He couldn't believe how his nerves were tingling up and down his spine.

The passion was so real and uninhibited that he was on top of the world. But like most things in life, all good things must come to climatic end. Hand in hand they walked to the bed. Adrian helped her undress and kissed her naked flesh.

They lay down, slowly kissing and caressing each other's bodies. They melted together as if they were one. The night faded away into a cavalcade of pleasure and desire.

The hours passed by as if only minutes had elapsed. The night grew long and the passion peeked to its greatest heights. The romantic night had passed and Adrian quietly got dressed as his goddess slumbered.

He opened a beer and lit a cigarette. He went to the laundry room and put his clothes in the dryer. The music was still playing softly in the back ground.

He relaxed on the couch and thought to himself, "I know I was well aware of all my surroundings last night. I also know that when I leave her today, Christine will be alive and well. This is a night I will remember forever. I didn't blackout or lose my memory, and I didn't hurt her in any way."

Adrian was cataloguing all the events in his mind to ensure that Christine was safe and sound. He heard the buzzer on the clothes dryer and took his stuff out. He then put on his shirt and sweater and went to the couch to put his coat on. He took a few last gulps of beer and left the apartment.

People were bundled up a bit more today; winter was around the corner. Adrian lifted up his collar to brave the winds. It was a seven-block walk back to the G-Spot. He finally arrived at Trixie's bar and opened the door.

Trixie greeted him at the entrance and said, "Where were you last night?"

Adrian snapped. "I don't have to tell you anything! I was fine last night. I didn't get sick or anything like that!"

Trixie apologized, "I'm sorry Adrian for stepping out of bounds with you last night. It is none of my business who you see. I'm sorry, please forgive me."

Adrian went to give her a big hug and a kiss on the cheek. He said, "I think I'm going upstairs for a cup of coffee. Are you going to pop by for a little visit later?"

Trixie nodded her head and said, "Ok...I'll see you later."

"Monday morning, September 17th, 2002" read the newspaper in small print. The larger print that plastered the front page read, "Cop's daughter rescued from serial killer."

Matt took a sip of coffee. He was thinking of the quiet day they had yesterday while visiting Emily in the hospital. The poor kid had sure gone through hell! She was extremely lucky to be alive.

The officer alerted Matt and said, "Mr. Parsons has just driven up the driveway. Would you like me to let him in?"

"Yes, of course let him in."

There was a quick knock at the door and in sauntered Mike. He cheerfully said, "Good morning, Matt. What a great day to be alive!"

Matt looked curious. "What the hell is wrong with you?"

"I'm just very happy that Emily is safe and sound."

"Yeah...so am I."

"Well, today is the big day. We get the DNA test results today." Mike poured himself a coffee. He took a seat at the kitchen table.

Matt replied, "Well, the tests should show us something. Too bad we have a back up of things yet to be tested. It will take weeks before we get any results."

Mike took a sip of coffee and asked, "How was my little munchkin yesterday?"

"Well, she didn't sleep too well. She had a nightmare, and she needed some painkillers to make her comfortable. The visit itself was nice. It was great to have the family back together again."

"5124 code 10-35 at E 72nd St. and Davis," the dispatcher crackled on Mike's radio.

"It looks like Adrian is at it again," Matt said.

"I'll see you later." Mike said. He sped up the strip towards town and turned onto Davis Ave. He could see patrol cars surrounding the apartment. He got out of his car and ducked under the yellow tape. He was met by the Captain.

The Captain said, "Christine Korsakov, age twenty-one. It has the same MO, but no twenty dollar bill. There was no immediate ID, but we found her cheque book. The head is basically missing and she is in that damn foetal position.

The one thing we do have is Adrian's fingerprints all over the place. She's been raped and her naked body is on the bed.

The apartment looks like the two of them were quite casual before he killed her. There was no struggle except for the normal bruising."

Mike said, "Thank-you for the briefing, sir."

He then took the elevator to suite 507. He walked carefully so as not to disturb any possible evidence.

The whole crew was up there taking pictures and gathering evidence. Again, everything was the same except there was no twenty dollar bill. The apartment was used, but not rummaged through or anything like that.

"This is number seven," Mike mumbled under his breath. "I wonder how high this guy is going to go!"

He walked around and took notes, and got dates for when the tests results would be ready for review. This one looked different somehow. It looked like they were having a good time. The stereo was still on low. Mike was going to ask around to see if anyone had seen them around last night.

Mike took to the streets and stopped at bars and stores and asked the regular street life for answers. The couple had been sighted at a convenience store at about three am.

The description, however, did not match Adrian's, unless he had changed his appearance. Mike radioed in for a sketch artist to come to the store for a description.

He finally made it to "Wet Dreams," where he got the same description of the man that was already reported. It did seem that Adrian had changed his appearance, which was why he had been so hard to find. Some of the locals on the street made the same observation and reported what they had seen to Mike.

The two of them were having a night on the town. They were cheerful, and somewhat romantic towards each other.

It didn't make sense - why would he kill her?

Mike was seriously thinking that Adrian was not the killer, but that he might be being set up. He thought, "Why doesn't Adrian just turn himself in, and we can work it out."

It was possible that there were two of them, and Adrian was the lure. Adrian got close to the victim, and lured her into a trap.

Then his partner murdered her. Mike started coming up with several scenarios.

The partner concept seemed to be what they should be working on. Mike just remembered that he had to check Adrian's name against the shrinks in town. He went back to the car and drove to the station.

Adrian was watching the news when a segment of "murder number seven" was being investigated at Christine's apartment. He blew a fuck'n fuse! "I fuck'n know for a fact that I didn't fuck'n do that!!"

There was a knock at the door and he cautiously asked, "Who is it?"

An angry voice said, "It's me, Trixie! Open the fuck'n door!"

Adrian opened the door and yelled, "It wasn't me! I had the most wonderful evening with her! I wouldn't harm a hair on her head! I'm being set up for the fall! Someone is following my every move. He takes advantage of my situations, and commits murders with my signature on them!"

Trixie yelled, "You are a liar and a murderer! I trusted you and gave you everything, and you go ahead and kill one of my girls!"

Adrian was getting pissed off and said, "I didn't kill anyone! I know it for a fact, I'm innocent! I am absolutely positive she was alive and well, when I left her apartment this morning. She was sleeping like a baby, and her head wasn't bashed in either!"

"Ok...Let's say that you are telling the truth. Who would want to do this to you?"

"I don't know. Maybe my activities fit his schedule. I have strange habits and tendencies, but I'm not a killer."

"How about if you just don't remember?"

Adrian sat on the couch and lit a cigarette. "I know that I remember last night, but I'm not sure about the others. I did try to rape you, and I don't remember that at all. I don't know, Trixie. I really don't."

Trixie said, "I saw on the news broadcast that they now know that you have changed your appearance. They flashed a sketch of you on TV. I think you'd better change your clothes and take a shower."

Adrian agreed and went to the washroom to clean up. Even though it was quite early in the morning, Trixie poured herself a gin and tonic. She went to the chesterfield and sat down to watch the news. The whole city was afraid of this guy, even though it seemed that his targets were sex trade workers.

Trixie was not sure if she could trust Adrian anymore. He was capable of anything. She wasn't even sure if she believed him that he was being set up.

That seemed to be a far-fetched story. She was in a dilemma, wondering if she should maybe turn him in. She was not sure. What happens if Adrian was telling the honest truth? He would be crucified with all the circumstantial evidence against him.

Then an innocent man would sit in prison instead of getting the help he needed. Trixie decided to support him, and love him to the bitter end. He was, after all, her brother.

Matt got up from the kitchen table to get another coffee. Through the window, he could see the Captain drive up. He said to the uniformed officer, "Let him in."

The Captain knocked on the door and opened it. "Hi, Matt. I'll have one of those too."

Matt pulled out another cup and filled it with coffee. They both sat down at the table.

"I have an appointment for you and Marilyn to see Doctor Jason Freemont at one pm. Can you make it?" the Captain said.

"That will be fine. Marilyn and I will be there."

"We did find number seven this morning. Adrian's prints were all over the place. We have a hunch that Adrian might have a partner."

Matt said, "I don't think the perpetrator is the partner type. Who ever he is, he is working alone. There have been seven murders and one attempted murder. There hasn't really been a break for us. All the loose ends are tied up. It would be much sloppier if there were two of them working together."

The Captain asked, "Do you still think its Adrian?"

Matt said, "I don't know anymore. However, he has been at the crime scene several times. This is more than coincidence."

The Captain took a sip of coffee and said, "I'm going to put a uniformed officer outside Emily's room as a safety precaution. I will sleep better knowing that she is under guard."

"Thank-you, sir. I also feel better about it." "We couldn't get a trace on the call. He was using a cell phone." The Captain finished his coffee and said, "I asked the doctor to do an assessment on you to see if you are fit enough to return to work. We will play it by ear. Ok...Matt?"

"Yes, sir. That sounds good to me."

"I'll talk to you later. Take care." The Captain then left through the back door to his car.

Matt got up and grabbed another coffee and sat down. He was not one hundred percent sure that Adrian actually did the murders.

> Leaving the house is a safety precaution to ensure that there is no physical violence. I am afraid that the mental scars that I have given my wife may never heal.
>
> Those scars that she has felt from my behaviour are something that I don't want to happen again. Time and time again, the same behaviour puts fear into the hearts of my family.
>
> As much as I truly love my family, this monstrous behaviour still exists. The worst part of behaviour is that I have never been under the influence. At the time of the outbursts, I have always been absolutely clean.
>
> It was always been the alcohol that would calm me down to a safe level. In fact, all of my episodes start off without the influence of alcohol. I am actually screwed up long before I take the first drink.
>
> Am I an alcoholic? Yes...of course I am. There is no denying that! I tend to turn to alcohol to solve my problems. Unfortunately, it does temporarily help. I am always able to calm down and I always recognize my limit.

ADRIAN

I normally do not use alcohol on a daily basis. Whenever a depressive or manic episode appears, my consumption soars. The one thing that is sad. I drink very large quantities before any effect is noticed by others or me. I am always in worse shape when I enter a bar than what I am when I leave.

I just may be defending my drinking habits. I may also try to deny that I have a serious drinking problem. I have been born amongst drug addicts and alcoholics. These things were a daily staple.

Even my severely mentally ill mother hit the stuff pretty hard. My life seems to revolve around this woman that I barely know. She was apparently diagnosed with manic depression some time ago. She never told me anything about it. Then again, that would have been very difficult for her to do.

My birth mother and I have never spent more than thirty days together over a forty year period. In honesty, I don't have any real love for her. I cannot love a person when there was no bond established. It seems that she loves me, but I am unable to feel any love for her.

How can I love this woman? I have a very hard time getting over her mental disabilities. When I see her, all I see is a severely ill woman.

This woman could not be my mother. Her bond for me is stronger than what I have for her. The first two weeks we were together didn't mean anything to me. I was only a baby at the time.

I don't remember anything because of my age. Is it actually wrong that I don't love her?

Many members of the family are surprised that I don't have an unconditional love for her. I have more love for my dearly departed gold fish I had when I was six years old than I did for my own mother. I did not see her again until I was twelve years old. I knew my goldfish for two years.

It may be possible; this is the connection I must make in order to heal. I have no will to ever see her again.

Another thing is that I really do not want to see the rest of the family either. The amount of time that was spent apart from them has buried the affection that I might have once had.

In honesty, I have no love for anyone who has loved me all their lives.

The love in my heart died many years ago. I really do not feel love in my heart for any one or myself.

My thoughts and emotions seem to change rapidly. My train of thought changes so often, I really don't know what to believe anymore. What effects do the current medications provide?

Through out the years, the results are basically the same. These medications do not stop an episode from occurring. Once an episode has started, even increased medication cannot eliminate or curb the illness. An episode has never been stopped by medications that I have used so far.

The one thing that I believe that has happened because of the medication is the continual cycle has been broken down into three or four episodes a year. I believe the medication has allowed a few recovery periods. It has allowed some short periods of good mental health during the year.

The amount of time that I have good mental health is for about three or four months per year. The remainder of the time is not affected by treatment.

Prior to constant treatment of these medications, there were no periods of good mental health. The cycles would create a continual loop right into the next episode. The illness was continuous without any relief. There were more hospitalization periods.

The personal injuries grew more and more severe as the episode continued. The hospital stays were longer and the treatment was more aggressive. I was not able to recognize the illness like I can today. The concentration and control of my thoughts and actions were impossible.

ADRIAN

It actually seems that the treatment had positive affects in controlling the amount of time and the severity of the illness.

During the continual cycles, the episodes were very frequent and very difficult to control. The personal harm was also continual with no thought or plan to carry out those actions.

Those actions just happened, there was no choice. There were no consequences or feeling involved, not physically or mentally. The years were marked by memory loss, loss of control of my physical actions and sexually hyperactive.

There were no morals involved to save myself from more inflictions and uncontrolled behaviour. There was a six year period in my life that disappeared into a blur of chaos. The actions went unchallenged and the truth wasn't important enough to investigate.

Many horrible things happened during those six years. This is a time of my life that will remain my secret forever. It will be carried to my grave without a word spoken.

                                  Journal
                          September 16th, 2000
                             MADMAN

Chapter Ten

At the Azario Manor sat an elderly, tall, salt-and-pepper-haired man. He was exquisitely dressed in a white suit and Italian white shoes. He sat on the veranda, drinking his tea and looking over his acreage. A large goon watched every movement ensuring no harm came to the old man.

The mansion was luxurious with fifty suites, games rooms, and dining rooms. It had everything a man could ever dream of. The Italian artwork was original and priceless. It adorned the walls and ceilings in every room. The grounds were immaculately manicured, and numerous fountains flowed with the gentle rush of habituated water.

The old man signalled for a refill of tea. His command was fulfilled without delay by the ever-observant butler. Mr Azario was wondering how business was going in the east, especially New York. That was the largest money-making city in the east, next to the several gambling joints and hotels he owned in the west.

His network of deals spread from one coast to the other. Money meant power, and Azario had both. He was a ruthless man, and didn't believe in excuses. He had been in business for almost sixty years. He knew what had to be done to make things work. He never left a loose end, and he always trimmed off excess waste.

Azario had been paying close attention to the news in New York. He was interested in what was happening on the strip. If they had a serial murderer there, that meant a great deal less cash flow. Everyone would be too scared to hit the clubs and streets for action.

Azario could not have some one screwing up his business dealings! This little shit would not destroy what Azario had built after all these years. It didn't matter if his name was Adrian Eisner.

Meanwhile, back in New York, Adrian got out of the bathroom wearing a stylish, three-piece suit. He didn't look anything like the old Adrian Eisner. He walked up to Trixie and gave her a kiss on the cheek and said, "I didn't do it."

Trixie turned her head and looked at him. She said, "I know. I believe you." The bar downstairs should be filling up

ADRIAN

with the noon crowd. Trixie got up and said, "Do you want to come down for a drink?"

Adrian checked his watch and said, "Sure...why not? It's better than sitting up here."

They locked up the apartment and went downstairs. The shows were in full swing and the music was blaring. The laser and light show kept the place bouncing with excitement. They two took their regular seats and ordered the usual.

Trixie said, "We have to come up with a plan to find out who is doing this to you. I think we have to use live bait and see if we can catch this bastard in the act."

Adrian's eyes widened. "You mean that I am going to put some innocent girl at risk of having her head bashed in by a lunatic?"

"Hell no! I'll be the girl."

"No fuck'n way! I am not going to allow you to be put at risk!

This guy has killed seven times already. What makes you think that you can survive?"

"Relax, I've got this." She dug into her purse and showed Adrian a 38 revolver.

Trixie explained, "Don't worry it is registered. I carry it for night time deposits to the bank."

Adrian was shocked and said, "What do you plan to do, once you find him?"

Trixie shrugged her shoulders. "Well, it would be self defence. I'd kill the bastard!"

Adrian shook his head and said, "No way! I can't let you do it! I'll turn myself in and plead guilty, before I would let you go after him."

"Don't be silly. The first sign of danger and I'll nail him right between the eyes."

Adrian was getting enraged. He said, "What if you don't get that shot off? He will kill you!"

"I'm a big girl now. I can make my own decisions."

Adrian stood up and said, "I've had it with you! I love you, and you are going to throw your life away! I can't take it anymore!" He left for the elevator. He went to the apartment to change back into his old grubs.

He grabbed a beer and sat down on the chesterfield. Nervously, he lit a cigarette and took a sip of beer. He was not sure what his next move should be.

Should he leave the apartment and become homeless? Perhaps he should go up to the first police officer he saw and give up.

All these thoughts were swirling around inside his head. He was unable to make sense of the confusion.

His body was shaking and he took a big gulp of beer to try to calm himself down. He was losing his ability to stay within reality.

He was becoming severely agitated. His muscles were tight and he was perspiring heavily. He did not even recognize the apartment. He drank his beer, and noticed there was a bar in there. He went and helped himself to another beer.

He had to calm down or he would totally lose it! There was one way. He ran to the kitchen and grabbed the sharpest knife he could find. He bared his left arm and sliced the inside forearm from one end to the other. He then let out a sigh of relief and took a couple of breaths.

The blood was flowing rapidly onto the linoleum. Adrian was now aware of his surroundings. He had snapped back into reality.

He grabbed a couple of towels, wrapped his arm up tightly, and proceeded to clean the floor. This was the only way he could snap back into reality. It was a method which helped ground him back into reality. As vulgar as it seemed, it really worked.

He threw the towels into the washer and started it up. He peeked at the gouge in his arm and saw that the tendons and major arteries were still intact. It was nothing more than a healthy flesh wound about one and a half inches deep.

Now that he was calm and relaxed, he grabbed his beer and took a nice long gulp. He had regained his composure and returned to normal once again. He went back to the chesterfield and lit another cigarette.

His breathing was back to normal and life went on.

The bleeding had stopped and he threw the other two towels into the washer as well. He buttoned up his sleeve and rolled down his sweater. There was no pain, just a sigh of relief. It actually felt good.

ADRIAN

Now he could think clearly about what he had to do. He pondered for awhile; the murders had almost always happened when he was in the company of a young woman. He could resist the temptation for such company, which would eliminate the targets.

He could also buy a gun on the street, and stick around until the bastard showed up. There was no way that he was going to jeopardize Trixie. She was all he had in life. He decided to get changed back into the suit and go buy a gun. If he died in the process, there was no real loss.

Now that he had changed, he put on his sunglasses and was ready to withdraw money from the bank. The day was still a bit chilly; the hookers were basically wearing long johns. Adrian thought that a thousand dollars should do it.

That would be his last withdrawal; the bank would soon have contact with the police about Adrian's last location.

This was a risky move. They could push the silent alarm, lock the doors and have armed guards on him in seconds. Suddenly, the plan seemed like a failure. He had to get money some other way.

He could use the ATM. However, it had limited amounts. Maybe he could buy a cheap gun for a couple hundred. It was possible; he could do it over a two day period.

Adrian went to the bank across the street and used the ATM. He hid his face from the camera and withdrew two hundred fifty dollars. Now he could hit the streets for his search.

He looked at the corners to see if any young men were just standing around. He walked up and down Davis, trying to determine who were the druggies, pimps and salesmen. He was propositioned several times for drugs and he asked back whether they also carried merchandise.

There hadn't been any takers yet, but Adrian kept on checking the street. A scruffy looking kid came up to him and asked, "Watcha look'n for?"

Adrian looked around before answering. "I need a piece." The kid grabbed Adrian by the arm and said, "Follow me." The kid led him to a back alley where several of his friends were waiting.

One of the other guys said, "What do you want?"

Adrian replied, "I want something cheap, and some ammo too."

They pulled out a towel, unfolded it and put it onto the pavement. There laid several weapons of all different types.

The scruffy kid said, "Pick one."

'What are the prices?"

"Pick one and I'll tell you."

Adrian picked out a 38 revolver. "How much?"

The kid replied, "I'll let you have it for two hundred for the piece and fifty bucks for the ammo."

"That's a little steep. I'll give you two hundred and you throw in the ammo. If you do that, you've got yourself a deal."

The kid put out his empty palm and Adrian filled it with two hundred dollars.

The kid gave Adrian the weapon and a box of shells and said, "Nice doing business with you; now take off."

Adrian quickly put the merchandise away and went back to the G-Spot.

He went to his regular table, took off his coat and sat down. The waitress waved at him, and went and got him a mug of draft. Adrian lit a cigarette and waited for his beer. The beer came and Adrian thanked the cute little waitress. Now he needed a plan that didn't include Trixie.

Adrian took a sip of beer. It was obvious that this guy was watching his every move. Why couldn't he ever notice that someone was watching him? He had to be careful that Trixie didn't start following him, and get herself in shit.

She was damn determined to get this guy herself. Adrian was punishing his brain, trying to come up with an idea of how to set this guy up.

Meanwhile, back at the station, Mike was running a history check on Adrian Graham Eisner on the computer. He was born December 4th, 1960. He was born under the name of Marcus Adam Azario. His father was Frank Thomas Azario and his mother, Karen Lillian Jessup. Mike mumbled under his breath, "Holy shit!"

His step sister was Donna Cheryl Azario. He also had one brother alive, Jonathan Raymond Azario and one deceased, Franklin Roland Azario.

ADRIAN

Mike couldn't believe what he was reading! Everything was falling into place! Still mumbling to himself, he said, "It's a fuck'n family reunion!"

He read that Eisner was raised by an aunt and uncle and was later placed in a foster home because of behaviour problems. He had a history of mental illness dating back to 1972. His last doctor was Doctor Ken Stuart. Doctor Jason Freemont had taken over the case file at Belleview.

Unfortunately, there was no diagnosis of Adrian's problem in public files.

Mike went to the Captain's door and knocked.

The Captain answered, "Come in."

Mike opens the door and said, "I need a search warrant for Dr. Jason Freemont's files on Adrian Eisner slash Marcus Adam Azario."

The Captain looked up at him with astonishment. "Azario! Are you sure?"

"Yes sir, it's all in public records."

The Captain sat back in his chair and said, "Christ, I don't like the way this is going at all! I'll get you your warrant! However, I have to phone Matt right away! Will you please excuse me, this is private."

Mike backed out through the door, closing it quietly.

Mike thought to himself that he had discovered a major break through in the case. Now he had to wait for the warrant. Since the killer might be an Azario, a good place to check would be the Azario Mansion. Mike grabbed his overcoat and headed out to the mansion for more leads.

Upon arriving at this multi-million dollar wonderland, he noticed the guards at the gate. He stopped and said, "Special Task Force, Detective Parsons to see Frank Azario."

The heavy set guard said, "No one enters the grounds without an appointment."

"If you prefer, I'll come back with a warrant and a truck load of officers to search for Marcus Azario," Mike said.

The guard stepped back and called the mansion on the intercom and explained the situation. He came back and said, "Mr. Azario is out of town; we can have him call you when he returns."

"When will that be?"

The guard smiled and said, "He'll be back in about four months."

Mike took offence to the guard's attitude and said, "Ok, I'll be back later today with a warrant and a posse!"

The guard shrugged his shoulders. "Warrant or no warrant, you are not coming into this compound!"

"We'll see about that!"

Mike backed out of the driveway and returned to the station. He was steamed that he couldn't get any information at the mansion.

Maybe Dr. Freemont would have better news. He got out of the car and went into the station.

The Captain greeted him at the entrance and said. "Mike, here is your warrant for Adrian's file."

Mike took the warrant and said, "Thank-you sir. Do you think you can get another warrant to search the Azario Mansion for Marcus Azario?"

The Captain looked at Mike. "Did I hear you right? You want to search Frank Azario's mansion. It will never happen!"

Mike looked surprised. "Why not?"

"We can't start a war in New York City."

"We could have the State Police down here with their battering ram and bulldoze that place down!"

"No, we can't. There would be too much blood and we would fail in our objective. We just want to talk to the guy, not kill him. Sorry, Mike. My hands are tied."

Mike was pissed off and said, "Where is the justice?"

The Captain replied, "It's not worth the bloodshed. Now, that's the end of it!"

Mike turned around and stormed out of the station in a huff. He couldn't believe that some people were so powerful that they could avoid prosecution. How can justice work if everyone is not treated the same? They could escape justice, just because their name is Azario.

With warrant in hand, Mike arrived at the hospital.

He went up to Dr. Freemont's office and showed the receptionist his badge. He gave her the warrant and said, "I would like the file on Adrian Graham Eisner."

The receptionist said, "Just a minute please. I have to check it out with the doctor." She phoned his office and explained.

Dr. Freemont sprang out of his office and confronted Mike. "What makes you think that I am just going to hand over my files?"

Mike snapped back, "That warrant that I handed to your receptionist, signed by Judge Worthington, says that I am responsible for the recovery of Adrian Eisner's medical record."

Dr. Freemont was furious. He shouted, "What gives you the right to take my personal file? It is doctor/patient confidentiality."

"If you don't give up the file voluntarily, I will have a squad of officers' rummage through all your files, and we'll find it ourselves," Mike said.

The doctor's face was as red as a beet as he said, "Cindy, give him the file on Adrian Eisner!" He stormed back to his office, swearing under his breath.

Mike leaned over the desk and smirked.

The receptionist pulled out the file and said, "Here you go. This is Adrian Eisner's file."

"I want to thank-you for all of your help," Mike replied.

He went to the waiting area in the office, and sat down to check the records. He was quickly skimming the file to see if he could find something of importance. The thing was loaded with character profiles, mental capacities, and evaluations.

The guy didn't seem to take to treatment very well. He'd been plagued for pretty well his whole life.

Mike did find a warning in the file. "Patient is highly impulsive, capable of violence if provoked, and sexually hyper."

Well, the murderer fits the same description. Mike quickly closed the file, and went back to the station.

Meanwhile, Matt was getting ready for the one o'clock appointment with Dr. Freemont. He called to Marilyn and said, "Are you almost ready, honey?"

"I'll be down in a minute."

Matt was just having his last sip of coffee, as he turned the burner off.

Marilyn came down the stairs looking radiant. Matt looked her over and said, "You look beautiful, honey."

Marilyn smiled and said, "I want to thank you for your kindness, dear."

They left by the back door to the car.

As they were driving to the hospital, Marilyn asked, "What was the phone call about?"

"You wouldn't guess it in a million years! Adrian Eisner had his name changed when he was a baby. His name was Marcus Adam Azario."

Marilyn was shocked. "Is there any relationship between Marcus and the Azario you killed a couple of years ago?

Matt nodded his head and said, "Yes, they were brothers."

Marilyn sat up and said, "This could all be about revenge for killing Frank Jr.!"

"I think you got the same picture as I did, honey. I think that is why we are the killer's target."

"Are you sure Adrian is the killer?"

"No, there is one more possibility that we haven't checked out yet. There is one more brother; his name is Jonathan. Not only that, there is also a step sister named Donna. I don't know. It might be that the whole family is involved.

However, we can't go into the mansion for questioning without starting another Waco, Texas. The Captain doesn't want another disaster like the Davidian Camp."

"What are you going to do now to stop the murderer?"

"First, we have to positively identify him. This is all speculation."

The couple arrived at the hospital parking lot. They parked the car and went into the hospital. They took the elevator to the forth floor and went to the reception desk.

Matt said, "We have an appointment, Matt and Marilyn, to see Dr. Freemont at one o'clock."

The receptionist said, "Please have a seat; the doctor will see you in a minute."

The couple sat down and they each picked up a magazine.

They barely got comfortable when the doctor came out of the office and said, "Matt, I would like to see you first. Please come in."

Matt walked into the office and sat in the chair next to the desk.

The doctor closed the door and sat down in his office chair. "Well Matt, how are things going for you? I understand that you are going through some very rough times right now."

Matt replied, "It has a lot of room for improvement. My family is under siege of a madman.

ADRIAN

We are under police protection. My daughter was raped and beaten. I am also trying to catch this guy, but I can't because I was suspended by the force. So, my plate is quite full right now."

"How are you coping with the added stress?"

Matt smiled and said, "I've been drinking a lot more beer. My wife and I use each other to lean on. If we need to talk, the other will listen."

The doctor was surprised at the healthy approach and said, "That sounds very good. Do you have anyone else you can lean on?"

"I have my protégé, Mike Parsons; he's a great support system to me. He found and saved my daughter. I have a lot of respect for the man. I also have my Captain. When push comes to shove, he is always in my corner backing me up."

"It sounds like your success in coping with this extra stress is due to an excellent support team," said the doctor.

"I seem to be handling it much better than I thought I was capable of. I feel quite confident that I can handle this."

The doctor was writing down notes on the assessment form and said, "I have one important question for you, that I want you to answer honestly. What would you do if you met up with this guy one to one?"

Matt sat and thought about it for a moment and said, "That's very difficult to say. It all depends on the situation."

The doctor wrote down the response. "Well, Matt. I can't find anything wrong with you. You are handling the stress very well. I don't see anything that would get in the way of your job."

As Matt was listening to the doctor, he got a glimpse of a file that had a recognizable name.

The name was Ken Stuart. That must be Dr. Freemont's patient. Matt barely heard a word when he blurted out, "What ever happened to Ken Stuart?"

The doctor was surprised by the interruption and said, "Are you here for my help, or are you on business?"

"I'm sorry; he was just my old doctor. I just wondered what happened to him."

Dr. Freemont said, "I'm not obligated to talk to you about other doctors or patients without a warrant."

Matt thought to himself that the doctor was pretty tense about something.

"Fine. So I'm doing well and I have the stress under control. What is the bottom line?"

The doctor said, "Before I was rudely interrupted, I was saying that I don't see any reason why you cannot return to full duties again. I am recommending that you return to work ASAP."

"Thank-you, doctor. This is the type of news I like to hear."

"You can now send Marilyn in."

Matt went to the door and left the office. He went to the waiting room and said, "Honey, the doctor would like to see you now."

Marilyn put down her magazine and smiled at her husband as she passed.

Matt sat down and picked up a magazine. About fifteen minutes passed, when someone caught his eye. His eyes widened and he said, "Hi Dr. Stuart. It is strange meeting you here."

The tall man lowered his head and sat as far away from life as possible. He never uttered a word, and his head was pointed at the floor. The poor man looked like he was shaken up quite badly.

"What the hell happened to him?" Matt wondered. He thought he had better just leave him alone. It didn't look like he was very talkative right now. Besides, Matt could smell the booze reeking off of him.

A few more minutes pass by and Marilyn came out of the office. She said, "I have to stop by the pharmacy and pick up a prescription."

Looking concerned Matt said, "Is everything alright?"

"I'll be alright; I just need something to calm me down for awhile."

Matt got up, took his wife by the arm and went to the elevator. They went to the car and got in.

Matt was worried that Marilynn was finding it a little harder to manage the stress. She looked alright; he always thought that she was stronger than him.

"Would you like to go for a late lunch? I'm a little hungry."

Marilyn smiled and said, "I would like that. Where do you want to go?"

ADRIAN

"I feel like having a big bowl of soup and a sandwich on a day like today."

"I would like that too. There's a nice deli only a few blocks from here, and it has a pharmacy right next door. I can put my prescription in first, and have our lunch. By the time we finish eating, the pills will be ready for pick up."

Matt replied, "Excellent plan, my dear. You tell me where it is. I'm not familiar with this deli."

She smiled. "Don't worry. I'll guide you."

At the G-Spot, Adrian had just ordered himself another mug of draft. He was sitting back and watching the afternoon crowd fill the place. Trixie came out and sat across from him. She ordered a gin and tonic.

"Well, how are you doing?" she asked.

"I'm doing alright. I'm just sitting back and enjoying my beer."

"Have you given any thought on how we are going to catch this guy?"

"Are you still on that? We...are not going to do anything! Get that thought out of your fuck'n head!"

The drinks arrived and she took a sip. She said, "You can't stop me!"

"I'll shoot you myself if I have to."

Looking amazed Trixie said, "You wouldn't do that!"

Adrian said calmly, "Try me." He then pulled out the weapon and pointed it at her.

When he saw the shock on her face, he put the gun away. Trixie gasped, "How the hell did you get a gun?"

"You can get anything you want off the street within a half hour."

She freaked and said, "What the hell are you going to do with that?"

"I'll do the exact thing that you said you were going to do. It will be self defence."

"That is not a registered firearm!"

"When was the last time an Azario did something legal?"

Trixie got up in a huff and slapped him across the face. Adrian thought that was a pretty good comeback. She huffed and stormed back to the dressing room.

Adrian thought to himself, "Touché." He lit a smoke and took a sip of beer. He then decided to watch the shows for the afternoon.

Back at the station, Mike was going over Adrian's file. He was writing down notes as he reviewed the documents. The diagnosis was severe manic depression; he had a character defect and he was psychotic.

That seemed to qualify as being a nutcase. He had all the characteristics of being a killer, but there was no mention of any crimes. It did mention that he was sexually hyper; however there was nothing in the file that indicated any assaults or felonies. Mike was expecting to see some concrete evidence, and there was none.

It seemed that Adrian had been extremely ill for many years, and somehow kept it under control. It was possible he did not mention any crimes for the fear of getting caught. Any way, the file was basically useless.

They already knew that the killer was a psychopath. There was nothing that actually linked Adrian to the murders, except circumstantial evidence.

The Captain poked his head out of his office and said, "Mike, come in here. I want to talk to you."

"Yes sir." He went to the Captain's office.

"Close the door and have a seat," the Captain said. "We have the lab results and the DNA report back. In the four of the murders, Adrian's semen was found smeared on the clothing of the victims.

The semen found on the twenty dollars bills was also Adrian's. His finger prints were found at two of the murder scenes. That proves that Adrian was at five murder scenes. However, he is not the rapist. It proved conclusively that it wasn't him!

There is good news about this. The DNA retracted from the bodies does prove that the samples came from a sibling of the same mother. That means that our rapist is Jonathan Azario. He is our second suspect for the murders."

Mike took in all this information and said, "How do we go about bringing these two guys to justice?"

"We will issue the old man arrest warrants for Adrian and Jonathan. Then we will play it by ear."

"He's out of town and won't be back for months."

ADRIAN

"Don't worry about that. I'm sure he will get the message, and he'll be back in New York by noon tomorrow."

Mike was very excited that they now had names for the murderers.

It would take some time for the other results to come through for the other cases.

At least, they were sure of these. Unfortunately, if the killers were hidden within the mansion, they might never get them.

Mike asked, "Is there anything else, sir?"

"No, but I'll get you those warrants for you. You can go back to the mansion and serve those documents. While you wait, you can run a history check on Jonathan Azario."

"Yes sir. I'll get right on it." Mike then left the office and went to Records and pulled out the history on Jonathan Raymond Azario.

The computer pulled up the file. Born October 9th, 1958, Jonathan had been raised by an aunt and uncle. He had a history of mental illness that stretched over most of his life.

In 1974, he had murdered the entire family and killed nineteen people at Gregory James High School. He was found not guilty due to an insanity plea.

He was remanded in a psychiatric facility for ten years, then released, and disappeared from the face of the earth. There was no financial trail or crimes committed since then. From 1984 to 2002, no one had heard or seen Jonathan Raymond Azario. Mike now knew he was very capable of murder, and that this was probably his man. The history proved that he was very ill. He would be a very dangerous man if he were still alive, and on the streets!

Adrian was sitting back, enjoying the show, when he noticed that three lovely ladies had just come into the bar. They had taken a table nearest the first stage.

They were probably checking out the competition, or they were new dancers wanting to learn the ropes.

All three of them were extremely pretty; it was still unknown if they could perform on stage.

The ladies ordered their drinks and they noticed that Adrian was staring at them. They felt uncomfortable with that, so they turned their backs to him.

The little gesture didn't ward off Adrian. He had always wanted three women at one time. These three would do fine. He was studying their fine lines and skin tones, imagining what they would look like in a dimly-lit bedroom.

Adrian then ordered another beer and lit a cigarette. He watched closely as the excitement down in his pants grew.

He saw Trixie bring the ladies their drinks and talk to them for a while.

It looked like Trixie had business dealings with the trio. They didn't have to pay for their drinks. Adrian was hoping that they might perform on stage tonight.

Trixie glanced at Adrian and quickly went back to the conversation with the three women. It was obvious she was still pissed about the Azario remark. Too fuck'n bad. Adrian was thinking that tonight might be the night to take down that murdering son of a bitch.

Under the table, Adrian took out the firearm and shells. He loaded the weapon and ensured that the safety was on. Once he was done, he quickly tucked everything away. His beer arrived at the table and he gave the waitress a tip and said, "Thank-you." She smiled and went to the next table.

He was still watching the ladies and Trixie gab it up. Finally, Trixie grabbed the long haired brunette by the hand, and took her into the dressing room.

Adrian was thinking, "Now, comes the moment of truth. We get a chance to see if she could dance as well as she looks."

Several acts went by. Adrian was still watching the two remaining ladies at the table. The lights went dim and the music slowly faded. Suddenly, in a flash of sparks and smoke, the stage lit up like a roman candle.

The brunette was on stage making her debut. She exploded into action staying in perfect sync to the music. Her long curly hair bounced to the beat of the music.

She was very energetic and precise in her movements. She obviously knew what she was doing. Her beauty was something to admire. She had long succulent legs and a tight ass. Her breasts were plastic, but they still looked nice.

She was fantastic; she could easily be a headliner. In a burst of white light, she disappeared off the stage. The crowd went electric with applause. She really brought the house down.

ADRIAN

Moments later, she walked past Adrian's table and looked at him for a reaction to her performance. There was none. She smiled and went to the dressing room where Trixie was standing with open arms. That was pretty good! She had impressed the boss.

It was still pretty early in the evening, but Adrian wanted to go out and feel the night time air.

He finished his beer and put on his coat.

He left through the main entrance, into the cool night time air. The poor hookers were freezing their tails off.

Adrian decided to go to the convenience store for a twelve of beer and some cigarettes. The store clerk was carefully watching Adrian. Adrian noticed that the clerk was acting nervous.

He put the beer on the counter and asked for two packs of smokes. He could see very clearly that there was a poster of him on the wall.

He quickly grabbed his stuff and high tailed it back to the apartment. It was obvious that the police would be around looking for him soon. Back at the apartment, he took off his long overcoat and popped a beer. He wasn't sure if the police would check the bar or not, so he thought he would stay up here for a while.

There was a knock at the door and Adrian cautiously went towards it. "Who is it?" he said.

The voice on the other side said, "It's me, Trixie. Open up."

Adrian opened the door and asked, "What's up?"

"The police were just here. They did a full-scale search of the premises looking for you. What set them off?"

"I went to the store to buy beer and cigarettes, and the clerk recognized me from a poster he had on the wall."

"You better stay low for a while; I'm not sure how long they are going to stick around."

"How are you doing?"

"I'm feeling better. I guess it was kind of stupid of me to think that I should go on a manhunt."

Adrian agreed. "That was not one of your brightest schemes. However, the brunette you put on the floor was fantastic. She will do very well for you."

"Thanks, I think she'll be one of my headliners in very short time."

"Would you like a drink?"

"Thank-you, I think that would be very nice, right about now."

Adrian poured her gin and tonic and they went to sit on the chesterfield.

"You really wouldn't shoot me, would you?" Trixie asked.

"I would if I really had too."

Trixie smirked and said, "Look what kind of brother you turned out to be!"

"I'm only trying to protect you from getting yourself killed. That's all. Do you think that it is clear to go downstairs tonight?"

Trixie shrugged her shoulders and said, "It should be alright. They already did their massive search of the place.

Just be careful tonight; they might pop back in later." They drank up their drinks and went downstairs. Adrian went straight to his table and ordered another beer.

He took a look around and the three ladies were still there. He was wondering if the other two ladies danced as well. They had all the right parts in all the right places.

He would love to see them on stage. Adrian was curious whether the police had left or not - he really wanted to go out tonight.

His beer arrived and he gave the waitress a five dollar bill for keepers. She smiled and went back to work. He lit a cigarette and eased into his chair.

He was watching the show, when he noticed Trixie trying to sneak out the front entrance without being noticed.

He mumbled to himself, "Damn!" He didn't even have his overcoat; it still got pretty chilly at night.

He had to follow her. Adrian ran out of the front and looked up and down Davis Ave. He saw nothing. He decided to walk up and down to see if she took to an alley.

Maybe she would try the school. Adrian ran down and looked down the alley. He found her; she was entering the school yard.

Adrian thought to himself, "What the hell is going on?" He stayed within the shadows, and got a little closer.

He watched her light a cigarette and stand there in the open. Either she was waiting for someone or she had put herself there as a target.

ADRIAN

Adrian went to the other side of the alley. He slowly crouched down and followed the shadow to the back of the school. He thought he would come up behind her. He just had to make sure her hand wasn't on the gun when he startled her. Adrian was in position. He was just waiting for both hands to be visible. He sprung like a tiger and grabbed her, locking her arms to her side.

Trixie screamed blue murder. Adrian yelled at her, "You stupid bitch!! I snuck up to you with no problem. The murderer is probably a lot better than I am when using stealth. You wouldn't have had a chance! You would be dead right now!"

Adrian let loose his grip on her and Trixie quickly turned around and slapped him in the face, "You bastard!! I just pissed myself!!"

Adrian yelled back, "You're lucky that is all that happened to you! What the hell do you think you are doing?"

"I'm going to prove that you are innocent, that's what!"

"We better get out of here. We made a lot of noise. The police will be here any minute."

"I'm not moving! I'm staying right here!"

"You are a stupid, stubborn bitch! I can't handle you any more. I'm going inside. Go ahead! Get killed! See if I really care!"

Adrian spun around and went down the alley, towards Davis Ave. He quickly disappeared into the shadows. Trixie was left standing in the cold, soaking wet, but determined.

Adrian was pissed off, but he was also cold. He decided to go to the apartment and get his coat and gloves. Maybe, by the time he returned, she would have come to her senses.

Meantime, Trixie was lighting another cigarette.

Her bare, wet legs were freezing in this weather. She was trying to keep warm, when she saw the silhouette of a man coming towards her. She yelled, "Forget it, Adrian. I'm staying right here."

The figure came closer and Trixie was slowly trying to make out who this guy was. He looks very familiar.

The voice said, "Don't worry, it's me."

"What the hell are you doing out here?" Trixie said.

"I went to the bar to tell you something, and they said that you slipped out. When I came out, I heard yelling. I then followed the voices and found you standing here alone."

"What's so fuck'n important that you had to come all the way out here?" Trixie slightly turned her back to light a cigarette, when all of a sudden she saw a bright flash of light. She crumpled to the ground, bleeding severely from the head.

The ground quickly soaked up the dark crimson liquid. She laid deathly still. Adrian was running back to the school yard when he saw a man standing over the fallen woman. His baseball bat was raised above the head, ready for another blow to Trixie's already battered skull.

Suddenly, a gun shot fired. The man with the baseball bat fell to the ground. He dropped his bat and quickly got up and limped his way back into the shadows. Adrian fired a second shot, but it had no effect.

Adrian quickly ran to the convenience store and used the desk phone to call 911.

He yelled into the receiver, "I need an ambulance and the police to come to Carrolton Elementary. A woman was assaulted with a baseball bat, please hurry!"

He ran in a panic to Trixie's side and held her bleeding head. "Please sweetheart, don't die! Don't leave me now! Please don't leave!" He could hear the sirens getting closer. In tears he stood up and yelled, "Hurry the fuck up! Don't let her die!"

He laid his head onto Trixie's chest and cried like a baby. The flashing lights were now shining on them. He turned his head to the ambulance attendant and said, "It's about fuck'n time! Don't you care if she lives or dies?"

A police officer took Adrian off to the side. Adrian explained, "I am the man that you are looking for. My name is Adrian Eisner and that is my sister. Please officer, save her!"

Adrian put his hands over his head and clasped his fingers. He said, "Be careful officer, there is a loaded thirty eight revolver in my right hand coat pocket.

I fired twice. I hit him in the leg with the first shot and I missed on the second." The officer turned Adrian around and proceeded to handcuff and read him his rights.

Within minutes of the initial officers arriving on the ground, the whole area was surrounded by cop cars and yellow tape.

ADRIAN

Adrian said one more thing. "I would like to exercise my right to remain silent." The officer tucked down his head before putting him in the back seat of the cruiser.

Later on that night at the Azario Manor in L.A., the phone rang. The butler answered and said, "Sir, you have an urgent call from New York."

Frank Azario said, "Thank-you, Charles."

He stayed quiet for the entire time he was on the phone, and he quietly hung up a few minutes later. "Charles, get my jet ready to go. I'm going to New York, tonight!"

Chapter Eleven

Mike arrived at the scene and was greeted by the Captain. The Captain said, "This is getting very strange, Mike. It's a family feud. From what I made of it, Jonathan took the bat to Donna. As he was in the process of finishing her off, Marcus fired two shots. One was a hit in the leg and the other was a miss.

Marcus slash Adrian has turned himself in, and he is fully cooperative. I now believe that Adrian has been innocent all this time, and that Jonathan is the rapist and murderer.

Adrian has chosen not to speak to us tonight, but has promised a full statement tomorrow after lunch. However, he did request to see his doctor. Apparently, he hasn't been on any medication for awhile and is having a terrible time with his illness. The forensics team found a blood type that doesn't match Adrian or Donna. It looks like we will have the DNA evidence to charge Jonathan with all of the rapes and murders.

There is one other thing. I have reinstated Matt tonight; he is back in charge of the case. You can pick him up at the regular time tomorrow morning."

Mike said, "Thank-you sir, I will. There is one other thing, sir. How is the woman?"

"She is going for surgery to relieve the pressure on the brain. There is a severe fracture and swelling. They are going to keep her in an induced coma.

They are doing this to cut down as much brain activity as possible, until the swelling goes down. It is unknown if there is brain damage, and to what extent.

She is alive; she can thank Adrian for that. I have to finish a few things off here. You can go home, and I'll see you tomorrow."

Mike then went back to the car and drove off. He was thinking he might get a few more hours sleep before he had to go to work. He was wondering how they could get their hands on Jonathan; they didn't even know what he looked like. Perhaps, Adrian could fill them in on some information.

ADRIAN

Later in life, treatments were used on a more regular basis. Those years of hell were left behind. Slowly the behaviour improved. Those years of being totally out of control were now subdued by several types of treatment. With treatment, I was able to regain my sense of morality and control of myself. Today, the amount of time that I am totally out of control is greatly reduced, but not eliminated.

Even the short periods that I am out of control are still unacceptable. A lot of things can happen in eight to ten hours. The medication today seems to stop me from destroying myself. It feels like my morality and control is just hanging on by a thread.

It is the biggest time bomb set to blow my life into kingdom come. The exception is that you cannot see the timer. The only way to stop the disaster from happening is to defuse the bomb. That's me!

I also do not know when this will happen. I just know it will. It does seem that it will be soon. This treatment seems to be the most important, and possibly the last chance to cure the condition. It seems that there is no room for failure.

It is my conscience that is warning me of severe danger. This is the first time that I am extremely desperate to end these episodes.

The time is growing close and my nerves are starting to tense up. Is this a warning that my life is coming to an end? Perhaps, this is why God has called upon me.

The last three to four months have been full of discoveries. This is the first time that so many secrets and mysteries have been unlocked and discovered by me. If this treatment fails to stop the next episode, there is no fear. It has been a devastating experience as well as interesting.

So much has happened that I may never discover some of the miracles that have become part of my life. I do not feel saddened that I have this illness; it almost feels like a *blessing. I was meant to have this life, and to experience it the way God always wanted me to.*

*Journal
September 17th, 2000
MADMAN*

It was a brand new morning and Matt had just rolled out of the fart sack. First things first. He'd have a quick cup of coffee, and then he would get cleaned up for work. Downstairs he went. The uniformed officer said, "Good morning sir. Good to have you back on board."

Matt replied, "Thanks, it's good to be back."

He started up the coffee machine, and went to the back step to get the paper. The paper read September 20th, 2002. Matt was surprised that there was no story in the paper about Adrian and the shooting. They must have gagged the story, because it would interfere with the investigation.

The coffee was ready and Matt got up and poured himself a cup.

He sat back down and took a sip. From the corner of his eye, he could see that Marilyn had come down the steps already showered and dressed.

She came into the kitchen, and bent down to kiss her husband on the cheek. She went and got herself a cup of coffee and sat down. "Is there anything in the paper, dear?"

"No, they must have gagged the story. There is nothing about it in the paper."

Matt stood up, took the last gulp of coffee and said, "Honey, I'm going up to take my shower. I'll be down in a bit."

"Ok dear."

Several minutes later, the uniformed officer said, "Mrs. Ruzo, Mr. Parsons has just driven in."

"Thank-you please let him in."

There was a quick knock at the door and then in flew Mike. He was beaming from ear to ear and said, "Good morning, Mrs. Ruzo. Sorry, I mean Marilyn."

She smiled and said, "That's better! Good morning Mike. Would you like a cup of coffee?"

"Sure! Don't get up. I'll get it myself."

ADRIAN

He poured his coffee and sat down in his usual spot. He noticed the still-empty spot where his little munchkin usually occupied.

"How is Emily?"

"She is doing remarkably well. She doesn't like the hospital very much. She also can't wait until she can sink her teeth into a juicy hamburger. She is already tired of pureed food. It's just the normal complaints you would expect from a twelve year old."

Mike smiled and said, "That's my little girl!"

From the kitchen, you could hear thunder as Matt came down the steps all primed for his first day back. "Good morning, Mike," He said.

"Good morning! Do you think you are ready to go back to work so early?"

Matt refilled his cup and said, "Sure, I'm ready. We are just that close from closing the case. I feel great about it." He sat down and took a sip of coffee.

Mike warned, "There could still be some problems before we actually get our hands on him."

"I know that. I wasn't born yesterday! I know there may be a long haul ahead of us before we catch him."

"It will be interesting to see what Adrian has to say today. He must have had quite an experience trying to get away from us."

"I'm more interested in yesterday's shooting, and the location of Jonathan.

He has a bullet in his leg, and he hasn't checked into a hospital or clinic. Don't you find that strange?"

"Not really; he knows we are checking out those places for him. He probably dug it out himself."

"He's more ingenious than what I give him credit for. He is also more dangerous than I thought. A psycho like that probably doesn't even feel physical pain."

"He probably doesn't feel much of anything. Things like guilt, remorse or morals don't play out in his mind.

He is a true killing machine, and that's about it." Mike got up, poured himself another coffee and asked, "Marilyn would you like another cup?"

"Yes please."

Mike came to the table and poured her another coffee. He said, "Well, that's it for this pot." He then turned off the machine and sat down.

"What did the doctor say last night?" asked Matt.

Mike replied, "He said Adrian is on a severe mania with psychotic tendencies. In other words, he is unfit to stand trial if he is ever charged with anything."

Matt asked, "Do you think that anything he says today will actually be fact, or will it be a hallucination?"

"I don't know if we can trust his word. Even if he believes it to be the truth, I don't think we can quote him."

"That leaves us in a pickle. I have a suspect and he is totally useless."

"The girl won't be any good to us. They are going to keep her in a coma for awhile. We don't even know if she will remember her own name, never mind anything else. She did pull through the surgery alright. However, only time will tell."

Matt said, "That really pisses me off! We are stuck. We know the guy's name, but no one has seen him in the last ten or fifteen years or so. He must be either dead or under an alias. We need the names of every employee who works for Frank Azario.

After we get the names, then we check each one against the computer and weed them out."

"How are we going to get the names?" asked Mike.

"I don't know yet. I have to think on that one. The Azario Mansion is the best place to start, but I don't think they will give us the list voluntarily.

They didn't respond to the arrest warrant. I don't think they will help us by offering us information."

"It is affirmed that Frank Azario landed in New York early this morning. We will give him a dingle, and see if he will at least talk about his daughter. Donna and Emily share the same room. They are protected by two uniformed officers. Even Frank Azario is not allowed in for a visit. The Captain is not taking any chances; she is our star witness."

Meanwhile at the Azario Mansion, Frank was catching up on the news about the slayings involved around the strip. He sat in a luxurious tea room over looking the immaculately manicured grounds.

He could not help but wonder how Donna was doing.

ADRIAN

He looked at the arrest warrants, thinking that it may be possible that both his boys are involved. Frank had never seen Adrian in his life. He had taken off before Karen had the baby. Adrian had been adopted by Frank's sister and her husband, Harold Eisner. It was there that he grew up for twelve years before being released to Child Protective Services.

The old man had plans for this son. The plan would be ruined if Adrian went to jail, or if he was incarcerated in a hospital for the rest of his life. Frank had to find out the truth, before the police did.

He summoned several of his men to be his personal task force. He wanted them to gather information on Adrian, and the murders. Frank Sr. would make his judgement once all the facts were in. If he had to, he would kill Adrian and Jonathan himself.

Back at the lock up, Adrian was enjoying his breakfast. He had had a great sleep, due to the fact that he was finally back on his medication. It would take six weeks for the medication to kick in full strength, but he already felt better.

He had a good talk with Dr. Freemont last night. The doctor was trying to make him recollect his memory, and see if he had killed those people. But it was to no avail; the doctor was unsuccessful trying to recover any memory. He couldn't even remember trying to rape Trixie.

Adrian really did not know if he was guilty or not. The one thing was he never owned a baseball bat. He didn't even remember ever seeing a bat around, either. He did know that he had shot a man in the leg, while he was about to kill Trixie. He was prepared to tell the police everything.

It was Adrian's hope that they would find the truth one way or another. He didn't want a lawyer present; he thought they were the biggest crooks around.

The guard came around to pick up the breakfast dishes and said, "Are you all finished in there?"

Adrian replied, "Yes sir, the breakfast was delicious, thank-you." He then handed the guard the tray. He was baffled as to who would want to pin those murders on him. He couldn't think of a reason why it had to be him.

Not unless he really did commit the murders. It would all come out in the wash, when he talked to the police. Adrian was thinking that he was ready to face the music now, and not wait until after lunch.

He yelled, "Guard!!...Guard!!"

The guard heard the call "What do you want?"

"I'm ready to talk now."

"Ok, I'll pass it on to the Captain and we'll get it set up for you."

"Thank-you, officer."

Mike and Matt pulled into the station and got out of the car. Mike said, "Cross your fingers. I hope we have a good day today."

Matt replied, "That all depends on what Adrian has to say."

They went inside and were greeted by the Captain. "Hi you guys. Welcome back, Matt. Well, the morning is starting well. Adrian is willing to talk right now. The interrogation room will be ready in ten minutes. He seems willing to get this out in the open, so play it by ear. Don't spoof him."

Matt said, "Don't worry. We'll take it easy on him and just let him talk. We need all the information he can tell us. Are you taping the interview?"

"Yes we are. We don't want any screw ups, so it will all be on film. That's why you have to wait a few minutes."

The guard came out to see the Captain and said, "The interrogation room is ready, sir."

"Well boys, good luck."

The detectives went to the interrogation room and waited for the guard to bring Adrian. A few minutes later, he arrived under guard and in shackles. He sat down in front of the two detectives.

Matt said, "My name is Detective Ruzo and this is Detective Parsons. Good morning Adrian."

Adrian replied, "Good morning detectives."

Matt said, "Adrian, I want you to gather your thoughts on September 8th, 2000."

Adrian laughed. "I can hardly remember yesterday, and you want me to remember a date? You have to give me a better clue than that, detective."

Matt rephrased the question. "Do you remember Allison Rachel Chambers from two years ago?"

"I don't remember the name, sorry."

ADRIAN

"How about a young woman who was raped and had her head crushed in? Near her body was a semen-stained twenty dollar bill, with your DNA on it."

Adrian replied, "I remember giving three women twenty dollar bills, but they were not stained."

"Adrian, tell us how you think those bills got stained with your semen."

Adrian replied, "Actually, two of the women were at the same location. They both happened about the same way. I was walking up Davis Ave., looking at hookers and I got a little excited. When I get excited, I become quite impulsive. I saw a beautiful young woman and grabbed her hand.

I then shoved it down my pants. When she grabbed me, I creamed all over her hand. I then gave her a twenty dollar bill for her trouble. I grabbed a cab and went home. The other one happened about a week or so back."

Matt said, "Tell us about the young woman in the apartment who was found raped and murdered."

Adrian explained. "She was working on one of the corners when I spotted her. She was very beautiful and I got sexually aroused. I watched her all night. When she was done for the night, she went to the convenience store for some groceries.

I followed her home, and snuck through the security door. When she got to her apartment and started to pull out her keys, I came out and asked her if I could help pay for her groceries. She smiled and put her hand down my pants and jerked me off. I then gave her a twenty and went home."

"Did she jerk you off inside the apartment or outside?"

"Outside."

"Tell us about the girl in the school yard. Your semen and fingerprints were found at the scene".

Adrian replied, "There was a girl at the school yard. She was working the corner when I was having a few beers. I was feeling lonely and I paid her one hundred dollars to keep me company.

Her name was Pam. I don't know her last name. Things got a little out of hand and she gave me oral sex. When she finished, I gave her a twenty dollar bill. Then I grabbed a cab and went home."

Matt asked, "What do you know about the two cops that were murdered?

Adrian said, "They stopped me for my ID. I gave it to them. I saw them later in the G-Spot with you two guys doing a search for me. I didn't see them again. I never touched them."

"How about the woman in the apartment with all your fingerprints plastered all over?"

"She was a real nice girl. Christine was her name. She was a stripper at the G-Spot. I was drinking beer in the school yard when she came up to me. We got interested in each other and we hit a bar together. We then went to her place and had a beautiful evening.

We made love and I returned to the G-Spot in the morning. She was very much alive when I left."

"What can you tell us about the rape and beating of Emily Ruzo?"

"I don't know anything about the little girl. I only know what I saw on the news. I never saw the girl in my life."

"Why did we find a bloodied paper towel with your blood type on it at the scene?"

"I don't know. Someone must have found it at the school yard or something. They probably kept it, and planted it later."

"Are you injured?"

Adrian stood up and lifted his shirt and removed the bandages. He said, "I have another wound on my left arm." He then bared his arm.

Matt was shocked at the size of the wounds and said, "Those are very serious wounds. Who did this to you?"

Adrian replied, "No one, I did them myself. That is a method I use to shock myself back into reality. It really works well."

Matt commented, "There is serious infection in those wounds; we'll get you a doctor. You have to get those wounds fixed up. You can sit down again, Adrian."

Matt was very shocked at how Adrian was reacting to the barrage of questions. He was doing very well and seemed to be very cooperative.

"What can you tell us about Donna Azario?" Matt asked.

"She is apparently my step sister. I only met her couple of weeks ago, while I was in a bar. She followed me a couple of times, and then the relationship grew. She told me that I am an Azario too.

She also told me that I have one brother who was killed by a cop, and another older brother named Jonathan."

"Have you ever met your two other brothers?"

"Never."

Matt sat back, took a deep breath and said, "Are you telling me that you never met your real family except for Donna?"

"Yes sir, that is exactly right."

"How did you get the gun?"

Adrian explained. "I was wandering up and down Davis, when I was approached by a kid. He asked me what I wanted. I told him.

He then sold me a 38 revolver and a box of shells for two hundred dollars. I was on the lookout for a weapon not longer than half an hour."

"Tell us what happened last night when you fired two shots from that weapon."

Adrian explained. "Trixie had the stupid idea that she could catch this guy on her own. We argued several times that it was too dangerous. That is why I bought the gun in the first place; I had to protect her from making a stupid mistake. She wouldn't come back to the bar with me. So, I went to get my coat and gloves and go back to talk some sense to her.

When I returned, I saw this man with a bat raised over his head. He was getting ready to hit her again. I fired one shot and he fell down and dropped his bat.

He then got up and limped to the shadows. I fired a second shot, and it had no effect."

Matt asked, "Where were you hiding all this time?"

"That's the only question that I refuse to answer. I'm sorry."

"Well, Adrian, we still have circumstantial evidence that proves that you were at most of the crime scenes. That means that you are still a suspect. We can charge you for possession of an illegal firearm. We can also charge you with discharging a firearm in city limits."

"Can't you have those charges dropped? I told you everything I know!" Adrian said.

Matt stood up and walked around a bit. "We will let you walk out those doors today, if you help us out."

"How can I do that?"

"Frank Azario is back in town. There is no doubt in my mind that he is going to track you down. He also needs some questions answered. We will clear you of all charges and publish it in the newspaper and on TV.

Azario will then accept you, and bring you back to the mansion. You can be our bloodhound. I want you to sniff out your brother, Jonathan. We want a list of names of the people who are employed by Frank Azario.

Try to get all the information you can, and relay it back to us. We want to reveal Jonathan's fake identity."

Adrian asked, "Isn't it a little dangerous to put me in that situation?"

"Yes, it is extremely dangerous. However, Azario is going to make it happen either way. We don't have to do anything. The ball is in his court. All you have to do is stay visible.

We will try to keep an eye on you, but you will basically be on your own. We can't use a wire tap; if they found it they would kill you. Do you agree with these terms?"

"That is pretty dangerous work considering that I can quietly serve out my time for a couple of minor charges."

"You are still a suspect; we can always charge you for those crimes when the time comes. Take it or leave it."

Adrian replied, "Fine, I'll take it."

I can feel that my time on this earth is fast approaching its final chapter. My head is spinning with thoughts that I cannot control. I cannot control my hunger. I am trying to resist, but the evil is too powerful for me to stop. I think it is almost time to feed again. What dark force has taken over my body and soul? How can this possibly be happening to me? My dear brother will either be dead or incarcerated for life. I will not have to worry anymore. My future is secure. With him and that slut out of my life, I will have what is rightfully mine. I wonder if the bitch survived or not.

I haven't heard anything on the news lately. The story has been put on the back burner. I don't understand why! I am big news in the city; they have to pay attention to me! They just have to!

ADRIAN

I think it is time to have a little chat with Matt in the future. I haven't heard from my little buddy in a while. I hope he is keeping well. I wonder how Emily is. She was a nice piece of ass! I'd love to do her again! Maybe next time, I'll give the mom a whirl. Matt would love that!

I can't forget about Matt. I have to do something extra special for him. I will never forgive him for what he did to my brother.

That fat son of a bitch will soon meet his maker. This has been nothing more than a little game; it is time to raise the stakes a bit higher.

Matt must learn and accept the sins that he has committed and beg for forgiveness. I want him to beg on his knees and cry for mercy. I want to see his sins spill to the ground. His precious time is soon coming to an end. He too, will beg.

He is a bit of a pain in the ass. I heard that he has been put back in charge of the case. I'll just have to try a little harder to make everyone understand me. No one knows what it is like, no one cares! I will make them all listen to me, I speak the truth.

I have been given a gift from God. It is my obligation to fulfill his wishes.

Soon, everyone will know the truth. Only a few have been chosen by these sacred hands. Many more are needed to show the world that they are in God's hands. They must accept him into their dark souls.

They have had it much too easy in their miserable lives. They must repent. They have to go down on their knees, and beg for forgiveness. They have to shed tears of sorrow, before accepting everlasting joy into their hearts. Their wretched souls have to be made aware of their sins. They have to be struck down by God, so that others can learn. This is the only way!

Soon, all of New York will be captivated by God's love and spirit. They will all beg for forgiveness. He may spare them, if they shed real tears. They have to learn the truth about themselves!

They are all sinners. They must all feel God in their hearts. He is the only one that can grant them eternal peace. I can help, by showing them the way of the Lord, and deliver them from evil.

*Journal
September 20th, 2002
MADMAN*

Adrian showered and the doctor did the necessary repairs to his body. The papers were being processed so that he could be released under his own recognizance; that was, providing he adhered to a strict list of regulations.

He had to stay in contact with the detectives as directed by the schedule. Most importantly, he had to discover the alias of his brother. Somehow, being in a mansion full of murderers made Adrian's stomach a little queasy.

He was not sure how he was going to gather all that information without getting himself killed.

The place was loaded with guards, and finding the time to rummage through the payroll would be difficult. He had to get close to the old man to gain his trust. He had to work his way up the ladder slowly to gain acceptance. Once the trust was in place, then he could go to work.

Adrian's medication was keeping his mind focused. It was surprising how much relief there was with only a couple of doses! His mind was clear, and he was ready to take on the dangerous task.

It would be interesting to meet his biological father for the first time in his life. He wanted to see what kind of man he really was, running off and abandoning a mother and son.

The guard came to the cage and said, "Mr. Eisner, the paperwork is ready for you to sign." Adrian was then led to the reception desk and had the cuffs and shackles removed.

The two detectives met Adrian at the desk. Matt said, "Here is a little gift for you."

Adrian put out his right palm and Matt handed him a cell phone. Matt said, "You probably won't have any access to phones while you are in the mansion, so you can use this one. It is activated and ready to go. The number is in the box."

ADRIAN

Adrian got a shiver up his spine. He knew that once he left those doors, he would be all alone. He signed the paperwork and collected his belongings.

Matt said, "The envelope that the clerk gave you has everything you need to know. The schedules and everything is in there."

"I guess my Dad will soon have his men looking for me," Adrian said.

Matt responded, "I'm sure of it. You can bet that as soon as we release the news, the ball will start rolling. Just take it easy. Take your time and do it right."

Adrian said, "I sure hope things turn out. I'm not used to this cloak and dagger stuff."

"Don't worry, you'll do fine. I know it. You are free to go. Good luck, Adrian."

Adrian turned around and gave a quick wave and left through the front doors. The first thing he had to do was get home and get rid of this paperwork, before Azario's men picked him up. He grabbed a bus and then transferred down to the strip. After a long bus ride, he arrived at his destination. He got off the bus and walked down Davis Ave. to the G-Spot.

Once arriving at the bar, he was greeted by the cute waitress that he had seen frequently.

She said, "Hi Adrian. We haven't been properly introduced. My name is Gina. I'm the assistant manager. I'll be running the bar while Trixie is away. Don't worry. Trixie told me everything about you. I'll help you out any way I can."

"Thank-you Gina! I am very pleased to meet you. I think I'm just going to go upstairs for a while. I'll talk to you later."

Adrian went upstairs and finally got into his comfortable surroundings.

He got himself a mug of draft and lit a cigarette. He went to the chesterfield and turned on the TV.

There he was. There was a press release on the news stating that Adrian Eisner had been cleared of any wrong doings. Police were on the look out for Jonathan Azario. Adrian thought to himself, "Well that should do it. The old man should be releasing the hounds by now." He decided to go on about his own business, and they would find him soon enough.

Frank Azario was watching the news and caught the special bulletin. He watched intensively, then sat back in his chair and smiled. Everything was going to work out just fine. Azario snapped his fingers and a servant rushed to his side. "Yes sir."

Frank said, "Have Al come and see me right away."

The servant clicked his heels and disappeared. Several minutes later, a voice said, "Yes sir, you called for me?"

Azario threw an old newspaper at the hulk of a man and replied, "You see the man on that front cover? His name is Adrian Eisner. Bring him to me, unharmed. No rough stuff. Search the whole city if you have to, but be quick about it! I am not a very patient man."

"Yes sir. I'll get right on it." Al turned around and quickly left.

Azario also had to get rid of this murderer. He was bad for business on the strip. The old man knew his secret identity and was going to do a little digging of his own.

He had to be absolutely sure that his older son was responsible for those killings. This would be done discretely.

Only Donna and Frank Sr. knew of his alias, and one of them may never recover. No one else in the world knew who he was.

Back at the station, the two detectives reviewed the tape with the Captain and a profiler.

Matt asked, "Steve, by looking at this guy, can he be our killer?"

The profiler said, "He has the same characteristics and mentality of a serial killer. I would say it is highly probable that he can be your man, but not right now. He is too coherent. He was highly focused on the conversation, and he was telling the truth according to what he believes."

Mike said, "Would only two doses of medication improve one's mental health that effectively?"

"No, it usually doesn't help as profoundly as it has in Adrian's case. However, you cannot rule it out. Some combinations of medication work extremely well."

"So what you are saying is, two days ago he would match our profile as our man. Then today, he was exonerated. This all happened because of two lousy doses of medication?"

ADRIAN

"That's about it. It is possible that you released the murderer."

Matt slapped his forehead and said, "Shit!! There is one thing left unanswered. Who did he shoot yesterday? We have actual proof that he shot a man last night. We have blood, weapon, and powder burns to make a solid case. Adrian shot and wounded a man last night! Who the fuck is the murderer? We still don't know!"

The Captain said, "There is one thing I want checked out.

Matt, I want you to find out from Freemont what drugs he gave Adrian, and at what dosage.

Come back to me with the results, and we will have our expert go over the findings. I already know that Freemont will not be pleased. So wait around for a half hour and I will get you a warrant."

"Yes sir!"

Mike walked around like a caged animal. "I can't believe that Adrian can be our man! He was too damn straight with us! He was calm, relaxed..."

Matt interrupted, "Just like a psycho!"

Mike's mouth dropped in astonishment. "Then, it can be true!"

Matt nodded his head in agreement.

"I need a coffee!" Mike said.

Matt yelled at the disappearing detective, "Get me one too!"

Steve looked at Matt. "I only said it was possible. I am just like you; I don't have any proof, except for the profile."

Matt thought to himself, "We need to find Jonathan as fast as we can!"

A few minutes later, Mike returned with the coffees. "What do you think? Did we release the killer?"

Matt said, "I don't know."

Back at the G-Spot, Adrian was catching the noon show and having a beer. To his surprise, those same three women were back at the same table. Adrian was still hoping that the other two would dance.

As long as the brunette went on stage, Adrian would be happy. The same thing was happening again. They noticed Adrian staring, and they turned their backs on him. That was ok, they had nice asses too.

Adrian lit a smoke and took a sip of beer, when he noticed three huge men in suits enter the bar. It didn't look like they were coming in for the entertainment. Adrian sat still, not knowing if he should go upstairs or not. He was already shaking with fear.

How the hell was he going to pull this off? The leader lifted his sunglasses for a moment and looked around. He made a quick signal and all three turned around and left. Adrian thought to himself, "Thank fuck for dark corners!" He had pretty well shit his drawers. They were huge!

Adrian quickly gulped his beer and ordered another one. He'd never been so scared in his life. He wasn't so damn sure if this was a good idea. Maybe, he would bail out of the deal, and take the charges. He was trembling, nervously waiting for that mug of beer.

Finally the beer arrived, and he took a couple of big gulps to soothe his nerves. He was seriously thinking about phoning Ruzo, and tell him that the deal was off.

He was wondering how he could keep his cool, while under such stress. He had never been able to fight off the nerves before. What made him think he could do it now? He drank his beer slowly. Maybe, he would find courage at the bottom of the mug.

Adrian ordered another mug, and sat back. They would be back for him. This time Adrian had to make himself more visible, and get it over with.

He thought he would start to watch the shows to help him calm down. His beer arrived and he lit another cigarette. He was starting to relax.

He was not sure if he should just stay where he was, or go out looking for them.

He decided there was no reason to advertise; they may think that they were being set up.

The best bet was to continue with his normal activities, and let them catch up.

But just as he was calming down, the same three men came back in. This time they were walking around the bar. Adrian's heart started to beat faster.

There were visible signs of sweat beading off his forehead. He took a couple of deep breaths as the trio was fast

ADRIAN

approaching his table. The leader caught a glimpse of Adrian and referred to the newspaper photo.

He approached the table and said, "Do you mind if we sit down with you?"

Nervously, Adrian offered them their seats.

The leader turned to the bar, and signalled for a round of drinks.

He said, "My name is Al. I work for Mr. Azario. He would very much like to talk to you today. First of all, we'll have a round of drinks, and then we will go to the mansion for a visit. Don't be nervous Mr. Eisner; he just wants to talk to you."

Adrian felt much more at ease this time than he had an hour ago. The drinks arrived and Al paid with a hundred dollar bill. He told the waitress to keep the change.

Adrian was pleasantly surprised that Al actually had a sense of humour. The hour passed and he was ready to meet the old man. They got up from the table, and went to the limousine waiting out in front of the bar.

Well, this was it! Adrian was going to meet his father for the very first time in his life. The only thing was he couldn't let the old man know that he had already been informed of that fact. Adrian still had to protect Trixie.

The car pulled into the long winding driveway, until it reached the front door entrance. The chauffeur got out and opened the doors for his passengers. Adrian noticed that basically everyone was carrying a weapon. That heightened the danger aspect that much more.

The doors swung open and Adrian stepped into a grand entrance. The place was luxurious, nothing out of place. Everything was immaculate.

Al said, "Wait here Adrian. I will tell Mr. Azario that you are here to see him."

A few minutes later, he returned and said, "Follow me this way, Adrian."

Al led Adrian to the tea room, where he saw a tall, elderly man sitting down, sipping his tea.

Al said, "Mr. Azario, this is Adrian Eisner."

Adrian stood tall and said, "It's a pleasure to meet you sir."

Mr Azario signalled to Al to leave the area, and allow the two men their privacy.

"Have a seat, Mr. Eisner. I presume you are wondering why I had Al bring you here."

"Yes sir, I am a bit curious."

"Do you know who I am?"

"All I really know is that your name is Mr. Azario."

"I will give you a quick run down. I am a frugal businessman. I have business interests from coast to coast and in several countries around the world. This is my extended family. We are a very tight group run with a firm hand.

I have invested almost sixty years of my life to create this empire. My interests are many and very profitable, and I want to keep it that way."

Adrian said, "I'm not a businessman; I don't know the first thing about it."

Frank said, "That is why I had you come here. I understand that you had all of your criminal charges dropped."

"Yes sir."

"I am starting to become an old man, and the day will come when my empire will be handed down. I have decided to hand it down to my second eldest son. Mr. Eisner...You are that son."

Chapter Twelve

Even though Adrian knew that Frank was his father, he was still stunned to hear that he would be left to run the empire. He said, with shock, "Sir, are you absolutely sure about this?"

"Yes, the mother that raised you for twelve years is my sister. With proper training, you will also rule the empire as I have done. It will be stressful, and need long hours to accomplish many tasks.

It will not be easy. I will have you watched constantly to ensure that you obey all of my rules. It will not be a cake walk. It will actually be the hardest thing that you have ever done in your life. However, the rewards are bountiful and rewarding."

Adrian said, "Sir, I'm grateful, but don't you think you could have found somebody more suitable than me?"

Frank said, "Yes, I have a number of employees who would be more suitable than you. However, they do not have the Azario blood running through their veins. Blood amongst family is very important to me.

You will be brainwashed to think and act Azario, and then you will become one! You must promise me that no one knows what I have told you today. If I hear it through the grapevine, I will have you strung up and shot. Do you understand that promise?"

"Yes sir, I understand very well."

"You will have privileges, but don't get greedy. It will depend on what you do. The rights and privileges you will earn will be for your dedication and loyalty to me."

I will be known to you as Mr. Azario. You will be known as Mr. Eisner or as Adrian.

At this time it is not important for you to know your siblings or crap like that. It will all be business. You must work very hard and take it very seriously. This is a deadly business which will shake you down to your boots.

You better be fuck'n ready for it, Adrian. I'm not pulling any punches with you. Either you do what I say, or I will kill you myself. Do you understand?"

Nervously Adrian said, "Yes Mr. Azario, I understand."

Frank said, "It's settled then. I want you in a quality suit tomorrow morning at 8:00 o'clock for breakfast. You are dismissed for the day; Steven will take care of the details for you. Good day."

Adrian stood up and went to the tea room doors. Steven was waiting for him. "Follow me this way, sir. I will show you to your quarters."

They climbed a colossal spiral staircase to the balcony above. The doors were made of antique teak. They approached a double door and Steven opened it for Adrian. "These are your quarters, sir. I am sure that you will approve. I will be back in five minutes with a chalk and tape to take your measurements, sir."

Adrian walked inside and was amazed. The suite had a huge sunken living room with fireplace. It had a full size bar.

The dining room had a table and chairs for twenty people. There was an industrial kitchen with an on-call staff twenty-four hours a day.

It had five bed rooms and six bathrooms. The entire place was twice the size of most houses.

Antique furniture and original Italian art adorned the walls and nooks. This place was a mansion within a mansion!

It also had a large office with all of the modern equipment that a person could imagine. The master bedroom had a fireplace, walk-in closet, and an in suite bathroom.

The room also had a living room suite facing the grounds through a large picture window. There was nothing left out. It had a bar, fridge and coffee pot designed right into the room.

A servant met Adrian at the master suite and said, "Mr. Eisner, my name is Doris. I am your personal servant; I will help get you into a routine around this place."

"Thank-you, Doris."

There was a knock at the doors, and Doris answered. It was Steven.

"Sir, if you would please step this way. I will measure you for your wardrobe."

"Yes, of course."

"Your wardrobe will be in your closet by 7:00 pm."

Adrian asked Steven, "Would you be able to get this prescription filled, since there is no bus service way out here?"

ADRIAN

"Yes sir, I will have the driver pick it up for you. Sir, you do have full access to the city via your chauffeur. He will take you anywhere at any time."

"Thank-you, Steven."

Steven handed Adrian an envelope and said, "There is one last thing, sir. This is an advance on your salary.

There is one-hundred thousand dollars in that envelope; you will have to earn the rest. Those are orders from Mr. Azario."

"I understand."

Steven finished taking down the measurements, shoe size, etc. "Will there be anything else, sir?"

"Yes, I would like a car brought around to the front in ten minutes please."

"Yes sir, I'll get right on it." Steven then left.

Adrian didn't like the way things were going. He was hesitant about what his job would entail. He had been showered with royalty, but he was sure that his job would be extremely morally demanding. He wasn't ready for this job; he would be on a tightrope the whole time he was here.

Adrian told Doris, "I will be out for the evening; I'm not sure when I will be back."

"Don't be late for tomorrow morning with Mr. Azario." Doris warned.

Adrian assured her, "Don't worry; I'll be ready for breakfast."

He left the suite, went to the waiting car and got in.

The chauffeur said, "Where to, sir?"

Adrian replied, "The G-spot." The car then drove off.

Adrian was worried sick about what was about to happen in his life. He was being moulded to become a creature which he dare not describe. Ruzo was going to flip when he heard about this!

He might be put in situations that violated the law, or even worse, commit murder. Adrian had to find out what to do next. The car pulled up to the bar and the chauffeur got out and opened Adrian's door.

Adrian entered the bar, went to his favourite table and ordered a draft. He lit a cigarette, pulled out the cell phone and dialled Detective Ruzo. The phone rang and Ruzo answered. "Hello."

"It's me Adrian; I'm in a lot of shit. You have to pull me out now!"

"Calm down! It can't be that bad."

"Oh yeah!! The old man is going to train me to be the head man of his organization! Do you know what kind of things this guy will expect me to carry out? I'm not a killer, and I think that is what he has planned for me!"

"I don't like the way things are turning out. It looks like if you are given the order to kill, that is exactly what you will have to do.

You can't jeopardize the case, or get yourself killed. That won't do us any good at all. You have to stay alive, and do what you have to. You have to become accepted as one of theirs."

Adrian yelled, "I'm not a killer! I can't do that!!"

"Not only may you have to do it, you will be forced to like it. Adrian, you may have to do some pretty rotten things; don't turn bad on me."

Adrian was starting to cry on the phone and said, "I'm going to be the head boss of an evil organization, and you don't want me to turn bad! It has to be one way or the other."

Matt said sombrely, "I'm sorry, Adrian. I hope we don't become enemies."

"I hope not too, Matt. Please...get me out of there!"

"I can't. I don't have the power to help you, only God does."

Adrian replied in shock, "Oh...fuck off, Matt!!" Adrian turned off the phone. His beer arrived and he took several deep gulps.

He was shocked that the police were powerless against this guy. He was shaking like a leaf.

He didn't have his prescription yet, and he was running out of places to cut himself. His head was spinning out of control.

He drank faster and ordered another beer. Thoughts were spinning all around him and he was in a total daze. He was falling deep into his own private world, where no one could find him. He took a couple of sips of beer and became transfixed with the woman on stage.

It was the beautiful brunette. Her every move was calculated and precise. The music was moving her, and the lights were glistening off her muscle-toned body. Adrian couldn't take his eyes off of her.

His icy stare pierced right through her, and penetrated deep into her soul. His groin swelled with desire and his heart ached for lust.

A calm darkness filled Adrian's soul. Whatever happened now was pure coincidence. The show abruptly ended with a loud bang, followed by ecstatic applause. The brunette bounced off the stage, walked past Adrian's table and smiled.

She went toward the dressing room. Adrian stared at her tight ass as she quickly disappeared. His beer arrived and he took a sip and lit another cigarette.

The trance was intensifying. He was so deep into his mystical world; he might never come out of it.

The next lady passed the table and went to the stage. The lights were down low and there was no music. The place was as black as Adrian's heart. The stage exploded with white light and smoke.

The music blared out as the young woman jumped into action. She was fast paced and very exotic.

Adrian's passion grew with every second that passed. The bleached blonde was almost unbearable to watch. Adrian was fighting his compulsions with all of his strength.

He stood up abruptly and stared at the stage. In a split second, he changed direction and raced for the suite upstairs. He opened the door and ran to the bathroom where he dropped his drawers in front of the sink.

The sexual desires were unbearable; this was where Adrian could safely live out his desires and fantasies.

The tensions built to an extreme high where he could no longer hold up against the pressure. Suddenly the mirror would bear witness to the soils of this pent-up pleasure.

Adrian took several deep breaths to regain his strength. Once recovered, he pulled up his pants, and retrieved some window cleaner from under the sink. He sprayed the mirror and wiped it clean with a towel. Feeling a bit more relieved, he put the towel into the washer. He then went back downstairs to watch the shows.

I can't believe that father has allowed that gutless shit in as his protégé. He doesn't have what it takes to run a business like this. The empire rightfully belongs to me. I have what it takes to do the job right.

One day we will meet each other, and I will be victorious. That day is soon coming to a close, and he will pay the ultimate price for his sins. He will bow before me and beg for forgiveness. God will smite him down like the others.

They will all pay the price with their lives. They must learn to understand the truth and accept it as their own. New York will soon bow at my feet with tears in their eyes.

They will chant my name, and beg for each day that I grant them to live. No one will escape my clutches.

My head is full of racing thoughts and my soul is dark. I have the power of the dark side within me. My heart aches for God's strength to endure, but too no avail. I am powerless; I am unable to fight the dark evil that dwells deep inside of me. Soon, everyone will understand me and believe in the truth.

Journal
September 21st, 2002
MADMAN

Back at the station, the two detectives returned from Dr. Freemont's office. They came back after serving a warrant for more information about the medication he had given to Adrian. They went down to the lab for conformation about this medication.

Dr. Roland Taggart was the head scientist in the lab. Matt gave him a list of meds and said, "Tell me about these medications."

Roland said, "This is an excellent cocktail of medication to ease the patient of mood swings and psychotic behaviour. The anti-psychotic and the dose prescribed should eliminate all symptoms of psychosis.

The high doses of mood stabilizers should calm the patient and keep him at an even keel. These medications should stop the mood swings. This is the course of action I would take to treat someone with severe manic depression."

"Thank-you doctor; you have been very helpful."

Mike turned to Matt and said, "Well the medication was alright. Now what do we do?"

"Now we wait for Adrian to check in, and see what's happening next."

"What happens if he starts to like his new job? He could become more dangerous than his father."

"I know. I would hate for him to get tangled up in this. Adrian is not such a bad guy, but he needs medical attention. Without his medication, he would be perfect for the job. He would be ruthless, and he wouldn't have any morals. He would be out of control. Adrian would be a monster and he would have the power to back him up."

"I presume there is no way we can help him get out."

Matt shook his head and replied, "None."

Matt said, "Adrian is caught in the middle of this whole situation. I didn't think the old man was going to hand over the reigns. That changes everything; we may never find the killer now."

"We still have something that Adrian wants real badly."

Matt looked confused and said, "What?"

"We have his sister. Once she wakes up, we can use her as a playing chip."

"According to the doctors that are treating her, she will be out for a long time. Even when she does wake up, she might stay a vegetable for the rest of her life."

"Think positively, Matt. We are stuck, and we need a glimmer of hope. I think the girl is the only way to getting close to the Azario's."

"I just hope Adrian can stay sane enough so that he can help us. Right now, he is our only chance of identifying the murderer."

Meanwhile back at the G-Spot, Adrian sat quietly and stared at the woman on stage. His libido was not out of control as it was a little while ago. He was a bit calmer.

He took a sip of beer and lit a cigarette. He noticed at the entrance that the brunette's two friends had just arrived. They moved their way to their favourite table and sat down. Gina noticed the two ladies and quickly got their drinks made up. Momentarily, the brunette arrived and gave her friends big hugs and she sat down.

Gina went to the table and delivered the drinks. Adrian stared at the trio, and he didn't take his eyes off of them. He was taken back by their beauty and grace. He fantasized erotic moments involving all three women and himself.

He entered the world where dreams come true.

The brunette caught Adrian staring, but this time she got up and went to Adrian's table. "Hi, my name is Jennifer. You must be Adrian Eisner; Gina told me about you and said that you were harmless."

Adrian said, "I'm very pleased to meet you, Jennifer. Please excuse me if I tend to stare; I just find you and your friends very attractive. Please enjoy yourself and don't let me bother you."

"I noticed that you are in here all of the time. Maybe, I'll sit down with you later and have a drink."

"I would like that. I'll talk to you later."

Jennifer left Adrian to go and rejoin her friends. Adrian thought, "Not only is she beautiful, she also seems to be a very nice woman." He had to be careful; the murderer could be in there watching his every move. If Adrian got too close to Jennifer, she may become the next target.

Adrian decided to go for a walk and maybe pick up a twelve of beer. He put on his overcoat and went outside.

The wind had picked up and it was a little chilly. He noticed there was another limo parked behind his. Adrian's driver got out to open the door for him.

Adrian said, "I'm not leaving yet, I'm just going for a walk. Whose car is that?"

The driver said, "It's one of ours. However, I am forbidden to tell you who the passenger was. It's company policy, sir."

Adrian walked up Davis Ave. to the convenience store. He picked up a twelve of beer, and two packs of cigarettes.

He noticed that the scantly dressed hookers were having trouble keeping their skirts down with the wind blowing. He took the back alley and went to the school yard. He sat down against the wall, popped a beer and lit a cigarette. The fresh

ADRIAN

air was clearing his mind. It was a bit chilly, but he was dressed for it.

Adrian had had a few beers when he heard a noise in the alley hidden by shadows. He could not make out what was making the noise. He stood up and yelled, "Who's there?" There was no answer.

The silhouette of a man wearing an overcoat and brimmed hat appeared out of the shadow. Adrian could not make out the face, he was too far away and it was dark out.

The silhouette slowly moved, and pulled out a baseball bat from under his overcoat. The figure stood still with bat in hand and stared at Adrian.

Adrian yelled, "Jonathan, let me see your face. I can help you." The figure stood deathly still, without uttering a word. He slowly put the bat back under his coat and stepped back into the shadows and disappeared.

Adrian's heart was pumping a million times per minute. He was scared, but the figure had decided it wasn't time yet. The murderer had just made a guest appearance. This was a little too spooky for Adrian. He picked up his beer and cautiously walked back to the G-Spot.

Upon arrival at the doors, Adrian checked up and down Davis Ave. He looked to see if the murderer is following him. The coast was clear, and he moved indoors and up to the suite. He opened the door to the suite, and put the beer on the kitchen table.

He pulled out the cell phone and called Ruzo. The phone rang and Matt answered. "Hello."

Adrian said, "Matt, it's me, Adrian. The son of a bitch was at the school yard not less than ten minutes ago! He was watching me drink beer. He stepped out of the shadow, and revealed his bat! Then he disappeared again. I didn't get to see his face."

"He's playing head games with you Adrian. I'll send a couple extra cars in the area for a patrol. Where are you now?" Matt said.

"I'm at the G-Spot on Davis."

"Don't worry; I'll take care of everything. Try to relax and have some fun."

"Thanks, Matt. Good-night." Adrian shut off the cell phone and went back downstairs.

He ordered a beer and lit a cigarette. Jennifer was watching and gave him a smile and a wave. Adrian was thinking, "I wish she wouldn't do that. The bastard might be in here." He carefully scanned the dimly lit bar for any signs of the killer.

He couldn't see anyone who looked suspicious. Everyone was watching the show or laughing with friends.

Adrian was carefully watching the door to see if anyone walked in matching the description. He noticed that two uniformed officers came in and walked around the bar. They were working on his tip.

They were checking out the crowd for possible suspects, but came up short handed. They then left. Adrian felt a little more relaxed knowing that the cops were around. It seemed that he could at last relax. He started getting comfortable and took off his overcoat.

The two ladies that were with Jennifer were saying their farewells and left the bar. Jennifer grabbed her drink and came to Adrian's table. "Do you mind if I sit with you? I don't like to drink alone."

"Be my guest. Could I buy you a drink?"

Jennifer nodded and said, "Yes please."

Adrian signalled Gina for another round.

"Do you like my acts?" Jennifer asked.

Adrian grinned from ear to ear and said, "Yes, I certainly do!" He snickered with a boyish grin.

Jennifer caught on and blushed. "I take it from your grin that you really enjoyed the show."

Adrian burst out laughing; he almost split a gut. "I'm sorry dear, but you hit the nail on the head! Yes, I really, really enjoyed your show. I think that you are very beautiful."

Jennifer had a devilish grin on her face. She took off her right shoe without anyone noticing, and placed her foot between Adrian's legs. There was magic happening under the table.

Gina popped by and brought the drinks.

Adrian paid for Jennifer's drink, and in a high pitched voice, he said, "Thank-you."

All three burst out into laughter and Gina left to serve the next table. Jennifer's foot was in a deliberate rhythm. Adrian

ADRIAN

almost didn't know what to do with himself. He was climbing the walls, and couldn't express his pleasures in a public place.

Suddenly his back arched and he gave off a silent relief of pressure. He was gasping for breath.

Jennifer smiled and took a sip of her drink. Adrian caught his breath, and took a big gulp of beer. Then he lit a cigarette. He smiled and whispered. "Where the hell did you learn that?"

Jennifer smiled back and said, "It is one of my many talents."

"Thank God, I have a long overcoat to cover up with."

"I have to go for awhile. I'll be back soon."

"Where are you going?"

"I have a little business to take care of. Don't worry. I'll be back in no time." She went to the change room, grabbed her coat and left through the front entrance.

Adrian couldn't believe she would do that!

He was excited all over again. He took a couple more sips of beer and sat back. He started watching the show, while he was waiting for Jennifer. These women were not half as talented as Jennifer. He found them interesting, but not overwhelming.

Adrian would like to get to know Jennifer a bit better. He really liked her. Several shows had gone by and there was still no sign of Jennifer. It had been quite some time; she should've been back by now.

Suddenly, Adrian could hear sirens that seemed to be very close. It sounded like they were coming from the back parking lot.

Adrian went to the rear exit and opened the door. To his amazement, he saw an ambulance and cop cars; yellow tape was being strung up. There were cops everywhere!

Adrian walked outside and was halted by a police officer. The officer said, "I'm sorry sir. No one can go beyond this point."

Adrian's heart sank to rock bottom. He was just hoping it was not Jennifer! He was actually praying that it was not her. Adrian told the officer, "I might be able to help identify your victim. My lady friend was late coming back to the bar."

The officer asked, "Who are you?"

"My name is Adrian Eisner; here is my ID."

"You were our murder suspect for weeks!" the officer said.

As the two were conversing, Mike and Matt showed up at the scene. Adrian said, "I hope that I am wrong, but I think I can guess who you just covered up."

"Who do you think it is?"

"Her name is Jennifer. She works here at the bar as a stripper. You can find her last name, and details in her file.

Just ask Gina, she will give it to you. Let me see the body, I might be able to give you a positive ID."

Matt grabbed Adrian and said, "Ok, but I have to warn you. If this is our guy, her head will be mostly missing. It may be very difficult to handle."

"I'll be ok. I just have to know if it is her."

Adrian and the two detectives ducked under the yellow tape, and went towards the body. The coroner walked by Matt and said, "It happened about ten minutes ago. She is still warm."

Matt asked, "Are you ready?"

Adrian took a deep breath and nodded his head. Matt quickly pulled off the blanket. Adrian's eyes widened with extreme shock. He spun around, and viciously threw up his guts.

Matt asked, "Is that Jennifer?"

Adrian nodded to affirm the identity. He was on his hands and knees, and was very slow to rise. Matt grabbed him by the arm and took him back behind the tape.

"Are you sure that this is Jennifer?"

Adrian wiped his mouth with his sleeve. "Yes, I'm positive! That is Jennifer. I recognize her clothes! That is what she was wearing when she left the bar."

"What are the details of your contact with this woman? Don't leave anything out."

Adrian told Ruzo everything. He told them they might find semen stains on her nylon by the foot area.

Matt told Adrian, "You know the routine, don't leave town. Keep in contact with us. You can go now, Adrian." Adrian knocked on the rear exit and the bouncer let him in.

Mike said, "I'll go talk to Gina, and get some more information."

"Ok, that sounds like a good idea. I will be working out here." Matt said.

ADRIAN

Matt went back under the tape and went to the body. He lifted the blanket and revealed her partially naked body.

The coroner came up to Matt. "She's been brutally raped; there are bruises on her knuckles. You may also notice that her head is basically gone. I will have to reconstruct her jaw and teeth to make a positive ID."

Matt said, "Thanks doc."

He then took a look for himself.

There was no twenty dollar bill, and the MO was exactly the same as the rest. Forensics would take care of the details, but Matt already knew everything he needs to know.

Mike came back and said, "Her name is Jennifer Anne Lewis. She is twenty two years old. She was born February eighth, nineteen eighty-one. She lives at apt. 502, 52St. west. It is at the Shangri-La Apartments. Adrian's story checks out. He was in the bar at the time of the murder."

"I bet that son of a bitch is watching us right now. He is playing with our heads, especially Adrian's. The poor guy has enough trouble as it is, without this guy making things worse. We can't do much out here. Drop me off at home, will ya?"

"Sure, I'll take you home."

The two walked back to the car and disappeared.

Meanwhile, back in the G-Spot, Gina was trying to console Adrian who had been crying hysterically since he came in. They were all taking the news real bad. They cancelled the shows for the night, and the bartender had announced last call.

This was their way of paying their respects to Jennifer. Everyone had loved her; she was the nicest girl that anyone had met. The G-Spot and staff would deeply miss her.

Adrian got up and downed his beer. He grabbed his coat and left through the front doors. He noticed that the second limo was still there. That meant that the son of a bitch was still here, somewhere. Adrian didn't care anymore; he just wanted to go home.

The chauffeur opened the door for him and asked, "Would you like to go home, sir?"

"Yes, please. I have had enough!"

Upon arriving at the mansion, Adrian noticed that the old man was still awake. He could see him in the glass-enclosed tea room. He got out of the car and went upstairs to his suite.

On the kitchen counter, he saw that his prescription had been filled. He took his medication, and poured himself a draft from the bar. Adrian doubted that he would get any sleep, especially after what had happened tonight.

He went to the bedroom to check out the wardrobe. To his amazement, there must have been fifty thousand dollars worth of suits, coats, and hats. A suit, coat and shoes had been laid out by Doris.

Adrian had less than six hours before he had to face Mr. Azario. He figured he should get a few hours sleep anyway. He went to the chesterfield, lit a cigarette and took a sip of beer.

He had to wind down a bit; he was too hyper to sleep. Poor Jennifer, he really liked her a lot! It was too bad he only knew her for a short period of time.

She would have been a headliner in no time; she was very good at her job. Adrian started to quietly sob. He would really miss her; she had left a big impression on him.

Adrian put out his smoke and gulped down the rest of his beer. He went to the bedroom, got undressed and went to bed. There he lay awake, thinking about how terrifying her death must have been.

Jonathan was a monster and he had to be stopped! How could a man do such a thing, and survive his conscience? Adrian turned off the light and fell into a deep sleep.

Later that morning, Matt woke up and went to the bathroom for his morning routine.

After about a half an hour, he was dressed and ready to face yet another day. He went downstairs to make coffee. A uniformed officer said, "Good morning sir."

Matt replied, "Good morning." He went to the coffee pot, poured in the water, and measured out some coffee for the filter. After the machine started to brew; Matt went to the back step to retrieve the morning paper. He sits down and reads the headlines. "Eisner questioned and released after eighth murder!"

Matt thinks to himself, "Adrian might not survive living in the mansion if Azario still thinks that he is the murderer." Number eight already, and still no identification of Jonathan's alias.

Adrian had to get that information as soon as possible, before Azario did. Azario would have him killed in a blink of an eye, and he wouldn't hesitate about taking out Adrian too.

The uniformed officer said, "Mr. Parsons has just pulled up. Would you like me to let him in?"

"Yes, of course. Let him in."

There was a knock at the door and in barged cheerful Mike.

Matt asked, "Why do you always look so damn happy in the morning?"

Mike replied, "It must be my happy-go-lucky character, I guess."

"Well stop it; you're depressing me!"

Mike went straight for the coffee pot and poured two cups of coffee. He gave one to Matt and then he sat in his designated spot.

He asked, "How was Emily when you saw her yesterday?"

"The doctor came in during our visit, and said that she can come home today."

Mike smiled ear to ear. "I'm very happy for her, Matt. She will be very glad to come home."

"We are happy for her too. That kid has been through a lot, and she is finally coming home. The doctor said that she still has trouble sleeping, because of the nightmares. We are hoping that they go away after she's been home for awhile."

"What do you make of the latest victim?"

"It is obvious that Adrian is being constantly followed. It also seems that anyone who comes close to Adrian usually dies. This guy is breaking down Adrian piece by piece. There has to be reason why he just doesn't kill him. It seems he wants him to go off the deep end instead."

"What reason would Jonathan have for keeping him alive?"

"The old man is preparing for retirement, one way or another. Maybe there is a clause in the will or something. It may stipulate that he must remain alive. Otherwise, the empire leaves the family.

The pieces are starting to fall in place. The daughter may never be the same, and would never be able to run the empire. If Adrian is locked away in a loony bin for the rest of his life, the whole kit and caboodle goes to Jonathan."

Mike said, "However, this is only speculation. There is no proof of this."

"We don't have it yet, but maybe Adrian can get it for us." said Matt.

"Adrian has to toughen up a great deal to pull this off. If he does toughen up enough, we may never be able to stop him either."

"I know, and then we are left holding the bag."

Matt took a sip of coffee and said, "We have to keep Adrian on our side, somehow. He is going to be forced into bad situations, which may just rub off on him"

"So far so good. He is still keeping contact with us."

Marilyn came down the stairs as the men were talking. She walked into the kitchen and said, "Good morning, Mike."

Mike held his cup up as a salute and said, "Good morning, Marilyn."

She grabbed a coffee and sat down. "Are you going to be able to slip away for awhile, so that we can bring Emily home?" she asked Matt.

"I should be able to take an hour off or so, sure."

Marilyn smiled at Mike and said, "My baby is coming home."

Meanwhile, Adrian had just wakened. It hadn't been much of a sleep, but it was better than nothing.

He popped into the shower, and started getting ready for his first lesson on how to become an Azario. He had had trouble sleeping; it seemed that the medication didn't take affect very well last night. He could usually sleep like a baby. Maybe it was all the excitement that made him restless.

He finished up in the bathroom, and went and got changed. He really liked Steven's taste in clothes. The smoked grey, three piece suit looked dashing on him.

Now he had enough time to have a quick smoke.

He didn't want to get killed on his first day on the job. Actually, he wasn't all that fond of the killing idea, anyway.

There was a knock on the door. It was Doris reporting for work. "Good morning, Mr. Eisner. How are you today?"

"I'm fine, thank-you. You did a fine job picking out my suit this morning, Doris."

"Thank-you sir."

ADRIAN

Adrian looked at his watch and butted out his cigarette. He then made his way down the stairs to the tea room. Upon his arrival, he had to rely on the darkness in him to carry this through.

He noticed that Mr. Azario was sitting down. There was an empty chair and a gun with a holster on the table. In front of Mr. Azario was a chubby, nervous old fart. Al and a few of his men were closely standing guard behind the nervous old man.

Adrian knew what he had to do. Thoughts were spinning out of control in his mind. He was slipping into his own private world. Darkness had overcome his heart and soul.

He made his entrance and said, "Good morning, Mr. Azario."

Frank looked at his watch and said, "I see that you made it on time this morning. I would like you to meet Tony Lorenzo from Chicago. He runs my operations on the east side of the city."

Without thinking, Adrian took off his coat and slipped on the gun and holster. He then put his suit jacket back on and said, "It's nice to meet you Mr. Lorenzo." He extended his hand in a friendly gesture.

Tony nervously shook hands with his sweaty palm. Adrian sat down in the empty chair.

Frank said, "Mr. Lorenzo has been skimming profits off me for some time now. I don't like people cheating on me, especially one of my own men. Today, we are going to correct that problem. Aren't we, Mr. Eisner?"

Very calmly and coldly, Adrian said, "Yes sir. It will be corrected."

Frank said, "Al, take this piece of crap outside. I don't want any mess in the tea room."

Adrian followed the group outside. Tony was shaking like a leaf; he knew his time was up. He got down on his knees and cried for a second chance.

Adrian's heart was cold and his soul was black. He slowly pulled out the gun and pointed it at Tony's sweaty head. With deathly calmness, he pulled the trigger. Tony's body straightened up momentarily from shock then fell over on its side. Adrian took out a handkerchief and wiped his hands and face of the splattered blood.

He calmly said, "Al, would you mind getting rid of this garbage and have someone clean this up?"

"Yes Mr. Eisner. We will do it right away."

Adrian buttoned up his coat and walked inside the tea room and sat down.

Frank asked, "Would you like a cup of tea?"

"No thank-you, sir. I prefer to have coffee."

Frank signalled Steven and told him to bring a carafe of coffee. He reached into his inside coat pocket and pulled out an envelope which he handed to Adrian and said, "You catch on very quickly. I like your style."

Adrian put the envelope into his pocket and said, "Thank-you sir."

The coffee arrived and Adrian thanked Steven. He made up his coffee and took a sip.

Frank pulled out the newspaper and said, "Give me your gun." Adrian opened his coat and withdrew the weapon. He handed it to Azario.

Frank said, "Take a good look at this headline." He took the gun and pointed it at Adrian's head. "You better have a good fuck'n reason why another one of my girls is dead."

Calmly Adrian said, "Someone is trying very hard to pin the murders on me, but has failed. The real murderer is still out there, while I'm trying to keep my head on straight."

Azario withdrew the weapon and handed it back to Adrian. He said, "You're telling me that you are not involved in these murders?"

"No, I'm not involved. That is why I am cleared of any charges. I wasn't even near the girl last night when she got killed. I have proof that I was inside the G-Spot when it happened."

"In that case, I have a big job for you. The strip has lost forty percent of its profits since the murders have started. There are property transfers on your desk.

I am transferring all of the properties on the strip to your name. When you're done with the paperwork, you will be the new owner of the strip.

Your job will be to get those properties back onto their feet. I also get a twenty percent cut on those properties. The more money you make, the more money I will make. Everyone will be happy. To raise the profits, you have to remove the threat that is scaring off all of the customers.

I want the fuck'n bastard on his knees, snivelling before me. I don't care who the bastard is. I want him terminated. Do you understand?"

"Yes sir. I understand."

Steven came down with breakfast and served the two men. It seemed that Adrian's black heart saved him this time. He suspected that getting Jonathan would be much harder than he expected.

Adrian had to choose who he was going to be loyal to. He started to eat his breakfast and was wondering how he could draw Jonathan into the open. There must be something that he really wanted.

Adrian finished his breakfast and said, "I want to thank-you for the breakfast, Mr. Azario. I think I should be getting some paperwork done for you. If you will please excuse me, I will leave now."

"Yes, you go ahead. You have a lot of business to take care of."

Adrian stood up, pulled down his jacket and left to go upstairs. He got to his suite and opened the door. He saw Doris was busy cleaning the place.

"Doris, would you mind making me a pot of coffee, and bring it to my office when it is ready?"

"Yes Mr. Eisner. I will get that for you right away."

Adrian went into his office and saw about two hundred files on his desk, each containing one single property.

This was going to take a couple of days to review and sign. Now that he was going to be the new owner of the strip, what would his priorities be? Most likely, try to find a way to get Jonathan to come forward and be identified.

If only last night Adrian could have seen his face. That would have made it a lot easier. He might have to try that again, only this time he will a gun to take him down with. He might be forced to kill his last surviving brother. It would all be for the sake of the empire!

The little bastard got the keys to the golden gates. He thinks he is all so mighty - wait until a few more of his slut girlfriends' fall upon my feet. He didn't handle it all that well yesterday, poor sap. The wrath of God will be upon those sinners.

I am here to show them the way to an everlasting life with God. They have to beg for mercy, so that their black hearts can be cleansed of all the sins they committed during their miserable lives.

Soon the kingdom will be mine to rule as I wish. New York will stand to hear my voice. My life has been a blur, but I am finally remembering the horrid past. I too, have had darkness visit my soul.

Six years of my life disappeared without a trace, not one single memory. Now the darkness returns to its rightful owner. It is an overwhelming comfort to be within the shadows of the night. To walk among the deadened souls of our city is pleasing to me.

The outcasts of society are my peers. The dieing are my friends. The smell of rot gives me pleasures and memories of a time almost forgotten. I am doing everyone a favour. I am doing it for them and for my Lord.

Society has lost track of the importance of life. Then again, they have also forgotten the importance of death. It is time to celebrate life with a clean slate, a time to be reborn. They should welcome death with open arms. They just don't understand. No one does.

One by one, they are learning the way of the Lord. This will continue until the time arrives for me to be side by side with God. That will be a glorious day.

My time is not up yet; there is much to do in so little time. There are many more that have to be shown the way to eternity.

The sinners are many, and not all will be saved. New York City will be the only place in the world, which will find true peace.

Now, I must shake Adrian down to the core until he is nothing more than a shell of a man.

Father won't take a second glance at him by the time I am finished with him. Farther won't have a choice, but to choose me as his successor.

ADRIAN

I had Adrian shaking in his boots last night when we met. I may not be as gentle the next time we meet. This man is weak in the flesh and in the mind; I should be able to make him crumble like a cookie.

I can't wait until the time arrives that I meet Matt, one on one. He will pay for what he has done to this family with his life. He thinks that all that police protection will save him.

I have gotten through before, and I will do it again. The fat bastard won't even see it coming. I will avenge my brother's death, even if it means that I will lose mine.

Journal
September 22, 2002
MADMAN

Back at the station, Matt and Mike were going over the preliminary reports of last night's murder.

It was all old news; there weren't any new leads that would help identify Jonathan's alias. Matt said, "I don't know how he gets away with it.

I had extra patrols in the area, and he still slipped in and out without being noticed."

"Maybe, he uses disguises to slip away."

"That's possible. He must be doing something, so that he isn't noticed. Let's do a little review of what we have so far. We have eight murders; six of them were sex trade workers. Two were strippers and the other four were hookers who worked on the strip.

Two murders were caused by two officers getting too close. There was a rape and two attempted murders. One was Emily because of revenge. The other was Donna Azario."

Mike said, "Wait a minute. What do you mean revenge?"

Matt explained. "I never told you before, because I thought it was none of your business. Two years ago, when the first murder took place, my partner and I almost caught the culprits in the act. There were two of them. There was a gun fight. One got away, and I killed the other."

"I guess his name was Frank Azario Jr."

"You're a smart boy. Yeah...that's who it was alright. It almost started a gang war between the police department and the Azario Empire. Now, we know that Jonathan was the second man."

"You should have told me, Matt. This is a very important factor to the case. He's going to try again; you must know that by now."

"I know. The last time, I had mailings and threats on the phone promising revenge one day. I lost my mind after a few weeks of torment, and was put in Belleview for three months.

I just couldn't handle the pressure anymore. I just cracked up. Now, he is back.

He's playing games with me and jeopardizing my family. I am ready for him this time; I know I can handle him."

"You still should have told me before. We can't hold things back from each other. Your whole family is at risk, and so are you. He must have something planned to get his revenge. You are in a lot of danger. You shouldn't even be on this case; it is too close to home."

"This case is much too important to abandon. I have the expertise and the desire to get this bastard off the street. The Captain thought the same way as you. He later realized that it was the best thing for everyone if I stay on."

Mike said, "Your family is a target; I can't believe you didn't tell me!"

"I'm sorry; I didn't think it was any of your business."

"Of course it was my business! I'm working side by side with you. I should know if your life or mine is in jeopardy."

"You're right, Mike. I should have told you. Now you know, let's get back to the review. Adrian had contact with all of these people prior to their death, with the exception of Emily. Jonathan must be watching Adrian's every move. Perhaps, we should have Adrian tagged as well. With a constant police presence around Adrian, the killer couldn't possibly strike.

If he does strike, there are chances that we will catch him red handed. I'll put a tag on Adrian, twenty-four hours a day. That should do the trick."

Back at the Azario Mansion, Adrian finished enough paperwork for one day. He got the pile down to less than half; he would be able to finish up tomorrow.

ADRIAN

Now, he had to plan out how he was going to catch Jonathan. Adrian could try to lure him into a trap and shoot him between the eyes.

Unfortunately, the old man wanted him alive for awhile. Maybe, he would just put a hole in the other leg. He should try to get the files for Ruzo, but it was too soon for that. He couldn't put his neck on the line yet.

He said to Doris, "Can you get Michael to bring the car around front, please? I will be out for the evening."

"Yes sir, I'll get him right away for you."

"Thank-you, Doris."

Adrian grabbed his coat and went to the front doors, where Michael was waiting with the car. Michael opened the door for him and they drove off. Michael asked, "Where to, sir?"

"The G-Spot."

Adrian was watching to see if there was another limo following. He did notice they were being followed, but not by a limo.

They arrived at the bar, and Michael opened the door for Adrian, saying, "Have a good evening, sir."

Adrian got out of the car and watched the other car park about a block away. "Thank-you Michael. I will see you later."

He walked towards the other car. When he reached it, he tapped on the window. The electric window rolled down, and Adrian asked, "Who are you, and why are you following me?"

The man in the car said, "I am Detective Mitchell. You are on twenty-four hour surveillance so that the killer cannot get close to you. It will perhaps stop a murder from happening."

"I sure wish you guys would keep me informed of these things. Besides, you did a horrible job following us. You stuck out like a sore thumb." Adrian turned around and went back to the bar.

He got to the bar, opened the door, and went inside. He went to his favourite spot and ordered a beer.

Gina brought the beer and said, "Well, if it isn't the prince of death himself! You're starting a bad reputation around here. Everybody who gets close to you either dies or goes to the hospital."

"Knock it off! I didn't ask for your opinion!" Adrian said.

Gina went off in a huff. However, she was correct in her observation. Adrian scanned the bar to see any recognizable faces of the regulars. He was looking for people who had been at the bar every time he had been there. He did recognize several regulars, but they don't quite fit the murdering type.

Adrian noticed that Detective Mitchell was in the bar keeping a close eye on him. Maybe the police presence was a good idea; he could relax and have a good time.

It didn't look like many people were willing to associate with him right now. Adrian could understand that people didn't want to get involved with him while the murderer was on the prowl. He lit a cigarette and started watching the show.

The bar had bad vibes ever since Jennifer had died last night. The place would never be the same without her. The crowd wasn't very good today either; the word must have got out. The old man would shit himself if he knew how bad business was today.

Adrian thought he would put his head out the front door and see if there was another limo parked out front.

He went to the door and opened it a crack. Sure enough, there was another limo out front. Either it was Azario keeping track of him, or it was Jonathan.

Adrian went back to the table and started drinking his beer again. Some time had passed before Detective Mitchell came to sit down with him.

Adrian said, "Do you know what would happen if Azario caught me talking with you? How stupid can you be? You have to watch me inconspicuously."

The detective said, "I just got news about your sister; they are going to wake her up tonight. The swelling went down, and now they are going to check for brain damage. Come with me and I'll take you there."

Adrian quickly downed his beer and grabbed his coat. They left the bar and went to the car. Adrian was taking a big chance driving around with this guy. Azario might have had one of his men watching him.

They quickly drove off. Momentarily, the second limo followed. Adrian checked the back window and said, "Shit! An Azario limo is following us."

The detective said, "Relax, you probably will never step foot into that mansion again after tonight."

"Yeah...That's because I will be a dead man! I don't mean to be rude, but I don't like you Detective Mitchell."

"Don't worry, I'll check out the limo when we get to the hospital."

They finally arrived, and the detective dropped Adrian off at the front doors of the hospital. "I'll catch up with you later. I'm going to check this guy out," he said, and drove off to the parking lot.

Adrian went into the lobby and was met by Mike and Matt.

Matt said, "Well, this is the big day; let's go up and see what happens."

They took the elevator to the fifth floor and checked in with the receptionist.

Adrian said, "We are here to see Donna Azario."

The receptionist said, "Go around the corner to room 512. The doctors are with her now tying to get a response."

"Thank-you."

They came up to room 512 and saw several doctors checking her out. It is obvious that there was no response, yet. Adrian walked in, pushed the doctors out of the way and said, "I'm her brother."

He took her hand and gently kissed it. He slowly massaged her hand and whispered, "Trixie...it's me Adrian.

Please wake up, sweetheart. I need you, Trixie. You have to come back."

The doctors decreased her IV in hopes that the reduction of medication would trigger a response to wake up. Adrian looked closely at her face and he could see that her eyes were moving behind those heavy eyelids.

Adrian said, "She is starting to come around."

The doctors worked feverishly to balance out her medication.

"Sweetheart, please wake up. I need you back. I can't do this on my own." Adrian could feel her hand tightening gently around his. Her eyelids start to flutter and her angel eyes opened. Adrian put his arms around her and said, "I love you, Trixie."

She smiled and whispered, "I love you, Adrian."

Adrian was so excited that she knew his name. "Do you know who did this to you?" he said.

Trixie whispered, "Jonathan."

"We know it is Jonathan. What is his alias?"

Trixie took a deep breath and said, "His name is Dr. Ken Stuart."

Matt said to Mike, "Get an arrest warrant for Jonathan Azario alias Dr. Ken Stuart! I want every cop on the Azario grounds, pronto!!

Adrian held Trixie closely; tears were streaming down his cheeks. He finally had some kind of hope to live for. His sister had come back to him.

An orderly came in and said, "I'm sorry Mr. Eisner, but we need to assess Donna's condition."

Adrian kissed Trixie gently on the cheek and said, "I'll be here when you come back, sweetheart."

Trixie smiled and waved as her gurney was wheeled into radiology.

Chapter Thirteen

Matt and Mike were in the parking lot when they heard a scream. They ran towards a woman who was between two parked cars. She was screaming hysterically. There on the ground, was a man in the foetal position, his head barely recognizable. From the clothes and the empty holster, they knew it was Detective Mitchell.

Matt got on the radio and called for backup and a forensics team. Mike said, "We must be closing in on him; he's running scared now! I'll take a perimeter search of the parking lot and see if I can find something."

Matt, who was consoling the shocked woman, said, "For heaven's sake, be careful!"

A gurney was rolled out of the emergency entrance to pick up the hysterical woman and give her medical attention. Matt examined the wallet and made a positive ID. This was in fact Detective Mitchell. Matt could hear the police sirens coming closer.

The first person on the scene was the Captain. "Who's the victim?"

"It was Detective Mitchell, and his weapon is missing. Mike is searching the parking lot alone. Can we have some back up?"

"They're on the ground now."

The Captain handed Matt a couple of warrants. "One is an arrest warrant for Jonathan Azario, and the other is a search warrant for his residence. Go find Mike and you get all the men you can, and surround that fuck'n mansion. I want these papers served in person to Frank Azario!"

"Yes sir. Thank-you sir."

The Captain turned around and started barking orders; within seconds a detailed search was on the way.

Matt found Mike, and they got into their car and sped off to the Azario residence.

Matt put out an all units call to set up tactical positions around the Azario residence. The squads were dispatched. Every piece of weaponry was pointed at the mansion. This was the largest law enforcement dispatch ever in New York City's history.

Matt said, "What do you think, kid? Do we have him on the run?"

"I think so. The hunt is on!"

They arrived at the mansion gate. There were hundreds of cops taking up fire positions on the mansion.

There were snipers, tactical teams, and armoured cars littering the whole area. It looked like a parking lot at a police convention or a donut shop.

Matt turned to the guard on duty and said, "Get Frank Azario on that thing of yours! I have warrants for the arrest of Jonathan Raymond Azario, alias Dr. Ken Stuart, and to search the residence! I also have the back-up to make it happen! Do you understand? Tell him it is Matt Ruzo. I'm sure he will want to see me today."

The guard disappeared for a few moments, came back and said, "Mr. Azario will see you now, Mr. Ruzo. You can take a small group of men to search his suite. Please, drive carefully." The pistol-packing guard opened the gate and sneered.

The entourage parked out front and were met by Al and his men. Al said, "Mr. Ruzo, please follow me.

Your search team can follow Steven. He will show them to Dr. Stuart's suite."

The two groups split up, and the two detectives were taken to the tea room. Frank was sitting quietly in the tea room, having a glass of sherry. Al introduced the two men to Azario. Frank said, "Well Matt, which of my sons are you planning to kill tonight?"

"I'm not planning to kill anyone. I want this to go as smoothly as possible, and then we will leave." Matt handed the warrants to Azario.

"Tell me Matt. Do you have proof that Jonathan has committed these crimes?"

"Yes we do. We have a material witness who made a positive ID on Jonathan, alias Dr. Ken Stuart."

"Who is this witness?"

"I can't give you that information, but the source is reliable."

"What makes you think that I am going to honour two lousy pieces of paper?"

"You will honour it because you want him stopped as bad as we do. By the way Frank, how is business on the strip?"

ADRIAN

Azario quickly grew angry and blurted out, "Don't get cocky with me you fat piece of shit! I'll have you gunned down right where you fuck'n stand!"

"Let's keep this down to a quiet conversation. No one has to get their shit tied up in a knot. I know that the murders have hurt the business. Besides, they were all your girls.

I also have other proof beyond a reasonable doubt, that Jonathan is guilty."

Suddenly, one of the officers came running into the tea room. Al and his men quickly drew their weapons.

Azario signalled them to put their guns away. The officer said, "Lieutenant, I think you better come and see this!"

Matt struggled up the stairs and went to the suite. It was a disaster area. There was garbage and clothes strewn everywhere. Liquor bottles and weapons of all sorts littered the suite.

The officer took Matt to the closet and pulled out two empty metal cases marked "Anthrax." Matt took a step back and said, "Holy shit!!"

The officer said, "There are twenty canisters missing. That is enough to destroy the whole city if it was administered properly. According to the journal on the computer, that is exactly what Jonathan is planning to do. He is planning to give New York City a chance to repent its sins and join God in eternal peace!"

Mr. Azario said, "How do you think he is going to administer that stuff?"

"I think the best way of doing that is by poisoning the water supply to the city," Matt said. Mike stated, "He could poison the Croton water system coming into New York City via the Richmond Tunnel. Or he could choose the Jacqueline Kennedy Onnasis Reservoir via the No.3 Tunnel in Central Park. They are heavily guarded. However, if he got through, he could administer it through the reservoir. That would be the easiest way to take down this city."

Matt said, "Contact the New York City Water Department and warn them of the impending threat. Have them go on high alert."

Mike said, "I'll do that."

"Mr. Azario, we have a real tough situation here. It might turn ugly and people may get hurt," Matt said.

"I would prefer if you brought him here. I would take care of it myself."

"I can't do that. That would make me an accessory to murder. I will try to bring him in safely. There is one thing I want."

"What is that?"

"I want all of his medication bottles that you can find, with the most recent dates on them."

The search team were frantically looking for medication and any other clues.

Matt got on the radio and called to terminate the stand off. He directed all units to report to their posts.

He made contact with the State Police to keep their eye on the Croton Dam for possible infiltration. He told them to be on the look out for a Jonathan Raymond Azario. He gave them a warning of the chemicals involved, and emphasized not to let Jonathan reach the water.

Matt said, "Thank-you, Mr. Azario, for being very cooperative. I'll keep in touch as things progress."

Azario extended his hand out as in truce, and Matt accepted. Matt and Mike went down the stairs and back to the car. Mike said, "Do you think he went there right away?"

"No, his plan is not complete yet. He still has a few things left to do. I presume he is finding a place to crash for the night, and stay low. Tomorrow is another day. We end today with victim number nine. We have enough officers at both reservoirs to handle him, if he decides to change his plan."

Meanwhile, Adrian was waiting patiently for Trixie to come back from her cat scan in the waiting room. He looked down the hallway and he could see that they were bringing her back to her room. He stood up and quickly went to her side. The orderly put Trixie back in bed and took the gurney away.

Adrian asked, "Did they say anything about your condition yet?"

"Not yet. The doctor will come by a little later and tell me."

"You sound like you have all your marbles and you're looking alright. I think you are pretty damn lucky! You did find out who it was, but it almost cost you your life. You could've died that night, if I hadn't shot him in the leg."

"So...you are the one responsible for saving my life."

Adrian shrugged his shoulders and said, "I guess so."

Trixie gave him a big hug. "Thank-you."

Meanwhile, in a seedy hotel on the strip, Jonathan lay waiting for his moment. He laid out an old duffle bag full of his weapons of choice, plus the twenty canisters. The headlines tomorrow would be plastered with his name. Tomorrow, New York City would know who he was. Jonathan had the whole city at siege.

It wouldn't be long before he could walk through those gates and take what was his. The plan was working just like clock work. Jonathan already dumped the limo and driver in Queens and took the bus here.

Now, it was time to do some celebrating. He put on his coat and locked up the room.

He then walked a couple of blocks to the convenience store for two dozen beer and cigarettes.

He had the same dirty habits that all three of the brothers shared. It seemed very common among the Azario family. The siblings all had substance abuse issues, and mental illness - except for Trixie. "Her mother wasn't a stupid bitch like mine," Jonathan thought.

He got his goods and went back to the hotel. There he lay among his arsenal, drinking beer, and having a cigarette. He was on top of the world. He had beaten the cops again.

Jonathan felt invincible. He had been given a gift, and he was using it to his full advantage. God was waiting patiently for him to fulfil his task. He was near the end and the excitement filled his heart.

Jonathan pulled out his cell phone and the electronic voice modifier, and called Matt. "Good evening, Matt. How are you doing tonight?"

Matt said, "Jonathan, or should I say Dr. Ken Stuart? You don't need that electronic gadget anymore. We know who you are, and it is just a matter of time. You are running out of places to hide. It's soon coming to an end, Jonathan."

Jonathan replied, "I couldn't agree more with you, Matt. How is Emily? She was great! We'll have to meet again."

"You won't get within ten feet of the house, without getting a bullet in the head."

"I've slipped by you guys a dozen times already. What makes this any different?"

"I know how your sick mind works; I'll be ready for you!"

Jonathan was getting angry. "No one can stop me now! I'm on a roll! A fat slob like you can't do it; who else is there? That's right! There is no one! Your time is coming, Matt.

Watch yourself! Good-night, Matt." Jonathan then turned off the phone.

He lit another cigarette and laughed out loud. Everything was perfect; all he needed was a little action tonight. He put his weapons back into the bag and put it in the corner. He put on his coat and opened it wide.

There was a make-shift long pocket and strap; he slid the bat inside and strapped it in. He filled his pockets with a half dozen beer. He slid a 38 revolver into the back of his pants and covered it up. Now, he was ready to wet his Willie.

Jonathan walked up Davis Ave. to check out the ladies.

He was pleasantly surprised at all of the naked flesh that was out tonight.

He walked amongst them staring at their bodies. He was getting tense between the legs and started to play with himself.

A beautiful young blonde said, "I'll take care of that little problem of yours."

"Alright miss, follow me." He grabbed her by the arm and took her back to the hotel.

They got into the room and she said, "That's two hundred bucks for the night, sweetie."

Jonathan's back was facing her. "Fine." He took out his wallet and threw the money on the floor behind him.

She became annoyed and grumbled, "You could've handed me the money; I'm not trash, y'know."

The darkness of his blackened soul was unleashed. There was fear and panic in the heart of the defenceless woman. She didn't stand a chance against this evil fury which was thrown at her. The assault was brutal and unrestrained.

Jonathan pulled out the bat from under his overcoat and finished what he has started. Jonathan has taken his fill and delivered her soul to his Lord.

His breathing was returning to normal and he was starting to calm down. He opened a beer and took a big gulp. He then lit a cigarette. The calming effect was making him quite tired. He took off his bloody clothes and took a shower.

ADRIAN

He then went into a small knapsack and put on fresh clothes. He stared at the bloody corpse on the bed, and took a sip of beer. God should be pleased that he had another soul for his kingdom. Jonathan then packed up all of his things and left the hotel to find another one to sleep in. He needed to rest for a long period of time and regain his strength again.

He walked down Davis Ave. for a few blocks until he came across another hotel where he checked in. He didn't worry too much about his identity; it hadn't been publicized yet. Jonathan went to the elevator and pressed the ninth floor. The elevator stopped and he went to room # 908.

He opened the door, put his stuff down against the wall and locked the door. He then took out the weapon and put it on the night side table and got undressed. Once in bed, he closed his eyes and withdrew himself from his devilish life for one more night.

Adrian woke up refreshed after a good night's sleep. He put on his robe and went into the kitchen.

Doris said, "Good morning Mr Eisner. Would you like a cup of coffee?"

Adrian nodded his head and said, "Yes please. I sure can use one right about now."

Doris poured him a cup and put it on the kitchen table in front of him.

Adrian responded, "Thank-you, Doris." He got up and went to the kitchen counter to pick up his cell phone. He sat back down, took a sip of coffee and lit a cigarette.

He then called Matt. The phone rang and Matt answered. "Hello."

"Hi Matt. It's Adrian calling. How are you today?"

"It's a little too early to tell right now, I haven't had my coffee yet."

"I stayed with Trixie last night until the doctor kicked me out. He said that she is a very lucky lady. She does not have any brain damage; the scan showed a clean bill of health. She just has to stay in hospital for observation a little while. She will be back to normal in no time!"

"That's wonderful news Adrian. I'm very happy for you. However, your brother is a lot more dangerous than ever before. Do you have a newspaper? Take a look at it."

Adrian picked up the paper from the kitchen table and saw a big picture of Jonathan. The headline read, "Serial Killer Plans to Poison New York City."

Adrian said, "Ok, I read the headline. How is he going to do this?"

"He has twenty canisters of Anthrax; we figure he's planning to poison the water system in God's name. He believes that he is on a mission from God."

"Don't laugh! I had similar thoughts myself. He really believes this, it seems very real to him. How did you find out?"

"We searched his suite last night and found the empty boxes and a journal.

He also has plans to put you in the loony bin or kill you. It seems he is still pissed at me for killing your brother."

Adrian's mouth hung open like a barn door. In shock, Adrian said, "You mean it was you who shot Frank two years ago?"

"Yes, I thought you already knew that."

"No, I didn't. How would I know that?"

"I'm sorry Adrian. It was self defence. Frank Jr. shot at me first. That's why Jonathan raped my daughter and left her for dead. He is out for revenge.

Both of us, as well as my family are on his hit list. So be careful Adrian. He wants the empire to go to him, instead of to you. That's why he wants you in the loony bin. If you and your sister are out of the picture, he figures that it will go to him."

"Let me get him. We're brothers with the same mother and the same illness. I know how he thinks and where he will go in certain situations. I can find him better than you can.

Our illness is almost identical; we have the same thoughts and delusions. What better chance do we have but to let a psycho go after one of its own? If you put reward posters where I tell you, you will shut a great many doors on him and put him into hiding.

I know exactly where he will go to do that. He is now at war, so anything goes. Jonathan's back is up against the wall, and there are no more places to hide. You know better than I do, he is going to fight to the death!"

"I can't let you go after him," Matt said. "Only cops are allowed to do such things. Your own sanity is very questionable as well. You can't do it!

ADRIAN

Just stay where you are and keep your head down. Don't make yourself a target; he is extremely skilful."

Adrian said, "Either you let me do this with you, or I will do it on my own."

"Sorry Adrian, we have to separate in our ways. If I catch you out there going after him, I will throw you in prison for a long time."

Adrian then replied, "I believe that our relationship is now terminated. Good-bye, Matt." Adrian shut off the phone and threw it against the wall. The phone exploded into hundreds of little pieces.

Doris peeked around the corner and said, "Don't worry sir; I will get that for you."

"You're very kind. Thank-you."

Adrian then went to get cleaned up for a very big day. He was to ask the old man for a few favours today. The first thing he needed was a reward for information leading to the capture of Jonathan Azario. A hundred thousand dollars should keep the public's eyes peeled for Jonathan's whereabouts.

Since his targets were all around the strip, Adrian was going to plaster a wanted poster on every store window and pole from one end to the other of Davis Ave.

That should keep Jonathan away from the strip and put him into hiding. All Adrian has to do was flush him out into the open.

Adrian would be waiting in the wings for that to happen.

He finished his morning ritual and got dressed in the suit that Doris had laid out for him.

He went back to the kitchen, grabbed another coffee and lit a cigarette. He then started to read the cover story in the paper.

Meanwhile, at the Ruzo residence, Matt had been awake for a good half hour. He was enjoying his first cup of coffee. He was upset that he had blown it with Adrian. He was an excellent source of information. He even would have had use for him in the future to take Frank Azario down. He didn't have that inside edge that Adrian had. Matt was pissed off at himself, but he had no choice. He couldn't allow a civilian to get involved in a police crackdown.

He was glancing at the front page story. All of New York City was well aware of this madman and his plans to destroy the city. Matt figured that everyone in the city would be drinking bottled water from now on.

He heard a strained voice from upstairs. "Daddy, can you come and get me, please?"

"Ok sweetheart, I'll be right there." Matt got up, went upstairs, and picked up Emily. He carried her downstairs and put her in a wheel chair.

Emily kissed her father on the cheek and muffled, "Thank-you, Daddy. Can you please get me my mush and juice, please?"

Matt smiled and said, "It sure is nice to have you home, pumpkin." He got her breakfast and put it on a tray in front of her.

"Thank-you."

"Sweetheart, when Mr. Parsons shows up, can you keep him entertained while I take a shower?"

"Ok, I will."

Matt went upstairs. Ten minutes passed and the on-duty officer said, "Miss Emily, Mr. Parsons has just driven up. Should I let him in?"

Emily smiled and said, "Yes please."

There was a quick knock at the door and in flew Mike.

He went straight to the wheelchair and gave Emily a big hug and kiss on the cheek. "Welcome home, munchkin! I am so glad to see you!"

Emily was so excited to see her knight in shining armour. "It's real nice to see you Mr. Parsons! I missed you."

Mike went to get a cup of coffee. He sat across from Emily, just like the old times. It was all smiles; words didn't need to be said. Besides, it was still very difficult for Emily to talk with that wire on.

Matt stomped his way down the stairs and went to the kitchen. "Good morning, Mike. How are you?"

"Not bad. I had a good sleep."

"I had a call with Adrian this morning. Our little deal fell through. He won't be able to help us anymore. He wanted to join forces and I said no."

"Do you realize how important he is to us? You should have been able to do something to keep him on our side!"

"Legally, there is nothing I can do. If I catch him taking the law into his own hands, I will burn him."

ADRIAN

The dispatcher on Mike's radio interrupted. "1L1, 5124 there is a 10-35 at 320-3856 Davis Ave."

Mike responded, "1L1, 5124, 10-4."

"The dirty bastard did it again!! Let's go see what kind of mess he left for us this time," Matt said.

The two detectives ran out of the house and got into the car. The siren echoed in the early morning. The red flashing light lit up the street as the two detectives raced towards the strip.

Meanwhile, Adrian was making the last touch ups to his tie before meeting with Mr. Azario. He took one last glance in the mirror and went downstairs to the tea room. He stood at the entrance and asked, "Mr. Azario, may I speak to you for a moment?"

Frank signalled Adrian in. "What can I do for you, Adrian?"

"Sir, I read the paper this morning and I know how to get Jonathan. We have a lot of things in common. I am sure I can end this quickly. However, there is a great possibility that I will have to kill him on the spot."

"What do you need from me to get the job done?"

"Sir, I need two hundred thousand dollars to get the job done."

"Isn't that a lot of money for a single hit?"

"According to some of my figures, you lose ten times that amount every night that Jonathan is on the loose. This is actually pocket change, and half of it is reward money for information leading to his capture."

Adrian exposed his weapon and holster and said, "I need hardware that is a bit more powerful than this pea shooter. I need something that will deliver a good punch at a good distance. Those are my requests, sir. I will take care of everything else."

"You must know who Jonathan is to you? Are you ready for such a task?"

"I know he is my brother. I am ready to do what is necessary."

"What makes you so sure you can pull this off?"

"We are brothers, and we grew up under the same circumstances. The two of us have the same problems and thoughts.

I know exactly what he is thinking and where he will go if provoked a little. I'm just going to eliminate a few hiding places, and draw him out into the open."

"You sound very confident of yourself, Adrian."

"Yes sir, I believe that I am the only one who can do it quickly and efficiently. Soon, the strip will be back to normal and the profits will rise again."

Azario sat back in his chair and took a sip of tea. "Alright, I believe you. You are very convincing. I give you my blessing to do whatever is necessary to take Jonathan down.

Steven will take you to the weapons room, and you can pick out whatever you need. He will also give you two hundred thousand dollars in cash to carry out the task. But I am warning you, don't screw this up! Now, go and get it over with!"

Adrian replied, "Yes sir." He turned around and left.

Frank Azario was in deep sorrow. Another son would soon be lost. God save his soul.

The two detectives arrived at the hotel. It was cordoned off with yellow tape and the flashing lights lit up the whole block. They got out of the car and were met by the Captain.

The Captain said, "Room 320. You will find Crystal Allison McGuire, aged twenty-three. It is Jonathan's MO. He didn't take her ID this time. Everything is the same, except it looks like he had a shower and cleaned himself up before he left. I got a call from a patrol officer in Queens; they found one of Azario's limos abandoned. The driver was in the trunk with his head bashed in."

Matt said, "That brings the magic number up to eleven. Jonathan is now on a rampage and on the run. Somehow, I think I should have agreed with Adrian."

Mike said, "There is nothing we can do about it now. Let's go upstairs and do our thing and get out of here."

"You're right. Let's go."

The two detectives went to room 320, and there she was, on the bed. She was gagged, naked from the waist down and in the same position as the others. Forensics was taking samples and photos.

"He must have some demons in him to do such a thing as this. I've been on the force for a long time, and I have never seen anything as horrific as these murders!" Matt said.

ADRIAN

They were taking notes of their observations for a report to the Captain. They went over the room and the bathroom. They found some blood on the floor, where Jonathan had gone to clean up.

The main focus of attention was the body and the blood splatters. They took all of the particulars of the ID found in her bag, and wrote them down.

Now, they had to check the other guests to see if they had seen or heard anything strange last night.

After that, they would check the strip and ask the girl's colleagues if they saw who she went with last night.

Lastly, they would call the next of kin and give them the bad news. Mike decided to go downstairs, and ask the clerk about a few details concerning timings. This would take them the rest of the morning to finish up.

Back at Jonathan's hotel, he finally woke up. His morning ritual was going to include a radical haircut. He went and got his electric shaver from his knapsack, and proceeded to the washroom. He activated the trimmer and shaved off his thick mane.

The change was incredible; however, it was only temporary.

He had to get out of the hotel and off Davis Ave. before he was recognized. He finished cleaning up and got dressed. He picked up his weapon from the night stand, and put it in the back of his pants. He packed his bags and took the elevator down to the lobby to check out.

He went to the front desk and said, "I'm Dr. Stuart. I'm checking out of room #908."

He pulled out a huge roll of bills marked in two denominations of hundred dollar and thousand dollar bills. He flipped up three hundred dollars, and told the clerk to keep the change.

He grabbed his bags and hastily left through the front doors.

He took the back streets and alleys along side Davis Ave. until he came across a used car dealership. He needed a car to finish his work, so he entered the lot. Just like shit to a stick, a salesman appeared out of nowhere.

This time Jonathan did need help and welcomed the salesman with a handshake.

"I'm looking for a special car with a solid motor."

The salesman asked, "Did you have any particular car in mind?"

"Yes, an old police car is exactly what I'm looking for."

"We usually don't have too many of those in stock, but I do have one you can look at. Please come this way."

Jonathan followed the salesman down the many rows of cars until they approached a white, old police car.

The salesman said, "The one thing about these cars that people don't like is that someone else has to open the back doors for them. They can't get out by themselves."

Jonathan said, "That's alright, it will do just fine. I see that this old beast still has its security cage on."

"Yes, we kept it on because it's a bugger to take those things out. You're welcome to try, if you buy the car."

Jonathan lied. "I think I will keep it in. It is a perfect space for my dog to ride in."

"What kind of dog do you have?"

"A German Shepherd."

"Is it friendly?"

"No way! That's why I think the cage is a perfect idea."

"I'll let you have the car for forty-five hundred."

Jonathan pulled out the roll, pulled out five thousand dollar bills and handed them to the salesman. The salesman was somewhat taken back by this, but quickly shrugged it off. They went to the office to finalize the deal and insure the car. Shortly after, Jonathan was driving down Davis Ave.

Everything was working according to his plan. He was mobile again, and not so easy to catch now. He headed towards the shopping centres.

There was an old Army Surplus store down there which would have the necessary equipment that he needed to carry out the next phase of his plan.

Jonathan reached his destination, and turned into the driveway. He entered the parking lot and found a parking space near the stores. He got out of the car, locked the door, and went into the surplus store. He pulled a paper out of his wallet with a shopping list of equipment to buy.

He purchased everything from clothing, tent and supplies. He bought enough equipment to survive in the woods for a lifetime. Then he went back to the car and changed into camouflaged fatigues and Army boots. He went to the closest garbage can, and dumped his twenty-five hundred dollar suit. He wouldn't need shit like that any time soon.

Then he drove to the eight hundred and forty acre greenery, known as Central Park.

This was where he was going to lay low. He would change locations several times a day, so that the police patrols didn't take notice of him. Jonathan parked the car, and took a stroll through the park. He might find something of interest or even have a little fun.

Back at the mansion, Adrian followed Steven into the weapons room. Steven asked, "Sir, what do you have in mind? I may be of some assistance."

Adrian replied, "Yes Steven, I believe you will. I need a sniper rifle with a scope and ammo. A 44 will do nicely, and a few assault rifles for Al and his boys."

Steven opened up the steel doors and Adrian walked into a bloody armoury. There was everything in there! Hand grenades, rocket launchers, and any other weapon your little heart may desire. The police department would be foolish to try to take the mansion; they would never succeed.

Steven said, "Follow me this way, sir."

Adrian walked closely behind.

In several racks, there were all types of sniper rifles. There were rifles from every part of the world. Adrian, being true to his flag, picked up an American rifle and scope.

"That's the latest weapon on the market, sir. It's our finest to date."

"I'll take this one."

"Excellent choice, sir."

"Can you now show me a 44 and the assault rifles?"

Steven walked a few aisles and picked up a pistol and ammo. He walked a couple more aisles and picked up four assault rifles and a truck load of ammo.

"Will there be anything else, sir?"

"No, Steven. That should do for starters."

"Very well, sir."

They walked out of the weapons room and Steven locked it back up.

Adrian said, "Can you have these taken up to my suite?"

"Yes sir, right away."

"Thank-you."

"Wait here, sir. I will go get your money."

"Yes, of course."

About ten minutes later, Steven arrived with two hundred thousand dollars in cash and handed it to Adrian.

"Thank-you, Steven. That will be all for now."

Steven designated two men to take the weapons to the suite. He then disappeared to do his numerous duties. Adrian went to the suite and grabbed a coffee. He made a beeline to his office. There he scanned a picture of Jonathan. He saved one picture and used the computer program to alter the second picture.

He made the second picture of Jonathan with a bald head. Adrian knew that Jonathan would try to drastically change his appearance. He took the two pictures and put them side by side. He made a poster, requesting information leading to the capture of Jonathan, and offered a hundred thousand dollar reward.

This should be big enough incentive for the public to search out that bastard! Soon, everyone would be tracking him down. Adrian went to the copy machine and made two thousand copies.

He took his coffee cup to the kitchen for a refill. Doris had already made a fresh pot for him. Adrian was very grateful.

He asked Doris. "Is there a way that you can have these posters plastered on every pole and business window down the whole length of Davis Ave?"

"Yes sir. My husband is a coach for a kid's hockey team. I'm sure a small donation to the team will inspire the young lads to put those posters up."

Adrian pulled out two thousand dollars and said, "Here, take this for the team. However, I want them up tonight. I will be checking."

"Thank-you sir! This is a lot of money!"

"It is just a little insurance that they do the job right."

It was mid-day and Doris made Adrian a soup and sandwich for lunch.

It had been a long time since Adrian had a good tuna sandwich, and home-made chicken soup. His wife used to make that for him. Adrian often thought of Carol, and wished they were still together. He missed her.

ADRIAN

Even though things were not perfect between them, they had still loved each other very deeply.

Maybe down the road, he would have the courage to talk to her. He just wouldn't be able to handle it right now.

It hurt too deeply. He had many regrets about things that he should have done. If it wasn't for the fact that he was so ill, maybe things would've been much better. He was deeply saddened by her absence, and a tear fell into his soup.

The two detectives finished up at the hotel and were on their way back to the station.

Matt said, "I need to talk to Adrian. There is something wrong."

"What?" Mike said.

"Adrian didn't sound like the same man we had in the cell. He seemed completely different in his character. I don't think his medication is working. The pills that Freemont gave Adrian at the station worked extremely well. Adrian is just not himself right now; he is even psychotic.

I want the medication that he has to be examined by our lab. I have a very strange hunch that we will be surprised by the results. I already had Jonathan's medication sent down. That's what we are going to check first, when we get back to the station."

They arrived at the station and parked out front. They went inside and hurriedly went downstairs for the results. Matt opened the lab door and was met by Dr. Roland Taggart.

The doctor said, "Matt, I found something very interesting about these meds."

"What did you find?"

"They are all placebos; they are nothing more than sugar pills. Jonathan's psychotic rage is not his fault.

He has been tricked into thinking that he has been treated. Dr. Freemont is the one responsible for Jonathan's behaviour. Bring in Adrian's medication to me; I'm sure I will find the same thing."

"I knew it! Something was terribly wrong with Adrian when I talked to him on the phone! That means that Dr. Freemont is guilty of eleven counts of second degree murder. He is the real bastard behind all of this. Jonathan is innocent due to his insanity and so is Adrian. "We have enough evidence to arrest Freemont, right now," Mike said.

"I'm going to see the Captain right now about a couple of warrants."

Excitedly, the two detectives bounced into each other while racing upstairs to the Captain's office.

Mike shoved Matt out of the way, and got there first. He hastily knocked on the Captain's door.

"Come in."

The duo came in and Matt said, "Sir, we have a major break through on the case! Dr. Freemont has been prescribing sugar pills to Jonathan and perhaps to Adrian as well! That means that neither one of them is guilty of any crimes. They are both insane."

The Captain said, "That would mean that Dr. Freemont is indirectly involved with eleven murders. We could charge him with eleven counts of second degree murder.

I don't really know his motive, but I want him in a cell, pronto! I'll get you three warrants; I also want you to rip his house apart for any clues to what the hell is happening."

"Yes sir, it will be my pleasure," said Matt.

Meanwhile, Jonathan was enjoying the afternoon when he thought he could use a cold beer right about then. He got back into the car and headed down towards the strip. He arrived out in front of the G-Spot; he could see a whole troop of boys putting posters up.

He got out of the car, and ripped a poster off the nearest pole. He mumbled under his breath, "Fuck'n Adrian did this!"

As far as he could see, the boys were putting posters up all over Davis Ave. It was not safe to hang around this neighbourhood anymore, it was too risky. Jonathan got back into the car and quickly turned up a side street to avoid detection.

Davis Ave. and the strip were all off limits. This changed everything; he could never go there again.

The little bastard really threw a wrench into his plan; he had to change a few things now. He drove to Brooklyn to the nearest liquor store where he bought several bottles of whiskey and four dozen beer. He wanted to stock up, so that he didn't have to make too many public appearances.

He took his cart full of liquor and went to the car. He opened the trunk and stashed away his nectar. He grabbed a couple of beers before closing the trunk, and returned to the driver's seat. He popped a beer and lit a cigarette. He was deep in thought about what he was going to do next.

Unfortunately for Jonathan, Adrian was very well protected. The chances of getting Adrian had dwindled away. The little bastard had dug himself in pretty good by closing off Davis Ave. Jonathan could never step back into the mansion until Adrian and the old man were both dead. That was the only choice left. He had to kill them both.

However, one part of the plan was still unchanged. Matt would soon feel the wrath of God upon him! Tomorrow was the day that they would meet face to face. Revenge would be sweet, and the Azario name would live on!

Jonathan threw the empty beer tin into the back seat and opened another one. There he sat, emotionless and unremorseful for what he has done. His thoughts swirled like a hurricane.

His mind, heart and soul were numbed. Jonathan felt dead inside. There was no stimulation until it was time to feed again. Then it happened automatically, without thought.

God's kingdom would soon have all the souls that you can imagine. An entire city would crumble under Jonathan's lead.

Meanwhile, Adrian was in his office finishing up the property transfers. They were all ready for finalization; he would have them delivered to Mr. Azario's office right away. He got up to stretch his legs.

He went to the living room, and poured himself a cold draft from the bar. He lit a cigarette and took a couple of puffs. He figured that with the hiding spots quickly disappearing, Jonathan would soon be forced into the woods. The closest woods right now were in Central Park.

After he got a little further into his plan, Jonathan would then move out of town. Adrian was sure of it. That's what he would do.

Jonathan would move to the Croton Dam Plaza, and hide out there until it was time to poison the water. He probably had enough supplies to last him months.

Once the population started to die off, he would just come right back. That was basically what he got out of the conversation with Matt. The only water supply for the city came from those two reservoirs.

Central Park was much too risky to try to poison the system there. There were too many people in there; he would never get away with it. He would have to go to the New Croton Reservoir. Adrian didn't quite know Jonathan's next target. He was too well protected to be in immediate danger himself. It had to be the Ruzo family.

Adrian was thinking, maybe he should stick around Matt's neighbourhood throughout the night for a little insurance. He might be of some assistance.

He couldn't use the limo; that would set Jonathan off. Maybe Steven would like to get out of the house and go shopping for a car.

Adrian asked Doris, "Can you get Steven up here please? I have an important errand for him."

"Yes sir, right away."

Adrian went and filled up his mug with draft. Several moments passed and there was a knock at the door. It was Steven.

"Yes sir, you summoned me."

"Yes, I want you to buy me a vehicle that can stand up to rough terrain. Here is forty thousand dollars. I don't care what it is; just make sure it is tough. Don't be long, I want it for tonight."

"Yes sir! I will have it parked out front for you."

Adrian sat down at the kitchen table, and wrote a list of things that he would need for that night.

He gave the list to Doris and said, "Make sure that I have all of this stuff by tonight. We might be away for a while. Tell Al and three of his buddies to plan for a camping trip tonight. Make sure that they meet me at the crossroads of Highway 129 and Batten Rd. They should stay hidden until I arrive."

Doris said, "Yes sir, I will get a hold of Al right now."

"Thank-you, Doris."

Adrian took a sip of beer and was contemplating what would be going through Jonathan's mind right then. He was putting himself in Jonathan's shoes. He made several plans around what Jonathan might do next. He studied the plans and memorized them. He thought that there would probably be a murder tonight.

Chances were, Jonathan's time table would be clear till at least the next morning. That would leave him with about

ADRIAN

eighteen hours of spare time. He would become very agitated waiting for the right time to go after the Ruzo family. He would absolutely kill that night.

Doris said, "Mr. Eisner, I have dinner ready for you. Would you like to eat at the table or where you are?"

"Thank-you, Doris. I will have it right here in the kitchen."

She placed down a ginger beef stir fry with rice, Adrian's chops were watering with anticipation. One thing about Doris, she was a wonderful cook.

Still thinking about Jonathan and referring to the paper, he started to eat his dinner.

He figured that it would be a nice evening for a drive around Central Park. It was very obvious, that was where Jonathan would be.

Meanwhile at Belleview, Matt and Mike were greatly disappointed.

Matt said, "We must have tipped him off when we asked about the medication."

The office door had a sign on it, "Office space for lease."

Mike said, "Well, that's two wasted warrants. Do you think he flew the coop?"

"It sure looks that way."

Suddenly, Matt's cell phone beeped. Matt answered, "Hello."

The Captain on the other end said, "You'll never believe this."

Matt interrupted, "I know the house is empty."

"How did you know?"

"The doctor's office has a 'For lease' sign on it."

"Shit! He can be anywhere by now."

"The best thing to do is let the Feds take care of it, especially if he has left the state."

"First, I'll put out a state wide search, and then I'll call the Feds if there is no result. I'll talk to you later, Matt. I'm going back to the station now."

"Yes sir, I'll see you there." Matt then turned off the phone. "Just as I thought! Freemont packed up the house too!"

"We are still no further ahead than we were a week ago!" Mike said.

"I know. It is very frustrating to me too. I just wonder where Jonathan is. Let's take a drive along the strip, and check out some of the bars before we call it a night."

Mike said, "Ok, hopefully we will get lucky tonight, and put the bastard away."

They reached Davis Ave., and parked the car. They took a look around, and all they saw were hundreds of posters of Jonathan.

"Well, one thing is for sure. There won't be any more murders on Davis Ave.," Matt said.

"That's true, but where is he going to go next?"

Adrian finished his dinner. He gave Doris a little hug and said, "Thank-you, Doris. That was delicious."

There was a knock at the door and Doris answered it. It was Steven.

"Sir, your vehicle is out in front. Would you like to come down and take a look?"

"Yes Steven, that sounds like a fine idea."

The two men went downstairs and through the front doors. Adrian's eyes nearly popped out of his head.

"Steven, old boy! I didn't know you were up with the times! It's a fuck'n Hummer!!"

"Is this sufficient, sir?"

Excited, Adrian said, "It is fuck'n perfect!"

Steven then handed Adrian the keys and the change from the purchase.

"Thank-you, Steven. You did an excellent job!"

Adrian went inside where two men were waiting for him. One of them said, "Sir, we have the equipment that you asked for."

"Thank-you, gentlemen. Would you take that stuff, and pack it in the Hummer?"

"Yes sir, we will take care of it right now."

Adrian was almost ready; he just had to pack a few other things. He would still have time to hit the G-Spot for a few beers. He went upstairs and grabbed a few clothes that were more suitable for the outdoors.

He changed into blue jeans, a tee shirt and a sweater.

He had a good sportsman's jacket, which should keep him warm during the cool night air. Not forgetting, he grabbed the 44 and the sniper rifle. Now he was ready for the hunt.

ADRIAN

Adrian did not seem affected by the fact that he was setting out to kill his last brother. He had taken to his new responsibilities very well. He seemed to have some fight in him. He seemed to fit in. He was still having disassociated episodes; however, they were tending to work in his favour.

His mind lost touch with reality and he entered the Azario world. This was a world where the rules were meant to be broken. This world had the stimulation that kept Adrian bound to his duties, even if it included murder.

He was packed and ready for a night on the town. Then after that, it would be all business. He went downstairs and hid the weapons under some equipment. The vehicle was already packed. Adrian got into his new vehicle. He pulled out of the driveway and headed towards the strip.

He arrived in front of the G-Spot, and locked up the vehicle. He went inside and headed towards his favourite table. He managed eye contact with Gina, and she started to get his usual draft.

She came to the table, put down the beer and asked, "Did you put those posters up?"

"Yes, I did."

"Good idea! As you can see, business has greatly improved already!"

"Good! That was the whole idea."

Gina smiled and went back to take more orders.

Mr. Azario would be pleased at the profit margin tonight. The place was booming, and it was still early in the evening. Part one of the plan was working, and so would part two. Now, it was time to hurry up and wait. It was now Jonathan's turn to move.

Adrian lit a cigarette and out of the corner of his eye, he noticed Matt and Mike made an appearance. He got up and moved towards the entrance to get their attention. They noticed him, and followed him to the table.

Matt said, "I need to talk to you Adrian. You have been cheated."

"How?"

"Dr. Freemont has been treating Jonathan with placebos. In turn, Jonathan is acting this way because he is not being treated for his illness. I believe that your pills are nothing more than sugar too. Let me have your pills so that I can have them tested for you. Then, I'll help you get the treatment you need."

"That's why I have been so screwed up! I was wondering why the medication wasn't working. I used to have good results with the medications before. What is going to happen to Dr. Freemont?"

"He has disappeared on us. When we catch him, he will be charged with eleven counts of second degree murder."

"Good! That bastard ruined my marriage and my life. I hope you hang that bastard for what he did to us. But that means that Jonathan is innocent, due to his insanity."

"Yes, that's right. He needs medical attention, not a life in prison. I noticed that business has picked up since you put the posters up."

"Yes, it is working like a charm."

"I told you Adrian; don't take this into your own hands. I will jail you, and throw away the key. If you're smart, you will tell me where I can find him!"

"I already gave you a chance, Matt. You declined my offer, and now the deal is off."

"I'll throw you in jail for obstruction of justice."

"I am working on speculation, just like you are. I don't have any hardened evidence. So, that means jail is out of the question. You have to do better than that! Are you boys off duty now?"

"Basically, we came here to look for Jonathan, and you scared him off the strip."

Adrian waved to Gina and raised three fingers. Gina nodded and brought three drafts to the table.

"They're on the house, cheers!"

The detectives grabbed their beers and raised their mugs in a salute.

Adrian said, "Don't worry, Mike. Jonathan is getting caged in. He doesn't have that many places to hide anymore; that will make it much easier to find him."

"It also diverts more people back into your business," said Mike.

"That's true. It has several advantages."

"When are you going to give up the business? Your job with us is done."

"My business with you is done. However, I still have a lot of work unfinished."

Matt warned, "Don't get tangled in a mess that you can't get out of, Adrian."

Adrian replied, "If you are within a hundred miles of Frank Azario, you are already involved. Do you get my drift?"

"We will help you get out of there," Matt said.

"You don't have the slightest idea what this guy is capable of doing. It is impossible to just walk out on him, without getting yourself killed. Once you enter those gates of his, you automatically become a lifetime member."

"Does that ruin our friendship?" asked Matt.

"It certainly wouldn't look good on your record having an acquaintance with the mob. It would damage your career. It has to be a work-related relationship. It just won't work out for either one of us."

"Too bad our work puts us on either side of the coin. I presume that we are enemies now."

"Both of our jobs require us to act against each other; there is no other way."

Matt replied, "I'm very sorry for this, Adrian. You're right. In that case, I hope I never see you again. Cheers!"

Matt finished up his beer and left the bar with Mike.

Adrian felt saddened that he had to brush Matt off like that. It was the only way; they just couldn't associate with each other. He actually liked the detectives. They seem to be fairly decent people with good morals.

He knew that the next time they met; their relationship would be much different. It was business from this point forward.

Adrian ordered another beer and lit a cigarette. Several minutes passed and Gina delivered the beer to his table and asked, "Are you alright? It looks like you lost a friend."

"I did. I lost two of them."

Gina patted Adrian on the shoulder and said, "Sorry." She then went off to serve the other tables.

Adrian turned his attention to the shows to try to relax and forget about what had just happened. He took a sip of beer, and quietly slipped out of reality. He became powerless to his fantasy world. He slipped deeper and deeper into his disassociated state. This was how he had to feel when he kills Jonathan.

He had to withdraw from his morals, and allow the darkness to take over his heart and soul. Adrian had now transformed himself into a murderer. Now the only thing left to do was to go and find Jonathan.

Chapter Fourteen

Meanwhile, Jonathan was cruising along Central Park West Dr., looking for a place to sit down and have a few beers. He found a place to park, and grabbed a twelve of beer and walked towards Shakespeare Gardens to relax.

He found some underbrush nearby and nestled himself inside. There he opened a beer and lit a cigarette, and was watching out for any attractive ladies that may pass his way. He sat quietly, like a predator stalking his prey. It was already nightfall, so his position was well guarded from the police.

Jonathan's mind was on autopilot. There was no thought involved, he would only react on impulse. He just had to feed his starving hunger. He grew tenser as time passed him by. The agitation caused him to drink several beers to calm his nerves, so that he could react when the timing was right.

The population in the park had dwindled; people were settling in for the night. Still, there were potentials in the park. Jonathan lay in waiting, as he saw a lone young woman approaching nearby.

It looked like she was a working girl. This was perfect for Jonathan. He patiently waited as she almost came within arm's reach. While her back was turned, Jonathan pounced and gagged her mouth with his left hand.

He quickly drags her into the brush and out of sight. For an instant, the vulnerable woman prayed to God for mercy. She knew now, that by the eye contact that was made, that she was face to face with Satan himself.

The evil that empowered this beast was no match for the poor woman. The viscous assault was more of what an animal would do, rather than a human being.

Jonathan pulled out the baseball bat and sealed her fate. After Jonathan fed his desires and sent her soul to God. He left the mutilated body in the brush as a trophy. He picks up his beer and walks back to the car. He gets in and opens a beer and lights a cigarette. Jonathan sits back deeply into the seat.

He slowly captured his breath and strength from his exhilarating triumph. God would be pleased that another lost soul had found her way to the heavens. Jonathan recovered and finished his beer. It was now time to leave the park.

He turned on West 86th Street and headed towards Matt's house. He would sleep there for the rest of the night.

He would patiently wait for the right moment to put an end to Matt's happy family life as he knew it. Even though, he had just finished his feast, Jonathan was still hungry.

He was on an incredible high; nothing could stop him now. He could foresee the future, where he would see Matt beg for his life.

Meanwhile back at the G-Spot, Adrian had just finished his beer. He figured that the witching hour had arrived. He got up and went to the car. A quick spin around Central Park and then Adrian would move off to the second part of the plan.

After fifteen minutes of driving, Adrian arrived at the park and entered West 81st Street. He drove slowly, keeping a close eye out for Jonathan.

Upon passing Belvedere Castle, Adrian noticed flashing lights by the lake. He drove towards the lights and saw that the police had the road blocked off. The whole area was full of cops.

It looked like part one had already taken place. Adrian turned around and went back the way he came. It looked like he was right; Jonathan had been there.

Back at the Ruzo residence, Matt woke up and went downstairs to make coffee. He grunted at the on-duty officer and grabbed the filters and coffee. With his eyes barely opened, he made coffee. He then went to the back step to get the paper.

He sat down and looked at the front page. It looked like Jonathan was known to everyone in New York now. That reward had the whole city scrambling to find this murderer.

Matt was disappointed with the way things had turned out with Adrian. He should have known that once he got in, he could never get back out. Adrian was a good man; it was a shame he had to deal with people like Azario.

A muffled voice came from upstairs. "Daddy, Can you come and get me please?"

"I'll be right there, sweetheart."

Matt got up and went upstairs to pick up Emily. They came downstairs and Matt put her in her wheel chair. He went back to puree her breakfast. Emily then wheeled herself to her spot at the kitchen table.

Matt said, "Here you go, sweetheart. Your mush awaits you."

"Yuk! I can't wait until I get this wire off, and eat decent food again."

The on-duty officer said, "Mr. Parson's has just driven up. Shall I let him in?"

"Of course you let him in. You do the same thing everyday. Why not today?"

There was a quick knock at the door and in flew Mike. He went straight to Emily and gave her a peck on the cheek. "How is my munchkin today?"

Emily smiled and said, "I'm fine Mr. Parsons, thank-you."

"Good morning Matt."

"Good morning Mike."

Mike went and took a couple of cups from the cupboard, and poured two cups of coffee.

"Here's your coffee, Matt."

Mike then sat across from Emily and smiled. Mike took a sip of coffee and said, "Well, what's on the agenda today?"

"Well, I guess we tighten the noose on Dr. Freemont, and see if he makes a public appearance. We'll do the normal routine investigation on him, and see if we can find a motive."

Marilyn came downstairs and went to the kitchen. "Good morning, Mike."

"Good morning Mrs. Ruzo."

"Oh...Mike. You are just too kind. Loosen up a little. It's Marilyn."

Mike laughed and said, "Yes Marilyn, I will try to remember."

Marilyn poured herself a coffee and sat down.

"Oh...Matt, is there enough gas in the car? I have to go grocery shopping today. We are getting pretty low on everything."

"Yes dear, I filled it up last night. However, I don't want you to go out alone anymore. It is too dangerous. Jonathan is closing in on us and we might be next."

"Can I have a police escort?"

"Our resources are already working double shifts tying to catch this guy.

We can't afford to have an escort to take up valuable time. You could take one of the officers from the house. The only thing is that Emily wouldn't be as well guarded."

"I don't like that idea. She has been through enough already. I have to go shopping today. The store is only five minutes away. I'll be there and back in no time."

"I don't like the idea, but please be careful. The first sign of trouble get back to the house as fast as you can."

"You worry too much, dear. I'll be careful."

Matt's cell phone beeped and he answered. "Hello."

The Captain said, "The son of a bitch moved to Central Park. They found a body matching the same MO as what we have before."

Matt replied, "That is out of our jurisdiction. I guess someone else will be working on that one with a little cooperation from us, of course."

The Captain said, "Yes, the 22nd Precinct will take care of it. We will clue them in on what has happened over here."

"Thank-you for the update, sir. I'll see you a little later."

Matt turned off the phone and said, "The bastard got another one last night in Central Park!"

Mike said, "It sounds like a logical place to hang out. I bet Adrian already knew that."

"I think he knew, too."

Matt got up and said, "I'm going to get ready for work. I'll be back in a bit."

"Don't rush, we have lots of time."

Matt then stomped his way upstairs and disappeared from sight.

Mike got up, picked up the coffee pot, and topped up the two cups. He put the pot back and sat down again. "Well, munchkin, are you catching up on your school work?"

Emily said, "Almost there, I might catch up by tomorrow."

"Good for you! I knew you would come out of this just fine!"

Emily smiled and said, "Thanks Mr. Parsons."

After about thirty minutes of chit chat, the boss stomped his way back down the steps. He went to the kitchen and said, "I hope you guys didn't drink all the coffee!"

Marilyn said, "Mike was kind enough to leave you a cup, dear."

ADRIAN

Matt raced to the machine and poured himself a cup. He then turned the machine off and sat down.

Matt said, "He's up to twelve murders already! When will he stop?"

"He won't stop on his own; we have to stop him ourselves.

"According to the journal, he won't stop until the number reaches into the thousands. The State Police have the New Croton Reservoir covered, and the 22nd Precinct has the Jacqueline Kennedy Onnasis Reservoir covered."

The two detectives finished their coffees and Matt said, "I'll see you tonight. I shouldn't be late."

He went over and kissed Marilyn and still had one left for Emily. The two men left by the back door and drove off.

Marilyn said, "Honey, are you going to be alright, when I leave you with the officers?"

"I'll be fine; I can take care of myself."

Marilyn went about her morning chores, while Emily pulled out her school books.

A couple of hours passed and the chores were all done. Marilyn went to the closet and got her coat and purse.

She went to Emily and gave her a kiss on the cheek saying, "The stores are open now. Is there anything you need?"

Emily glanced up from her home work and said, "No, I don't need anything, Mom."

"Ok, I'm off. I won't be long."

She went to the car and backed out of the driveway. Marilyn barely made it two blocks, when this stupid driver of a parked car pulled out in front of her. The idiot then slammed on the brakes and Marilyn crashed right into the back of the car.

Marilyn was furious. What kind of idiot would do such a thing? She opened the car door, and stomped her way to the driver's window of the car in front. She started screaming at him, and the driver got out of the car.

He was wearing a camouflaged outfit, with blood stains all over it. Marilyn gasped when she realized what was happening. She stood in shock, unable to move. Her nightmare had come true; she was face to face with Jonathan.

Jonathan grabbed her quickly and opened the back door to throw her inside. He wrestled with her to get handcuffs on her wrists and ankles. Once that was complete, he slammed the door, and went to the driver's seat.

He drove off and turned north onto the highway. The whole incident only took a couple of minutes; no one noticed what has just happened. Marilyn's car was left abandoned with the driver's door wide open.

Jonathan made his way out of the city limits and pulled out the cell phone.

He punched in the numbers and the phone rang.

Matt answered. "Hello."

Jonathan said, "Good morning Matt. It is a beautiful day for a drive!"

"What the fuck do you want?"

"It's not what I want. It is what you want! Here, listen to this."

Marilyn yelled, "Don't worry about me! Just get the bastard!"

"Did you get that, Matt?" Jonathan asked.

Matt said, "If you hurt her I..."

Jonathan quickly cut him off. "What? Kill me, like you did my brother! At least I am giving you a chance, which is something that Frank never fuck'n had! Here's the fuck'n deal, Matt. Call off the guards at the New Croton Reservoir.

If I happen to see one cop, your wife will die a very brutalizing death! Meet me on Croton Dam Road. Meet me in the middle of the dam, and I will let you see your wife for one last time! I want this between you and me, and God! I hope you enjoy your drive upstate. I'll see you soon."

Jonathan shut off the phone and laughed out loud as he drove. Marilyn silently sobbed in the back seat.

Matt put away his phone. It looked like he had just been hit by lightening.

Mike tapped Matt on the shoulder. "He has Marilyn, doesn't he?"

Without a word, Matt nodded his head.

Mike said, "Matt!! Snap out of it! We got to go and get her!"

Matt shook his head and tried to shrug off the shock. "Wait! We have to pull the cops out of the area or he will kill her. I'll tell the Captain."

Matt ran to the Captain's office and knocked.

"Come in."

Matt blurted out, "Sir, Jonathan has my wife as hostage and he is on his way to the New Croton reservoir. If he sees a single cop out there, he will kill her."

The Captain said, "I'll call the State Police and have them pull out! I will tell them the situation. I will also let them know that you are working in partnership with them. Now, get out of here and go get your wife!"

The two detectives almost blew the doors off the station, and they squealed their way upstate. Matt was so nervous, he was trembling and shaking like a leaf. Mike was racing towards 9A and then North with lights flashing and siren blaring.

In the meantime, Jonathan had just arrived at the meeting point. He was preparing for one of his final acts. He got out of the car and opened the trunk. He then pulled out the duffle bag. He started to pull things out, when he finally found the canisters.

He took the bag over to the concrete railing and started setting the canisters in a long row about ten yards above the water mark. He pulled out rifle parts and ammo.

He quickly put the rifle together, because he knew that Matt should be coming very soon. Jonathan swung the rifle over his shoulder, and put the rest of the stuff in the trunk.

He opened the back door, and released Marilyn's ankles from the restraint. He pulled her out of the car, and dragged her to the front of it. Jonathan grabbed the revolver that he had stuck in the back of his pants and put it to Marilyn's head.

"Now be a good fuck'n girl, and I won't have to get nasty on you."

Marilyn's lips trembled with fear. Her legs were hardly strong enough to hold her up. There they stood and waited. A half hour has passed and in the distance, Jonathan could hear a siren. "Well, it looks like your old man is here. It's show time!"

"You'll never make it, Jonathan! Give yourself up! They can help you!"

"They can help me by repenting their sins!"

Jonathan looked down the road and saw an unmarked car racing towards the dam. The car reached the dam and started to slow down. It carefully stopped in front of him. The two detectives stepped out of the car with their hands up. They slowly moved towards Jonathan.

Jonathan said, "That's close enough, Matt. I told you that this was between you and me! Why did you bring him along?"

"He is my partner. He follows me everywhere I go. We can end this peacefully; no one has to get hurt. We can talk it out."

"There is no time for words, except for you to beg for forgiveness."

"You're wrong! You are very ill. I can help you! Dr. Freemont had you taking placebos and the result is this. You then started the killings!"

"I don't believe you! It's a damn trick to save your ass!"

"It's true! He tricked you, and now he is on the run," Mike said.

"I want the two of you to slowly take out your guns from the holsters, and place them down in front of you."

Reluctantly, the two detectives did as they were instructed.

Jonathan said, "Good, now kick them towards me."

Again, they did as they were told.

"Matt, get down on your knees and clasp your hands."

Matt was getting extremely nervous now; he shakily went down on his knees. It looked like Jonathan had this carefully planned.

Jonathan said, "Now, pray like you have never prayed before! Repent your sins and beg for forgiveness!!"

Jonathan pointed the gun at Matt's head and said, "I said fuck'n pray, you bastard!!"

At that instant, Marilyn stamped her high heel deep into his boot. Jonathan was temporarily off guard and Marilyn broke free to run to Matt's side. As Jonathan pointed the gun at Marilyn, Mike sprang in front. The gun went off and Mike fell like a ton of bricks, face first.

Mike took the shot in the centre of the chest. Marilyn screamed and cried as she hung on to her dear husband. Matt's head lowered in sadness and defeat.

Jonathan then pointed the gun back at Matt's head and said, "You can at least save your soul or burn in hell!

Matt said, "I'd rather burn in hell than listen to you!"

Jonathan screamed at the top of his lungs. "You mother fucker, burn in hell!!!" The hammer pulled back and suddenly a shot rang out.

ADRIAN

Jonathan straightened up like a pin; his eyes were wide as saucers. A trickle of blood flowed from between his eyes. He fell to his knees and dropped to the concrete.

Matt got up and grabbed his gun, searching for where the shot came from.

As he looked at Jonathan again, he could see that the back of his head was missing. Matt told Marilyn to lie flat. He scanned the area, and there was no sign of anyone.

He ran up to Mike and took a pulse. "Holy shit! He still has a pulse."

He turned Mike over and was amazed at what he saw. "Wait a minute! There is no fuck'n blood!"

Matt ripped open Mike's shirt and gasped. He turned to Marilyn and said, "The fucker is wearing a bullet proof vest!!"

Marilyn sprang up with all smiles and ran to Mike. Matt started to shake the shit out of him.

"Wake up you bastard!!"

Mike slowly woke up and said, "Whoa, take it easy. I think I have a few broken ribs."

"You bastard! You're wearing a vest. You scared the fuck'n shit out of me!!"

"Sorry, I wasn't going to chase down this lunatic without one of these on. I see you got him. How did you manage that?"

"It wasn't me! I don't know where the shot came from. I'm going to the car to call the troopers in."

As Matt walked to the car, he noticed five men getting into a couple of cars. One of the cars was a limo. He watched them drive down Quaker Ridge Road and disappear.

This was the end of the terror, which had put New York City into a nightmare of horror. Matt made the call and told them to bring disease control and the hazardous materials squad with them. He went back to his wife, and held her closely. They had never loved each other like this before. They had never known how lucky they really were, until it was almost gone.

Later that day, Adrian walked up the steps and into the mansion. Mr. Azario was waiting at the other side of the door and met him. Mr. Azario stood there without saying a word, and Adrian nodded. He walked upstairs to his suite, and the old man followed.

Adrian turned around and said, "Can I help you, sir?"

"I would like to come in and have a drink with you."

"Yes sir, I think that is a wonderful idea." Adrian opened the door, walked straight to the bar and said, "What will you have, sir?"

"I'll have a scotch on the rocks." Frank went and sat down on the chesterfield.

Adrian made up the scotch, and poured himself a draft. He handed Frank his drink and said, "Sir, I have something I would like to discuss with you candidly."

"Go ahead, speak freely."

"Thank-you, sir. You have been very good to me, sir. I really appreciate it. However, I don't believe we were cut from the same cloth. We are two very different people.

You are very business orientated and firm, and I am the opposite. I don't think I have what it takes to be the next boss of this empire. I have a difficult time with my morals, and it gets in the way of some of the work that may be required to be done."

Frank said, "You're a smart man. Adrian; you have done very well from my point of view. You handled a couple of tasks like a professional. I believe you want me to release you from the grip I have on you. I have to deny that request for the time being.

I want you to run the strip to the best of your ability.

I have noticed that business had already jumped last night, since you put the posters up. That was a brilliant idea. I need you, Adrian.

I need you as a protégée, and as a son. I had to give up on two sons already, and I'm not about to let you slip through my fingers. I missed the chance to see you grow up, and I'm really sorry for that. Unfortunately, I can't change the past. I do have the power to change the future."

Adrian said, "Sir, my character is all wrong for this kind of work. I am a caring and meek man."

"That's true. However, you are extremely capable to do what is necessary. You took care of Jonathan when you had to, and I know you can handle any challenge that is thrown at you."

"I can handle challenges when I'm forced to, but this not something I like to do. I'm not a killer by nature. I was forced by you, and the situation."

ADRIAN

"Things will be more legitimate for you from now on. You will run those businesses and not be involved in the politics of my interests. There are restaurants, hotels and other small business holdings that you now own. Run those businesses and leave the killing to me.

I need you involved in my life; I am a lonely man who has a lot of catching up to do."

Adrian said, "What are we going to do about the cops? They will be here soon to ask questions."

"I told you. Let me take care of the politics and I'll talk to the cops."

"Did you want another drink, sir?"

"No, that's enough for me. I just had to talk to you for a little while."

Adrian stood up and said, "I want to thank-you for allowing me to speak my mind, sir."

Frank got up and said, "We'll talk again, soon. By the way, you did an excellent job today. Bye for now." Mr. Azario went to the door and let himself out. Adrian then went to the bar and poured himself another draft, lit a cigarette and sat down. He felt a little better that he didn't have to kill any more.

He thought that when he got a new doctor and the proper medication, his own character and demeanour should all return. Perhaps he could return to a normal lifestyle, and start fresh.

Meanwhile at the hospital, Mike had just finished getting his ribs taped up. He got dressed and went to the waiting room to meet Matt and Marilyn.

"How do you feel, Mike?" Marilyn asked.

"It hurts like hell."

Matt said, "It could've been a lot worse. You were so lucky; I just can't put words to it."

"You know very well who shot Jonathan," Mike said.

"I know who it was, but I don't think we will be able to charge him. Not only was he ill at the time, he also came to the aid of a police officer. If it wasn't for him, we would be all dead by now!"

"We still have to make a case and bring him in. It is up to the DA's office if he gets charged or not."

"I want to go to the Azario Mansion and talk to Adrian" Matt said.

"Do you think we will get in?"

"I think Frank has a little better understanding of what we are all about. I think the old man will let us in."

"What are going to do about Freemont? He is responsible for the whole thing."

"The Captain put out a state-wide APB on him. We just have to wait and see."

The three of them left the hospital. Matt thought he would stop by the impound first. Marilyn's car was probably there. So they went to the station first and went around the back to check out if the car was there. They found it and Marilyn had to pay the fees and towing before getting it back.

She signed the paperwork and said, "I'll see you tonight, dear." She gave Matt a kiss and drove away.

Mike said, "Should we go to the mansion now?"

"Yeah...I think that is a good plan."

The two detectives went around to the front, got into the car and drove away. Twenty minutes later, they arrived at the Azario Mansion. They were stopped by the guard at the front gates. Matt said, "Tell Mr. Azario that Matt Ruzo is here to see him."

The guard said, "One moment." He disappeared for a few moments and returned. "Mr. Azario is waiting for you in the tea room. Please drive through." He opened the gate and Mike drove to the front of the mansion.

Matt noticed the Hummer in the driveway. It matched the description of the car he saw at the dam.

They entered the mansion and were met by Steven who led the two detectives to the tea room. The two men entered the room and stood in front of Azario.

Matt said, "I want to thank-you for seeing us on such short notice, sir."

"Don't mention it. How can I help you?"

"I'm not sure if you know this yet, but Jonathan was killed this morning. Some one sniped him while he had us at his mercy. The killing was basically an act of aiding a police officer. Whoever the killer is, he saved our butts. I think Adrian did it, and I want to talk to him."

"Are you planning to make an arrest today?"

"No, we have to check with the DA to see if we have a reason to arrest or not. I just want to talk to him."

ADRIAN

Azario picked up the phone and had a short conversation with Adrian.

"Very well, Steven will take you to his suite."

"Thank-you sir."

They followed Steven up the stairs to Adrian's suite. Steven knocked on the door and Doris answered.

"The two detectives would like to talk to Adrian."

"Please come in. He is waiting for you."

Adrian was sitting at the bar. "Would you gentlemen like a drink or a coffee?"

Matt replied, "I could go for a coffee, thanks."

Mike said, "I'll also have one of those, please."

Doris went to the kitchen. She came back and gave the detectives their coffee.

Matt said, "Adrian, I'm going to cut through the bullshit, and come straight out and say it. Did you kill Jonathan this morning?"

Adrian replied, "You do realize; I don't have to say a word without my lawyer present. You don't possibly believe I would admit to such a thing."

"I recognize the Hummer. I saw it this morning at the dam along with a limo. There were five men. It was too far away, so I didn't get a chance to see the faces. However, I do suspect you."

"Are you going to arrest me?"

"Not right now - not until we finish gathering evidence. I told you not to take matters into your own hands. Off the record. I know it was you, and I would like to thank-you. You saved us from our doom."

"Off the record, you are very welcome."

"I presume we are enemies from now on. If I see you again, it will be all business."

"I guess so. I don't think we are going to run into each other anyway. I am running the legitimate end of the business. I'm the new owner of the strip. It will take all my time to ensure that everything runs smoothly."

"I'm glad to hear that."

"I'm not very good at this cloak and dagger shit anyway. It just isn't me."

"I guess we should go, Mike. We have a lot of paperwork on this one."

Mike agreed. They bid farewell and left.

Adrian went to the bar, poured himself a draft and lit a cigarette. He could not help but think that Freemont was the real bastard responsible for everything that had happened. He went to the kitchen and sat down. He figured that he was going to take the afternoon off, and go to the G-Spot.

Doris had other plans and said, "Here you go Mr. Eisner. Eat up! I made you lunch."

Adrian smiled and said, "Thank-you, Doris."

Adrian loved pasta primavera, and Doris knew how to do it right. He was in deep thought while he was eating his lunch. It looked like the case was basically closed.

The police would eventually catch up to Freemont. The rampage was over and the city could go back to its normal routine. Adrian was very relieved that the whole thing was over. He was hunted like a dog and forced into hiding. Then he was forced into the mob.

The worst thing of all was that he had to kill his only surviving brother. This was a lot of shit to go through in a very short amount of time. Adrian was surprised that he was able to handle it, even while not being treated medically.

He finished his lunch and said, "It was a delicious meal Doris, thank-you. Can you have Michael meet me out front in about five minutes?"

"Yes sir, I'll get on it right away."

Adrian went to the bedroom closet to get his coat and made his way downstairs.

He waited a couple of minutes out front, when Michael pulled up in the limo. Michael got out of the car and opened the door for him. Michael popped back into the driver's seat and asked, "Where are we going?"

"Take me to the G-Spot, Michael."

The car then pulled out of the driveway, and made its way to the strip. They arrived at the bar, and Michael got out and opened the door for Adrian. When Adrian got out of the car, he noticed there was another Azario limo parked out front. Adrian was curious as to who it might be. He opened the door and was surprised at what he saw.

There was a big crowd gathered around near the back of the bar. Adrian couldn't make out what all the excitement was all about. There were balloons, streamers and confetti strewn

ADRIAN

all over the bar. Adrian made his way to the crowd and pushed his way through to see what was happening. He finally made it to the centre and was shocked at what he saw.

Trixie was back! Adrian tapped her on the shoulder. She turned around and jumped into her brother's arms. They were very excited to be back together again. They hugged and kissed and wouldn't let go of each other.

Adrian said, "I love what you did to your hair!"

Trixie laughed and said, "It's a wig, silly! I'm as bald as a cucumber under this rug. I just thought I might look a little more human this way."

"You look beautiful! I am so glad that you are alright. Do you want to go upstairs for a quiet drink?"

"Yes please, I'm starting to get a headache from all this noise."

The two took the elevator and entered the suite. Adrian turned on the lights and they both got a terrible fright. There, in the middle of the room, was Dr. Freemont with a gun.

Freemont said, "Close the door and please come in. Adrian, take your gun out of the holster and place it on the floor. Trixie, you can do the same thing. I know you carry a piece in your purse."

They both did as they were told.

Freemont said, "Now, you can both kick the weapons towards me."

They again obeyed his order.

Freemont picked up both weapons and said, "Don't let me be a terrible host, please go get yourself some drinks. I'll have bourbon, Adrian."

Freemont was closely watching the pair get their drinks; the gun sight never left Adrian. Trixie had a gin and tonic for herself and brought the bourbon for Freemont.

Freemont said, "Just put my drink on the dining room table and have a seat on the chesterfield."

Adrian got his beer and went and sat beside Trixie.

With the gun trained on Adrian, Freemont said, "I would have never thought in a million years that you would have survived, Adrian. You are much tougher than I anticipated. I thought Jonathan would have got you the same time he nailed this bitch beside you."

Adrian jumped up in a rage.

Freemont pointed the gun at Adrian's head and said, "Easy now! Don't forget who is in control of this conversation. Now, sit fuck'n down!"

Adrian regained his cool and sat down. "How did you get in here or even know about this place?"

"That was the easy part. Jonathan was very resourceful; he took an imprint of Trixie's keys. They did live in the same house, you know. With a few suggestions and playing with the medication, Jonathan was wrapped around my little finger. He was my pawn, until you killed him this morning." Trixie's mouth hung open in shock as she grabbed Adrian by the arm and asked, "Is that true?"

Adrian nodded his head and said, "Yes, it's true."

Freemont said, "He was doing everything the way I wanted it. All I had to do was read the morning paper. He carried out my commands, without question."

"Why did you go through all this trouble?" Adrian asked.

Freemont said, "That's easy. All I've ever wanted was the money and the power. I would have had it all, if it wasn't for you. You did not break as easily as Jonathan.

Since I controlled Jonathan that means that I would have had the control of the money and power to do as I wish.

Eventually, I would have had Jonathan commit suicide, and I would have been in full control. It is a very simple idea; it was working perfectly. Now, I am here to avenge Jonathan's death, and destroy you for what you did to me! You took away my dreams! They were so close to coming true and you ruined it all!

Jonathan told me that this place is soundproof. That is very convenient for me. I plan to keep Jonathan's legacy alive by taking over from where he left off. I am much more dangerous than he was. The city will never have a restful night again. I'll be kind to you; you can have one more drink before I kill you. You can refresh mine as well."

They got up from the chesterfield and went to the bar. They were pouring their drinks when they heard a yell. "Freemont!! Put the gun down!! It's the police!!"

Freemont turned to fire, but Matt was too fast on the trigger. Freemont flew back and fell onto the coffee table breaking it into hundreds of pieces.

ADRIAN

Matt ran to Freemont and disarmed him, and then checked his pulse.

Matt looked at Mike and shook his head. Freemont was dead and the rampage was finally over.

Adrian grabbed his fresh beer, took a big sip and said, "How did you guys know about this place, or that Freemont was here?"

Matt said, "We had a state-wide APB on him, and he was noticed by a detective. He followed him here and watched him go upstairs; then he radioed in. We came down as fast as we could, and the rest is history."

Mike called in for forensics and the others to come down and do their thing.

Trixie said, "That means that it is really over now."

Matt said, "Yes, it is truly over now. You are a free man, Adrian. The DA cannot find any charges that would hold in court. You are not going to be charged for murder."

Adrian smiled and said, "That's great news! I want to thank-you guys for everything you've done."

Matt said, "The precinct is starting a mental health awareness program. This is to show officers how to detect, and handle people with mental disabilities. The idea was conceived because of this particular case. Adrian, you are our poster boy. You've been through hell, and you still made it through all right. The station has a lot of respect for you, thanks."

PATRICK J. SCHNERCH

Part Two

Chapter Fifteen

It was early evening and Trixie and Adrian both took the rest of the day off. They were downstairs at their favourite table having a few drinks. The police were just finishing up their investigation upstairs. The body had been wheeled out only a few moments ago.

Trixie and Adrian gave their statement to Matt and Mike so that they could wrap up the investigation. It shouldn't be much longer, and the police would leave. Then the G-Spot could go back to normal.

Adrian asked, "Well, how does it feel to be back in the saddle again?"

Trixie said, "Oh...it's wonderful to be back! Everyone was so nice to me. It was a great welcome home!"

"Unfortunately, you also had a startling welcome by Freemont. We both didn't need that. I feel very relieved that he is gone for good. He was a very evil man, and he almost got away with it."

"We don't have to worry anymore. It's all over. How did you manage to cope so well?"

"I used my mental illness to my advantage. My mind and soul would shut off at just the right time and allow me to enter a world that I was able to control. It was extremely dangerous to do, but it saved my butt several times."

"What are you going to do for a residence? The police said that the suite is off limits because it is a crime scene. They said it could be weeks before we are allowed back in there."

"I guess you don't know, yet. I now have a suite at the mansion.

Mr. Azario has taken me on as a protégée and new owner of the strip. I had the properties transferred to my name a couple of days ago."

"Oh...That is wonderful news! I am so happy for you."

Trixie raised her glass for a salute.

They touched glasses and Trixie said, "Welcome to the family. I'm sure you will be very happy there. I know that I am happy you're there."

Adrian said, "Mr Azario has been very generous to me. He has bent over backwards to help me out. I have a beautiful suite, personal servant, chauffeur and all the money I need. It is wonderful. However, I really had to work for it. I had to deal with the devil to gain acceptance by your father."

"That's the way it is with my father. He doesn't give hand outs. You have to really earn your keep. You're lucky he has accepted you so readily. He usually doesn't do that."

"Maybe things are a little different for me, since I am his last surviving son. He could've loosened the reins a little, so that I would stay on."

The police were just coming down and Dr. Taggart said to Trixie, "We are finished here for today. However, it is still a crime scene and the area is off limits till further notice."

"That's fine. No one will go in there, I promise. Thank-you, Dr. Taggart."

The police left through the front entrance and Adrian and Trixie could relax for the night.

Adrian said, "I want to thank-you Trixie for believing in me. You were the only friend I had during this whole ordeal.

I would've been totally alone, trying to clear myself from the overwhelming evidence that was mounting up against me. I don't know what I would've done without you."

"You are very welcome. You saved my life. I guess we can call it even. It was one hell of a ride though. Jonathan was a monster. It is too bad that he had to die because of Dr. Freemont. He was the real monster.

I didn't realize how serious mental illness can really be. I didn't know it could be so devastating. I guess you need to see a doctor soon, so that you can get treated properly."

"I would like to do that tomorrow. The sooner, the better. I would like to get back to normal as soon as I can. It has been a terrible strain on me. I'm just getting too tired from it."

Trixie turned around and signalled to Gina for another round. Adrian lit a cigarette and gave one to Trixie. They were so happy that things turned out for the better.

Gina came to the table and delivered the drinks.

She smiled and said, "It is so nice to have you back Trixie."

"Thank-you Gina, it's nice to be back."

Gina skipped off to serve the other tables.

Adrian asked, "Did you see you Dad yet today?"

"No, not yet. I'll see him later on tonight. I just want to relax and have some fun tonight."

ADRIAN

From the corner of his eye, Adrian noticed six large men in suits enter the bar. Five of those men had baseball bats.

Adrian whispered to Trixie, "I think we are in big shit. Try to stay calm."

Slowly the patrons were quietly leaving the premises.

They could sense that there was trouble brewing. The men came up to where Adrian and Trixie were sitting. The leader said, "My name is Miguel. I work for Mr. Manicotti. He is not very pleased with the string of events that has taken place today. Dr. Stewart and Dr. Freemont were very dear friends of Mr. Manicotti.

Mr. Manicotti has decided it is time for a new business arrangement. You will now be paying a thirty percent protection fee on each of your businesses on the strip."

Adrian said, "We don't need your protection. We are very capable of supplying our own. You can tell Mr. Manicotti to shove it up his ass!"

Miguel pulled out a magnum, pointed it at Adrian's head and said, "Nobody bad mouths Mr. Manicotti, not even you trigger man."

The rest of the patrons had been paying close attention to what was happening in the back corner. Even the die-hards had already left. Now the place was empty, all except the unwanted guests and the staff.

Adrian said, "What makes you think I did it? It was a private conversation."

Miguel said, "We also know that you are the new owner of the strip. By the way things are working out for you tonight; I'd say that your protection is inadequate. Take the thirty percent deal and save yourself a lot head aches. If you don't, the property value on the strip will plummet and you will have no choice but to sell at below market value to Mr. Manicotti."

"I won't be pushed around and forced into selling the strip! It will never fuck'n happen!"

Miguel snapped his fingers, and the goons went to work. Baseball bats were flying, destroying everything in their path.

Mirrors, bottles of booze, everything was getting smashed into hundreds of pieces. The stage floor was ripped up, the lighting and sound systems were wrecked. Nothing was safe, the décor, the bar; everything was being dismantled piece by piece.

Trixie went to sit beside Adrian and wrapped her arms around him. Her head sank into his shoulder and she sobbed. "I thought it was over, I really did."

Adrian whispered, "Don't worry; they won't get away with this."

Miguel waved the goons off, and the rampage ended. Nothing was left intact. The whole place was destroyed.

Miguel said, "You and the old man are as good as dead! Watch your fuck'n backs! You will regret for what you did to Mr. Manicotti's friends. He holds the two of you responsible, and he will avenge their deaths! As a little insurance so that you do not retaliate against Mr. Manicotti, we are taking the girl with us. If you decide to retaliate, she will be killed."

Miguel grabbed Trixie by the arm and ripped her away from Adrian. Adrian yelled, "You won't fuck'n get away with this! I fuck'n promise you that!"

Miguel had his arm around Trixie's throat and they backed out of the bar. He still had a steady aim at Adrian's head.

Miguel said, "Remember, if you try anything funny, the girl dies! Thanks for the entertainment. I had fun tonight. Cheers!"

They left the bar and sped away. The phones were ripped out, so Adrian went next door to call the police. After making the call, he returned to the bar. Thank God, they hadn't touched the draft machine!

It was still functioning so Adrian filled up his old mug and lit a cigarette. He anxiously waited for the police.

Adrian wondered what they could do. They had Trixie and the old man's hands were tied. Otherwise Adrian would burn the Manicotti mansion - burn it down to the ground!

If they accepted the offer, it would be just a matter of time before the businesses would fail from the extortion. They would be forced to sell at cut rates. The empire would greatly suffer from such an impact. It may never recover from that loss.

The police arrived. A uniformed officer said, "What happened here?"

Adrian said, "I want to talk to Detective Ruzzo about this."

"We can handle this one on our own. We don't need the Special Task Force involved in a vandalism case."

"This is not a simple fuck'n vandalism case! Get fuck'n Ruzzo down here, right fuck'n now! I will only talk to him!"

ADRIAN

The officer got on the radio and contacted Matt. Matt agreed to come down.

"Detective Ruzzo is on his way sir."

"Thanks."

Adrian went to his corner to sit down and wait for Matt. The Police were assessing the damage and taking notes of what they found. Adrian couldn't believe it!

He had thought it was over. He didn't think that Jonathan had friends who would seek revenge. What the hell was Jonathan doing associating with Manicotti anyway?

Adrian didn't know who this Manicotti was, but he damn sure knew that he would find out. It seemed that Dr. Freemont was also involved.

Maybe, they would have to look at the big picture to see what was really going on. Why was Manicotti so pissed? It must have meant a great deal more to him than friendship. Adrian went behind the bar and poured himself another draft and lit a cigarette. He then went back to his corner to sit down. About ten minutes passed by before Mike and Matt has arrived.

Matt said, "Holy shit! What happened to this place?"

"Have a seat gentlemen, and I'll try to explain. I shouldn't be associating with the cops on this anyway. I'm taking a big gamble telling you two guys. You have to promise me that this is unofficial. This conversation will never become known to anyone except the three of us. You have to promise me, or the deal is off."

Matt said, "Fine. This is an unofficial visit. Now, tell us what the hell is happening here."

"Do you know Mr. Manicotti?"

"Sure, we know him. He is the mob boss over in Little Italy. The Manicotti's and the Azario's have been at each other's throats for almost a lifetime. They are mortal enemies."

"Well, Manicotti sent his goons over here with a few messages. First of all, they want a thirty percent protection fee on each property along the strip. That high price would put the strip out of business. It would become worthless, and then Manicotti will come from behind and buy the property dirt cheap.

This bit of damage you see tonight is just the beginning. There will be more. Manicotti is pissed that his two friends were killed today. They said the old man and I are dead men.

It seems Jonathan and Freemont were associates of his. Now Manicotti is seeking revenge. They took Trixie tonight. They said if we retaliate, they will kill her. They must never know that I told the police, or that will be the end of Trixie."

Matt said, "I can't just sit on this! There is a hostage taking, extortion, and a gang war about to erupt, and you want me to stay quiet! There is one thing that usually happens.

The police don't have the resources to get involved into gang wars. We do nothing more than clean up the mess and catalogue the dead. Our main concern is the innocent victims that may get caught in the crossfire. We usually handle the mob with evidence rather than with fire power. There would be just too much blood shed if we did it any other way."

Adrian said, "So what am I supposed to do, lick my wounds and let Manicotti destroy the Azario Empire!"

Matt said, "If we stepped in now, they would kill Donna in a flash! I am keeping an eye on you, Adrian. If you are involved in any crimes, I'll haul you off to jail so fast, it will make your head spin!"

Back at the mansion, Frank Azario was in the tea room, enjoying a sherry. He was still saddened about Jonathan. Maybe, he would feel better after the funeral when Jonathan could finally rest in peace. It had been a stressful few weeks for the Azarios. Maybe Frank could take off somewhere and have a holiday in Europe or something.

He was slightly startled when he heard, "Mr. Azario, may I speak to you? This is extremely important!"

"Yes, of course Adrian. Please tell me what is on your mind."

Adrian put his finger up to his lips to signal Frank to be quiet. He knelt down, looked under the table and found an electronic device. He got up, put it in Azario's hand and said, "Manicotti."

Frank's face turned beet red with rage and he yelled into the device, "You are not going to get away with this Manicotti! Consider yourself a dead man!"

Frank summoned Steven. "Get Al over here, right now!"

Steven said, "Yes sir!" He ran back into the mansion with the urgent message.

Within a minute or two, Al raced to Mr. Azario and said, "Yes sir, you summoned me?"

Frank said, "Al, you know what this is, don't you? I want this house torn upside down to find all of its brothers and sisters. Destroy them all! I want this fuck'n house bug free by the time I go to bed! This is Manicotti's idea. Clean it up, now!"

Al snapped to attention and said, "Yes sir! I'll take care of everything!"

Adrian then said, "Sir, it gets a lot worse than that. Now, we can speak freely.

Manicotti sent his goons to the G-Spot tonight. They know that you and I talked about the hit on Jonathan. Jonathan and Freemont were associates of Mr. Manicotti. Now Manicotti is seeking revenge on the two of us for their deaths."

Azario said, "Fuck'n Jonathan was a traitor to his own father! He's the one who probably planted all these bugs. We were under surveillance by Manicotti the whole fuck'n time! He is lucky he is dead, or I would do it all over again!"

"That's not all, sir. They destroyed the G-Spot. It's nothing more than a pile of rubble inside - everything is gone. They want a thirty percent protection fee. Once the businesses fail from the high prices, then Manicotti would force me to sell at a cut rate.

The worst thing that happened is that they took Trixie. She is now being held hostage. She was going to surprise you tonight that she was released from hospital. They gave us a warning. If we retaliate in any way, they will kill her."

Azario went ballistic; he got out of his chair and screamed obscenities. He went right off the deep end. There was no way of consoling this man. You couldn't get close to him because of his flying appendages. The pain was much too real for him to handle.

Adrian sat down in the chair and quietly sat there while his father was throwing a tantrum. He was just waiting for him to calm down. Maybe, together, they could figure something out. They seemed to have their backs up against the wall for the moment.

Suddenly the phone rang. Azario was awakened from his rage and raced to the phone. "Azario."

"It's been a long time Frank; we should keep in touch more often."

"Manicotti!! What the fuck is this all about?"

"I'm taking you down, Frank. It's nothing personal, its business. I like your neighbourhood, and I'm going to take it all away from you. However, you did have two of my closest friends killed today. Now, that I take personally. I'll let you in on a little secret.

I know you are in the middle of house cleaning tonight; I have some very interesting taped conversations of you and your associates. There is everything on it, like conspiracy to commit murder, murder, extortion, drug import and distribution, prostitution and much more. I have a nice little package ready to go.

The police will have enough evidence to crush your empire. Then I'll come along on the sheriff's auction block and buy it up. After that, I can expand my empire to include most of Manhattan. To let you know that I am a considerate man, I will give you a grace period until you bury your son. After the funeral, it will be time for you to pay the piper.

Just a reminder, don't do anything stupid. I have your daughter, and she will be the first one to go if you try something. I think I might give her a little shot of something to calm her nerves. She is a bit on the edge."

"One way or another Manicotti, I am going to make you pay for this with your life."

"You are in no position to give me an idle threat. You can't back up those words, Azario. I believe our conversation is over. Good-night."

Azario hung up the phone quietly and took a seat in his regular chair. He took a shot of sherry and poured himself another glass. It looked like Frank was pinned to the corner. He just sat there in shock, not knowing what to do.

Adrian said, "Sir, please excuse me, but I think I should get to learn a little more about this Manicotti guy. I think if I had all the information you have on him, perhaps we could fight back."

Azario looked at Adrian quite sternly and said, "Give it a fuck'n break! I just lost a son today, and now my daughter's life hangs in a basket. I don't think I can handle another family death. I'm getting too old for this!"

ADRIAN

Adrian said, "Sir, I bet my bottom dollar that if all of your resources were pooled together, you could make good on your promise to Manicotti. However, I will need to have access to those resources."

"I thought you did not want to get involved in this area of my business."

"Sir, I am taking this as a personal matter. I will do everything in my power to put an end to this once and for all! You are my family and nothing comes in between family, especially not a Manicotti. Please excuse me, sir. I think I need to relax a bit before I go to bed. Good-night, sir."

Azario said, "Very well, Adrian. I will see you in the morning."

Adrian went upstairs to the suite. Once inside, he went to the bar to pour himself a draft. He could see that the place was nice and clean, it was done before Doris took off for home. He really liked her; she was a very sweet woman.

Adrian took off his shoes and went to the kitchen. He sat down and took a sip of beer. He lit a cigarette and already had an idea on how to take Manicotti down. However, it would be very messy. They would have to get to Trixie first, before setting off any alarms.

That meant that some people would have to infiltrate the mansion without being detected. They would have to be extremely efficient at what they were doing. There was no room for mistakes. Adrian was not sure if Azario had the resources that Adrian needed to pull this off.

Poor Trixie, she fell victim for the second time. The poor girl had been through enough to last her a lifetime. Adrian just hoped that she was alright. He prayed that he could get to her first.

Meanwhile at the Manicotti Mansion, Trixie was being held prisoner in a lavish room. The door was locked and the windows barred.

There was also a guard on the outside of the door. There was nothing in the room that could aid her in an escape. The door opened and several men entered. The first one through the door is Manicotti himself.

"Good evening Donna. It is nice to see you. The last time we met was at your mother's funeral," he said.

Trixie said, "Well, you're the bastard that put her there in the first place!"

"That was an accident, my dear. She was at the wrong place at the wrong time. Your father was our real target."

"What kind of dealings did you have with Jonathan and Freemont? Why should you care so much that they are dead?"

"They were not only my friends, but they were also business associates. Jonathan had a very big part concerning this take over of the Azario Empire. He gathered information on your father's dealings which gave me the leverage I need to shut him down. I couldn't have done it without his dedication.

Dr. Freemont was the puppeteer. He had control over Adrian and Jonathan. For exchange of a piece of the pie, Freemont was preparing Jonathan for the big fall.

I would start a corporate take over and Freemont would soon be in rags. They were both fundamental in my success today.

I still had plans for them, and your brother and father ruined those plans. Now, I have to deal with your father directly. It is all about business. I want to expand my empire to include most of Manhattan. Now, I am in the position to take it over, and there is nothing your father can do about it. You must understand dear. It is nothing personal, it's strictly business.

Miguel, our guest looks to be a bit on edge. Will you give her a little something to calm down?"

"Yes Mr. Manicotti. Right away."

Suddenly, four men grabbed Trixie and threw her onto the bed. They were holding her down tightly while Miguel injected a syringe into her arm.

Manicotti said, "Now, that's much better. She will be much happier now."

He laughed and walked out of the room with his goons following close behind. The door was locked and Trixie was all alone.

She could see that the room was spinning out of control. The light left trails behind. The sounds were slowed down to a monotone level. Her muscles were so weak that she could not move them. The spinning continued, even while her eyes were closed. Trixie was totally helpless; she couldn't even scream for help. She was at the mercy of Manicotti.

ADRIAN

Back at the Ruzzo residence, Matt picked up his coffee and went to get the paper off the back step. He sat down and thought that it was so nice that they didn't need the police protection anymore. They had their house back to normal and safe.

He opened the paper. The headline read, "We Got Them!" He took a sip of coffee and read the story.

Just like clockwork, he heard, "Daddy, can you come and get me please?"

"Ok sweetheart, I'll be right up."

Matt got up and went to bring Emily downstairs. He put her in the wheelchair and went to make her breakfast. Maybe today, Emily might like pureed pears for breakfast. He put the pears in the food processor and got a glass of milk. When everything was ready, he put it out on the table for her.

She wheeled herself up to the table and said, "Thanks for the breakfast, Dad."

"You're very welcome, pumpkin."

There was a quick knock at the door. Mike was as cheerful as ever. He ran to Emily and gave her a kiss on the cheek. "Good morning munchkin. How are you today?"

"I'm fine Mr. Parsons. How are you?"

"I can't complain; it's a beautiful day outside. I also get time to spend with my munchkin. Life can't get any better than that!"

Matt said, "Good morning, Mike. You know where the coffee is."

"Good morning, Matt." Mike went and got himself a coffee, sat down and said, "You know we have to tell the Captain about Adrian's little secret."

Matt said, "I know. We have to tell him that the city is at the brink of a gang war. Unfortunately, the first cop to stand foot on the Manicotti grounds and Donna is dead. We need a different approach. We have to do something safe."

"Do we have the resources to assault the mansion and save the girl?"

"We do have swat teams, but there is a high possibility that she will be dead before they get to her.

We'll tell the Captain this morning about the situation. I presume he will alert the 5th Precinct of the impending danger."

"All we can do is wait and see what happens, and pray that the girl is alright."

"I just wonder how involved Jonathan and Fremont were with Manicotti. Was the whole idea conceived by Manicotti? Maybe Jonathan and Fremont were nothing more than pawns in the big picture. I bet there was a lot more going on than what we are led to believe."

"We can't even put extra patrols on the strip. That would set off Manicotti that the police are involved. We actually have our hands tied."

"I'm going to take a shower and see if I can think of something." Matt then went upstairs.

Back at the mansion, Adrian was already in his suit having a coffee and a cigarette in the kitchen. He had a very busy day ahead of him. Adrian had to call up an architect to redesign the G-Spot. He also had to set up contractors for the job. He wanted the G-Spot up and running as soon as possible.

After that was done, he had to find a new doctor and see if he could get started on medication as soon as possible.

The next thing to do was to make a plan on how to save Trixie, and put an end to Manicotti once and for all. This was going to be a very thought-out plan.

Adrian would impersonate a building contractor and get the floor plans of the Manicotti mansion from city hall. Once he got the plans, he would plan the rescue minute by minute.

The plan would include defence against roving patrols, guard dogs, perimeter guards and the interior guards. The plan had to be precise and fast with no mistakes. It had to be perfect.

Thoughts were spinning in Adrian's head as he entered his own world. He envisioned the assault to be devastating with a high death ratio. His world was full of darkness, and his soul was black. Manicotti's empire would crumble in one quick blow. This was not a time for morality or guilt. The main focus was to destroy everything in his path. That was the only way to stop Manicotti for good!

Adrian stared at the wall while he was engaged in his disassociate state. Nothing could enter his world. As far as Adrian was concerned, Manicotti was already a dead man! All they had to do now was follow through on the Azario promise.

ADRIAN

Adrian puffed on his cigarette and was startled that his coffee cup was empty. He was awakened by this realization and was now back in the world of reality. Even though he was back in the real world, the Azario promise remained unchanged.

Adrian got up, poured himself another coffee, sat down again and lit another cigarette. He was wondering how the funeral arrangements were going. The morgue had said that the family could take possession of the body after the autopsy that is scheduled for early this morning.

Steven was handling the funeral arrangements. He was sure it would be a big spectacle. All the crime bosses across the country affiliated with the Azarios would be here. There might also be some guests from overseas.

Funerals were big events in these woods. Adrian was sure it would be held at one of the grand cathedrals near by.

Mr. Azario would ensure that security would be tight. Manicotti had given them a grace period to grieve, but Adrian was sure that the shit would hit the fan shortly after. Adrian couldn't stand the feeling of being defenceless against this guy! The businesses in town were finally open, and Adrian called the architect.

The phone rang and Adrian heard the secretary's voice say, "Armstrong Architects. This is Charlene speaking."

"Good morning Charlene, I would like to make arrangements to see an architect today."

"What is your name?"

"My name is Adrian Eisner. I live at sect 1326 west. It is the Azario Mansion. My number is 727-1185."

"We have an evening timing that I can book for you. It would be at 7:00 pm with Mr. Armstrong."

"Could you Have Mr. Armstrong meet me at 3146 Davis Ave.? It is known as the G-Spot."

"Yes sir, I will make sure he meets you there."

"Thank-you for your help, Charlene. Good-bye."

Adrian then called Taber Construction. "Taber Construction. This is Ron Taber speaking."

"Good morning Mr. Taber. I want to know what your schedule is like in the next month or so."

"What kind of a job do you need to get done?"

"I need my bar to be gutted and renovated as soon as I get the plans from the architect."

"I should have a crew just finishing up on a small job, around that time."

"Can I have a clean-up crew as soon as possible to clear everything out of there?"

"I could have one there tomorrow morning. Where are we going?"

"You are going to 3146 Davis Ave. It is known as the G-Spot. I will meet your crew there at 9:00 am to let them in. You can reach me at 727-1185. My name is Adrian Eisner."

"Ok. They will be there first thing in the morning. Good-bye."

Now, the most important thing to do was to find a doctor. Adrian thumbed through the phone book and saw that a Dr. Moss had an office nearby.

He dialled the numbers and a female voice said, "Dr. Moss's office. You are speaking to Crystal."

"Good morning. My name is Adrian Eisner. I want to know if Dr. Moss is taking in new patients."

"Yes he is. Would you like to make an appointment?"

"Yes I would. It is a bit of an emergency, I am a manic depressive. I haven't been treated for a long time and I am suffering very badly from it. I need an appointment as soon as possible."

"In that case Mr. Eisner, we had a cancellation early this morning. Can you make it down here in twenty minutes?"

"Yes, I'll be right there, thank-you. Good-bye, Crystal."

Adrian asked Doris, "Can you have Michael meet me out front, right away?"

"Yes sir. I'll get right on it."

Adrian went to the bedroom closet and got his coat. He quickly raced downstairs and ran out the front doors to meet Michael. Michael opened the door for Adrian, and then he returned to the driver's seat. "Where would you like to go, sir?"

"Take to the Richmond Medical Arts Building at 1488 Terrace Drive."

"Yes sir, I'll get you there in a few moments." The car drove off.

About ten minutes later, they arrived at the medical building. Michael opened the door for Adrian who went inside

ADRIAN

and checked the directory. He went to the third floor and found Dr. Moss's office.

"Good morning Crystal. My name is Adrian Eisner. I have a 9:30 appointment with Dr. Moss."

Crystal looked at the clock and said, "You just made it on time. I'll tell the doctor that you are here. Please have a seat."

Adrian sat down and grabbed a magazine. No sooner than he sat down, the doctor called for him.

Dr. Moss said, "Adrian please follow me this way."

Adrian lowered his head, shuffled himself into the office and took a chair.

Dr. Moss said, "Well Adrian, why don't you tell me why you are here today?"

"I have been diagnosed with bi-polar depression, anxiety, disassociation, and psychosis. I have not been treated for a long time and I am having a difficult time coping with day to day activities."

"Why were you not treated?"

"My doctors were Ken Stuart and Jason Freemont. I was on placebos for months."

"I recognize the names now. You guys were in the papers and the news for weeks. That must have been very traumatic for you, even under normal circumstances, never mind being severely ill at the same time."

"I really need your help badly."

"Adrian, I am very surprised you survived your ordeal. What was your saving grace?"

"Quite honestly, it was the booze. There was lots of it, too."

The Doctor looked shocked and said, "How much is a lot?"

"I drank morning, noon, and night. I guess I drink about twenty mugs of draft a day."

The doctor's eyes widened and he said, "It doesn't matter how much medication I give you, it just won't work while you are drinking!

The booze will keep you in a constant depression and the medication won't have a chance! You have to stop drinking!

After a prolonged use of alcohol, your brain becomes damaged. I will refuse to treat you unless you make some drastic changes. You are an alcoholic and you need help now. Here is a number of the Awareness Society; call them today.

They offer drug and alcohol counselling on a one to one basis as well as group sessions.

Here is a number for another excellent support group. They are called The Centurion Chapter. They help people with a dual diagnosis such as you have. You have a severe mental illness and you are an alcoholic. They often go hand in hand; it is very common for the mentally ill to also suffer from substance abuse."

Adrian then told the doctor of the experiences he has been having mentally.

After that, the doctor said, "I agree with your previous diagnosis. As you well know, I can't treat you for the disassociation, but I can treat you for the psychosis and the bi-polar depression. I can only treat you if you stay off the booze. Do make myself perfectly clear?"

"Do I need to go to a de-tox centre?"

"We will let it go for a month, and see how it is going for you. We will make a decision then, whether you need to or not. Here is your prescription and here is your appointment for next month. I'll see you next time. Good luck."

"I thank-you very much, doctor."

Adrian left the office. As he was going back to the car, it felt like somebody had dropped a ton of bricks on him. It had never crossed Adrian's mind that one day he would have to give up his booze.

This was a real shock to him; he didn't know how he would manage. He had always trusted the booze to help make life a little easier to cope with. Adrian was now scared of the unknown. What would happen now?

He made it back to the mansion and up to his suite. He couldn't help himself; he went straight to the bar for a draft. It quickly calmed the anxiety that he was feeling. He grabbed the phone and took out the paper that the doctor gave him.

He called the Awareness Society. The phone rang and a lady answered. "Awareness Society, this is Lucy speaking. How may I help you?"

"Good morning Lucy, My name is Adrian Eisner. I am an alcoholic and I need help."

"We have an open house on Tuesday from 1:00am-4:00pm.

It is a first come, first serve basis. We will set you up with a councillor, and we will help you with your recovery."

ADRIAN

"Thank-you very much, I'll see you next Tuesday. Good-bye, Lucy."

Adrian had one more call to place. He dialled the Centurion Chapter.

The phone rang and a young woman answered. "Centurion Chapter. This is Francis speaking."

"Good morning, Francis. My name is Adrian Eisner. I have been diagnosed with bi-polar depression, Psychosis, Disassociation and Anxiety. I am also an alcoholic. I heard that your organization help people with dual diagnosis."

"Yes, we are a self help group who meet twice a week at the Alexander Centre on Wednesdays from 4-30pm-5:30pm.

We also meet on Fridays from 6:00pm-7:00pm. You must be drug and alcohol free to attend these meetings. The address is 651 Charlotte Ave."

Adrian said, "Thank-you Francis, you have been very helpful. Good-bye." Adrian hung up the phone. He took a glance at the paper with all the information that he had just received. This was going to be one hell of a tough journey.

Adrian lit a cigarette and looked at his mug of draft. He was thinking that soon he would be going through life on a different, unfamiliar path. It was a very scary feeling to change direction in your life and not have a crutch to temporarily hold you up. Adrian took a sip of beer and thought long and hard.

Chapter Sixteen

Back at the Manicotti Mansion, Vincent Manicotti was enjoying a glass of wine and a cigar in his parlour. He thought to himself, "I've waited many years for this day to happen! The day is soon approaching that I will run almost all of Manhattan.

The little chunk of business I run in Little Italy is not prosperous enough. There isn't enough business. Besides, Azario made his empire from my loyalty in the old days, when we were friends. It was my muscle that got the contracts signed and set up a healthy profit margin.

Most of the empire was built on my blood and sweat. That ungrateful bastard Azario didn't do a damn thing but relax and watch the money roll in. What the hell did I get for my effort? Just a tidbit here and there, nothing much to speak of.

I was Azario's top muscle man; I ran the show! I have diddly squat to show for it, except this little racquet that I now run in Little Italy. Azario put me in charge here to set up prospects; I ran the show for years. That bastard made millions off my efforts!

Then I decided it was time for me to work for myself, rather than Azario. I raised the cash and the manpower over the years so that I could become strong enough to pull out of Azario's grasp.

Finally, the day arrived where I was able to break free. Azario and his wife were having a night on the town. They were hitting all the high class night spots, and having a time of their lives. As they were approaching the car, a sniper fired upon them. The woman's head exploded like a ripe melon.

Frank was rushed into the car and escaped the assassination attempt. He left his dead wife on the side walk for the police to clean up.

Our relationship turned into a battle, ever since I put a hit on him. I hate Azario, with a passion!

This time, I finally have him. I have the power to take him out of the picture now. He will now pay dearly for how he treated me. Another assassination attempt is almost impossible; he has never left that mansion of his, ever since that fatal day. I too, am heavily guarded against such things as an assassination attempt.

Azario will die! When his sacred empire crumbles and he is put onto the street, no one will care if he dies then.

He will be a bum, scrounging for loose change. I will get my revenge!"

Manicotti poured himself another wine and admired the décor in his parlour. He had done very well for himself. Business was good. However, once he took Azario's empire over, business would then be great. He will become the most powerful mobster in the United States and perhaps the world.

Manicotti said, "Ramon, have Miguel check on our house guest and see that she is comfortable."

"Yes sir. I will tell Miguel immediately." Ramon then took off in a hurry to repeat the message to Miguel.

Back at the station, Matt and Mike were about to knock on the Captain's door. Matt took on the task, and the Captain answered, "Come in."

The two detectives walked in and Matt said, "Sir, we don't think that the case with Jonathan and Freemont is over.

Apparently, they were tied in with Vincent Manicotti. They busted up the G-Spot last night and made serious threats to the Azario's. We think that the two families are about to engage in a gang war. Manicotti has taken Donna Azario as a hostage. He is seeking revenge for his two dead buddies."

The Captain sat back in his chair and thought for a moment. "I want twenty-four hour surveillance on the Azario family. I want to know anything there is to know.

I want to know who enters and leaves the compound. I want to know ahead of time if Azario plans to retaliate. I will tell the 25th, so that they can do the same on Manicotti. At least we want to warn the public before the bullets start to fly. There isn't much more we can do, other than referee the game."

"Yes sir, we were afraid of that."

"Sorry gentlemen, a rescue attempt would mean certain death to the girl. We have to stay out of it."

"We know sir, thank-you."

The two detectives left the office, and Matt closed the door behind him.

"Excuse me Mike; I'll be in my office setting up the surveillance for the Azario Mansion."

"Sure, I'll talk to you later."

Matt went into his office and closed the door.

Meanwhile at the Azario mansion, Adrian was having a draft in his suite. He was feeling very lonely. There was something in his life that was missing.

He had a luxurious home, money and cars. He thought he had it all; then why was he so bloody sad? He was a free man and there were no charges pending.

He should be on top of the world. Adrian knew what was tugging at his heart. He was missing Carol. He was still deeply in love with her. Adrian sank his face into his hands and cried.

Doris came up to Adrian, put her caring hand on Adrian's shoulder and said, "What's wrong sir? Can I help you?"

"I'm sorry Doris; I am having a serious time with the blues right now. I really miss my wife."

"Well, why don't you call her?"

"I think it is all over; we will never be back together again."

Adrian was sobbing very heavily; his heart was broken. He missed the days that they were together. He especially missed the times when he wasn't so ill.

He remembered the picnics, and the family days with the dog on a nice walk. They used to go window shopping and eat hot dogs at the food kiosks. Just being together and holding hands were the most memorable times in his life. He was afraid that he had lost it all.

"I don't even know if she will talk to me," Adrian said.

Doris said, "You'll never find out unless you try. Is she home right now?"

Adrian looked at his watch and said, "It's four o'clock; she might be home now."

"Tell me her number, sir. I will call her right now for you."

"Her number is 727-1128."

Doris dialled the number and was waiting for an answer. It rang about five times when she heard, "Hello."

"Is this Mrs. Eisner?"

"Yes...who is this?"

"My name is Doris. I have somebody waiting to talk to you, one moment please."

ADRIAN

Doris then handed the phone to Adrian. He took the phone, and broke into heavy sobbing and said, "Carol it's me, Adrian."

Carol burst into a sob and said, "I'm sorry, honey. I should have trusted you! I am so very sorry! I should have never called the cops on you! Please, forgive me! I miss you so much. Please come home!"

Choking back the tears, Adrian said, "I love you, sweetheart. I really do. I miss you so much that my heart is breaking. I want to see you tonight. I will pick you up. Bring the dog with you. We have a lot to talk about."

Carol sobbed heavily and she said, "Don't you want to come home with me? I need you at home with me! Please, come home!"

"I want to come home, sweetheart! I really do, but I need to talk to you tonight. I will explain everything. Bring Blackie with you; I want the whole family together tonight. I will pick you up at 8:30 pm. You can phone in sick tomorrow. This is very important. Don't eat dinner; we will have that together. Please trust me, honey. I love you very much."

"Ok, but I really want you to come home!"

"I know honey. We will talk tonight. I'll see you guys at 8:30 sharp."

"Ok, I'll see you tonight. I love you, honey. Bye."

"I love you too, sweetheart. Bye."

Adrian silently put down the receiver and got up to see Doris. He put his arms around her and sobbed. He gave her a kiss on the cheek and whispered, "Thank-you."

After a few minutes, Adrian let go of his embrace with Doris and said, "Doris, I have a very big favour to ask of you..."

Doris interrupted, "Yes sir, dinner for three at 9:00 pm. You would like a nice romantic dinner for two with champagne. You would also like dinner and biscuits for the four legged member of the family as well. Yes sir, it will be my honour to do this for you two."

"Yes, how did you know?"

"I have a loving family too; women just know these types of things."

"I will give you five times your salary for helping me out tonight. I really do appreciate it, thank-you."

"You don't have to do that sir. That is a lot of money."

"You are worth your weight in gold, Doris!"

"You'll have to excuse me sir. I have a lot of things to do before dinner tonight."

"Yes of course. You do what you have to and I will stay out of your way."

Adrian went to the bar and poured himself a draft. He went to the kitchen table and let go a sigh of relief. He lit a cigarette and took a sip of beer. He was so relieved that Carol wanted him back! That made him very happy. Unfortunately, Carol's morals were quite high.

He didn't know how Carol would react to his forced induction into the mob. She wanted everything to be the same as it was. Adrian didn't blame her for that either. He wanted the same thing as she did.

He would give up this luxury in a second, if he could have one single day with Carol. She meant everything to him, and now he really knew what love meant. Adrian was deep in thought, hoping for the day that they could stay together under one roof as husband and wife again. He truly missed her.

He started to cry and a tear drop fell onto the kitchen table. He cried because he knew Carol would not accept taking part in a mobster's life.

For as long as he was held captive in the mansion, there would never be a life with Carol. Sadness filled his heart again, because he already knew what was yet to be. Adrian looked at his watch. It was already twenty after six. He had to get ready to see Mr. Armstrong at the G-Spot. Then he was going to pick up Carol.

Adrian was on his way out when Doris called to him. "Sir! Where are you going that you are dressed like that?"

"I'm going to see the architect and then I'll pick up Carol. What's wrong with my clothes? It's a three thousand dollar suit!"

"You're not going to pick up your wife in those rags! Go look in your bedroom. I laid something out for you."

Adrian went to his bedroom and was shocked. Doris had laid out a long tailed tux, top hat, cane and a dozen roses. Adrian smiled, and quickly got changed. He excitedly went to the living room all decked out.

Doris applauded and said, "You look charming, sir. Michael is already awaiting you out front."

"Thank-you Doris, I'll see you later tonight." He ran downstairs to the waiting limo. Michael already had the door open for him.

"Michael, I would like to go to the G-Spot," he said.

"Yes sir. I'll get you there in no time."

About fifteen minutes later, they arrived at the bar. Adrian got out and was met by Mr. Armstrong.

Mr. Armstrong jokingly said, "Sir, you didn't have to get all dressed up for me."

Adrian laughed and said, "No...I have a very important engagement after our meeting."

Adrian opened the doors. For a little over an hour, the two men took measurements and discussed the details of how Adrian wanted the renovation to look. Once the two men were happy with the improvements, they shook hands and separated in their own ways.

Adrian got back in the car and told Michael, "I would like to go to 2031 Oak Street."

"Yes sir, right away." The car drove off to Adrian's old house. Once they arrived, Adrian got sentimental about the old house. He remembered how hard the two of them had worked to buy this place. Michael opened the car door.

Adrian was very nervous; it was like a first date. He saw Carol peek through the drapes as the car rolled up. Adrian put on his top hat and grabbed the flowers. He then walked up the sidewalk and rang the front door bell.

The door opened and they both broke down in tears. The top hat quickly fell off as they embraced into a heart-felt hug. They were smothering each other with hugs and kisses. It continued for several minutes. Their love was very deep indeed.

After a while, when they let go their embrace, Adrian bent over to pick up his top hat and put it back on. He then handed Carol the beautiful bouquet of roses.

"Thank-you Adrian, they are beautiful! Come in for a second and I will put them in water. You could go greet Blackie. He is dying to see you!"

Adrian opened the kitchen door, and the dog flew out with heightened excitement. There were hugs, pats and licks galore. The love was mutual. They had been buddies for over ten years now. Finally, they were reunited.

Carol said," Well, he certainly remembers his dad. You see Adrian, you belong here."

"I know I do, honey. I know that very well. Anyway, are you two ready for a little ride?"

Michael had two doors open, one for the dog and one for the handsome couple.

The dog quickly raced towards the open car door, anxiously waiting for his car ride.

Carol said, "Adrian, I think you have a little explaining to do. What is with the tux, limo, and chauffeur?"

"I have a lot of explaining to do. Wait, there's more!"

Once everyone was in the car, Adrian said, "Take us home, Michael."

Carol looked stunned and questioned, "Where is home?"

"You'll see, honey."

Carol could see a gigantic mansion as the car turned into the driveway. She was in utter shock. She just couldn't fathom what was happening.

They pulled out in front of the mansion and Michael opened the two doors. The dog raced out and peed on one of the supporting pillars.

Carol yelled, "Blackie! Don't do that!"

"It's alright. Don't worry about it," Adrian said.

He noticed that Mr. Azario was in the tea room and thought that it might be a nice idea if they met each other.

Adrian led Carol to the entrance of the tea room and asked, "Sir, may I see you for a couple of minutes."

Mr. Azario said, "Yes of course, please come in."

All of a sudden the big black lab raced up to Mr. Azario and gave him a big kiss on the lips. Adrian's eyes popped out of his head; he thought that Azario would have them all killed on the spot. Frank smiled and laughed and asked, "Who is your big friend?"

"This is my four legged son, Blackie. He really seems to love you, sir."

"Well Blackie, welcome to the mansion. It is a pleasure to meet you old boy!" Azario patted the dog lovingly, his eyes glistened with joy. He looked up and saw Carol. "Who is this lovely lady?"

ADRIAN

"Sir, this is my wife, Carol. She came to visit me tonight."

"It is a pleasure to meet you Carol" Azario took her hand and gave it a gentle kiss.

"I am very pleased to meet you, sir."

"Are you staying the night Carol?"

"I don't know, sir. I'm still not sure what is going on."

"Well, if Adrian doesn't ask you to be our guest, I will do it for him. Please stay the night; you are more than welcome here in my house."

"Thank-you sir, you are very kind."

"I will not take up much of your time. You kids have a lot of catching up to do. Now, run along. Have fun."

Adrian said, "Good-night Mr. Azario."

Carol said, "Good-night sir, and thank-you."

The two climbed the spiral staircase, hand in hand.

Adrian opened the door for Carol, and when she stepped into the room, she was traumatized; there were roses and flowers of all types filling the suit. There were soft-lit scented candles which gave off a romantic atmosphere.

Soft classical music was softly playing in the background. There was a doggy bed. Even the dog's place mat had a candelabra on either side of it!

The place was luxurious. The place settings were elegant. Even the dog shared the same setting as the humans.

Nothing was left out. Doris came to the door and said, "Good evening Mrs. Eisner. My name is Doris. May I take your coat?"

Carol said, "We spoke briefly on the phone, didn't we?"

"Yes we did."

Carol took off her coat and handed it to Doris. Adrian also took off his coat. "Thank-you, Doris."

Carol was taken back by the whole experience. She had never seen such glamour in real life before. "Is this where you live all the time?"

"Yes, it is. May I show you around the suite?"

Adrian led her around and as each moment passed, Carol became even more amazed. In the master bedroom, even to Adrian's amazement, there were rose petals scattered all over the bed.

There was a chilled bottle of champagne beside the bed and roses all over the room. It was beautiful and very romantic. Carol's heart filled with overwhelming joy. She kissed her dear husband and whispered, "I love you, honey."

"I love you, sweetheart."

They embraced each other tightly and kissed. Their souls were alive and their hearts were warm. The moment was meaningful and had depth. They were truly in love.

Adrian led Carol to the living room and sat her down on the chesterfield. He went to the bar and pulled out a chilled white wine and poured two glasses. He sat down and handed her a glass.

"I want to thank-you sweetheart, for coming over on such short notice."

"I would have done anything to see you, honey."

They touched glasses and made a toast to each other. They were talking when Doris said, "Mr. and Mrs. Eisner, your dinner is being served."

There were two chairs nestled together on one end of the gigantic table. The couple sat down and Doris brought out the meal. It was poached salmon with lemon sauce and rice pilaf with asparagus. The meal looked wonderful. Carol loved salmon. The couple talked and laughed as if this was their first date. Doris filled the dog dishes with dog food and water. Blackie was very happy with his meal; he gobbled it up like lightening.

Doris came back about an hour later and said, "May I take your plates?"

"Yes please, Doris," said Adrian.

Doris cleaned off the table to make room for the couple to relax and have desert. She came back to the table with two tall glasses of strawberry sherbet with whipping cream. She placed one in front of each person and said, "I hope you enjoy this light desert."

Adrian said, "It looks wonderful Doris, thank-you."

They ate their deserts and Adrian got up from the table, went over to Doris and gave her a big kiss and hug. "You did a wonderful job tonight Doris. Everything was perfect, thank-you very much."

"You're very welcome sir. It was my pleasure. Your wife is a very charming woman, sir. I will quickly clean up and leave you two alone for the evening."

"Wait here Doris. I will be back in a moment."

ADRIAN

Adrian raced off to the bedroom and came back a couple of minutes later. He grabbed Doris's hand and put something in her palm. "This is to show you how much I appreciate you."

Doris opened her palm and looked. She was shocked; there was ten thousand dollars in her hand. "Sir, I can't accept this! This is my job! It is way too much money!"

"I'm your employer and you will take the money. It is the least that I can do for your family; please take it."

Doris gave Adrian a kiss on the cheek and said, "You are a very generous man Mr. Eisner, thank-you."

Adrian went back to his wife. They moved into the living room for a serious chat.

"I guess, you are wondering what this is all about," Adrian said.

"I am very concerned about all of this. I'm still waiting for an answer, on why you can't come home with me."

"I'll try to tell you as much as I can. Mr. Azario is the grand-father of a crime family. His empire has been built from other people's pain and anguish. He is a very powerful and dangerous man.

He had me picked up and inducted into the family against my will.

This was not my choice. He has a hold on me that I cannot discuss with you at this time. He wants me to be his protégé, and become the new ruler of the Azario Empire. He will not release his grip on me. If I left on my own, he would have me hunted down and shot like a dog."

"Why you? You do not have a mean bone in your body. You wouldn't be able to do it, you have a good conscience," Carol said.

"I'm sorry; I can't tell you why he picked me. He would have me killed, if I told you. He said that with training and brainwashing that I will soon learn the ropes. However, I don't have to do anything illegal, because I am the new owner of the strip."

"That part of town is disgusting! Why would you want to run those types of businesses?"

"I didn't have a choice. The decision was made by Mr. Azario. At least, I don't have to do anything against the law."

"This whole place was built with blood money! What happened to you Adrian? You had good morals and a strong conscience!"

"I am forced here! I don't have a choice, unless I want to die. It is either his way or death! There is no compromise!"

"There has to be a way out. You have to come home with me!"

"I already asked him if he would consider letting me go. His answer was no.

I know you'll not agree to what I am going to ask you, but I'm going to try anyway. You and Blackie can always stay here with me. There is no problem that way. I just can't leave this place."

"Within time, your duties will slowly increase to the immoral side of the business. You will be no better than him.

When you take over the empire, you will have become a monster. I can't live like that! I want it the way it was. I want the three of us back in our own little house, just the way we were. I will not live with a mobster!

I refuse to live here with you if that is the way things are going to be. I'm sorry honey; I love you with all my heart. I just can't go against my own morals. He doesn't have a grip on me; I can walk out that door and never return!"

Adrian's heart shattered and he started to cry. "Sweetheart, I love you so much. I need you. I can't live without you, Carol! I will stay on the right side of the fence. I will do everything in my power to keep you."

"I'm sorry Adrian. I will not lower my morals for Mr. Azario. I will stay tonight to say my farewell. If you can ever be released from his grip, please come home. We will start all over again and live happy lives together."

Adrian's fear had come true. Carol would not accept him being a mobster. He was deeply hurt that he had been rejected by his own wife, and would spend the rest of his life alone. He buried his face into his hands and sobbed heavily.

Carol snuggled close and held him tightly. He turned around with tears running down his face and hugged her as closely as he could; he didn't want to ever let her go.

He knew that when tomorrow morning arrived, she would be gone forever. The moment was spiritual and tender; they

ADRIAN

melted as if they were one. They knew each other's thoughts and feelings without a word spoken.

Their hearts reached out to each other and there was a sense of need.

They depended on each other for love and support. It was a very sad day. Their feelings for each other would soon be nothing more than distant memories.

They loosened their embrace and Adrian said, "I know where you stand, sweetheart. How about we temporarily forget about the mess I am in? Let's remember the happy times we had. Would you like a drink?"

"Yes please, I would really like one."

Adrian mixed her a Brown Cow, and he poured himself a draft. He went back and sat down beside Carol and handed her the drink. They talked about their wedding day and how beautiful it had been. The conversation covered their entire lives together. They remembered the good times and even some of the bad.

They talked and drank to the early morning hours. Adrian had very deep feelings for Carol. He softly touched her face, and gave her a long sensuous kiss on the lips.

The romance was still alive after twenty-one years of marriage. They gently touched and caressed each other. Their kisses were slow and full of emotional impact.

Adrian stood up and grabbed his wife's hand. They slowly moved to the bedroom and gently undressed each other. They climbed upon the bed that was littered with hundreds of red rose petals. The sensuality continued for hours.

Their love for each other was unbreakable. There was real life between the two melting hearts. If only this night could last forever! The love would last forever, but the relationship wouldn't. This was their last act as husband and wife. That was why every moment was treasured deep inside.

This was a memory that Adrian would cherish for the rest of his life. Adrian woke up at six a.m. He had had less than two hours sleep, but he had to open the doors at the G-Spot for the workers coming. He got cleaned up and put on a brown woollen suit. Carol was sleeping soundly. Adrian would just leave her there. She could leave when she wanted.

Adrian went to the kitchen where Doris poured him a coffee.

"Good morning sir. How was your evening with Mrs. Eisner?"

"It was wonderful. It was like a fairy tale. It was just beautiful, thank-you again."

He sat down, lit a cigarette and took a sip of coffee. He was in dreamland about the perfect evening he had had with his wife. It was like a second honeymoon. He beamed with the memory.

Doris just smiled, as she knew that her boss had died and gone to heaven. He looked so happy. They made a very nice couple.

Arian grabbed a pen and paper and wrote down a lovely note to Carol, expressing how special last night had been to him. The final words told her that he had a never-ending love for her, and that he would never forget.

He finished the letter, reminding her that if she changed her mind about staying, he would always be there. He left it on the kitchen table, got on the phone, called Carol's work place and told them that she was sick and wouldn't be in.

Then he got up, poured himself another coffee and went back to sit down. He only had about a half hour before he had to leave. It was sad that he wouldn't get a chance to see Carol off. He sure was going to miss her.

After a couple more quick coffees, he said, "Doris, can you have Michael meet me out front, please?"

"Yes sir, I'll get him right now." Adrian grabbed his coat and took one last look at his beautiful sleeping wife. The tears started running down his face and he left quietly.

Doris was putting the finishing touches on the suite and returned it back to normal. She was proud of her accomplishment. Her boss was extremely happy with her work. She never had a boss before that was as nice as Mr. Eisner.

A couple of hours passed and Doris was taking her break. Carol got up and saw that Adrian was gone. She panicked, ran to the kitchen and yelled, "Doris, can I use your phone? I'm late for work!"

"Don't worry Mrs. Eisner. Adrian called your work this morning and told them that you are sick."

"Where is Adrian?"

"He had to go to work this morning, but I think he should be home shortly. Oh...excuse me Mrs. Eisner. You're still naked."

Carol blushed and ran back to the bedroom.

Doris was just finishing up a bacon and egg breakfast for her. When she came back dressed and said, "I'm sorry Doris, I was in such a panic I didn't realize that I didn't have any clothes on."

"Don't worry about it; I've seen it before. No big deal. I think you should have a seat right there in Mr. Eisner's chair. I've prepared a nice breakfast for you, eat up!"

Doris put the plate in front of Carol and said, "Mr. Eisner left you a note. It's right in front of you."

Carol was enjoying the breakfast and started to read the note. Her eyes welled up in tears. She could never stop loving him, no matter what. She just couldn't live with him right now. Her heart was broken, and life would never be the same without him.

"Are you alright, Mrs. Eisner?"

"What kind of man is Mr. Azario? He is the one responsible for our separation from each other! We are husband and wife! We are supposed to be together! I want my husband back home with me!"

Doris was shocked. She had no idea that this was going on. She was horrified that Mr. Azario would do that. "I am very saddened for you Mrs. Eisner. Mr. Azario can be very stubborn in his ways. I wish I could help you."

"There is nothing that any one can do."

Carol finished breakfast and said, "I'm going to go now. I want to thank-you for the unforgettable evening I had last night."

"It was a pleasure meeting you. Let me go get your coat."

Doris went to the hallway closet and brought out Carol's coat. Carol stood up and put her coat on. She bent over and gave Doris a kiss on the forehead and said, "Take good care of him for me, Doris."

Carol put the leash on the dog and said, "Good-bye."

She then let her self out. She closed the door behind her and cried heavily. She couldn't believe that it was going to end this way. Their marriage vows promised that they would be together till death do them part.

Carol sadly went down the stairwell. When she reached the bottom, she noticed that Mr. Azario was in the tea room.

She was going to give it one more shot. She was going to face Azario head on. She stomped her way to the entrance of the tea room and announced, "Mr. Azario, may I see you for a few moments?"

"Yes Carol, of course. Please come in and have a seat. Would you like some tea?"

"Yes please."

Azario signalled to Steven to bring another cup. Steven promptly returned and placed the set in front of Carol.

Azario looked concerned and said, "You were crying, dear. What is wrong?"

"That is why I came to talk to you, sir. I don't know what kind of grip you have on my husband, but he is supposed to be at home with me. We are supposed to live out our lives together as husband and wife."

"You are more than welcome to live here in the mansion with Adrian. You can live your lives together here."

"No...That won't work. My morals would not allow me to live here. We have a home! It's small, but we're very happy there. Please let my husband come home with me! I beg you, Mr Azario!"

"I will tell you a secret and then I want you to forget that I told you. I do owe you an explanation. I have three sons, two of them are dead. I have one son left that I hadn't seen in over forty years. I also have another daughter from a second marriage.

Adrian is that third son. The Azario Empire rightfully belongs to him. I am going to ensure that he is properly trained to carry out the duties as the new leader. Once that's complete and I am totally satisfied, I will retire, and leave the reins in Adrian's hands.

I never got a chance to meet him until just recently. He is a fine man.

I am very proud of him. I owe him, and all I have to offer is the empire. You see dear, I need him as badly as you do."

"Sir, he doesn't have what it takes to do the things that you do."

"On the contrary, he is extremely capable of doing anything that I have done. He does have a very dark side to him. I personally witnessed it. He might be gentle and sweet to you, but he is a fully-pledged killer. He has the instinct."

"I don't want a killer! I want my loving husband back!"

"I'm very sorry you feel that way dear, but I am not going to lose a third son. This one is staying here with me! I believe our discussion is over. Steven will show you out. We will have a car waiting to take you home. Good-bye Carol."

Carol stood up with tears in her eyes; she grabbed the dog's leash and stomped out behind Steven.

Azario sat back in his chair and poured himself another tea. The fact that he was destroying a marriage between his son and his wife did not concern Frank at all.

The empire must remain alive at all costs. He was not going to let this slip through his fingers. Adrian would be the next ruler of the empire, if it was the last thing that Azario ever did.

Steven returned to the tea room and announced, "Sir, several of your out-of-town guests have arrived for the funeral."

Azario said, "Keep them in the foyer; I'll be right there."

"As you wish, sir." Steven left to contain the crowd.

Azario got up and went to the foyer to meet his guests.

Upon his arrival, he noticed several of them were from overseas and across the country. He directed the crowd into the grand room for refreshments. Drinks were served by Steven and his staff.

Azario was talking to Juan Cortez when Juan said, "Sir, I understand you are in a bit of a pickle right know with Manicotti. I hear he has you draped over a barrel."

"Watch your mouth, or you will find yourself on the east side of Chicago with Tony Lorenzo!" said Azario.

Cortez's grin suddenly drained from his face. He knew he had stepped out of bounds with the boss. He knew he had to watch his step from now on. It was obvious that this was a touchy subject for Azario. Even Frank didn't know what his next step would be. All he knew was that his daughter's life was in serious jeopardy.

Frank left Cortez standing alone and went to greet Pauly Sabotinni and his wife.

"Pauly, I hear you expanded your business at Lake Tahoe. The profits from you this month were most impressive. Congratulations!"

Sabotinni said, "I thought that you would have been pleased with our expansion, sir."

"Yes, I was most impressed. Keep up the good work."

Azario then patted Pauly on the back and moved on to the next couple, Salvador Ramirez and his wife Catalina.

"Welcome to the United States. I am very pleased that you could make it for the funeral."

"It has been a long time since we have met, sir. We are sorry that it is under such sad circumstances. You must come back to Panama for a holiday."

"I am thinking of taking holidays soon but I wasn't quite sure where. I will give Panama some consideration, thank-you."

Azario walked around the room participating in idle chatter. This seemed to be very annoying to him. He had basically greeted all his guests that had arrived so far.

There would be a few more coming in a few hours. From the corner of his eye, he noticed that Adrian had just slipped through the front door.

Azario called for Adrian's attention. Grabbing his arm, he said, "Let's go up to your suite where it is quieter. I want to talk to you."

They walked to the suite and Adrian opened the door for Mr. Azario.

Adrian followed in behind and asked, "Sir, would you like a drink?"

"Yes please, a scotch on the rocks."

"It's coming right up, sir. What would you like to talk about?"

"There are a couple of things I would like to discuss."

Adrian passed the scotch to Azario, and went to pour himself a draft.

"Is there something wrong, sir?"

Azario pulled out an envelope from his coat pocket and said, "This is for the excellent job you performed yesterday. I am very pleased with the results."

Adrian took the envelope, placed it on the bar and said, "Thank-you sir."

"Your wife came to see me today. She seems to be very upset with me."

"Oh...Sir, let me apologize for her. I will make things right."

"Relax Adrian. It's alright, I understand. She wants you at home with her, and she begged me to return you to her.

I can see her point of view, but I don't think she understands mine. You are my only son; the empire will soon be yours. You must carry out my wishes. She is welcome to stay here with you, if she ever changes her mind."

"She will never step foot in this house again, sir."

"Adrian, you have to understand where I am coming from. Try to see it from my point of view."

"I'm trying sir, but this isn't a ma and pa-owned grocery store. This is organized crime - it is against our beliefs.

We just want our lives back the way they were. It was the three of us and we were happy. We had our problems too, but we worked hard to keep our marriage together.

Now, it is being broken up by an outside force which we cannot control."

"I'm very happy we can talk openly with each other. I'm sorry, but I have to deny your request. My empire is much too important to me. You are too important to me. I need you here by my side."

"I must be honest and say that I am very disappointed in your decision sir. You are personally responsible for our marriage break up. I can't forgive you for this."

Azario stood up and handed the empty glass to Adrian. "The conversation ends right here and now! You are going to be the next head of the Azario Empire! Good-bye!"

Azario stormed out of the suite. Adrian poured himself another draft, lit a cigarette and thought at least he wasn't shot for opening his mouth. This was one hell of a bad time to think about stopping drinking! He went to the kitchen table to sit down.

Now, it was time to forget all this and start thinking about Trixie. Once he had a sound plan, he could take it to Azario for finalization. Azario must act offensively or lose the whole empire to Manicotti.

Chapter Seventeen

The next morning, Adrian woke up from a restless night. He hadn't even had his prescription filled yet. He showered, shaved and got dressed in a suit that Doris had laid out for him the night before.

He went to the kitchen and sat at the table. Doris brought him his coffee. "Good morning, sir."

"Good morning, Doris."

Adrian lit a cigarette and took a sip of coffee. "Can you have Michael meet me at the front for 8:30 am?"

"Yes sir, I'll do that for you."

Adrian had to go to the open house at the Awareness Society today. It was the big day to see if he could get some professional help for his drinking problem. He certainly had second thoughts about that. He would go insane right now if he didn't have something to calm him down.

He had so many things on his plate at the same time he didn't know where to start. He needed his drink to slow things down, so he could handle these stressful situations.

He was staying away from Mr. Azario on purpose. The old man had been continually busy with business meetings, ever since the guests started arriving. Tomorrow is Jonathan's funeral; maybe by tomorrow night, the mansion might return to normal.

Adrian knew that Azario was still pissed at him. The old man couldn't even look him in the eye. Adrian was concerned about where he stood with the old man. He just didn't know.

Time had flown by, and it was almost 8:30. Adrian grabbed his overcoat and went out front to meet Michael.

He got in the car, and Michael returned to the driver seat. "Where are we off to this morning, sir?"

"Take me to #326, East 79th Street."

"I'll get you there right away, sir."

They reached the destination and Michael got out of the car to open the door for Adrian. Adrian walked into the building and checked the directory. He went to the third floor and found the door with the sign "Awareness Society."

He went inside and was greeted by the receptionist.

"My name is Adrian Eisner. I came in for the open house."

ADRIAN

The receptionist said, "If you would please fill out this confidential form, we will then set you up with a councillor."

Adrian took the pen and form and sat down. He filled out the form and returned it to the receptionist. He sat down and waited.

About fifteen minutes later a woman came out and said, "Adrian...My name is Bonnie. Please follow me."

They entered the office and Adrian sat in a chair beside the desk. Bonnie closed the door and took a seat at her desk.

"Tell me, how did you find out about us?

"I was referred to you by my psychiatrist."

"Explain to me why you are here."

"My doctor is trying to treat me with medication. However, with the amount of alcohol that I drink it renders the drugs useless. It is as if I am not being treated at all."

"How much do you drink?"

"About fifteen to twenty mugs of draft a day."

"That's quite a lot. Why do you think you drink?"

"I use it like a self medication. I use it to calm down and stay relaxed so that I can stay in control. I can handle stress much easier if I've been drinking."

"Are you under stress right now?"

"Oh...Yes, I am. My wife and I are having our marriage destroyed by a third party. My sister is in a life-threatening situation. My father is forcing me into the family business which I feel is immoral. I have to run a string of businesses and I have to ensure that there is a high enough profit margin. There are many more things that I playing on my mind. This is the only way I know how to cope."

"That seems to be quite overwhelming. Do you think that you would be able to handle it without alcohol?"

"Honestly...Not in a million years. I have been mentally ill for most of my life, and alcohol has been the only thing that can calm down the effects."

"Do you drink in the morning?

"Sometimes, I do. It doesn't seem to matter to me when I drink."

"Do you get the shakes?"

"No."

"Do you drink when you get upset or nervous?"

"Yes, I do."

"Do you drink everyday?"

"Yes, I do. I am a heavy drinker. I space my drinks well enough apart so that I don't get drunk, but I do drink all day and night."

"Do you get hangovers?"

"Never."

"Have you ever been late for work because you drank too much?"

"No, I am never late."

"Have you ever been in trouble with the law, because of your drinking?"

"No, I never drove while I was drinking. I also tend to keep to myself when I drink. I don't usually mingle with people so a confrontation never happens."

"Do you drink alone?"

"Most of the time I do like drinking alone. I like staying quiet and enjoy my beer."

Bonnie said, "This was an assessment on how to categorize your drinking habit. You scored very high and you are considered to be in a life-threatening position health wise. You scored as a serious alcoholic.

You are destroying your liver with prolonged and heavy usage. You are killing off your brains cells from the prolonged use.

My recommendation is that you get yourself admitted into a de-tox centre. It usually takes about seven days to rid the alcohol out of your system. We have drop-in group sessions every Tuesday from 6:30 p.m. to 8:30 p.m. just down the hall way from this office.

I also recommend that we meet every other week for one-to-one counselling.

You should continue your treatment with your psychiatrist on a monthly basis. This will keep your mental stability in check so that you won't feel that you need a drink to solve your problems.

There is a group that deals with dual diagnosis. It helps people with mental issues and substance abuse."

"I know about them. I phoned the Centurion Chapter, and I plan to attend their weekly meetings," Adrian said.

"Good, I see that you do have a will to get better. If you follow with these programs, it will help you to accomplish your

ADRIAN

goal. Our hour is up. Follow me Adrian, and we will set you up for your next appointment."

They walked back to the reception desk and Bonnie asked, "Lucy, can you make an appointment for Adrian to see me in two weeks?"

"Sure, I'll do that for you."

Lucy looked at the calendar and counted off the days. "Adrian, is 10:00 am on the 10th of October good for you?"

"Yes, that is just fine."

Lucy wrote out an appointment card and handed it to Adrian. "Ok, we will see you in two weeks. Bye Adrian."

"Thank-you Lucy; I'll see you then."

Adrian went back down to the awaiting limo. Michael opened the door for him, returned to the driver's seat and said, "Would you like to go home, sir?"

"No Michael, take me to the closest drugstore first. Then we'll go home."

After Adrian picked up his medication and they were on their way home. He was thinking that they would have to act fast on Manicotti before he struck first. Adrian had to convince Azario of the first strike approach. It seemed that the old man was hesitant on striking out. It should have happened already. Adrian was puzzled as to what was holding Azario back. What was he afraid of? Adrian had to confront him on this matter. The longer Trixie was held captive, the higher the risk that she would not survive.

The car pulled up in front of the mansion. Adrian got out and was met by Steven.

"Sir, Mr. Azario would like to see you in the tea room, right away."

"Thanks for the message, Steven. I'm on my way."

Adrian went inside to the tea room entrance. "Sir, you asked to see me?"

"Yes Adrian, have a seat."

Adrian sat down in the empty chair.

"We are having a formal luncheon with the guests this afternoon. I expect you to dress appropriately and I want you to wear your gun. We are entertaining for the bosses of the Azario Empire. We are going to announce your designation into the family."

Adrian was worried and said, "How do you think they will take the news that a rookie has risen to the top of the pack without the experience that they have?"

"I don't care what they think! This is the way it is going to be, and that's final!"

"Sir, I have a big concern. What are we going to do for Trixie?

"We will sit tight and wait for Manicotti to slip up. Then we'll nail him to the wall!"

"Excuse me, sir. Isn't that putting Trixie in danger? I've been working on a plan, and I believe we can save Trixie and put Manicotti out of business for good."

Azario said, "I am not going to risk the life of my daughter. There has been too much death in the Azario family already.

We'll see what Manicotti has up his sleeve first, and then we can make a plan. Perhaps we can gain a few bargaining chips of our own, and make a trade."

"That puts Trixie into direct danger. If we retaliate, he will kill her. If we attack him with a massive force before he gets a chance to kill Trixie, then we are in the position to destroy him once and for all."

"What happens if something goes wrong, and you don't get to her in time?"

"Then we burn him to the ground!"

"That is also extremely risky! There is no guarantee that you can get to her first! I will not put her life in jeopardy!"

"It seems that you are willing to allow the empire to fall Manicotti's hands. We have to strike, first!!"

"We have a grace period until after the funeral. I don't want to blow it, and have my daughter killed! Don't you fuck'n understand that? We are going to do it my way, and that is that! You have less than an hour to get ready for the luncheon. Now, go!!"

Adrian turned and walked out of the tea room and went to the suite.

Once inside, he asked Doris, "Do I have anything that is appropriate to wear for a formal luncheon?"

"Yes sir you do. I will lay it out on the bed for you."

"Thank-you, Doris."

Adrian went to pour himself a draft and lit a cigarette. He went to the kitchen table and sat down. He couldn't help thinking that Azario was making a very big mistake. They had to take a chance that Trixie may not survive. God only knew she might be dead already! Waiting around was not going to make things better. It would get worse, as time went on.

Doris came into the kitchen and said, "There is a black tuxedo on your bed, sir."

Adrian butted out his cigarette. "Thanks Doris."

He went to the bedroom to get changed; he noticed the tux had a burgundy sash and a bow tie. It was actually quite a distinguished-looking suit. He got dressed, went back to the kitchen and lit another cigarette. He took a sip of beer and sat down.

He still had about ten minutes before he had to go downstairs. He was concerned about his introduction as the next leader of the Azario Empire. Some of the guests would be pissed that they had been overlooked.

Adrian almost forgot - he ran to the bedroom, took off his jacket and put on his gun. One never knew; he might need it this afternoon. Once he got his jacket back on, he went to the kitchen to put his cigarette out. He then went downstairs to the main dining hall.

Upon his arrival, a servant handed Adrian a glass of beer. He noticed that no one else was wearing a sash except him and the old man. He also noticed some very dirty looks from the guests. He believed that this sash meant more than just an accessory to the tux. He then knew why the old man had told him to wear the gun.

Adrian walked among the black tuxedoes. No one introduced themselves to him; he just got evil stares. It was obvious that this was going to be a very tense afternoon.

Azario broke away from the crowd and seated himself at the head of the table. That must have been the cue for everyone to take their seats. Azario waved to Adrian and pointed to a chair that was on the right of him.

This was another indication to the guests that Azario had an announcement to make. Adrian took his seat.

Azario stood up and said. "I would like to say a special thank-you to our guests today. It is very good to have everyone here at the same time. This is a sad but special event today, but first we eat and drink."

Azario clapped his hands and an army of servants came out with covered silver trays.

The meals were spread from one end to the other. The wine glasses were filled; everything was extraordinary. The cutlery was made in eighteen carat gold. The place settings were also trimmed in gold.

Azario stood up and said, "I would like to propose a toast to my departed son, Jonathan."

Everyone else stood up, raised their glasses and took a sip. Azario signalled them to sit down. Everyone imitated Azario's every move. When he ate, that was the time that they were allowed to eat. No one was allowed to rise from the table until Azario did. It was a very militant meal of roast duck. After lunch, desert and drinks were served; Azario then stood up.

"I have an important announcement to make today. Many of you have been wondering when I will retire, and who will be the next leader of the empire. I can tell you that my retirement will commence once I am satisfied that I can hand over the reins. It will be in the near future.

Perhaps, it will be a year or two, or even sooner. It all depends on several things.

The one thing that I am positive about is who will be my successor. I have chosen Adrian Eisner. He is unknown to you, but I have my own very good reason why I chose him over any of you. In fact, it is none of your damn business why I chose Adrian. The fact is that he will be the next ruler of the Azario Empire. You don't need to know anything else.

Take a very good look at him. He will run the ship with the same firm hand as I have. He is more than capable of keeping you in line. I warn you, don't step on his toes. It will probably be fatal.

If you have comments about this, I recommend that you keep your fuck'n mouths shut!

What he says from now on, is the gospel according to Azario. What he says is what I say. Remember that! You will treat him with the same respect as you treat me. Another thing you should all remember.

There is always someone behind you, waiting to take your place. That is all I have to say. Please stretch your legs and help yourselves to drinks."

ADRIAN

Every one got up and the servants came around to refresh the drinks. There was a buzz in the room. It was a tense situation; Adrian could tell that the announcement did not go over well with the others.

They kept their distance from the protégé. Adrian would have to play hard ball with them to gain their support. As for now, while Azario was still in control, Adrian would just have to stand tall and keep cool. The guests continued drinking till early evening, and some of them were feeling pretty loose by then. Their liquid courage was building up, and their mouths were starting to flap carelessly.

The truth was coming out, that some of them were strongly opposed to Adrian's new post. Adrian felt that he was the target for the night.

He noticed that Azario had withdrawn himself from the festivities and had gone to the tea room. This was a cue to Adrian that he could also leave, and let the guests blow off their steam for one night.

Adrian went to his suite and changed into jeans and a sweater. He was going to go back to his roots tonight and relax. Doris had already left for the night.

He phoned downstairs and had Michael meet him out front. When he got outside, Michael was already waiting with the car door open. Once the two of them were in the car, Michael asked, "Where are we off to tonight, sir?"

"Take me to Wet Dreams on Davis Ave."

The car pulled out of the driveway and headed down towards the strip. Adrian needed a break from that kind of shit tonight. He wanted to catch a show at the pub and think things over. He had been under a tremendous strain lately. He figured that he shouldn't start taking his pills yet. He may have to call upon his dark side to handle some of the situations that were yet to happen.

They arrived at Wet Dreams and Adrian got out of the car and entered the pub. This was more like it! There were beautiful women, good music and lots to drink.

Adrian found a table near the back, hidden away in the shadows. He took off his coat and sat down. A waitress came by and took his order. He took a deep breath and relaxed. Shortly, his mug of draft arrived. He paid for the drink and gave the waitress a tip. He lit a cigarette and took a sip of beer.

Adrian was watching the woman on the stage. She was very good, and she was also quite beautiful. The place was really bouncing tonight. The business along the strip had sharply risen, ever since word got out that Jonathan was dead. Even the hookers were back out in full strength. Everything was back to normal for now.

That might be very short lived, depending on what Manicotti has planed to do next. Adrian thought that Azario would go in there with guns blazing and wipe out Manicotti. He didn't expect Azario to turn yellow.

Adrian was supposed to go to the support group at the Awareness Society that night. He knew they would have turned him away anyway, because he was drinking. You had to come in sober for those kinds of things.

Adrian had a million thoughts going through his head. He wasn't sure if he could handle it. He took a sip a beer and tried to calm down. He was starting to become agitated and tense. He was having fears of losing control. He could feel himself slipping away from reality. He signalled the waitress for another beer. He hadn't even brought his knife tonight.

The waitress came with the beer and Adrian paid her. He took a deep gulp of beer, but it wasn't working. He knew that his morality was gone and his dark heart had returned. He saw the world in a whole different perspective.

From the corner of his eye, he could see a group of men entering the bar. He recognized several of them.

They walked to a group of people sitting down, muscled out the patrons and took their table. Adrian knew who they were. That was Miguel and his hired muscle.

There was a fat man smoking a cigar that he didn't recognize. Miguel noticed Adrian and whispered into the fat man's ear.

Miguel got up and walked towards Adrian's table. "Mr. Manicotti would like you to join our table for the evening, Mr. Eisner."

Adrian would love to know who this fuck'n jerk stain was.

He accepted the offer and followed Miguel to the table. He grabbed an empty chair and sat down.

ADRIAN

Manicotti said, "This is a nice establishment you have here, Mr. Eisner. Let me introduce myself. My name is Manicotti. I understand you own all the buildings along the strip. How is your Dad doing these days? I haven't heard from him for a while."

"He's doing just fine. He keeps himself pretty busy these days. There isn't much time for idle chat."

"It looks like business along here is quite profitable. I should soon be a very rich man. I like the neighbourhood very much. I thought me and the boys would come down here and have a few drinks and get myself accustomed to my new surroundings."

Adrian said, "We don't care much for sudden changes; I think we're going to continue as we always have. This is our neighbourhood, and we are very happy here. The strip grew on us, we're very comfortable."

"Change is good for the soul, it keeps you alive."

"We have a philosophy of our own; if it's not broken, don't fix it."

"You just reminded me of something when you mentioned the word broken. By the way, how is the G-Spot coming along?"

"Very well, we decided to do some major improvements. The customers will be very pleased with the changes that we have planned for it."

"How is the family, anyway? Is everyone in good health?"

"Every one is quite well. Health and welfare of family members are very important to us. We take good care of each other."

"Have you heard from Donna lately?" Adrian replied, "We haven't heard from her lately, but we are expecting to meet up with her very soon.

We have very close ties. By the way Mr. Manicotti, how has your health been? You aren't suffering from severe migraines or heart problems, are you?"

"No, I'm as fit as a fiddle. My doctor says that I will live a long time."

"I think you should change doctors. I don't think you have that much time left at all. You don't look very well."

Manicotti was starting to get angry and said, "Listen here, you little shit! I don't take too well to idle threats, especially from scum like you! Remember, your days are also in jeopardy! I have the ball in my court. You and the old man are powerless to stop me! I also have the girl.

If her health and welfare are important to you, I would be careful about what you say or do."

"Since we're being candid with each other, I think you've made a very dangerous career move. Besides, I didn't give you an idle threat; it was a promise! I'm the type of man who sticks to his word."

"You and the old man are dead meat, and I will take the Azario Empire and make it my own! That is my fuck'n promise to you!"

Manicotti stood up and stormed out of the bar. His goons gave Adrian a dirty look and left.

Adrian got up, walked back to his old table and sat down. He ordered another mug of draft. His heart was full of fury and his soul was burdened with hate against Manicotti. The darkness was overwhelming. Adrian was going to enjoy watching Manicotti burn in hell.

His beer arrived and he gave the waitress a twenty dollar bill and told her to keep the change. He was very happy to have met Manicotti, because now he knew what the fat bastard looked like.

There would not be any mistaken identity when Adrian put a bullet into his plump head. Adrian was a changed man; he was becoming an Azario as each minute passed. The transition was very dramatic indeed. He was no longer the man that Carol once knew. Hatred was burning him up inside.

Azario would be pleased that he had made the right decision to pick Adrian as the front man. Perhaps he had known all along. Adrian no longer had any fear from any man. His nerves were slowly turning to steel. He sat at the table like a stone; he was mesmerized by his new-found power. He had no doubt that the Azario Empire would survive.

He just had to get the old man to listen to reason, and convince him that a first strike was necessary.

Manicotti would continue his mayhem until he was stopped. If they let him, Manicotti would gladly take it all. That was what he was counting on, and Azario was playing right into his hands! It made Adrian very angry that he wouldn't take a stand against that fat tub of lard!

ADRIAN

Adrian ordered another beer and lit a cigarette. His plan was complete; he knew exactly what had to be done. He had been working at it ever since Trixie was kidnapped. He knew the timing, the amount of men needed, and the equipment required. Everything had been carefully calculated.

Adrian's beer arrived and he gave the waitress another twenty dollar bill.

She got to keep the change from that one too. Adrian thought he would start to watch the show, and stop thinking about killing for awhile. He started to calm down a little and relax. The waitress came back and put another beer on his table.

"I didn't order this," he said.

The waitress pointed her finger to a table where a woman sitting alone waved. She said, "That young lady over there bought you a beer."

Adrian grabbed his coat and his two beers and went to the lady's table.

"Do you mind if I sit down?"

"Please do," she said.

Adrian sat down, extended his hand and said, "My name is Adrian. What's yours?"

"Lori. I'm glad to meet you."

"It was very kind of you to buy me a drink. Thank-you, Lori."

"It was my pleasure."

Adrian asked her bluntly, "Why did you buy me a drink anyway?"

Lori said, "You have been in the paper for two or three weeks, and I recognized you from your picture. When I saw you tonight, I became curious about what type of man you are. I have found your ordeal to be amazing! It was something out of the movies! Even New York City didn't have things like that happen before."

"It was quite the experience, I can vouch for that. Well Lori, what do you do for a living?"

"I'm a legal secretary for Huntington and Brown."

Adrian was impressed and said, "Good for you. That sounds like an excellent job."

"I like it. What do you do, Adrian?

"I own the strip. It keeps me very busy."

Lori looked surprised and said, "Do you own the whole thing?"

"Yes, the whole thing. It's quite a large chunk of property. It stretches all along Davis Ave."

"You must have a bit of money."

"I do have some."

"So what was it like hiding from the police all that time? They never did find you. You turned yourself in."

"It's not a very nice feeling at all. You are scared all time and you always have to look over your shoulder. You just never know who is watching you. It was a time in my life that I would rather forget."

"So the killer turned out to be one of your brothers, whom you never saw before in your life. That is fascinating! I was glued to the news the whole time. You should write a book."

"I don't have time for that kind of stuff; I am a very busy man. Besides, I don't need any more money."

"I've never heard any one say that before. Every one wants more money! I know I do."

"Even if you had a lot of it, you would soon find out that it doesn't buy you happiness. You can still be miserable even if you were rolling in the shit."

"Are you very happy, Adrian?"

"I must admit that I am quite miserable. There are other things in life which make me much happier than the life I am living now. For instance, family makes me very happy.

I love my wife and my dog and my little house. I would trade everything I have, if I could get them back."

"I sense that you are very sad and lonely. I feel that you are really hurting inside," Lori said.

A tear ran down Adrian's cheek. He wiped it away and ordered another round. He tried to hold back the tears and look brave for the young woman.

Lori grabbed his hand and said, "I'm very sorry Adrian; I didn't mean to hurt you. I presume your emotional wounds are quite deep and will take some time to heal. I wish I knew how to help you."

"I know how you can help me," Adrian said.

Lori was very curious. "What can I do?"

"It's very simple; all you have to do is be my friend. There are no strings attached.

A friendship and nothing more, that would really help me. I need some one to talk and share my feelings, so that I don't keep them all bottled up inside. There really is a way you can help."

Lori said with amazement, "You mean you don't want sex or anything?"

"No...I only want friendship."

Lori said, "What happens if I want sex?"

"I'm sorry. You'll have to find some one else for that."

The drinks arrived and Adrian paid the waitress, leaving a tip. It seemed that Lori was a little disappointed with that remark.

Adrian said, "Don't take it the wrong way. You are a beautiful woman and I am very flattered, but my wife already occupies my heart. Even though we don't live together anymore, I just can't bring myself to do that kind of thing."

"I understand, even though I've never been in love before."

"You are still very young; you have lots of time for that kind of thing. Once you really are in love, you will know it. It will hit you like a ton of bricks.

You will know from the very first moment you look at him that he will be the one. It is actually very beautiful."

"Adrian, I would love to be your friend."

"I am very grateful, thank-you Lori."

They exchanged phone numbers and addresses. Adrian finished off his beer and bid Lori a good-night. He then went home and called it a night. Tomorrow was the funeral and he wanted to be ready for it.

The next morning Adrian was sitting at the kitchen table having a coffee and a cigarette. He was already dressed in his black suit, ready for the funeral. It was supposed to be an open casket today. Adrian was not too sure how good a job the funeral director had done putting Jonathan's head back together.

Adrian butted out his cigarette and finished his coffee. He went downstairs and saw that all the guests were mingling in the foyer. He went out front where Michael was waiting. "Take me to St. Anne's Cathedral, Michael."

"Yes sir, we're on our way."

They arrived at the church and Michael dropped Adrian off at the front. He went inside. He carried out his Christian obligations and went to view the body, and pay his respects to the dead.

The altar was loaded with flowers. It actually looked quite beautiful. Adrian took a seat in the front pew and waited for the other guests to arrive. Moments later, Azario arrived. He then looked at his dead son, and sat down beside Adrian. Al and the boys were keeping watch, ensuring that there weren't any interruptions.

Al went to check the flowers and to his amazement, he found something that Azario would not allow.

He went to Azario, bent over and whispered. "Mr. Azario, there is a wreath of flowers on the altar from Vinny Manicotti."

Azario turned red with fury and said. "Al, Get rid of them! I don't want that shit up there!"

"Yes sir, I'll get rid of them right now."

Al went to the altar and grabbed the wreath. He went outside to the parking lot dumpster and threw them in. He went back in to continue his duties as security.

The guests all arrived and the priest conducted a high mass. After the service, the Azario's followed the casket out to the limo. The next destination was St. Benedict's Cemetery. The long funeral precession slowly drove to the cemetery. It was the longest string of limos ever seen.

They arrived at the cemetery and the casket was laid over the grave site. People gathered around for the prayers. Al noticed that seven more limos had pulled up and parked on the road just behind the crowd. Adrian also noticed and the two of them moved towards the lead car.

Manicotti stepped out of the first limousine. About twenty of his armed goons took up positions surrounding their boss. Azario saw the interruption and stormed off to see Manicotti in person.

Azario yelled, "You are not fuck'n welcome here! Get the fuck out!"

Manicotti said, "He might have been your son, but his loyalty was for me. I have come to pay my respects to a dear friend, who you had murdered. He worked for me, and I helped him.

Did you ever wonder how Adrian was followed for weeks, and could never see who was stalking him? That was simple.

ADRIAN

I had my boys do surveillance on his every move. They would then tell Stuart where he was. We worked as a great team.

Stewart, of course gathered the information about you and your business. All of his help paid off. Now, I am ready to crush you. You must understand; I have every right to be here."

Azario went ballistic. He took a swing at Manicotti and caught him in the chops. Manicotti didn't even flinch. He stood there like a rock, unaffected by the punch.

"You feeble old man, is that all you have to stop me with?"

Azario went hysterical. "You will pay dearly for thinking that you can push the Azario's around. Your life is as good as gone. I..."

Suddenly, Azario was interrupted by a severe pain in his chest. He grabbed his chest and crumpled to the ground in front of Manicotti. His colour was washed out and he lost consciousness."

Manicotti laughed out loud and said, "You better dig another hole! It looks like you will need it!"

Adrian stood eye to eye with Manicotti. "You are a dead man!! Get out of here!!"

Adrian then started CPR on the old man. Al got on the cell phone and called 911. Al and his men then took positions in front of Manicotti and his goons. They assured Manicotti that his presence was not welcome, and that he should move on before a gang war started right there in the cemetery.

Manicotti said, "Adrian, your time is up. Now, it starts."

Manicotti and his men returned to their cars and drove off. Azario lay there, fighting for his life.

Adrian worked feverously, trying to revive his father. The ambulance finally arrived about fifteen minutes later. The attendants pulled out the paddles to try to get a pulse. They shocked Azario once, and there was no response. They shocked him a second time and managed to get a weak reading.

They wanted to stabilize him before they moved him, so they put an oxygen mask on him and hooked him up to an IV. Only then were they ready to put him in the ambulance.

Adrian said, "I'm going with you!"

The attendant said, "Ok, but I want you to stay out of my way!"

Adrian called back to Al "When you are finished here, take the guests back to the mansion for the wake. I have something extremely important I want to discuss with you later."

"Yes sir, don't worry sir. I'll take care of everything!"

Adrian followed the gurney into the back of the ambulance and they rushed off to the nearest hospital.

They arrived at the hospital and a team of emergency staff was waiting at the doors. It didn't look good; Azario's pulse was barely making a reading.

Adrian got out of the ambulance and told the doctor, "You have to save him at all costs! I don't care what you do, but he has to remain alive!"

"We'll do our very best!"

They rushed Azario into the emergency room. Adrian was stopped at the waiting room by a nurse. "I'm sorry sir; you will have to wait here."

He nervously sat down. He needed the old man more than ever right then.

There was any army of family members who would rather have Adrian dead than be their boss. Manicotti was on the rampage; Trixie's life was in danger. Now, the old man was just hanging on by a thread. This was a lot of shit to handle all at one time!

Adrian sat quietly and waited. Over an hour passed by, and there was still no word from the doctor. Adrian noticed Steven and another man racing towards him. "Sir, this is Ron Mauler. He is Mr. Azario's lawyer. He has something to say that is very important."

Mauler said, "Adrian, Mr. Azario made it quite clear in his will. If he becomes incapacitated, you automatically have his power of attorney. I got off the phone with the doctor and he said that Mr. Azario is in very bad shape. If he survives, it will be a long recovery.

You are now the head of the Azario Empire. Please sign this form, and it becomes a legal document. It is reversible in the case that Mr. Azario fully recovers."

Adrian signed the form, and then he watched the lawyer sign it.

ADRIAN

Mauler said, "It is official. You are the man in charge as of right now."

Adrian said, "Steven, I want you to inform the guests that there will be a formal dinner party tonight at 7:00 pm. It is very important for all to attend. Tell Al to make himself available; we have a lot of serious work to do!"

"Will there be anything else, sir?"

"Just make sure that Michael is at the hospital. I may need him soon."

"Sir, I will take care of it."

The two men left to return to the mansion. This was it!

Adrian was the new leader of the Azario Empire! It had happened a lot sooner than what Adrian had anticipated.

He actually was very pleased that he was the new leader. Now, he was free to put his plan into action and save Trixie. Manicotti wouldn't even know what had hit him!

Adrian saw that the doctor has come out of emergency. The doctor said, "Mr. Azario is alive, but barely. He needs surgery on his heart. It is a risky surgery, but he will die without it. I need your consent to go ahead with it.

There is a fifty-fifty chance that he will die on the table. He is very weak.

He had a massive heart attack and it caused severe damage. If he even has another small attack, it will be enough to kill him.

If we can make the repairs before he has another attack, then I can foresee a full recovery. We are working against time and we have to act fast."

The doctor handed Adrian the form and Adrian quickly signed it.

Adrian said, "Good luck doctor, thank-you."

The doctor then raced back into the emergency room and was preparing his team for surgery. Adrian wasn't going to stick around to find out what happened. He had to get back to the mansion right away. He got up, went to the door and waited for Michael outside.

The car pulled up and Michael opened the door for Adrian. Once Michael was back in his seat, he asked, "Where are we going, sir?"

"Take me back to the mansion."

"Yes sir, I'll get you there right away."

Adrian was going over the plan in his head. He would really need Al's help with this. He had over twenty years with Mr. Azario, and had the knowledge of all the resourses available to them. Adrian needed highly trained men and lots of special weapons and equipment.

Al should be able to fill Adrian in on their inventory. The weapons room didn't have everything that Adrian needed. The car pulled up in front of the mansion and Adrian was met by Al.

"Sir, you asked for me."

"Yes Al, I need your help. Follow me."

Adrian led Al to his suite and asked, "Would you like a drink?"

"I'm not allowed to drink on duty."

"I'm your boss now. You can have a drink if you want one."

"I'll have a mug of draft."

Adrian was impressed and he poured two mugs of draft. He handed one to Al.

Adrian said, "Sit down; we have something very serious to talk about. We're going to rescue Trixie and we are going to hit Manicotti right where it hurts.

We are going to take out twenty Manicotti businesses and the mansion simultaneously. Little Italy and the mansion are going to turn into gigantic fire balls.

You have been with Mr. Azario for many years. I need to know where I can get about a hundred and twenty trained men and women.

I need equipment like sixty grenade launchers, with about a hundred and fifty of rounds of tear gas. I also need two hundred and fifty rounds of incendiaries. I need fifteen collapsible assault ladders, ninety assault rifles and thirty pistols.

Black commando outfits with hoods are a must. We will need four semi trucks with trailers. Get me a heavy machine gun for each of the trucks. I need four rocket launchers with lots of HE rounds.

I need raw hamburger, C-4, piano wire, and cross bows. I want all personnel to be equipped with a commando knife. One last thing, make sure we have a lot of first aid equipment. Do you think you can get me that all of that?"

ADRIAN

Al said, "You have three warehouses full of equipment and arms. I should be able to fill out your shopping list. However, only you can immobilize the troops. You will need the code book, which I will get for you right after this meeting.

Mr Azario has a mercenary battalion in Colombia to ensure that the drug lords are kept under control. You will need a company-strength force with mixed gender and age. They are able to deploy anywhere in the world within forty-eight hours."

Adrian said, "Good, we'll get the troops moving right away. It has to be explosive and conducted with precision timing. It has to go off as a surprise and catch them with their pants down.

I am very determined to put an end to Manicotti for good! He is a big pain in the ass, and I want him out of there! I have a detailed shopping list and plan right here for you. You and your men will be on full alert and armed to the teeth to stop any police aggression. Now, go get that code book and let's get those troops over here."

Chapter Eighteen

It was 6:30 pm. Adrian was dressed in his newly-cleaned tux and sash. This time around, Adrian sat at the head of the table. He took a sip of beer and lit a cigarette. It was now time to be an Azario. He was wearing his pistol, just in case something happened.

As he sat at the kitchen table, he stared at the wall in front of him. He could slowly feel himself drifting into his other world. His morals were washed away by the waves of darkness that overpowered him. His strength came from deep within his blackened soul. Adrian was now ready to take control of the Azario Empire.

He butted out his cigarette and took the last few gulps of beer. Then he went downstairs to the main dinning room. An observant servant quickly rushed to him to serve him his beer. The room was so quiet you could hear a pin drop.

Everyone watched Adrian's every move. He went and stood behind his chair. His posture was straight and his facial features, stern. He looked at his watch; the dinner would commence at precisely 7:00 pm. Adrian took a few more sips of his beer and finally sat down.

The guests gathered around the table and took their seats once Adrian was seated.

Adrian picked up his wine glass, stood up and said, "I would like to propose a toast to Mr. Azario. May he reign for many years to come."

The guests stood up and raised their glasses in salute. Adrian took a sip of wine and the guests followed suit.

Adrian said, "I would like to take a few moments of your time before dinner is served. Today's string of events will not be overlooked. We have our problems, and I am going to personally correct them.

I have a lot of work to do tonight and I asking you gentlemen to find other accommodations for the night. After dinner, you will have one hour to vacate the premises. I want you gentlemen to closely watch the time, for my request will be strictly enforced.

Please feel free to stay and have a few drinks, but I warn you to be observant. I hope you enjoy this special dinner in honour of Frank Azario. His favourite meal is steak and lobster, and that is our main course for this evening. Thank you."

Adrian clapped his hands and the meals were delivered piping hot and promptly.

Adrian then sat down and started to eat. The guests quickly acted on Adrian's cue to eat. An hour passed in silence; the air was feeling a little tense. The desert was served, followed by drinks.

Rudely, there was an address directed at Adrian.

Juan Cortez said, "We would like to take a moment of your time. A lot of us believe that we are much more suited for your position than a gringo like you. We are opposed to your command."

Adrian slowly wiped his mouth with his napkin and stood up. He walked up to Mr. Cortez who was still sitting down. Adrian opened up his jacket and removed his gun. Without hesitation, Adrian pointed the gun to Juan's head and coldly pulled the trigger.

The body flew backwards. Juan's brains were splattered all over the rear wall.

The guests finally started to pay attention to Adrian. He certainly had the floor at that point in time.

Adrian said calmly, "Mr. Cortez claimed that many of you have felt the same way. Would anyone else like to say something to me? Which of you think that you can take me on? There will be no fuck'n mutiny on this fuck'n ship!! If any of you want to redeem your return airfare like Mr. Cortez did, speak up fuck'n now!!"

Adrian stood still and carefully listened to see if anyone else felt the same way.

"It seems to me that Mr. Cortez was lying. I gave you gentlemen a chance to speak. I didn't hear a fuck'n word! Remember, this is the Azario family. This is not the Cortez Empire! It is fuck'n mine!! Gentlemen please mingle and have a few drinks before I ask you to leave"

Al asked Adrian, "Sir would you like me to dispose of the trash?"

Adrian replied, "That is a good idea Al, thank-you. Can you have some one quickly tidy up the mess as well?"

"I'll get somebody on it right away, Mr. Eisner."

Al then designated several of his men to the unforeseen chores. Within minutes, it looked like nothing had happened at all.

Adrian grabbed his beer and stood up. The remainder of the guests did the same thing. Suddenly, there was lots of chattering and commotion. Adrian was surrounded by the waiting guests who wanted to introduce themselves to the new leader of the Azario Empire. Everyone wanted to talk to the new man.

It seemed that they had suddenly changed their attitude towards Adrian. Could it have been something Adrian said?

The family was back together again as one big unit. Adrian let the party go for a couple of hours, and then he bid his guests farewell. Within the hour, the guests had all left as requested.

Adrian was on his way upstairs, when Steven said, "Sir, you have an urgent call from Lieutenant Ruzo."

"I'll take the call in the tea room. Thank you Steven."

Adrian went to the tea room and picked up the receiver. "What's up Matt?"

"You better get your ass down here! Manicotti's men just busted up Wet Dreams! You better tell me what's go on Adrian. Manicotti is really putting the screws to you guys. Am I to expect a fuck'n war or something?"

Adrian said, "Don't worry about it. I'll be right there."

About twenty minutes later, Adrian's limo pulled up in front of Wet Dreams. There were hordes of people around.

Police cars with flashing lights lit up the whole street. Adrian got out of the car and he suddenly heard a female voice. "Adrian!! Adrian!! I'm over here!!"

Adrian scanned the crowd and saw Lori running towards him.

"Oh Adrian...it was just horrible! They came in and took the place apart piece by piece! What's going on?"

Adrian grabbed her by the hand and ducked under the police tape. They were quickly stopped by a uniformed officer.

Adrian said, "I'm the owner of the building. Lieutenant Ruzo is expecting me, and she's with me."

The officer let them pass. They went into the bar where Matt and Mike were sitting at the only table and chairs left standing.

ADRIAN

Matt said, "Oh...shit. You're wearing the sash! Adrian...how could you?"

Lori whispered in Adrian's ear, "What does the sash mean?"

Adrian said, "I'll tell you later." He turned to Matt. "I don't have a choice. I am what I am. So, what are you going to do about Manicotti?"

Matt said, "We can't do anything, you know that. I'm sorry that the old man is sick. I hope it turns out for him."

"I do too, thanks. Well Matt, the only thing I can say to you is to stay away from me and Manicotti.

Don't get mixed up into something that you cannot handle. It's just an advance warning from me to you. Consider yourself lucky."

"Adrian! What the fuck are you going to do? Don't make me put you in jail."

"Matt, don't make me fight you. You'll never win! Anyway, what are you going to do here?"

"We're basically finished here. We have numerous witnesses. We have the whole breakdown of what happened. All we have to do now is board the place up. Then we're out of here."

"Since I'm not needed here, I'm going to take off. See you guys."

Adrian took Lori the hand, put her in the limo and they drove off.

Michael asked, "Do you want to go back to the mansion, sir?"

"Yes Michael, take us home."

They arrived at the mansion and Lori was shocked at what she saw. She had never in her life seen a house like that! Adrian led her inside and back up into the suite. She couldn't get over how beautiful the place was.

Once inside the suite Adrian asked, "Do you want a drink?"

"Sure! Do you have rye and ginger?

"Yes I do, it's coming right up."

"Is this place yours?"

"It belongs to Mr. Azario."

Adrian passed the drink to Lori. He went to the bar with his beer and lit a cigarette.

Lori was curious and asked, "You never told me before, what does the sash mean?

"There is no easy way of saying it, but I'll tell you anyway. Right now, I am boss of one of the largest crime organizations in North America or even the world. It is not something I am proud of or even wanted. I was forced into it. That's what the sash means."

"You mean that you commit murders, drug imports and stuff like that?"

"I'm not going to go into detail as to what our business is. That kind of information is confidential. I would like to talk to you on a personal basis, rather than talking shop."

Lori said, "You're in some kind of trouble aren't you? Those men destroyed your bar for a reason."

"Why are you so interested in my business?"

"I find it very intriguing. It's not every day that a girl meets a mob boss."

"I would prefer to keep my relationship with you on a personal level, not a professional one."

"I'm sorry Adrian, I didn't mean to pry."

"That's alright. I can understand your fascination with all of this. What were you doing at the club tonight?"

Lori said. "I was hoping to run into you. I had a great time with you last night and I was hoping we could catch up with each other."

"Well, we still managed to do that."

"Adrian, you seem worried today. What's wrong?"

"It was a very bad day today; everything hit me all at once. Now, I am licking my wounds and waiting for a fresh day tomorrow morning."

"Adrian, I think if you want me to be your friend, you shouldn't keep anything back from me. You have to learn to trust me, or our friendship will suffer. I'm not going to the cops or spreading it around. I'm not that stupid. I know you would have me killed if you had to."

"You are a smart girl. I didn't want to leak information just for those reasons. I certainly didn't want resort to violence. I try to keep that to a minimum."

"I get the feeling that something really big is about to happen. That's why you can't even trust me."

"I only met you last night for a couple of hours. I don't even know you yet. You have to earn my trust before I can reveal secrets; even my own staff doesn't know certain things. You have to understand, this is a very dangerous business. Sometimes the less you know, the better it is. It is a matter of self preservation."

"I am willing to take all the risks that are involved.

I believe you when you say it is dangerous. A true friend will take those risks."

"Why do you want to get involved? I didn't even want this position, I was forced into it. I didn't have a choice. You do have a choice and you are making the wrong one right now."

"I think you are in real big trouble and I want to help."

"I hope you realize that once you step through those gates, there is no turning back. It is a life-time commitment. The only way out is by death. Your morals would suddenly be put to the ultimate test.

You have to be mentally and emotionally strong to withstand the evils that go on inside these walls. You cannot show weakness. It is all business, and it is a dirty one."

Lori said, "I think I could handle it."

"There is no time to think. You just have to perform at a high standard at all times. Your life is at risk everyday. Today could be your last day, and you wouldn't even know it. Besides, you have a wonderful honest job right now. Why the hell would you consider a life of crime?"

"The job I have isn't all that great either. The money is not bad, but the people I work for are probably bigger crooks than you are. They are lawyers! Their jobs also discredit any morals and beliefs. It really wouldn't be that much different working for you."

"You are not going to work for me. You will stay at your present job and live honestly. This place will destroy you. You don't need to spend the rest of your life in prison or die. You are very lucky for what you have. Don't throw it all away."

"Can we still be friends?"

"Yes, of course we can. Just leave the business to me. Your friendship means more to me than anything else.

Maybe as time goes by, I may become more open with you. As for now, I just want to take it slow. You don't need to know my business dealings."

Lori conceded her argument and said, "I really do understand where you are coming from, Adrian. I just thought we should be straight towards each other, that's all."

Adrian said, "I am trying to protect you. Don't you understand? The less you know, the safer it is for you. You could be easily kidnapped for information about the organization. You could be raped and tortured. These things do happen! Anyway, do you want another drink?"

"No thanks, by the time I get back to my car it will be quite late."

Adrian got on the phone and got Michael to go up front and wait for Lori.

"Michael is waiting for you downstairs. He will drive you back to your car. Keep in touch; I had a very nice time tonight."

"It certainly was very interesting. Thanks for the drink. Maybe I'll see you tomorrow."

They both got up and Adrian walked Lori to the waiting car. They said their good-byes and Lori got into the car. Adrian gave a wave as the car drove off.

Matt woke up from a restful sleep. He got up and went downstairs.

The first thing he needed was a coffee, so he got the machine fired up. He went to the back step, got the paper and sat down.

It had been a few days already since he had seen Adrian at Wet Dreams. He wondered what he was up to.

The reports from the surveillance teams were frightening. There is a big storm brewing. Two more businesses of Adrian's had been destroyed in the last couple of days. Adrian still had not retaliated.

This was costing Adrian hundreds of thousands of dollars in lost revenue and repairs. Matt was afraid that Adrian was waiting for the right moment to strike, and then all hell would break loose. Matt's first priority was to keep the public safe from a war between the two empires.

Matt heard a muffled voice from upstairs. "Daddy, can you come get me please?"

He yelled up the stairs, "I'll be right there pumpkin."

He got up and went to get Emily. Matt then brought her downstairs and put her in her wheel chair. He then went back to the kitchen to prepare her breakfast. Emily—wheeled herself into her designated spot at the table.

"Here you go, sweetheart. Breakfast is served."

He placed Emily's breakfast in front of her, got himself a cup of coffee and sat down. He took a sip of coffee and gave off a sigh of relief. He just noticed that his eyes were finally starting to open. That must be good coffee, alright.

Matt could hear a car drive up; it must be Mike. Momentarily, there was a knock at the door and in burst Mike. He went to the wheelchair and gave Emily a kiss on the cheek and said his usual, "Good morning munchkin. How are you today?"

"Good morning Mr. Parsons. I'm fine."

"Good morning Matt."

"Good morning, how are you Mike?"

"I'm doing pretty well. I had a good sleep; all I need now is my morning coffee."

"Well, you know where it is. Help yourself."

Mike grabbed a coffee and sat down across from Emily. "I think the war is going to start soon.

I just heard on the radio that four bus loads of people just arrived at the Azario compound. Most of them were men, but there are a few women. There has been a lot of vehicle traffic going in and out. They also have four tractor trailers.

The activities on the grounds have increased by at least fifty percent."

Matt said, "We better tell the Captain about this. It is my guess that Adrian is going to do a massive attack, probably tonight.

We know that Manicotti has been in contact with Adrian on two occasions, which put the old man in hospital. Adrian is not going to let this go unpunished. I'm afraid to think what he has planned."

"Our fears have come true, Matt. Adrian is much more dangerous than the old man; he has real guts to stand up against Manicotti."

"I think Manicotti made himself a very fatal mistake trying to take on Adrian."

"We know Adrian is about to do something big; we've been watching his every move for days. Why don't we go and talk him out of it?"

"Adrian is an Azario now; he won't even let us in the compound. We are on opposite sides of the coin. He even warned us to not to fight him. I really believe that he would win, if it came to a showdown. I don't even think the Captain would allow any interference; too many cops would be killed."

"I guess we just sit back and let them go at it. I wish Adrian all the luck in the world."

Later that night at the Azario mansion, Adrian was going over the plans with the assault team leaders.

"I hope everyone had a good dinner. Now, it is time for business. You have already had your weapons and equipment issued to you. You also had several rehearsals today to familiarize your troops on what is happening tonight.

I have some new details for you. In front of you, there is a map of the grounds and floor plan of the Manicotti mansion. The map will show you where the entry points to the compound are. You can use the map to your advantage by choosing the ground, foliage and lawn fixtures as cover, until you get close enough to the mansion.

The floor plan indicates that there is only one room with bars on the windows. I will bet my bottom dollar that is the room that Trixie is being held in. The room is at the back in the east wing. I will lead the entry team to that room. You should know everything else from what you were given today.

There is one more thing. Everyone comes back, even the dead. No one is to be left there.

I want one hundred and twenty four people coming back to this compound when the mission is over. I believe that you will be busy with your final briefings and rehearsals. Are there any questions? Good, I'll see you at the marshalling area at zero hour. Good luck, you're dismissed."

Adrian then went to his suite. He poured himself a beer and sat at the kitchen table. He lit a cigarette and took a sip of beer.

If he was not careful tonight, a bullet would quickly put an end to his drinking problem.

Tonight was the night that Manicotti would fall. Adrian was ready for him. Mr. Azario had probably been waiting for this day for the last twenty years, and tonight the waiting would end. Adrian had pure evil pumping through his veins. The old

ADRIAN

Adrian was dead. This was the new Adrian, with money, power and might.

It was 02:30 hrs and all was quiet on Francis Ave. in Little Italy. There were several families of homeless people keeping warm at the burning barrels on the street.

It was very peaceful. There were a few cars parked on the street and a semi truck on the corner of Francis and Shepherd. Little Italy was probably not that busy tonight because of the cold snap they had been experiencing the last few days.

Meanwhile, back at the Manicotti mansion, all was quiet except for the gate guards laughing and having a coffee outside.

Suddenly from behind, two shadowy figures popped up out of nowhere and quickly cut the guards' throats. They quickly dragged the bodies out of sight and into the shadows. The only sound there was came from the gurgling of blood emptying on the ground.

Several teams of shadows quietly took position on the outside perimeter of the stone wall. On the other side was a roving patrol of dog handlers patrolling the grounds. The dogs were able to sniff any intruders out. They were getting very agitated, until finally they were released by the guards.

The Dobermans raced for the gate. They turned to the left and went along the outside wall until they were confronted by five pounds of raw hamburger. They stopped just long enough to hear several swishes of arrows cutting through the night time air. There were a few short yipes and it was all over.

Manicotti's guards waited for a few minutes, and then started to call their dogs back.

When there was no response, they followed the direction that they last saw the dogs. They drew their weapons and walked towards the back of the wall. Upon arrival they didn't see anything, not even the dogs. It was deathly quiet.

They noticed that the gate guards were also missing. As they turned to investigate, a loop of piano wire tightened around their necks quickly ending their precious lives.

Several teams of shadowed figures passed through the gates and spread out to the length of the mansion. They cautiously used the foliage and shadows as cover from detection. They noticed that there were three guards in the front, one on each second floor balcony and one in the centre.

The teams crawled their way slowly, so as not to make any sudden movement or noise. They used a hedge to hide their approach. They finally reached their destination at the assault line. They took their positions with cross bows at the ready.

Within seconds of each other, all three guards slumped to the ground. The assault teams remained where they were and waited to see if anyone had heard or seen something outside. The noise didn't alert anyone inside.

Several figures with assault ladders made their way across the grounds and up to the hedge. Three assault teams slowly edged to the rear of the mansion to do a reconnaissance. They observed that there were three more guards in basically the same location as the front guards.

The teams formed another assault line in front of their targets. Quietly the three guards slumped over into terminal sleep. Shortly after, three more ladders were taken to the assault line and put in position.

As if they were towed by a rope, all the ladders were put up into position to their assigned balconies. The assaults teams then reached the balconies and cleared the bodies to the sides. They took their assault positions and put on their gas masks.

The all-clear signal was given, and the grenadiers took their positions in front of their designated targets. They laid their extra ammo beside them at the ready and loaded their weapons. They then signalled that they were ready.

Adrian's team then took position at a balcony close to room that Trixie was being held in. This was a tense moment; there would probably be someone sleeping in the room that they were gaining entry into.

One of the team members quietly put a toilet plunger on the window located next to the lock. With a gentle steady hand, he cut the glass with a glass cutter. A quiet crack of the glass could be heard as the circle of glass was broken and removed. He slid his hand inside and slowly undid the lock. The door was then cautiously slid wide open.

Adrian quietly stepped in first and scanned the area. He saw that there was a man in bed, sleeping on his back.

ADRIAN

Adrian tip toed towards the man and drove a knife into his heart. He continued the search for others. After several minutes, he came back to the remaining team members and gave them the all clear.

They quietly entered the room and made their way to the door. Adrian got down on his belly and opened the door just by a crack. He looked to the left and took a chance by slowly opening the door, hoping that there wasn't anybody standing in his blind side. The door opened enough so that he could peek through the crack between the door and the wall. He looked down to the right; it was also clear.

The team opened the door and moved down the corridor in silence. They came to a turn to the left. Again, Adrian went down on his belly and slowly peeked around the corner. He could see a guard on the outside protecting a room. According to the map, that was the right room. The guard confirmed it by being there.

Adrian had to get the guard's attention so that he would come around the corner to investigate. Adrian stood up and signalled that they had contact. He backed up a little with his knife in hand and coughed loudly. He waited about thirty seconds, and the guard came around the corner. Adrian greeted him with a blade into the heart.

The body quietly slumped into Adrian's arms. He gently laid the corpse down, hidden around the corner. The team walked around the corner and took fire positions outside the door. The demolitions man placed a C-4 explosive and detonators near the lock of the door.

This was the moment everyone had anticipated; it was time to rock and roll.

Adrian gave the signal and the door blew off the hinges. Simultaneously all hell broke loose. The assault teams burst through the glass doors with automatic fire, instantly killing all occupants of the rooms, and conducted a systematic search for others.

Seconds later, a barrage of tear gas grenades flew right through the doors and windows of the mansion, causing havoc inside.

Radio contact was made, and the homeless families on Francis Ave shed their coats and fired several rounds each of incendiary rounds into the targeted businesses. The whole street turned into a roaring inferno.

The team entered the room and Adrian fired an automatic burst of lead into the chest of Trixie's captor. He carried the drugged woman to a corner in the room and covered her body with his. The demolitions man puts a stronger charge of C-4 on the barred window and blasted a large exit in the wall. Within seconds, a ladder was placed under the hole for the escape.

Adrian went down the ladder with Trixie over his shoulders under covering fire of the on-guard troops outside.

He was met by two of his troops who evacuated Trixie to the hospital for treatment. He then took up a fire position and gave the order to start the evacuation of the mansion.

Adrian got on the radio and had Francis Ave. to escape and evade. The troops pulled out of the building. Adrian gave the all-clear that all the troops were out of the building. He gave the order for the grenadiers to fire their incendiary rounds into the mansion. Within minutes, the whole place was burning wildly out of control.

Adrian gave the order to evacuate. Within seconds, three tractor trailers pulled up front with their doors open. The troops quickly boarded the trucks and heaved the heavy machine gun inside.

Adrian was the last man on the ground. He watched the Manicotti dream go up in smoke. He turned his back on the mansion just as a shot was fired. Adrian dropped to the ground and tried to see where the shot had come from. It was Manicotti; he had survived. The fat man was crawling on his knees, puking and sputtering from the tear gas and smoke. He couldn't have hit Adrian if he was standing right in front of him.

Manicotti said, "I will kill you for this Adrian!! I will come back and destroy you."

Adrian walked right up in front of the lump of shit and said, "You are never coming back!!"

Adrian then put the rifle to Manicotti's head and blew it off. He took one quick look at the mansion and ran to the last remaining truck. On the way back to the Azario mansion, there were tons of police cars lining the streets, but they weren't engaging. There were no blockades. They just made their presence known.

Upon arrival at the mansion, there were more police cars, but they allowed the trucks through.

Adrian thought that the police were not as stupid as he suspected. The troops dismounted and took up fire positions. Al and his men were armed and ready for World War III. Adrian was ready for any retaliation by the police. He stood out in the open and saw two men with their hands up, walking towards him. Adrian told his troops to hold their fire.

As they came closer, Adrian recognized Matt and Mike. He said, "You can put your hands down. No one is going to shoot you guys."

Matt said, "Manicotti did manage to hit you again tonight. I guess you can start to rebuild again. Is it over, Adrian?"

"This time, it is really over. I guess, you're not even going to try to arrest me, are you?" Adrian said.

Matt said, "Not a fuck'n chance!! We know what you did to Manicotti! His force was bigger than ours; we would be foolish to try. By the way, how did it go?"

Adrian smiled and said, "We didn't have one single casualty; we totally caught them with their pants down. It went like clockwork."

"I don't like what you have become Adrian, but I'm glad that you are alright."

"I don't like it either boys, but I am still stuck with it. I'm sorry to let you guys down."

"Take it easy, Adrian. We'll talk to you later," Matt said.

The detectives walked back to their car. Adrian gave three long whistle blasts to signal to the troops that it was over. There were loud cheers throughout the compound; no one could believe the force that Adrian was able to muster up. The drinks would be flowing that morning! It was a true miracle. Adrian really did believe in God.

It had been two days since the demise of Vincent Manicotti. Adrian was in the tea room, enjoying a mug of draft and a cigarette. The troops were on their way back to Columbia and he was enjoying the peace and quiet.

Steven came to the tea room and announced, "Sir, Mr. Azario would like to talk to you on line one."

Adrian waved off Steven and answered the phone. "Yes sir, you wanted to talk to me."

Azario said, "Yes Adrian, but I would rather talk to you in person. Can you come down to the hospital right away? It is urgent."

"Yes sir, I'm on my way. Good-bye."

Within the half hour, Adrian arrived at the hospital and went to the doorway of Mr. Azario's room. "Sir, you wanted to see me."

"Yes Adrian, please come in. I've heard that you have been extremely busy since my absence."

"A couple of things happened, sir. However they are all under control now."

"I heard you took care of that trouble maker, Cortez. I also heard that Manicotti is no longer a concern of mine. I must say, you certainly have more guts than I do. That was magnificent; it's been all over the news for the last two days. No one will ever push an Azario around ever again.

I am very proud of you. You also did something very special for me"

Azario clapped his hands. Adrian turned around and looked at the doorway. There was Trixie, as beautiful as ever. Adrian ran up to her and gave her a big kiss and a hug. He cried in her shoulder. He was so happy that she was alright.

Trixie said, "I just had my release papers signed. I'm going home today!"

"That's wonderful, I'm so happy that everything turned out!" Adrian said.

They just couldn't let go of each other. They were just thrilled with each other.

Trixie said, "That is the second time you saved my life; thank-you sweetheart. I really mean it. That was a very brave thing you did. I'm so proud of you!"

Azario signalled the two of them to join him at his bedside. He clapped his hands a second time, and this time it was Doris. Doris put out her hand behind the wall and out came Carol. Doris brought Carol to stand beside her husband. Doris then stood over Mr. Azario to make sure he got it right.

Azario said, "Doris had a long talk with me and made me understand that I made a terrible mistake."

Mr. Azario took Adrian's and Carol's hands and placed one into the other.

"I was very selfish thinking that I could force Adrian into the empire. He was held hostage and forced into situations against his will.

I was foolish to think that he would be happy with me. The whole time he was there, he was miserable and lonely. Then one day, when Carol came over, I could see the extreme pleasure in Adrian's eyes.

He was truly happy once again. That soon disappeared once I confirmed my will on him. You are so perfect for each other, and I am sorry that I came in between the two of you. Please accept my apologies."

Adrian said, "Those are very kind words sir, but we are still separated."

Azario said, "As of this very moment, you are released from my hold on you. You may now live in your little house with Blackie. I do expect my weekly visits from the two of you. I'm releasing my stern grip, but I still want you as my son. Al will take over the duties of the mansion.

Adrian, you are still the owner of the strip. I believe you have a lot of work on repairs to do. I'm sure you will do very well there."

Azario clapped his hands for the third time and in came Steven. Steven walked up to Adrian and gave him a very fat envelope and a set of car keys. Adrian recognized the keys. They belonged to the Hummer.

Azario said, "It's my way of saying thank-you and good luck."

Adrian started to cry like a baby, threw his arms around Azario and whispered, "Thank-you Dad; that is the nicest thing you could have ever done for me."

"You are very welcome, son. God-bless you."

PATRICK J. SCHNERCH

Part Three

Chapter Nineteen

Meanwhile back at the station, Matt and Mike were having a discussion with the Captain.

Matt said, "Sir, I just received word from our surveillance team that they followed Adrian and his wife to their home. I also received word that Adrian has been released from Azario's grip. That means that Adrian is out in the world on his own, without the protection of the old man. That leaves the door wide open to have him charged for murder, conspiracy to commit murder and twenty counts of arson. We can at least have one Azario in jail."

The Captain said, "I want the surveillance on Adrian to continue. I want you guys to gather all the information you can dig up and present it to the DA's office. We'll see what Andréa can do and see if she can make a solid case. Then Adrian will go down."

"There will be a bit of a problem gathering hard evidence," Matt replied. "We will never be able to recover the murder weapons because they are in the mansion. They'll never let us search the place a second time. Adrian is now known as a hero. No one in the mansion will cooperate and volunteer information that will be used to convict Adrian."

"The streets were full of officers. Didn't anyone witness a criminal act?" the Captain asked.

Matt replied, "They did witness the arson attack on Little Italy, except they had to keep their distance to avoid detection. They were too far away and it was dark out. No one was able to make a positive ID. The same thing happened at the Manicotti Mansion. It was even harder to see anything there because of the tall stone wall and the semi-truck that was parked across the driveway. Besides, they were all wearing hoods. They couldn't actually confirm whether Adrian was really there or not."

"You really don't have too much of a case. It has to be more convincing than that to satisfy the jury."

"We actually do know that Adrian was there. We met with him briefly at the Azario Mansion. He was dressed in a black commando outfit and he had a gun in his hand. His hood was off, and we asked if it was over.

He said yes and that they never lost a single casualty. He also said that they had caught them totally by surprise. Plus, we did meet him again at Wet Dreams.

When the place got trashed, he came by wearing the maroon sash. He admitted that he was in charge of the empire. The orders for the attacks had to come from Adrian himself. The whole idea of the attack just had to be from him."

The Captain said, "That is only circumstantial evidence. You don't have any real hard evidence to make a case.

Adrian was pretty damn smart. He pulled off a massive attack; the police force was on the ground and we didn't get a single shred of evidence. You have a lot of digging to do before you can make this thing happen. Now get out of my office. I have a lot of reports to go through."

"Yes sir, thank-you for your time."

The two detectives left the office and closed the door behind them.

Mike said, "I really don't think we are going to get too far with this. If we can get our hands on the weapons, then we would have real proof. We already have thousands of empty casings being collected for evidence. We even have several slugs of lead that were dug out of Manicotti's head. We do have some hard evidence. We just have to do the match ups."

Back at 2031 Oak Street, Adrian was getting reacquainted with Blackie. The dog had gone ballistic when his master walked through the front door. There were lots of wet doggy kisses and patting going on. It was these simple pleasures of life that truly made Adrian happy.

Carol walked by, patted Adrian on the bum and said, "Hi honey."

Adrian stopped playing with the dog and went to her. He looked her in the eyes and lovingly wrapped his arms around her. "I couldn't live without you, sweetheart. I missed you so much. I didn't realize how I took our relationship for granted, until it was taken away from me. I really do love you, sweetheart," he whispered.

The couple melted into each other, exchanging tender kisses. It was obvious that the feelings were mutual. The gentle hugs and soft smiles made Adrian happier each passing moment. He was truly home. His heart had filled with ultimate joy; he was very pleased to be reunited with his little family.

This was something that Azario could never do. He was capable of many things, but he was unable to provide happiness and joy in Adrian's heart.

Only Carol and Blackie had those qualities that Adrian held onto so dearly. This little old house was full of memories of good times. Adrian felt very lucky to receive a second chance at working on his home life.

He and Carol moved to the chesterfield and snuggled up close. Carol grabbed a blanket that was on the floor and covered them up. There they sat, all cozy, with Blackie lying at their feet. It was a wonderful feeling.

Carol said, "This is really nice honey, but I am concerned about something."

"What's wrong sweetheart?"

"I'm not very happy about how you received the car and money. I presume that Azario rewarded you with those things for doing some awful tasks. I don't like blood money. It really bugs me that you graciously accepted those gifts."

"I gave up my soul for that Devil. I earned every last penny. He owes me at least that much. He is incapable of making me happy in any other way, so he does it with gifts."

"I understand his reason for it. I just don't like taking gifts because of the blood that was spilled to get it. It is very wrong. I don't know the details, but I do know that you killed a man while you were there. Azario said he witnessed it and said that you were a cold-blooded murderer. That is not the gentle and loving man that I married."

Adrian reluctantly said, "I was a prisoner over there and I was forced into dangerous situations where sometimes my morals were challenged. Besides, I was also very ill.

I have not been treated with proper medication for a very long time. You would have done the same thing if you were in my situation."

Carol bolted up from the couch and yelled, "I would not!! I would never kill another human being, even if it meant that I would die for making that choice!"

"Oh...yes you fuck'n would! If you were in the same situation, you would have done anything to save your ass!! I'm not a fuck'n monster! I am the exact same person as what you married."

"No...Adrian, you have really changed. I'm not saying it is your fault, but I do think your morals have changed."

Adrian explained, "I just went through a very traumatic experience! It is bound to have some kind of effect on me! With time, I should be able to heal these wounds and gradually change back."

"How much time do you need? You've been seriously ill for more than twenty years. Do I have to put up with this for another twenty years?"

Adrian was hit below the belt. That one really hurt, especially coming from Carol. He had no control over his illness. She should've known better than to say that.

"No, you don't have to put up with it for another twenty years," he said. "It's your choice. Maybe you liked it better living alone than living with me! I thought we could start fresh and have a wonderful life together. It seems that your dreams don't include me."

Carol sat back down. "I do love you honey, but knowing that you killed someone really changes things.

I don't know what I'm supposed to do. I'm not even sure how I feel right now."

Adrian put his head into his hands and cried. One hour ago, he was the happiest man on earth. Then suddenly, his whole world was turned upside down. He loved this woman with all his heart but now he was getting the feeling that even she rejected him. Adrian felt terribly alone in his deep sorrow.

He got up and quietly left through the front door without a word uttered. Carol got up from the couch and went to the window where she watched her husband drive away. He was home for not even three hours and now she didn't know if she would ever see him again!

A tear ran down her cheek as she remembered the way he once was. She didn't know if her heart would ever allow her to love a murderer. Blackie came in and snuggled into her leg, offering his support to his companion. The two of them stood at the window, staring into the empty driveway. The sorrow was immense and Carol was not sure if she could ever make it without Adrian.

Back at the Azario mansion, Adrian drove up the driveway and parked in front. He entered the mansion and went straight to his suite. He walked in and saw that Doris was just getting ready to leave.

"What are you doing here sir?" Doris asked. "Shouldn't you be home celebrating your freedom with your wife?"

"I'm very sorry Doris; I'm not sure that your efforts to get us back together are going to work out. She believes that since I lived here, my morals have changed for the worse.

She thinks that I am evil because of some of the things that I had to do. She is not sure if she could ever love me the way as she once did."

Doris came over to Adrian and gave him a comforting hug. "You have to realize her point of view, sir. She now has doubts whether she could change her morals to match yours. You have changed, Mr. Eisner. Unfortunately, you had to make those changes. I also think you were getting a little comfortable with the power that you possessed. It seemed that the business was taking a grip on you, and Carol noticed it. She's not sure if things will ever be the same as they were."

"I think you're right Doris. I think I will just wait it out for a while and give her some time and space."

"I think that is a good idea," Doris said. "Maybe you will change back and she'll realize that and take you home."

"Thanks Doris, you've been a great help. Good-night."

"Good-night sir."

Doris left for the evening. Adrian was dying for a beer. He filled a mug and lit a cigarette, then went to the kitchen table and sat down. He wondered if he would ever heal the scars that he got from living in the organized crime world. He loved Carol so much; he thought that things would just fall back to the way they were. He had never considered how Carol felt. Maybe they just weren't ready for each other right now.

The beer seemed to be exactly what he needed in a situation like this. Adrian couldn't dream how chaotic his life would be without booze to calm him down.

The Awareness Society will have to pull a rabbit out of a hat before being able to get him off the booze. He had no idea how to kick the habit and stay in a safe mental state at the same time.

Adrian looked at his watch and saw that it was five-thirty. Lori should be home about now.

He pulled out his wallet and found a piece of paper with her number on it. He dialled the number and waited. After several rings, an out-of-breath voice said, "Hello."

"Hi Lori, this is Adrian. Did I catch you at a bad time?"

"No...not at all. I just got in the door when I heard the phone ring. That little jog made me lose my breath; I have to get in shape."

"If you don't have any plans, would you like to go out for dinner tonight with me?"

"That sounds like a real nice idea, Adrian. I would love that."

"I'll make reservations for seven and then we'll pick you up at six-thirty. I hope that gives you enough time to get ready."

"When it comes to food, I'm always ready."

"Good, I'll see you at six-thirty sharp. Bye for now."

Adrian hung up the phone, and then he dialled the restaurant for reservations. Now that everything was taken care of, he lit another cigarette and went to finish his beer before he got ready for dinner. He felt fortunate to have Lori as a friend. At least he had someone he could lean on in the time of sorrow! He finished his beer and went to the washroom for a shower.

Adrian finished up and got dressed for dinner. He still had time for one more beer. He filled his mug and lit a cigarette. He had to learn about how Carol felt about him and his business before they could progress. Doris was a very smart woman and she knew what she was talking about. It must have taken her a long time to get used to the things that happened at the mansion. Her morals were also tested.

If these walls could talk, there would be screams of horror. This was an evil place. But for reasons unknown, Adrian felt very comfortable here. He was very well aware of the terror that happened in this place. It just didn't seem to affect him anymore. Maybe, he really had changed. He had accepted this way of life living within the Azario mansion.

Although the transition was traumatic, it was very effective. He was able to conjure up the darkness from deep inside and use it against his enemies. Carol was right; he really had changed. He was starting to understand her point of view. He was not the same man as she married, he was an Azario now!

ADRIAN

Adrian phoned downstairs and got Michael to meet him out front. He went downstairs and moved the Hummer into the parking lot so that Michael could pull up front. Michael opened the door for Adrian and he got into the car. Michael went to the driver's seat and asked, "Where are we off to, sir?"

"132 E 69th Street."

The car pulled away and Adrian could not help but think about his sudden change in character.

He was worried that he would never find happiness in his life because of the trauma. He couldn't discuss this with his doctor, because of the illegal factors that would incriminate him. All he had was Lori.

He could tell her anything and lift this heavy burden that he was carrying. The car pulled up to Lori's house and Adrian got out of the car. He went to the front door and rang the bell. He waited momentarily and the door opened. Adrian was astonished and said, "Lori, you look magnificent!"

Lori blushed. "Thank-you Adrian, you look very charming yourself."

"Thank-you! Shall we go?"

Michael was waiting at the car for the couple to get in. He returned to his seat and asked, "Where would you like to go, sir?"

"Take us to Rafael's on Davis."

"Oh...that is a very swanky place," Lori said. "All the hob-nobs go there. I've never eaten there before. It's too rich for my blood."

Adrian said, "I want to treat you tonight. You are turning out to be a very dear friend and I want to show you how much I appreciate you."

"That is very sweet of you Adrian. I love your company too."

The car pulled up in front of Rafael's and the handsome couple got out of the car. Adrian raced to the front door and opened it for Lori. She was taken back by the beautiful décor and was very impressed.

A waiter greeted the couple and Adrian said, "We would like a table for the Eisner party at 7:00 pm."

"Yes Mr. Eisner, your table is waiting. Please follow me."

The waiter pulled out the chair for the lady and waited for her to sit down. He then did the same thing for Adrian.

"Would you care for something from the bar?" he asked.

Adrian said, "Yes, the lady will have a rye and ginger and I will have a mug a draft. I also want a bottle of your best wine for dinner."

"Thank-you sir. Marcel will be your waiter for this evening. I will ensure you get your drinks right away." He disappeared in a cloud of dust.

Lori said, "This place is fantastic! Thank-you Adrian!"

"Don't thank me yet. You haven't had your dinner yet."

Lori was all smiles. "What made you think about having dinner with me tonight?"

"I'm sorry, but it is for a selfish reason. I had a very sad day and I need a shoulder to cry on. You are the only friend I have that I feel comfortable doing that with."

Lori grabbed Adrian's hand and said, "I'll never turn you away Adrian. You can always count on me for support."

"Thank-you, I have no other place to turn and I have to get this off my chest or it will kill me."

Another waiter came to the table with the drinks and said, "Hello, my name is Marcel. I will be your server for this evening. Are you ready to order?"

"No, I'm sorry we haven't even looked at the menu. Can you come back in about ten minutes?" Adrian replied.

"Of course sir, I'll come back later to take your order."

"I guess we should decide on what we want to eat," Adrian said.

They opened their menus and Lori was surprised that there were no prices on the menu. She asked, "How do you know how much the meal is, if there are no prices?"

Adrian explained, "If you have to look at the prices, this is not the restaurant for you. Only the rich come here. Prices don't mean anything. That bottle of wine we have is worth twenty-five hundred dollars."

Lori was in shock and said, "Are you sure you can pay for this? This is very extravagant!"

"Of course I can pay for it. Pick anything you want. Don't worry yourself about the prices. I think I will have the roast duck in wine sauce. What will you have?"

"I'm going to try something I never had before. I'm going to have a rack of lamb," replied Lori.

"Excellent choice! They have a wonderful rack of lamb here; you'll really enjoy it."

ADRIAN

Adrian made eye contact with Marcel. He came to the table and Adrian ordered the meals and another round of drinks.

When Marcel had left, Adrian said, "Anyway, I'm not the leader of the organization anymore. I was pardoned by Mr. Azario. It was in everyone's interest that my wife and I get back together and start from where we left off.

Unfortunately, I drastically changed in character and my wife noticed it. She wants me to be the same as I was. I can't do that right now. I need time to heal. This whole ordeal had a traumatic effect on me.

My morals and character were totally dismantled. I really am not the same man as I was. I'm severely damaged from what has happened in the last little while.

I used to be a gentle, mild man. I didn't have the stomach to kill a spider. Now I am able to disassociate myself from reality and kill men in cold blood. I am starting to enjoy the money and the power and I'm not sure if I could ever change back to my old self.

I am scared of what I am about to become. My poor wife just cannot accept these severe changes and we are separated again. I've lost the love of my life because of Azario. I don't think I can ever again be happy without her."

"I never thought about that," Lori said. "Of course it had a major impact on you. I didn't realize the mental and emotional damage that this ordeal must have caused you!

I don't think it was your fault Adrian. I think you did the best you can to survive and you got damaged in the process. That is a humbling story. I'm sorry."

"That is why my heart aches so badly," Adrian replied. "I feel crushed and hopeless. I am all alone and I hate it. I want my wife and dog back!"

Adrian was already shedding tears. Lori was trying to console him, but he was too weak to fight back. She had never seen a man so distraught in her life! Afraid of falling apart in the restaurant, Adrian excused himself to go to the washroom and try to regain some stability.

There he fell to his knees and cried heavily.

The pain was just too unbearable to handle. It was eating at him inside and out. He felt out of control and helpless.

After a good long cry, he got up and washed his face. He straightened himself up, believing that he was ready to rejoin

Lori at the table. He went back and sat down, took a couple of big gulps of beer and lit a cigarette.

Lori grabbed his hand and asked, "Are you alright Adrian? Do you want to go home? We could always make it another night."

"No, I'll be alright. I feel much better now that I got a few things off my chest, thank-you."

"It must be devastating. I couldn't imagine what would happen to me, if I was in the same situation."

Marcel came with the entrées and placed them onto the table. Adrian was feeling much better and was ready to have a nice evening with Lori. There wasn't much talking during dinner. They were ravenous and the meals quickly disappeared from sight.

They were just finishing up their meal when Adrian asked, "How was your meal?"

"You were right!! This is absolutely the best meal I have ever had in my life! I never thought that food could taste so good!" Lori said.

Adrian got a big kick out of Lori. He loved watching her appreciate things; she looked very happy. This eased things up for him and helped put him into higher spirits.

Marcel came to the table to take the plates away. "How were your meals?"

Lori piped up, "It was fantastic, thank-you!"

"Would you like any dessert?"

Adrian said, "Yes please. May we have two crème de glace?"

"Yes, I'll be right back with your desserts."

Adrian took Lori's hand and said, "Thank-you for being there when I needed you. Your friendship means the world to me."

"No problem! Thank-you for the lovely meal. I really enjoyed myself."

Marcel came back with the desserts, refilled the wine glasses and went back to his numerous duties. The couple enjoyed the ice-cream and had a light-hearted chat.

Marcel came back and asked, "Would there be anything else, sir?"

"No thank-you. Just bring me the bill, please."

Marcel had the bill in his hand. He placed it on the table and thanked the couple for their patronage. Adrian pulled out a roll of thousand-dollar bills and put a few down on the table. The couple left the restaurant and Adrian took Lori home. He wished her good-night, and Michael then drove him home.

Once at the mansion, Adrian raced upstairs and grabbed a mug of beer and a cigarette. He went to the kitchen table. He looked at his watch and was thankful that it wasn't too late. He called Carol's number and waited for her to answer.

"Hello."

"Hi sweetheart, how are you?"

Carol softly replied, "Not very good! I cried all day. I still love you, you son of a bitch! I can't help but think that I am making a big mistake."

"I haven't been very considerate of your feelings and I would like to apologize. I didn't take into consideration that I have really changed. I couldn't accept that fact.

I pretended as if nothing happened at all and that life would go back to normal. I was foolish to think that. I'm sorry; I just took you for granted."

"I love you so damn much; it really hurts me to be away from you. However, my morals and my conscience are telling me not to go to you. There is a horrible battle inside of me; I don't know which way to turn."

"Is it ok if I visit you sometimes? I can't forget you! I will always love you. Wait, I have a great idea!"

"What's the good idea?"

"From now on, I'll get up at 5:00 in the morning and be at your house by 6:00. I could still feed the dog and let him out to pee. It will be just like it was. I'll put your tea on for you and we could have our normal morning chats. After you leave, I will take Blackie out for his morning walk. After we come back, I'll lock up the house and go to work. How does that sound?"

Carol sounded very happy about the suggestion but asked, "Isn't that too early for you?"

"Oh...no. I'm usually up at that time anyway. Besides, I don't start work until nine. I think it will be nice to have some contact with each other."

Carol thought that would be a wonderful idea and said, "I would really like that honey. I'll see you tomorrow morning, ok?"

"You bet, sweetheart. I'll see you tomorrow. Good-night."

Not far from the mansion at the local hospital lay a dying old man named Harold Eisner. Less than six months ago, he had been diagnosed with Non-Hodgkin's Lymphoma. The cancer was in its final stages. The man had lost about seventy-five pounds in weight; he was nothing more than skin and bones.

He had other conditions which inhibited him from having any other cancer treatment. He was just too weak to handle another round of treatment. It was just a matter of time. His wife, Lillian, had been by her husband's side practically the whole time.

Adrian had not really been close to the Eisners. Their relationship had frazzled after they put Adrian in a foster home. Many bad things had happened there and Adrian blamed them.

If he hadn't been put in the foster home, things would have been much better. It was for this reason that Adrian seldom visited them.

The Eisners had never attempted to visit or phone Adrian themselves. There was no birthday or Christmas cards, just nothing. They expected Adrian to crawl onto his knees and visit them. They thought all he wanted was money anyway.

Adrian had never hit it off well with Lillian, either. When he was a child, he remembered telling her he really enjoyed bacon.

One day, Lillian fried up three pounds of bacon and made the little boy eat it all. There were constant verbal threats and abuse. Adrian used to hide in his room all evening and never go out to play with the other kids. He stayed secluded away from the Eisners as much as possible.

His school grades plummeted and he failed Grade six. His self esteem was battered down and soon he became a loner. This progressed at school, making him a target for bullies. Everyday he would be beaten up or verbally abused by other children.

The emotional pain that Adrian felt as a child took a form that made the Eisners pay attention to his awkward behaviour. He was making a school project at home one evening. It was made of wood and there was cutting involved with a hand saw. While he was busy cutting a piece of wood, the saw jumped out of the groove and cut Adrian's left hand.

ADRIAN

There was no pain involved. As a matter of fact, this made Adrian feel good. As an experiment, he continued raking his hand with the saw until it was nothing more than raw meat. The feeling was elevating and pleasing. He remembered giving off a sigh of relief after cutting himself. It lifted him out of his depressed state and made him feel good for a limited amount of time.

Hair-pulling by the handfuls was also a habit that Adrian developed. Soon, the cutting and other habits became an addictive behaviour which got worse and continued for twenty-seven years. He visited his first shrink at the age of twelve. He was diagnosed with a dual personality.

The Eisners did not know how to deal with Adrian's behaviour and made him a ward of the court. He was then taken to a foster home where the real hell began.

Smoking cigarettes and drinking booze started at age fifteen. He tried anything, just so that he could escape from his emotional pain.

When puberty struck, he became a wild sexual machine. Luckily for him, he found a beautiful girl who also was just as enthusiastic as he was. He never came home at nights to the foster home and he started skipping classes at school.

Adrian was out of control. He was unleashed into the world without any restraints. Doctors worked on his mental state for years. They came up with a different diagnosis every time. Adrian spent his entire childhood in disparity and alone. The foster home was of no use for guidance or love; the foster parents did it only for the money. This place was a haven for highly-disturbed children, where they could run freely without consequence.

There were many dark secrets that happened there. Secrets that hadn't been revealed in thirty years since those dreaded days of Adrian's childhood. He was not sure if those secrets would ever come to light.

Physical abuse and verbal abuse were a daily event. There was always somebody getting the boom lowered upon them. The social worker was a piece of shit. He had no idea how the kids were treated, and he didn't care. This was hell for Adrian and he ran away at the age of sixteen to live his own life alone.

This was why Adrian did not feel any love towards the Eisners. He couldn't bring himself to love someone who had made his childhood a living nightmare.

The Eisners always blamed Adrian and never once considered that they may have made a mistake.

Adrian would visit the Eisners once in a while. Right away, Lillian would point at the scars on his arm and laugh. Then she would ask how he got them. She was evil minded and abusive to everyone.

The Eisners hadn't even told Adrian that Harold was on his death bed. They had no regards towards Adrian, whatsoever. Adrian was a compassionate man and would do anything to make Harold's life a little easier. He would never forgive them, but he didn't hate them.

Meanwhile at the Ruzo residence, Matt had just poured himself his first cup of coffee. He quickly glanced at the newspaper, but didn't find anything of interest. He couldn't help but think about Adrian. It looked like the police would be forced to act on him, before he became so powerful that he would become invincible.

Adrian had proved that he was a highly dangerous and intelligent man. He had the police backed in the corner the night Manicotti was murdered. He was invincible then. What would he be like in twenty years? They just had to take him down and lock him up for good. It was the only way.

A muffled voice from upstairs said, "Daddy, can you come get me please?"

"I'll be right there sweetheart." Matt yelled back.

He got up from his comfortable chair and went upstairs to get Emily. He picked her up, took her downstairs and placed her into her wheelchair. He went back to the kitchen to prepare her breakfast.

Emily followed close behind and wheeled herself to the kitchen table. After several minutes of preparation, Matt placed Emily's breakfast in front of her and sat down to finish his coffee.

He heard a car pull up into the driveway. After a couple of minutes, there was a quick rap at the door and in strutted Mike. He went over to Emily, gave her the usual morning kiss on the cheek and said, "Good morning munchkin. How are you today?"

"I'm fine Mr. Parsons. How are you?"

"I'm doing pretty well if I do say so myself. Good morning Matt."

Matt grumbled, "Yeah...yeah...good morning."

Mike raced to the coffee machine, poured himself a cup of coffee and sat down. "What do you have planned for today?"

"I think I know of a way to get some dirt on Adrian," Matt replied. "Do you remember that girl Adrian was with on the night Wet Dreams got busted up? I'm going to check on surveillance and see if they've been chumming around. If they're getting chummy, maybe we could put the screws to the girl and get some information on him.

I also want to drag in Adrian's housekeeper. I believe her name is Doris. She would have an earful of goodies on Adrian, especially in the last week or two. I want to push her especially hard, because I know for a fact that she knows a lot more than she will let on.

Forensics found some audio tape in a safe at Manicotti's mansion. It was stuck in a fire-proof safe with some papers and cash.

They are trying to see if they can recover any of the recordings because it did suffer some heat damage.

According to the papers, it looked like Manicotti was building a case against Azario and Eisner for the police. Manicotti was going to hit them legally and with force at the same time, crushing the empire. We should have the results today."

"I kind of liked Adrian," Mike said. "I feel a little two-faced sticking the sword in his back like that."

"So do I," replied Matt. "Unfortunately, we have to do it. It's the law and Adrian has broken it. The opportunity to get him off the streets is available now. We have to act fast."

"What if Adrian needs to be in a hospital rather than a prison?"

"That's up to the court to decide. All we have to do is bring him in and hand the case over to the DA. Anyway, I better get showered up or we'll be late. I'll be back in a while. Help yourself to another cup of coffee."

Later that afternoon, Adrian arrived back at the mansion after a full day's work with the architect and demolition crews down at the work sites. He had Mr. Armstrong drawing up the plans for all five bars that Manicotti's goons destroyed. He went to the bar, poured himself a mug of draft and lit a cigarette. He then sat down at his favourite spot at the kitchen table.

The phone rang and Adrian answered, "Hello."

Carol said, "Hi sweetheart. I have some bad news. Samantha just called and asked why you haven't been up at the hospital.

She said your father is on his death bed and they don't think that he is going to last any longer than a couple days."

"Why don't those fuck'n people tell me these things?" Adrian yelled. "What is their God damn problem anyway? Mom could've phoned me long time ago, rather than wait till the last fuck'n minute! Do you want to go to the hospital with me?"

"Yeah, can you pick me up?"

"I'll be there as fast as I can. I'll see you soon. Bye."

Adrian said to Doris, "Just leave my dinner on a plate. I'll put it in the microwave when I come back."

"Yes sir, I'll have it waiting for you on the counter."

Adrian rushed out the door and took the Hummer. He raced out of the driveway and quickly disappeared.

Less than fifteen minutes later, Adrian was honking his horn outside Carol's house.

She quickly came outside and locked the door. She ran to the car and gave Adrian a quick kiss on the cheek. They were off in a blur and on their way to the hospital. Adrian was pissed right off. He knew that he wasn't close to the Eisners, but they could've phoned and let him know about this.

They constantly kept him in the dark. Lillian had had a major heart attack that almost killed her and no one had said a fuck'n word to Adrian. He found out about it years later. They arrived at the hospital and ran in through the front doors.

Adrian went to the receptionist's desk and said, "My name is Adrian Eisner. Can you tell me where Harold Eisner's room is?"

"Mr H. Eisner is on the fifth floor, room #514."

"Thank-you."

They finally arrived at Harold's room and entered. Lillian was sitting down, holding Harold's hand. Adrian went and

ADRIAN

took a chair and sat on the other side by his father. Lillian just stared; she didn't say a word to them.

In a very weak whisper Harold said, "What are you doing here? I don't have any money. It's all going to her."

Adrian was just floored when he heard that. He pulled out a heavy wad of thousand dollar bills and said, "I have more fuck'n money in my pocket than you ever made in your fuck'n life!!

I don't want your fuck'n money! I came to see you! Why didn't you guys tell me you were sick? I would've been here a long time ago!"

Lillian said, "We seem to manage quite well on our own. We didn't need you to come down here and fight with your father at a time that he needs his rest."

Adrian blurted out, "If you had told me when he was first diagnosed, I could've helped you out. I could've driven you to the doctor's or something. Why do you do this to me?"

Lillian said, "You never bothered visiting us before. Why should you start now?"

"Not once in thirty years have you ever attempted to make contact with me! Why should I come crawling to you?" Adrian shouted.

The nurse heard the commotion and grabbed Adrian by the arm, saying, "Sir, I have to ask you to leave. He is dying! Don't you have any compassion?"

As they were walking out, Lillian yelled, "Don't come back! We don't ever want to see you again!"

Carol said to Adrian, "What the fuck is wrong with them? They're fuck'n nuts!!"

"I don't know," Adrian replied. "You think they would give it up already. Not them, they're going to fight me to the bitter end. Do you want to come over and have a dinner with me? Doris always makes more than I can eat. She left me a little something before she went home."

"Ok, I hope it's nothing fancy."

"Not tonight. It's just a good home cooked meal." The couple left the hospital and got into the car. Adrian couldn't believe that his Mom and Dad were still so screwed up, even after all these years. At least he had made an attempt. That was the best he could do.

About a half hour later, they arrived at the mansion. Adrian parked the car in the lot and they headed up to the suite. As Adrian opened the door, the suite still had that nice smell from what Doris had cooked earlier on.

Adrian went to the counter and said, "We're having chicken tonight. Do you want a glass of water with your dinner?"

"Yes, please."

"We'll sit at the kitchen table tonight. I'll just heat your dinner in the microwave for a few minutes."

Adrian put the plate in the machine and got Carol her water. He went to the bar and poured himself a mug of draft.

He went back to the table, sat down and said, "I told you there was lots of food. Doris cooks for an army. There's enough food for four people."

Carol smiled and said, "I like Doris. I think she is a little sweetheart."

Adrian smiled back, "I don't know what I would do without her. She has become a dear friend as well as a wonderful housekeeper."

The microwave beeped and Adrian got up, took the hot meal and placed in front of Carol. "Eat it while it's hot, sweetheart. Mine will be ready in a few minutes."

He then put his meal in the machine, set the timer and sat back down with his beer. Carol was carefully eating her dinner because it was still very hot. The alarm went off and Adrian joined his wife for a nice quiet dinner together. This reminded him of the good times that he and Carol used to have.

Carol said, "I'm very sorry honey, but I can't stay long tonight. I haven't had time to feed the dog or walk him yet. Can you take me home after dinner?"

"Sure sweetheart; that will be no problem. I understand that our boy has to be taken care of. We could always have dinner another day when we have more time available."

"You're going to have to tell Doris for me that she is a fabulous cook. This is delicious."

"I will make sure to tell her that. I'm sure that she would be very pleased."

The couple finished their meals and Adrian put the dishes in the dishwasher.

He gave the place a quick wipe and put on his coat. "Are you ready to go home sweetheart?"

ADRIAN

"Yes, I'm ready. Thank-you for the lovely dinner. That was very nice of you to invite me."

"It was my pleasure."

They left the suite and went off to Carol's house.

Meanwhile in the interrogation room at the station, Mike and Matt were relentlessly hounding Doris for information. They had had her there for two hours already and they were prepared to stay overnight. Poor Doris was frazzled and unprepared for such a verbal barrage and her nerves were giving out.

Matt barked, "We know that Adrian planned the attack on Manicotti. We know that Adrian is responsible for the forty-eight lives that were lost as well as numerous injuries. Mrs. Capelin, do you want all those deaths to be on your conscience for the rest of your life?"

"I don't know anything!" Doris said. "I clean and cook. I don't listen in on private conversations. It is none of my business and that's the way I like it."

Mike said, "If you don't volunteer the information that you know, we will have you subpoenaed, and the DA will rip you apart! You will be forced to tell the truth on the stand! Tell us the truth and we will let you go home tonight. Are you afraid of what Azario will do to you if you testify against Adrian?"

Doris was starting to shake and her bottom lip was trembling. Her eyes were starting to water and she was getting closer to her breaking point.

The detectives knew if they kept it up for another hour or two, she would crack.

Matt said, "Mrs. Capelin, do you want to go to jail for withholding information on a murder case? That's exactly what's going to fuck'n happen to you if you don't cooperate! We know that you are lying to us.

You know everything there is to know about everyone and their dealings in that mansion.

Your husband is waiting in the lobby, ready to take you home. Tell us what we need to know! You could be out of here within the hour. Your husband must be hungry, waiting for his dinner. You don't want to upset your own husband, do you?"

Doris's eyes were starting to tear and she softly replied, "No."

Matt said, "Adrian is a murderer!! Why do you want to protect him?"

Doris's voice cracked when she said, "I'm not protecting anyone. I am a housekeeper. I don't know anything."

Mike said, "If you don't know anything, why are you crying? Is your conscience starting to eat at you?"

"I just don't know anything."

"Are you willing to take a polygraph test?" Matt asked. "Then we will prove that you are lying to us. If you refuse to take it, it proves that you are hiding something from us. What do you say?"

Doris was sobbing. "No, I will not take the test. You cannot keep me here! I didn't do anything!"

Matt blasted out, "You are doing something!! You are protecting a fuck'n murderer!! I can hold you for interfering with a murder investigation!"

Doris was heavily sobbing; she just cracked. The verbal badgering had worn her down to nothing. She was mentally broken down by the two detectives and she just couldn't continue.

Matt softly put his hand on Doris's shoulder and said, "Doris, do you want to tell us the truth now?"

Doris nodded her head in a submissive manner and softly said, "Yes."

Matt was already dressed this morning. He woke up early and decided to get a head start on things. He went downstairs to the kitchen and poured himself a cup of coffee. He sat down and started to think about Mrs. Capelin. They really had put the boots to her last night. It was amazing that she was able to hold out so long.

The effort that they had put into the interrogation turned out to be very fruitful. They had enough evidence now to put Adrian in jail for conspiracy to murder.

Matt would still like to talk to the girl that Adrian was hanging around with. He was hoping for an open and shut case; he was going to gather enough evidence so that Adrian would never see the light of day again!

Forensics was not quite finished working on the contents of Manicotti's safe. They had promised that they would have it done by first thing that morning. The surveillance team said that Adrian was back living at the mansion; however he did go to work everyday.

That meant that there still was an opportunity to pick him up where he was alone and without the support of the mansion.

After they examined the contents of the safe, Matt was going to pack up the evidence he had and put it in a neat package for Andréa. She should have enough evidence to have Adrian brought in.

Matt could hear from upstairs, "Daddy, can you come and get me please?"

"I'll be right there, pumpkin."

Matt went and completed his morning ritual with Emily and she was already eating her breakfast when he heard Mike drive in; he patiently waited for the door to swing wide open. Sure enough, there was a quick rap at the door and Mike busted in. "Good morning everyone. How are you folks doing on this fine day?"

Matt and Emily both went on with the formalities and greetings. Mike went and picked a cup from the cupboard and poured himself a coffee. He sat down across from Emily and smiled. "That was one hell of a good shake-down we performed last night. It took her a while, but she eventually cracked like an egg."

"After a few hours of reviewing evidence, I am quite sure that we can pick up Adrian today."

"Hopefully he didn't seek refuge and stick around in the mansion. I would prefer to do this without any incidents," replied Mike.

"Mrs. Capelin probably told him the whole story. He must be well aware that we are now gunning for him. I'm not sure what Adrian has planned. His mind isn't working on all eight cylinders. He might not be all that eager to give himself up quietly."

Marilyn made her way down the stairs and into the kitchen. She grabbed a coffee and said, "Good morning Mike."

"Good morning Marilyn. How are you?"

"I'm doing just fine. It looks like it's going to be a nice day outside."

"It's fairly nice, but it is starting to be quite chilly first thing in the mornings. Before you know it, winter will be here."

The four of them continued with their idle chit-chat until it was time for the men to go to the station. Matt kissed his family good-bye and left through the back door. They then drove off to a new day.

A little later in the morning, Adrian returned back to the mansion after spending time with Carol and Blackie. He parked the car, went to the suite and opened the door. There he saw Doris sitting at the kitchen table with her head buried into her hands, sobbing heavily. On the table was an envelope with Adrian's name on it.

Adrian came in, put his hand on Doris's shoulder and asked, "What's wrong honey? Can I do something for you?"

Barely speaking words Doris uttered, "I'm very sorry sir, but by 5:00 pm today, I will have resigned my duties at the mansion. Here is my written notice."

Adrian was absolutely shocked and he barked, "You're not going anywhere! You are staying right here with me. What ever the problem is, we will work it out together!"

"I'm sorry sir. It has to be this way."

"No, it doesn't have to be this way! Tell me what's wrong and I'll see if I can help you."

Doris cried, "Oh…sir. I did a very bad thing to you last night! As my husband and I were driving out of the gates to go home, a car pulled in front of us and blocked our way. Two detectives came out and identified themselves. They wanted me to come to the station to talk to them.

They threatened me with jail if I didn't cooperate. The fat detective drove our car following the other guy to the police station. Once we got there, they put me in the interrogation room and badgered me for six hours for information about you, sir. They are building a murder case around you!

I tried not to tell them anything, but they were very aggressive and I broke down. I'm very sorry sir; I didn't want to hurt you. They forced me into it."

Adrian went to the bar; got himself a draft, lit a cigarette, and sat down on the couch. He sat silently and emotionlessly. He was slowly going into a disassociate state. Reality was slipping away and his own precious private world was returning. Nothing could harm him in here, not even the police. He stared at his cigarette as the smoke spiralled into the air.

Doris got up from her chair and went to Adrian. She put her hand on his shoulder and asked, "Sir, are you alright?"

There was no answer. Adrian was incoherent, deep into his own world.

Doris gave Adrian a good shake and yelled, "Sir!! Are you alright?"

Adrian snapped back into reality and said, "Oh...I'm sorry Doris. I didn't hear you."

"Are you alright?"

"Yes...I'm fine Doris. I know the police put a lot of pressure on you. Don't worry about me. You did the right thing, Doris."

"Sir, they want me to testify against you in court. I care for you sir. I don't want to hurt you."

"You have to do the right thing and that means that you have to testify against me. Don't lie on the stand for me; you have to tell the truth on everything you know."

"Sir, if I do that, they will throw you in jail."

"If I'm guilty, that is where I belong. It will be up to the court to decide that. You are not resigning today; it wasn't your fault. You are my friend and you are staying here with me and that is final."

Adrian got up from the chesterfield and went to the kitchen table where the envelope was lying. He picked up the envelope, tore it into several pieces and threw it in the garbage. "Tonight, you can sleep with a clear conscience that you are doing the right thing. Your husband and family will honour your bravery and morals. You are a good person, Doris. Don't throw that away."

Adrian went to the phone and called Al downstairs. The phone rang and Al answered, "Hello."

"Al, this is Mr. Eisner. I have a little problem. The police have enough evidence to put me behind bars. I expect that they are going to attempt to take me into custody soon. However, my schedule clashes with theirs and I am not willing to concede at this time.

I need eight armed men to be my escorts until this thing gets settled.

I'm going to work in a couple of minutes and I will require their services. Have them meet me outside and I will join up with them."

Al said, "No problem sir, they will be right there. Good-bye sir."

Adrian hung up the phone and then he looked at his watch and saw that it was time to go to work. He went to Doris, gave her a big hug and a kiss on the cheek and said, "We are friends forever. Friends never abandon each other. I'll see you tonight."

He then left the suite and made his way to work.

Back at the station, the two detectives were going over the evidence with Dr. Taggart. Dr. Taggart said, "Some of the tape is unreadable, but we do have Adrian asking Azario for permission to kill Jonathan. Azario granted the permission for the hit and supplied Adrian with money and weaponry for the mission.

There is quite a bit of evidence gathered on Azario himself. There is proof of everything from murder to drug smuggling and extortion. We even have Adrian on tape murdering an old crony that was sticking his hand in the till until he got caught by Azario. Azario ordered Adrian to kill Mr. Tony Lorenzo. There was nothing on the tapes about the massacre at the Manicotti Mansion. But at least you have evidence about two murders."

"Good work Roland, we already had evidence about the massacre, but we didn't have anything like this. You have been a great help," said Matt.

The two detectives went up stairs into Matt's office where he dialled the District Attorney. The phone rang and a voice said, "DA's office, Andréa Shelton speaking."

"Hi Andréa, this is Matt down at the station. I need you to review some evidence we have on an Adrian Eisner. We have him nailed cold and I want you to give us the go-ahead to bring him in."

Andréa said, "Ok, I just finished up a case this morning. This is perfect timing Matt. I'll be there in fifteen minutes. Bye."

Matt hung up the phone and said, "She's on her way."

Mike said, "Things don't look very good for Adrian right now. I don't see how he can get himself out of this one."

"There is no way out; we have him cold. You couldn't ask for anything better. We have more than enough evidence to put him behind bars for life."

The time passed quickly and Andréa walked through the station's front door. She walked to Matt's office and knocked on the door frame.

"Hi Andréa, this Is Mike Parsons. He is helping me out with this case. Mike, this is Andréa Shelton our District Attorney."

They quickly made their acquaintances and Matt said, "I want you to listen to these tapes. The first voice you hear is our suspect, Adrian Eisner. The second voice is Frank Azario."

After listening for a little while, Andréa said, "Azario just gave permission for a hit! Do you have any other evidence about this?"

Matt replied, "I witnessed five men getting into a limo and a Hummer.

The Hummer fits the description of Adrian's car and we have tire marks from both vehicles. We found our needle in the haystack. We retrieved the bullet and the shell casing from where it was fired. Unfortunately, we don't have the murder weapon. The next piece of tape is an order from Azario for Adrian to kill Tony Lorenzo."

"Was that a gun shot I just heard?"

"Yes it was. That was Adrian murdering Mr. Lorenzo. There is more. Have a seat and listen to this material witness."

Andréa said, "Oh...my God! You gentlemen hit the jackpot! There is enough evidence here to nail Mr. Eisner a hundred times over. Do you have anything else?"

"We have one more person we want to question."

"Fine, if anything else comes up, please keep me informed. Go and bring in Mr. Adrian Eisner. I want to see this son of a bitch."

"We're on our way Andréa, thanks."

Matt and Mike raced out of the station and went to Gyro's on Davis Ave. That was where the surveillance team was right then. The two detectives arrived and noticed that there were three limos parked out front. They were somewhat curious as to why there were so many.

They went inside and tried to stay out of the way of the demolition crew. They saw that Adrian was in the middle of the floor, talking to the architect. Matt walked up to Adrian and said, "Sorry to break up your meeting Adrian, but you are under arrest for forty-eight counts of murder and twenty counts of arson."

Suddenly, eight huge men circled Adrian and casually revealed their weapons.

Adrian replied, "I'm sorry gentlemen, but my schedule is booked up tight. I don't have time for you right now. My friends and I agree that we will have to do this another time. What do you think Matt?"

"Resisting arrest should not be taken lightly, Adrian. It just makes things worse for you. Turn yourself in now and come peacefully and I will put in a good word for you."

"Not today Matt, I will come to you when the timing is right.

I really have too many things that require attention before I go to the big house. I will fight you on this one Matt. My father is dying within the next day or two. The repairs have to be set up to go and my personal life has to be repaired as well. I am not going to jail right now. You will have to wait.

And how dare you to verbally attack my housekeeper? She was a nervous wreck when she came to work today. Couldn't you have taken it a little easier on her?"

"Sorry Adrian; we had to rough her up a bit. She wasn't cooperating with us," replied Matt.

"You will get your chance to sink your teeth into my back end at a more convenient time. Until then, you will have to excuse me. I am very busy right now."

Adrian signalled his men to circle the detectives and said, "My boys will see you to the door gentlemen. Good-day."

The two detectives were outnumbered and had no choice but to abort their attempt to arrest Adrian.

They didn't need to start a gun battle that they were bound to lose. Adrian was victorious this time, but his luck would soon run out. The detectives got into their car and went back to the station empty handed.

When they arrived at the station, Andréa was waiting to talk to Adrian. Matt went into the office where she was waiting and said, "He had goons protecting him, Andréa; we couldn't make an arrest. He claims he will come in when the timing is right and not before then."

Andréa said, "I don't understand why you didn't arrest him."

"They were ready for a shoot out; we were out numbered. It would've been a bloody battle and we would have lost. We couldn't arrest him; he was ready for us."

"When does he think the timing will be right?"

"It doesn't look like it will be any time too soon. He is pretty mixed up. He said that his dad is dying in the next day or two. I presume he was talking about Mr. Eisner," Matt said.

Andrea said, "I think that will work to our advantage and allow me to get a head start building up my case. This will allow me time to go over the evidence in detail.

Just keep surveillance on him and keep on with your investigation. We don't need him yet. I have a plan for Mr. Eisner."

Matt said, "We should tell you that he has a long history of severe mental illness. I'm positive that his lawyer will plea not guilty due to insanity. They have the proof to back up that plea. He really is that ill, and we have to find out a way to get around that."

"Does he require medication to stay stable?"

"Yes he does. Two of the murders were committed while he was on placebos. He was under the impression that he was being treated. However, I think he was medicated or should have been medicated at the time of the massacre."

"If he was medicated during the massacre, he is screwed. If he should have been on medication and didn't take them, that would also cause hardships for Mr. Eisner. We have to dig a little deeper into this insanity possibility. It could be difficult to convince the jury that he is guilty.

We actually need to know what medication he is on and the doses. We also need to know when they were prescribed and filled. That is something that you gentlemen can work on.

There is no doubt in my mind that the insanity plea will be the route his lawyer will take. It is the most solid defence they can possibly use for killing forty-eight people. They have no choice. We are going to counter their defence with brilliant detective work and an iron clad offence."

Matt replied, "Adrian was forced to murder Mr. Lorenzo. He was under strict family policies to obey orders or die. When the situation arrived, he had no choice but to kill Tony Lorenzo."

"Are we able to lay charges against the man that gave the orders?"

"Not a fuck'n chance. He's in the hospital recovering from a major heart attack. He has twenty-four hour goon patrols watching over him. They will not allow any contact with the police.

We already tried to do that. Adrian must have learned that trick from the old man."

"Is there anything else I should know about?" asked Andréa.

Matt replied, "We are unable to obtain certain evidence because it is within the Azario Mansion. They are so powerful that a piece of paper signed by a judge doesn't mean diddly-squat.

They would rather start a war with the police department than cooperate. They have the weapons and resources to turn us into chopped liver."

"Does that mean there is no ballistics?"

"Not a single one. We can't get the weapons to compare with in the tests."

"Were there any eye witnesses?"

"They couldn't make a positive ID of anyone because of the distance. Besides, they were all wearing ski masks in the black of night."

"You can't just assume he did it. We have to prove it beyond a shadow of a doubt. We need hard evidence that he was actually there.

I'm sorry gentlemen, but you have to do much better than that. The confession of the woman is only circumstantial evidence. I can't go in the courtroom half-cocked."

Matt asked, "How about conspiracy to commit murder?"

Andréa replied, "You might be able to get him with just the tape, but that is really pushing it. I would be a fool to go in there with only one witness. I need more than that. You boys really have your work cut out for you. With the evidence that you have, you can only hold him for twenty-four hours, then you have to release him.

Do you think that Mr. Eisner will talk in the interrogation room?"

ADRIAN

Matt said, "That probably wouldn't work either, especially if he is not under treatment. It would be like talking to a wall. I don't think we would be able to shake him down like the way it worked on the woman."

"As it stands now, Mr. Eisner will remain on the streets until we can gather more concrete evidence. I wanted to talk to him today and see whether I could make a deal or something. Unfortunately, you couldn't get him and you couldn't hold him. Sorry gentlemen, our meeting is over. I will see my way out. Good-day."

Andréa left the station empty handed. Matt and Mike thought that this was enough to put him away, but they need concrete proof to back it up. They were frustrated that all their efforts were not enough.

Matt still figured that the girl that Adrian hung around with might be of value. As for now, they would continue the surveillance and see if any hard evidence showed up. Until then, Adrian was a free man.

Chapter Twenty

Early that evening, Adrian arrived at the Awareness Society for the support group for men. This was the place where alcoholics met and tried to gain strength and fight their addiction. Adrian did not have a single clue on how to stop drinking. He was hoping that he could learn something from the others.

He went upstairs to the third floor and found the door with their sign on it. He opened the door and looked around. He heard men's voices coming from down the corridor and followed the sounds. There he saw several men gathered in a makeshift circle.

Adrian asked the men, "Is this the men's support group?"

They responded with a 'yes' and directed Adrian to sign in the attendance sheet.

It was almost six-thirty and the meeting should be starting very soon. Adrian was curious if this was all it will take to cure his problem or if it would have be more aggressive.

The councillor came in and took his seat of authority. They started off with their usual formalities and the councillor gave Adrian a break-down of how the group worked. The group session started with each individual doing a check-in to report how their past week had gone for them.

Adrian was surprised that most of the men were doing very well and had been sober for quite some time. They barely mention the word "alcohol." He did notice that some of the men were meeting-freaks. They attended several days a week at different alcohol programs and most of their spare time was involved with yapping all week long.

This was not the route that Adrian was willing to take. He didn't want to spend all his time stuck in a roomful of alcoholics! One or two meetings a week suited Adrian much better.

Finally, it was Adrian's turn to talk. He said, "My name is Adrian and I have choices. The way things are going for me, I don't see any suitable choices that can make me stop drinking. I do have an ultimatum with my physiatrist. Either I stop drinking or he will stop treating me for my manic-depression. Apparently, the amount of alcohol that I consume disables the healing effect of the medication.

For as long as I drink, the medications will never have a chance to do the job they were designed to do. It basically leaves me mentally disabled even while I am taking the medication.

Right now, I am having a terrible time with my mental condition which is rendering me out of control. That is my greatest fear, which has been a way of life for me for over thirty years. Many dangerous things can happen when you are no longer in control of your own mind and actions.

I also suffer from dissociated episodes where I lose touch with reality and enter my own private and secure world. This blocks the effects of the mental and physical anguish that I would be going through on the outside world. My mind and soul just shut right down and become unaffected by emotions or morals.

I am then at the mercy of my environment. The disassociation is my guide to what my actions may be.

The most usual emotion that I do get is the one between my legs. I become like a sexual animal stalking his prey. It is an uncontrollable urge which leads me into immoral or even illegal situations. It causes severe problems with my wife and other social affairs.

There is no choice available at this time. It is pure luck, even if I make it home alive that night. I cut my body to shock myself back into reality so that I can gain control of myself again. My moods linger on for months or even years in a depressed state with interruptions of mania in between.

It is emotionally and physically draining. It is relentless in how it batters down my self-esteem and confidence in myself. I am nothing more than an empty shell of a man, unable to continue my daily battle with mental illness.

This is why I drink fifteen to twenty mugs of beer a day. It helps keep the hurting away and keeps me calm. I tend to be able to stay in better control of myself when I have been drinking. It is pure survival for me. This self-medication approach is effective in keeping my sanity intact. Thank-you that is all I have to say today."

The rest of the people who hadn't spoken yet, all had their turn to speak up. After the check-in, those who smoke went for a smoke break for about ten minutes. They then gathered back into the room for the next part of the session. The councillor then took control of the group and started off with a topic and open forum.

The councillor took notice of Adrian's speech and tried to help by revealing that there really is a choice even if you are ill.

He said, "As time goes on and your recovery takes hold, something will click inside of you and cause you to open your heart and listen.

People can tell you over and over again that alcohol abuse is dangerous, but if you're only listening with your ears and mind, the message will never get through. You have to find things that you would rather do than drink.

Try to find something to do that alcohol effects the enjoyment of that activity. A choice has to be made. Do I want a drink or do I want to have fun or work? You can't have it both ways; you have to decide which one you would rather do. The more activities that are involved in your life that you enjoy, the less important alcohol will become in your life.

The more tools that you have in your toolbox; the easier it becomes to repair the damage. You have to make a decision before you get sick. It is too late once you are in an episode. You are unaware of your thoughts or feelings when you are ill. You have to catch it well enough in time before it starts, and make a conscience decision of what your heart tells you to do."

Adrian understood what councillor said and it hit him quite hard. He found the information to be exciting and hopeful. He was very pleased that he had gained some real helpful information. The only thing was, now he had to put those words into practice. That was when the hard part began.

The meeting ended with the normal routine that they practiced as a group. Adrian came out of the meeting feeling good about himself and hopeful for the future. It was very uplifting to hear those words of wisdom; maybe he did have a chance to change.

On the way home, Adrian thought hard about the meeting and thought it was time to make some changes. He decided to take his recovery slowly and start off by not drinking during the day. He thought that if he allowed himself to have his beer at 7:00 pm, which would be cutting his drinking down by over half the amount he normally drank.

It would be a long journey and this was his first step towards the ultimate goal of sobriety. One small step at a time is the way to go.

Adrian arrived home, poured himself a draft and lit a cigarette. It seemed that it really was true, that he really did have a choice in his life whether he wished to drink or not. Tonight, he chose to drink and was confident that his moderate approach would be more successful than going cold turkey.

He relaxed at the kitchen table and thought over what the councillor had said. It made a lot of sense. The phone rang and Adrian answered.

"Hello." Carol said, "Samantha just called honey. I'm sorry, but your father just passed away about fifteen minutes ago."

"I'm going to the hospital whether Mom likes it or not. No one will stop me from saying my good-byes. Do you want to come?"

"Your mother was quite clear that she never wanted to see you again. If you are still convinced that you are going down there, I'll go with you."

"I know what she said and she can go to hell. I'll pick you up in fifteen minutes. Bye sweetheart."

Adrian hung up the phone and drove to pick up Carol. They arrived at the hospital, went to his room and entered quietly. Lillian was hugging and crying over her dead husband.

The whole family was there, grieving for their loss. There wasn't a dry eye in the entire room. Adrian went up to his father, gave him a hug and looked down at his lifeless body. Several emotions were swirling within him and one of them was anger. He was still angry with Harold because he had put him through hell with that foster family he was living with as a child.

Lillian frowned at Adrian and said, "I thought I told you to never come back."

"You can't take this moment away from me, so give it up already. You grieve the way you want and I will do it my way, just give it a fuck'n break for Dad's sake."

Lillian was not happy, but she decided that Adrian could stay and mourn with the others.

Adrian said, "Mom, let me pay for the funeral and all expenses; it is something that I want to do."

Lillian wasn't going to pass up the opportunity to have her husband taken care of for free. She acknowledged the gesture and agreed that the funeral would be carried out to Harold's wishes.

Adrian stood at his father's side. For some reason, he didn't feel any sadness or sorrow for this man. He was almost happy that he was gone. It felt like a big burden had been lifted off his shoulders.

Adrian did regret not telling his father a dark secret, which had been eating away at him for over thirty years.

Now the old man would never know about the horrible mistake he made in getting rid of Adrian.

One by one, family members were filing out of the room after making their peace. Lillian and Adrian were the last people to finally have finished saying their farewells. Carol was pleased that Adrian had his own time to grieve as well.

"Mom, do you want a ride home? I'm going to be driving right past your place anyway," Adrian asked.

With tears still in her eyes, she accepted the offer. Adrian drove everyone home and returned to the mansion. He returned to the mug of beer that was left on the kitchen table and lit a cigarette.

He couldn't help but think of his torturous childhood living in that foster home. Since he got the news about his Dad, old memories were being stirred up and brought to the surface again.

His childhood days were haunting him all over again. The nightmares and memories were returning and putting Adrian into turmoil. The memories were still very fresh in his mind, even though it happened over three decades ago. Adrian couldn't seem to let it go; the emotional pain was still all too real.

He should have told his father about it.

Maybe the old man would have accepted the fact that Adrian would have been much better off staying with the Eisners. He was not quite sure if Harold would have even believed him anyway.

Harold was very set in his own ways and couldn't listen to reason. The Eisners truly believed that they were doing the best thing possible in the interest of the boy. Adrian didn't believe that story for one second; he thought that was a crock of shit.

He believed that they didn't know how to handle a twelve-year old with severe mental ailments. The easiest way to solve the problem was to get rid of the boy. That was the route that the Eisners chose and Adrian would never forgive them for doing that.

Adrian got up, refilled his mug with beer and returned to his seat. Rather than feeling sad about his Dad's passing, he was more mad than anything else.

Anyway, he had to connect with his Mom several times during the next few days to set up funeral arrangements. That would be a chore all on its own, trying to survive in the same room as Lillian.

Adrian felt good about paying for the funeral; he really wanted to help in the family's hour of need. He remained in deep thought and tried to calm down the anxiety that he was feeling. He was starting to feel agitated and hyper.

Thoughts were returning with a vengeance, making Adrian very nervous. He started to increase his beer consumption in an effort to calm himself down. Cigarette after cigarette, Adrian chain smoked, trying to ease his nerves.

Nothing was working. Perhaps, tonight Adrian would take his medication and that would put him in a more stable and controllable state of mind. It would also allow him to have a good solid sleep that he desperately needed. He needed all the strength he could muster to handle the next few days. He got up, took his medication and washed it down with a couple of gulps of beer. He decided to call it a night and hopefully tomorrow would be a better day.

The next morning at 5:00 am, Adrian woke up from a great sleep. The medication had worked like a dream. He headed to the washroom for his morning rituals. After his shower, he got dressed and ready for work. First of all, it was time for him to go to Carol's house and take care of the dog.

Fifteen minutes later, he arrived at the house. He opened the door and Blackie came and greeted him with a big waggy tail. He let the dog out into the yard so that he could do his business. Adrian then called him into the house and got his food and water ready. The dog went frantic for his breakfast; it was his favourite time of day.

Adrian got the coffee pot brewing and went downstairs for a cigarette. Carol should be up in about ten minutes.

He turned on the radio to listen to his favourite station. He smoked his cigarette and patiently waited for the coffee. He could hear Carol's footsteps on the creaky floor upstairs. He went upstairs and got a cup of coffee, returning back downstairs for a cigarette.

He had a bit of a dry mouth this morning, due to one of the side effects of the medication that he was taking. Other than that, he felt physically well.

However, when he sat alone, his mind conjured up those horrid memories of his childhood. He couldn't get rid of those thoughts. They were cutting right through into his heart and soul. Why was this happening now?

So many years had passed. Why were these hauntings returning back so vividly? It felt like he was reliving the past all over again. The feelings of a frightened and shocked little boy were playing over and over again in his mind.

It sounded like Carol had finished her shower, so Adrian butted out his cigarette and returned upstairs. Carol was getting dressed for work when Adrian said, "Good morning sweetheart."

"Good morning honey. How are you?"

"I don't know. Ever since I heard about my Dad being ill, terrible memories of my childhood have been resurfacing. I can't seem to shake it off. It is bugging the shit out of me. I almost forgot those memories; they haven't bothered me for years. For some reason, my father's passing has triggered them to return. I am reliving that pain all over again."

"What kind of memories are you talking about?"

Adrian was reluctant when he said, "It has been a secret for thirty years. I have never told anyone this. I feel that I have to talk about it so that the memories will disappear.

I was twelve years old and living in the foster home when I was sexually assaulted by my older foster brother. I had no idea what he was doing. Twelve year olds don't even know about things like that. I didn't know he was going to do that!

When he entered me, I flew into a shock and fought back. After a struggle, I was able to break free, out of harm's way.

I looked back at him and he was finishing off the job solo. It was witnessed by four other children. They just stood there emotionless and stared; no one ever spoke about that incident until today."

"Why didn't you tell me this before?"

"I never told you because it never bothered me until a couple of days ago. Men are somewhat reluctant about things like this. It stirs up a lot of emotions. You feel embarrassed, shamed and guilty all at the same time.

I feel like I should have known better than to listen to him. I should have never let it happen."

"You were only a kid! You didn't know what he was going to do. It wasn't your fault!"

"I know in reality that it wasn't my fault, but my heart tells me otherwise. I can't help but have those feelings."

Adrian went into the kitchen to make Carol her tea. She was shocked to hear that he had kept such a dark secret all these years. It must have been eating him alive, having never talked about this before.

He had so many tragedies in his life and yet he never spoke of this one. It was no wonder why he had so many emotional problems and why he drank so much.

Carol couldn't imagine herself going through such a life and not relying on drugs or alcohol. Adrian had actually done quite well for himself, considering all the obstacles he had to face in his life. He got married and bought a house. He was reasonably coping in the best way he could.

Adrian finished getting the tea and put it on the kitchen table at Carol's place setting. He sat down with a fresh coffee right across from where she sat. Carol finished dressing and came and sat down.

She said, "How do you feel, now that you told someone your dark secret?"

Adrian remarked, "I think this is only the beginning. It seems that I have to explore this in detail before the burden will lift off my shoulders. I am not sure what this will include, but I know that it isn't over yet.

The memories are still haunting me of that day at the swimming hole. We were innocent kids having fun, not having a care in the world. Then this happened.

This monster turned my whole world upside down. I thought that it really didn't affect me. I thought that I bounced right back like a trooper. I now realize that he must have done more damage to me emotionally, than I ever really believed."

"Do you have an idea as to how you can rid yourself of these horrible memories?"

"No, I don't have a clue as to where to start. I presume that telling you was a step in the right direction. I think it has to come out in the open before I can learn to accept what happened. Then it might change my feelings of guilt and shame."

"When do you see Dr. Moss? Maybe, you should tell him about it. He might be able to help you."

"I don't see him for another three weeks. I really can't believe that it is hitting me so hard now. Why didn't it affect me before? I just can't get it out of my head."

"Well, it was a very traumatic time of your life. Maybe you blame your Dad for the assault because he is the one that put you in the foster home.

It was Harold who put you in that position in the first place; that's probably why you are angry at him. You actually blame him for the assault."

"I think you hit the nail on the head," Adrian said. "That is exactly how I feel. I know that is the reason why I'm so angry at him. I have always blamed him for that."

Carol was carefully watching the clock so that she didn't miss her bus for work. Time flew by while they were engaged in this serious conversation. She got up and said, "Well, it's time to go back to that hell hole."

She went to the living room, put on her coat and knapsack and opened the front door. Adrian and Blackie were at the door to see her off. She and Adrian exchanged several kisses. Blackie received a real big send off. She then left and Adrian went back to the kitchen to fill his coffee mug. He went downstairs where he could enjoy his coffee and cigarette.

Meanwhile, back at the Ruzo residence, Matt was getting the coffee pot on. He took his regular seat and wondered how he could get some hard evidence to back up the tapes. They may just have to settle with a conspiracy to murder charge on Adrian.

That was the only real evidence they had. They needed more witnesses who could collaborate with Mrs. Capelin's story.

Matt was thinking that they might be able to lean on some more employees of the mansion. Unfortunately, most of them took residence in the mansion and getting near them would be impossible. He got up and took a cup of coffee before the machine finished brewing. He sat back down and was disgusted that they were stuck.

Somebody had to know something! It was a huge military assault and no one could prove who was actually involved.

Matt was even thinking of contacting Columbia to see if their police force could dig up information from the assault team themselves. Maybe a disgruntled soldier would be willing to give up some information on the assault.

If they could get names of who was involved in the massacre and link Adrian to it that would be the magic bullet that they were looking for!

Matt was deep in thought, when he heard Emily call for him. They did their normal routine and he put some breakfast out in front of his daughter. Matt thought that maybe the Columbia route might be the way to do it. He sat back down and thought hard about how they could go about this.

It would all start with a simple phone call. That would at least get the ball going. He could hear Mike's car pull up and knew that in a couple of minutes, the sickening cheerfulness of Mike would blow in like the wind. Sure enough, there was the quick rap at the door and the grand entrance.

"Good morning everyone! How's the gang today?"

Matt and Emily were both not as enthusiastic as Mike with their replies.

Mike shrugged his shoulders and got a cup of coffee. He sat down and said, "Matt, did you come up with any ideas of how we can make a case against Adrian?"

Matt replied, "I did come up with one new idea. I was thinking that we should get the Columbia police force involved and they can conduct their own investigation from their end."

Mike sounded unsure when he said, "I don't think that would ever happen. You have a corrupt police force trying to gather information from a battalion of six-hundred mercenaries. Even if the police are not corrupt, what do you think their chances are of ever getting an interview?"

"I never thought of that. It is the same situation with us trying to get Azario. I guess the mercenaries would also have a death penalty for traitors. That would probably be their code of honour.

Besides, they probably won't bite the hand that feeds them. Azario is safe, once again. I thought I had a good brainstorm going on there for a while."

Mike said, "I guess the best thing we can do right now, is to keep on watching Adrian and see if he makes any new contacts. He might confide in some one. A new idea just hit me. Why don't we shake down Mrs. Eisner? Maybe Adrian has told her something."

"That is a very good idea, but I think we should let their fragile relationship grow before we do that. He probably didn't tell her anything yet.

I think they are still busy mending fences between the two of them. They are still living separately. We will watch the relationship grow and then we'll bring her in."

"We could always give Mrs. Capelin another shot after some more time has passed. She might learn new information in some time as well," said Mike.

"We still have that girl that Adrian has being seeing lately. I think we should still keep an eye on them too, before we pull her in.

Anyway, I'm going to take a shower and get ready for work. Mike, give it more thought and see if you can come up with something."

Matt stomped upstairs to do his normal morning ritual.

Later that day, Adrian found himself at the Centurion Chapter. He opened the door and saw that Francis the receptionist was on duty. He remembered talking to her on the phone.

"Hello Francis. My name is Adrian Eisner. We talked on the phone briefly last week. I'm here for the self-help support group."

"Yes Adrian, I remember the call. Just go through this door and turn left. It is the third door on the right."

"Thank-you Francis."

ADRIAN

Adrian found the door and went in. He found himself a chair and took a seat. There were about ten people in there and the foreman introduced himself. He said, "My name is Joe, welcome to the dual-disorders support group. What is your name?"

"My name is Adrian."

Joe went over a brief introduction for Adrian's sake, since he was a newcomer. Then the group did a check-in around the table. There were addictions and illnesses of all types. These people were in some pretty bad shape socially.

There was everything from people being homeless to others trying to live on small disability checks. The drugs ranged from marijuana, rock cocaine to heroin. The types of alcoholics were also different. There were the daily drinkers, binge drinkers, and the wandering drunk type.

It was very sad to see these poor people who had fallen through the cracks of society. The breakdown of the medical system was not able to support the need of these people. There weren't enough hospital beds. These people could not afford their medication so they got mediocre medications that didn't cost as much.

These meds didn't do the job that the expensive drugs did. They got the cheap and insufficient medications, while the upper class got the good meds that people with money could afford.

It was Adrian's turn to speak, and he said, "My name is Adrian. I have been diagnosed with bipolar-depression, psychosis, and disassociation. My addiction of choice is alcohol. I am a daily drinker who can withstand large amounts of booze without really getting drunk.

The reason I came is because my medication won't work for as long as I am addicted to booze. I will remain ill forever until I can stop my addiction.

I have constant bouts with manias and depression in which I lose control of my mind and actions.

Anything can happen during these episodes. One thing that really scares me is that my libido goes out of control. I become sexually hyper and am compelled to screw anything at anytime. The feeling lasts all day and all night; I am always sexually aroused. It is a very dangerous situation that could lead to affairs or sexual assault. Neither of these conditions are acceptable behaviour as I see it.

I take six mg. of anti-psychotic that completely cures me of that problem. It also helps me fight against psychosis in which one time I rewrote the New Testament and thought that I was the new messenger of God.

I also am cured of that as well. I take four-hundred and fifty mg. of an anti-depressant, fifteen hundred mg. of a mood stabilizer, fifty mg. of tranquilizers and four-hundred mg. of anti-histamine.

As you can see, I am heavily medicated. It really makes one hell of a difference in my condition. The only thing that I suffer from now is constant bouts of disassociation. I lose total control when my mind leaves behind reality and slips into my own private world.

I become unaware of the outside world and enjoy the pleasures of my own safe place. Usually high stress will trigger these episodes and my mind just shuts off.

I am then unable to feel any pain or anguish that may be causing this stress. I cut my body so that it shocks my mind back into reality. It seems to be a little gross, but it is most effective.

I use alcohol to deaden any pain or anguish before it affects my mind. By staying calm and relaxed with booze, I then remain in full control of myself.

Medication cannot cure disassociation, but booze can get rid of the stress that triggers it. I am still not sure what I will be able to do about the stress if I don't have alcohol anymore. That is all I have to say, thank-you."

There was still some time left in the hour for an open discussion. The group decided to talk about Adrian's problem with stress and booze. They were trying to come up with ideas on how to cope with stress. There were some very good ideas, but you really had to be able to spot signs of trouble before you entered a stressful period.

The meeting ended with the group's normal rituals and everyone left the room feeling a little better than when they came in. Adrian felt very bad for those poor people. He had an entourage of three limos and those people either walked or had a disability bus pass. Their lives were so different, yet the illnesses were so similar.

ADRIAN

Adrian went back to the mansion a very humbled man. This experience was very enlightening and sad. He arrived at the mansion and went upstairs to his suite. He sure wanted a beer really bad!

He didn't know what he could do in the place of having a drink. He was confronted with making the decision whether he wanted to drink or not. He sat at the kitchen table and lit a cigarette. He thought long and hard about what kind of activities he enjoyed.

Suddenly, something struck him. He loved writing in his journal. He had tons of topics that could be covered. So many things had happened to him in the past couple of months that he could write forever! Adrian was driven with excitement and he raced to the computer in his office and started writing.

This was truly his love. Before he knew it, Adrian quickly forgot about the craving for a drink and was highly involved in his writing. The words flowed through his fingertips with ease. He wrote with passion and intensity. Time quickly slipped away; hours passed like minutes.

It was well past his promise of 7:00 pm where he would allow himself to drink. He had found his true passion.

Two days had passed and Adrian was getting dressed for the funeral. He couldn't wait until this was over! Spending all his time with Lillian was like living out a nightmare. Adrian didn't care; it was too late to resolve that matter. He might never be able to lift himself out of this burden. Maybe, if he had told his father, things might have been different between them.

Adrian lit a cigarette and sat down at the kitchen table. He had remarkable progress in cutting his drinking down by over half. He had kept his promise to himself for three days now. It was going to be a long journey to sobriety, but at least this was a good start. The meeting that he had attended gave him the support and ideas of how to make that conscious decision of not having that drink.

Adrian finished his cigarette, phoned Michael and told him to bring the car up front. He was going to pick up Carol and Lillian and then head off to the church.

About forty-five minutes later, the limo pulled out in front of the church with the three. They entered the church and completed their Christian rituals.

They gathered up their bravery, before walking down the aisle to view the body. Lillian was very shaken up by this experience; she almost passed out. Her legs were starting to give out on her. Adrian and Carol grabbed her by each arm and guided her to the first pew to sit down.

Adrian knew in his heart that it should have been a closed casket ceremony. Lillian insisted that she wanted it open, so that everyone could say their final farewells. Adrian understood Lillian's shock; the body didn't even look like Harold as he did when he was alive. Adrian could not recognize him as being Harold at all.

Poor Lillian was a wreck. Adrian wasn't sure if she could even make it through the ceremony. He didn't know how she would be when they had to go to the grave site. He hired a choir that were singing all of Harold's favourite gospel songs. The voices were beautiful and made the service seem more special for the sake of Harold and Lillian.

The eulogy was done by Harold's younger brother. He touched on Harold's past from a menacing youngster to a war hero in World War II. Most importantly, he mentioned that he had an unconditional love that was shared with Lillian.

Lillian broke down and sobbed heavily during the speech. The words were very beautiful and they all came from the heart. The priest said his final words and the service then proceeded to the grave site, the final resting place of Harold Eisner.

This was even harder for Lillian to handle. She cried in agony of a broken heart. She had truly loved this man and now he was gone. Adrian and Carol were holding up the semi-conscious woman from passing out completely.

The priest conducted the final prayers as quickly as possible to help alleviate the pain and suffering of the widow. The ceremony ended and the family were left alone, huddled together in their sorrow.

Adrian had made arrangements with the Women's Auxiliary to put on sandwiches, treats and coffee in the basement of the church. The guests then proceeded to the church, waiting for the arrival of the family members.

The family came into the small hall about a half-hour later and took their seats at a specially designated table.

ADRIAN

Adrian went to the table where the food was and got his mother something to eat and drink while she sat down. Lillian was bombarded with people expressing their condolences and sorrow. Adrian placed her lunch in front of her, but it didn't look like she would be eating for awhile.

Adrian and Carol then went to get their own lunch and coffees and sat down at the family table. The family received overwhelming sympathy from the guests.

Harold was a well-loved man and had touched many people's heart except for Adrian. Adrian did not have any love in his heart for this man, only anger.

Everyone thought that Adrian was strong to withstand the services and take care of the distraught widow. It wasn't like that at all. Adrian just didn't have any feelings for Harold whatsoever. He really didn't care either way if Harold was alive or not. The only reason he showed up at the funeral at all, was to have respect for his grieving mother.

After a few hours, the guests started to dwindle. Lillian was now ready to go home. The Auxiliary finished putting the food away and cleaned up the hall. Adrian thanked them for their help and gave them two thousand dollars for their service. He then left and took Lillian and Carol home.

Upon arrival at his suite, Adrian decided to break his promise for one day. The stress of the funeral and everything had taken its toll on Adrian. He entered the suite and poured himself a cold mug of draft.

He sat down at the kitchen table and lit a cigarette. Instantly, he felt the pressure easing with a couple of good gulps of beer. He was slowly drifting away into his own world. He stared relentlessly at the wall, sipping his beer and smoking his cigarette.

All was peaceful and calming while Adrian was in his own little piece of paradise. His mind, heart and soul were numb. Nothing could break through and hurt him now. There were no memories or thoughts, just a peaceful nothing. He sat emotionlessly with his wild stare.

Doris had noticed that Adrian was not responding to the noise or activities that she was involved with while cleaning the suite. She was not sure if she should try to wake him out of his deepened state of mind. He sure looked scary! That stare was piercing right through that wall. She decided to let him be. Besides, he wasn't hurting anyone.

The semi-conscious Adrian got up, refilled his beer and sat down again. He was oblivious to his surroundings and quietly drank his beer. Doris watched over him for the afternoon, to ensure that he was alright. She was making his dinner and kept one eye on him the whole time.

Doris finished the dinner and put the plate in front of him. Adrian didn't snap out of it. He was not even aware that his dinner was ready.

Doris walked up to Adrian and gave him a solid shake and said, "Sir!! Your dinner is ready. Eat it before it goes cold."

Adrian snapped out of his trance in a flash and almost put his elbows in his dinner.

"Eat up sir; don't let your steak get cold."

It took several minutes for Adrian to re-adjust to the sudden shock of reality. Once he got his bearings straight, he started to eat his dinner. He had now returned among the living.

Doris was starting to clean the pots and pans and asked, "Sir, what happens to you when you look like you are in a trance?"

Adrian replied, "It's called a disassociate state. I lose touch with reality and enter a safe place where stress and emotions can't harm me.

My mind basically shuts right off. It was caused by some kind of trauma when I was a little kid. It still affects me to this very day."

"I have never seen anything like it before. It is actually amazing that it still affects you after all these years. You must have some kind of demon in you, which will do that."

"You're right. I do. I am only starting to discover it now."

"Can you ever be cured of this condition?"

"I don't know. I have had it for over thirty years and I haven't been able to find anything that helped yet. Sometimes, the condition becomes useful and I can use it to my advantage. When the stress is too high, I just shut my mind off and carry on with the task. This leaves me unaffected by emotions or stress."

"So, you learned how to adapt."

"Yes I did. I've been under a lot of stress the last couple months or so, and my ability helps me from going insane. It's like a safety mechanism. When the heat gets too hot, the brain just shuts down."

"It sounds like it can be more useful rather than harmful."

"Sometimes it's useful and other times it can be very dangerous. You lose total control of yourself. You are no longer in the driver's seat and your fate is up in the air. You are capable of anything at this point; there are no boundaries that you won't cross. Morals or legally, none of these things are an issue when you are in this state of mind."

"Is that why you were able to do the things that you did recently?"

"Yes, I would have never been able to accomplish certain tasks normally. I have to call up my dark side and complete the task. It protects me from my normal moral values which would inhibit me from doing certain things. Without morals, you are capable of anything."

"That sounds very frightening sir."

"It is. This is especially true for the other person on the receiving end. It is most terrifying for them."

"Are you finished your dinner sir?"

"Yes Doris. It was delicious, thank-you."

Doris put the remaining dishes in the dishwasher. She then wiped down the counters and kitchen table. "Well sir, I am finished for tonight. I'll see you bright and early tomorrow morning."

"Ok Doris. Have a good evening, good-night."

Doris grabbed her coat and went to meet her husband out front.

Adrian relaxed with a couple mugs of draft when the phone rang. It was the front gate guard. He said, "Sir, a Lori Metcalfe has called for you. Should I let her in?"

"Yes, let her in."

Adrian hung up the phone and patiently waited for Lori to arrive. About five minutes passed and there was a knock at the door.

Adrian answered the door and said, "Hi Lori, please come in. It's a nice surprise to see you tonight. Do you want a drink?"

Lori replied, "Yes, that would be nice. I'll have a rye and ginger please."

Lori took a seat on the chesterfield and took off her coat. Adrian handed her the drink and he sat on the bar stool.

"To what do I have this honour of you visiting me?"

"I was bored sitting at home alone and I thought that a visit with a friend would break up the evening a bit."

"Yeah...I was bored myself. You were a beam of sunshine, when I heard that you were at the gate. So, how have you been?"

"Things are busy at work, but my evenings are usually quiet. I just veg out for a while, and then I go to bed. Nothing too exciting usually happens. How about you?"

"I buried my father today. That was enough excitement to last me a lifetime.

This week I had to have a working relationship with my mother, which almost killed me. We spent three days together making arrangements for the funeral. I am very pleased that it is over; now I can relax."

"I'm sorry to hear about your father. Maybe I should come back another day."

"No, don't leave. I want your company tonight. Don't worry about it. We were not that close. There was really no love lost between us."

"Why were you not close to your father? What made you drift apart?"

"We never were very close. When I was twelve years old, he put me in a foster home.

I started to resent him for that and we really split off in our different ways. I had a horrible childhood and I blame him for it. Even on the day of his funeral, I don't feel any remorse for being angry at him."

"The foster home couldn't have been that bad; they are sponsored by the government."

"Oh...yes it was. Everything that you can imagine happened in that house. It was a hellish nightmare living there. The kids were so traumatized by the experiences they suffered that no one opened their mouth. That house was full of dirty secrets. Only today, after more than thirty years, did I ever reveal to anyone my secret. This morning I told my wife about it for the first time."

Lori was curious and asked, "What was so bad that you kept it a secret all these years?"

Shamefully Adrian replied, "I was sexually assaulted by an older kid when I was twelve years old. The memories have just recently come back to me, since I heard that my father was dying. I unjustly blame my father for the assault. That is why I am so angry at him."

Lori was shocked and said, "That's a pretty big burden to carry for all of these years. How did you manage to survive it?"

"I'm not sure. Somehow, it didn't affect me at all, or I didn't think it did. I just carried on with life in the best way I could. Until now, the memories were buried deep inside. I never gave it a second thought. My dad's death triggered the pain and emotions to come back to me. I am having one hell of a hard time getting over it."

"It sounds like post-traumatic stress syndrome. You are reliving the emotions of a traumatic time of your life triggered by a close emotional tie to the event. That would be your father's passing. You are now experiencing the horror of that event, but only thirty years later."

Adrian was feeling a bit scared of what was yet to happen now. If this is true, how does he stop it?

"What do I do about it? I'm going nuts!"

Lori suggested, "I believe you need professional counselling from an expert in the field. They have such places for women; there has to also be one for men."

"I've been thinking about telling my psychiatrist about this; maybe he can help me. I don't think I can do it alone anymore."

"That's a good start. If he can't help you, he can refer you to someone who can. You need to talk to someone who knows what you are going through. They can guide you to recovery."

"Everything is happening all at once. I am on a program to help me stop drinking. I'm on another program to help deal with my mental illness and my addiction. Now, I have this problem. I can't seem to handle the overload; it's just too much."

Lori asked, "How did you handle yourself for the past couple of months? This was big news. It must have also been very traumatic being the head honcho of organized crime in the city. Yet, you were able to destroy Manicotti and his whole network all in one blow."

Adrian replied, "I have this special ability that when things are too stressful or emotional, I can shut off my mind and call upon my dark side. With no emotions or morals to get in my way, I am capable of anything. I use my disassociate state to my advantage to do whatever is necessary to do at the time."

"Even if it means murder?"

Adrian nodded his head and said, "Especially murder. I couldn't possibly do that if my morals were intact.

I am not normally a violent man; actually I tend to be quite charming. But when the high stress is eminent, the darkness takes over and I can become a killer."

"Did you personally ever kill anyone?"

"Yes, I killed seven men in the last two months. There was Tony Lorenzo who was swindling money from Mr. Azario. I was forced to kill him, because I would have been killed myself if I didn't follow Mr. Azario's orders. Then there was my brother, Jonathan. I was the only one who knew what he was thinking, because our emotional and mental capabilities were so similar. I was basically forced to kill him because of the rampage he had on the city. Someone had to stop him and I was the best candidate for that job.

Then there was a Mr. Juan Cortez who decided that he and others could run the empire better than me. The only way to stop a family mutiny was to kill Mr. Cortez and turn him into fertilizer. Soon after the incident, the other members followed my lead."

"What do you mean by fertilizer?"

"We strip them of their clothes and effects and burn them. Then we throw the body in the wood chipper that the gardener uses. We take the mulch, ashes and soil and mix them together. We then put the fresh fertilizer on the flower beds. Voila! We now have the most beautiful flowers in New York City, compliments of Mr. Lorenzo and Mr. Cortez.

Next, my sister was held captive by Manicotti.

The police wouldn't do anything to help, so I was forced to plan and conduct an assault on Manicotti. I killed one man in his sleep, while the assault team was getting ready to move in. I killed one unidentified guard in the hallway with a knife through the heart. Then I killed a man named Miguel with a burst of automatic fire. He was just about to kill Trixie when I entered the room. Fortunately, I got to him first.

Finally there was Manicotti and his revenge speech. I had heard enough from that asshole, so I blew his head off with automatic fire. That's it in a nutshell. I could have never been able to do those things normally. I dug out my dark side and did what was required at the time."

Lori said, "That is fascinating that you were able to do such things. All I see is a kind, gentle and caring man. Maybe one day, those memories will also come back to haunt you."

"I hope not. I have had my share of hauntings to last me a lifetime."

Chapter Twenty-One

That following Monday at the DA's office, two men in suits were waiting to see Andréa Shelton. They didn't have an appointment, but they were confident that she would really want to talk to them.

Andréa walked into the office and the receptionist said, "These gentlemen are from the law offices of Huntington and Brown. They said that they have something that you want."

Andrea said, "Thank-you Cheryl, let them in." The three entered Andréa's office and she said, "My name is Andréa Shelton. I am the District Attorney. How can I help you?"

One lawyer said, "My name is Charles Huntington. We understand that you are trying to build up a case against Adrian Eisner. I also understand that you do not have any solid proof. We have a business proposition for you, Miss Shelton. Allow us to join forces with you and we will disclose enough hard evidence to put Mr. Eisner away for a very long time."

Andréa thought about it and said, "Ok, what do you have?"

Huntington pulled out a tape recorder and put it on the desk. He plugged it in, put in a tape and said, "Listen closely."

Andréa couldn't believe what she was hearing. "Is that Adrian Eisner? How did you get this?"

The lawyer called Huntington responded, "Yes, that is a taped confession of Adrian Eisner. We had our private investigator befriend Mr. Eisner. Lori Metcalfe has been on the case for a couple of weeks already.

On Friday, Eisner felt he could trust her with the information and spilled his guts. Everything is on that tape. We will keep her on the case to see if there are any more developments."

Andréa said, "This is amazing! I am very surprised that he confided in her in such a short period of time. He must have been dying to unload his burden and picked her. Either Adrian is desperate or your investigator is very good."

Huntington replied, "The reason for his confession might be unclear. However, we do have solid proof that he committed murder and he planned the massacre on the Manicotti Mansion."

ADRIAN

The other lawyer said, "My name is Thomas Brown. This is enough information to bring him in and hold him until the trial starts. We are in the position where we can get him off the streets right now."

Andréa said, "Let's not ruin a good thing here. You have someone on the inside, don't blow it! We might be able to gather enough evidence to shut down the whole empire! Sit tight on this one, gentlemen. Miss Metcalfe is doing an excellent job; just let her continue at her own pace.

Adrian won't get away with what he has done. This new information was the shot in the arm that the case needed. Thank-you, gentlemen. Welcome aboard."

Meanwhile, at the Awareness Society, Adrian was waiting for his 10:00 o'clock meeting with Bonnie. She came out of the office and said, "Adrian come in. Have a seat. So, what has been going on for the last couple of weeks?"

"I am having a very difficult time. Controlling my alcohol problem seems to be the least of my problems right now."

"Why is that?"

"My Dad died last week and it has stirred some horrible memories of my childhood. I was sexually assaulted when I was twelve years old and those memories have all come back to me thirty years later.

It's as if I am reliving my childhood all over again. The moment I saw my Dad in the casket, there was this rush of tragedy overtaking my mind. I blame my Dad for the assault. If it wasn't for him putting me in that hell hole of a foster home, none of that would have happened. I am angry at him for putting me there. That's the only thing that keeps on haunting me. I drink to ease the pain and the rush of emotions that overwhelm me.

It was his incompetence as a father that led me to disaster. I had manic depression and instead of dealing with it like a nurturing father, he just handed his problem to someone else. He washed his hands clean of any memory of me being his son.

I'm also angry at myself for being so naive. I should have known better that to listen to my assailant. I should've figured out that he was up to no good. Why didn't a red light go on, when he told be to drop my bathing suit and bend over a rock? Why did I trust him that I was safe?

I had no idea what was happening. I didn't even know what an erection was. It totally surprised me; then panic set in and I fought to get away. Fortunately, I did manage to break free.

With my bathing suit wrapped around my ankles, I shuffled away from him. Looking back at him, I saw him masturbate. I felt humiliated and shameful.

The other kids just watched emotionlessly. It stayed a secret for over thirty years. It never bothered me before, but all of the sudden all those feelings and memories came rushing back. Only recently have I been able to talk about it."

Bonnie said, "It sounds like post-traumatic stress disorder. The link between your father and the assault is evident. Then, when your father died, it triggered off those memories of that horrible incident. You are experiencing the whole incident all over again.

There are grounding techniques that you can use to help you stay grounded from a disassociate state. That is a time when your mind becomes flooded with these memories; you can then bring yourself into the present time."

"A while ago, my doctor told me that I have a disassociation problem caused by a traumatic experience. I used to cut myself to ground myself back into reality. I either do that, or pick the scabs to ground myself."

Bonnie said, "Those things are very common among sexual assault survivors. It was a useful skill at the time of the assault; however it has out-grown its usefulness today. No one will hurt you now; you are safe here. Even the cutting and the scab picking were useful in keeping you in the present. Those skills are no longer needed. There are other ways to help you cope.

You can always look at a picture of your wife to keep you in the present time, or have some item in your pocket that you can touch and feel. Look around the room and keep your mind occupied with things that are in the present not the past."

Adrian said, "The thoughts just won't go away. My feelings are very raw right now. The alcohol helps me get through the tough times and allows me to relax. The stress and tension is too much to handle all at once."

"You are going through a very difficult time right now. What do you think would happen if you didn't have a drink?"

"I would get into a fit of anxiety and agitation that would constantly gnaw at me until I finally gave in and had that drink. I usually feel better after the second drink."

Bonnie asked, "If you feel better after only two beers, why do you drink more?"

"I don't know. Maybe it's not enough to totally put me into ease. I've cut down my drinking by over fifty percent. I drink only after 7:00 pm, except the day of the funeral.

My short-time goal is to go a week or two like this, and then cut it down by another fifty percent until I don't drink at all. I can handle a gradual decrease much easier than going cold turkey. It seems to suit me just fine this way."

Bonnie said, "That is excellent Adrian! I am very proud of you. You have had some very serious things happen and you are still able to stand tall and give it your best. Well done!"

Adrian replied, "I think if I take it one day at a time, I may be able to give it up.

The support group was very helpful and it gave me hope and that I do have choices. The councillor is very good at what he does. I was pumped up with enthusiasm and felt good about myself. It gave me strength that I never knew I had. I felt that I was ready to take on that long winding road that lies beyond."

Bonnie said, "Let's take a look at what steps you are taking to help yourself. You see your psychiatrist. You see me every two weeks. There is the men's support group every Tuesday. What else?"

"I go to a dual-recovery support group every Wednesday at 4:30 pm. My psychiatrist is once a month and that's it."

"What are your goals?"

"I want to remain dry. I want my relationship with my wife to improve. I want to participate with my wife and dog on walks in the park. Maybe, I could take a more active role in my house with chores. My ultimate goal is to have a nice picnic with my wife and dog. That is when I am sure that I am clear of this demon."

Bonnie said, "That sounds like a great set of goals. So, the picnic is the finale for you, is it?"

"When I am cured, I will have a picnic with the family to celebrate," replied Adrian.

Bonnie said, "Our time is almost up. We'll set you up with an appointment in a couple of weeks' time."

"Ok, that sounds fine."

Adrian received his new appointment card and said, "Good-bye."

Meanwhile, at the station, the two detectives were in Matt's office yakking up a storm.

The phone rang and Matt answered, "Special Task Force, Lieutenant Ruzo speaking."

The voice on the other end said, "Matt, this is Andréa. I've got some great news for you. We have a taped confession from Mr. Eisner admitting to the planning of the Manicotti massacre and seven murders. We have a mole on the inside."

"How did you manage that?"

"The law offices of Huntington and Brown were here to see me this morning with the news. That girl that you wanted to talk to is a private investigator working for their office. She befriended Adrian, and eventually he trusted her and talked. She was wearing a wire. Isn't that great news?"

"That is fuck'n excellent news!! We got him by the balls now!"

"We're not going to break up the party yet. We're going to allow her to dig around a little. Maybe, she can bring the whole house down."

"Good idea. She is already in there; we might as well let her snoop around a little longer."

"I just had to tell you the good news. I have to go now. I'll talk to you later. Bye."

Matt hung up the phone and said, "You know that girl that we wanted to talk to. Well, it turns out that she is a private investigator and she is working as a mole in the Azario Mansion. She obtained a taped confession from Adrian admitting to the planning of the Manicotti massacre and seven murders. It's all on tape."

Mike said, "That is great news. What are we going to do now?"

"We're going to let her dig a little deeper and see if we can get enough dirt to bring down Azario too. We're going to take advantage of this opportunity and play it out."

"Isn't this a pretty gutsy move for the girl to be so close to the Azario's? If they find out about her, she is as good as dead."

"That's her job. She was aware of the risks when she first became an investigator. Now, she gets a chance to prove herself."

Later that evening, Adrian was participating in the men's support group. They were doing their check-in. The other men seemed to have had a rather good week, with the exception of a few personal problems they were trying to work out. Adrian listened intensely as the others spoke.

Then it was his turn. "My name is Adrian and I have choices. I had a disastrous week. I did manage to cut my drinking down by half and found something that is more important than booze.

I enjoy writing. I have a journal that I write and it keeps me occupied and away from the booze. I decided to slowly wean myself off alcohol rather than go cold turkey. I believe this method will greatly increase my chances of success.

My father died and I'm being bombarded by childhood memories that terrorize my mind. I am having a very difficult time with a childhood nightmare that was triggered off by my father's passing. I was sexually assaulted when I was twelve years old. I went thirty years without it affecting me.

Now, all of the sudden, it has come back to me in waves.

I am reliving my past all over again. The emotions and feelings are all still very fresh.

I blame my father for the event, because he put me in the foster home. I was assaulted by an older foster brother. If he didn't put me in there, things would have been much different. I use the alcohol to ease the pain and agony that I feel inside. Temporarily, I feel much better. I am then able to cope with it and carry on as usual.

I am so overwhelmed with these thoughts and memories that it really affects my daily routine. I find it difficult to work, or even just to relax. Even while writing the journal, I have included the event in there.

I am hoping that with talking about it, I might be able to rid this nightmare out of my mind and finally live in peace. I never told a soul for thirty years. Not until this week have I ever breathed a word. Now, I am opening up and letting my feelings go. That's all I have to say. Thank-you."

The rest of the group had their chance to speak, and then it was time for a smoke break. Adrian was relaxing and enjoying his cigarette. He was not sure if by telling people about his misadventure, that it was really helping.

It didn't seem to make the burden any lighter. It was time to go back to the group. Adrian butted out his cigarette and rejoined the group.

The councillor asked the group if he could address Adrian's problem. He said, "You are suffering from post-traumatic stress. You have to understand that it wasn't your fault. What did you do when he assaulted you?"

Adrian replied, "I fought tooth and nails."

"You didn't participate in the action and you did the best you could under those circumstances. I presume he was much bigger and stronger than you, yet you did your very best to fight him off. You could not have prevented it from happening. He had you as a target and he took advantage of your vulnerability.

You were vulnerable because you were put in a foster home away from the people you loved and felt safe with. You were trying to establish yourself in your new surroundings. You were more trusting and desperate to make friends and get along with others. It left you susceptible to an assault. You didn't do anything to taunt or tease your assailant; you were an innocent child. It was not your fault."

Adrian replied, "I know that in my mind that it wasn't my fault, but my heart tells me the opposite. I feel at fault, shameful and humiliated. The pain is very deep inside and I don't know what to do to feel better. It is eating me alive."

The councillor said, "I think you need to talk to a councillor who is an expert on sexual abuse for men. They have special techniques to help ease the stress caused by such an event. Talk to your doctor and get a referral. I think you have to deal with this issue head on."

The councillor and the group continued on with several useful topics on how to control your anger so that it doesn't turn into a fit of rage. The idea is to deal with each single problem as it occurs. Don't let the anger build up to a point to where you lose control.

ADRIAN

Take care of these problems while you are in full control and you will avoid the problems of going into a rage.

The meeting was coming to an end and the group proceeded with their normal ritual. The group then ended for the evening and Adrian went home. He opened the door to his suite and went inside. He went to the bar and poured himself a draft. He went to the kitchen table and lit a cigarette, sat down and took a sip of beer.

The meeting was very informative and he was very appreciative of the group for allowing the councillor to help him deal with his problem. They were a good bunch of men who were trying their best to better themselves. Adrian admired their courage to be able to fight this demon under any circumstance.

Many of them also had very troubled lives and had made major changes.

Some had gone through hell and still managed to stay sober. Adrian could not imagine himself to be that strong willed. He was finding out that two or three beers were enough to ease his nerves. If he could cut back to that amount, that would be a major breakthrough in his recovery.

He was determined to make this work. He had everyone working so hard for him that he just had to be successful in his recovery.

It was difficult, especially with everything that was going on. He could've been a lump of shit passed out in an alley somewhere. But he survived, and didn't let things keep him down. He pushed on, past all the tragedies and still came out semi-normal.

This was just another bump in the road that Adrian had to overcome. He was determined to live beyond the dark memories and survive. With a little help, even this would pass.

Two weeks passed and Adrian was all dressed and ready for work. Tonight was the big night; the G-Spot would be open for business. Adrian hadn't even let Trixie see it yet. He wanted to surprise her at the party tonight.

This was the first of the five businesses to re-open since Manicotti's men destroyed them. It was a long haul to start from scratch and re-design the place. Mr. Armstrong and his crews had done an excellent job; Adrian was extremely pleased with the finished product.

He was getting ready to go over to Carol's and spend some time with her and the dog. He got his keys and left the suite. Upon his arrival at the house, he could hear the dog on the other side of the door. He knew that Adrian was home and that he was going to get his breakfast soon.

Adrian opened the door and Blackie came out with a big greeting. Adrian bent down and gave him a good rub behind the ears; the dog just melted like putty. When he was satisfied with his greeting, the dog went out, quickly did his thing and came back in.

Adrian went and got the food and water and placed it on the floor mat. He went back to the kitchen and got the coffee going, and then went downstairs for a cigarette. As he was waiting for the coffee to brew, he was thinking of the progress he had made with his recent problem.

He went to his doctor's appointment a few days ago and got referred to the Male Survivors of Sexual Abuse Society.

He had his first appointment yesterday, and it made a big difference already. He was taught ways of how to stay in the present period and not drift off into the horrifying past. It really worked and he was relieved that he now had a coping strategy to help him get over it.

Adrian had really progressed well with cutting down on his alcohol. He was down to two beers a night. That was a significant drop from the fifteen to twenty mugs he was drinking a month ago. He thought that tonight would be an exception to the rule. It was a special event and he was going to treat himself. He butted out his cigarette and went upstairs.

He met Carol in the kitchen and gave her a kiss. "Good-morning, sweetheart."

"Good-morning, honey. Did you feed the dog?"

"Yeah...he's been fed already and he had his pee."

Carol patted Blackie on the head and said, "That's my good boy." The dog was waiting to be rewarded for his good behaviour. He got his usual two dog biscuits after breakfast when everyone was sitting down. Today was no exception.

Adrian put the tea on for Carol, while she was finishing getting ready for work. He sat down, enjoying his mug of coffee.

ADRIAN

After several minutes, Carol and the tea were ready. She sat down and said, "So, tonight is the grand opening. Are you excited?"

"I'm excited and nervous at the same time. I just hope that Trixie likes her new place."

"Don't worry, she'll love it. You really worked hard on that place and money was no object. She has no choice but to love it."

"You're right. The place does look great. This morning we are getting all of our food delivered fresh. There will be lots of good yummies to eat.

I just have to get the new dishes and silverware put through the washer and put the trimmings on the tables. That will be that, until 7:00 pm tonight.

I'll be there all day anyway for damage control. Things usually go wrong on opening day and I want to catch them before they get out of control. I want the staff to be able to know how to use the new equipment, especially the cooks. I even put in new stoves, fridges and exhaust fans. Everything is brand new."

Carol replied, "Wow! You really did go full out on this."

Adrian said, "Only the best, nothing less."

Carol looked at the time and said, "Well, here I go again, another day in that hell hole." She went and got her jacket and knapsack and waited at the door for her send off from the boys. They said their good-byes and Adrian went to refill his mug. He then went downstairs for a cigarette. After a couple more coffees, he'd take the dog for a walk and then go to work.

He was very excited about tonight. He was really looking forward to the big bash. The entertainment had only the best women in the business.

Every one of them was a headliner. Adrian had booked the entertainment for tonight; he was pretty well an expert on the subject.

Meanwhile at the Ruzo residence, Matt was already dressed and having his coffee. Emily ate her breakfast and was studying one of her school books for a test. Matt heard Mike's car drive up and anticipated Mike's every move. Sure enough, it was the same old thing. After the salutations, Mike grabbed a coffee, sat down and said, "When are we going to make a bust on Adrian?"

Matt replied, "I think we will hit him tomorrow night. They are having that big shin-ding at the G-Spot tonight. I don't think tonight would be a good idea; we'll wait until things are a little calmer. We might be able to catch him alone tomorrow after noon, especially if he sticks to his normal routine.

Lori Metcalfe has done an excellent job for us. We did manage to get more details out of Adrian. The jury should be able to make their minds up that he is guilty."

Mike said, "The deliberation shouldn't take longer than a couple of hours. They just have to review the evidence and that should be it. We could all then say good-bye to Adrian."

"Well, it looks like the case is finally coming to an end and so is our partnership," said Matt. Once Adrian is behind bars, you will have passed your assessment and be re-assigned with a permanent partner. Then you'll start your new career as Detective Parsons. What do you think about that?"

"I don't know. I really liked working for you. We made a good team and I learned a lot from you. I'm going to miss our morning coffees and your family."

"Just because we won't be partners anymore, doesn't mean you can't come over for your morning coffee. We could still do that if you want."

"I would like that, thank-you."

"You did a damn fine job for your first detective case. You earned my respect and gratitude, especially when you saved Emily from that monster. You grew on me; you're a good kid. You will make a great detective."

Mike blushed and said, "I couldn't have done it without your leadership. You taught me a lot of things that the academy does don't teach. It just turned out that our case was a real tough one.

Now, we are ready to bag the last of the bad guys and wrap it up. I still feel bad that Adrian decided to make the wrong decision and end up with Azario. He was a good man. He had his medical problems, but he still had his morals."

Matt said, "I don't know if there was anything else we could have done to protect Adrian from Azario. What we do know, is that Adrian's final choice was to go back to the mansion. No one forced him back there; that was his own decision. That will be taken into account at the trial."

"Do you think Adrian called off his goons?"

ADRIAN

"The surveillance team has been reporting that Adrian has been travelling alone and unprotected for the last couple of weeks.

It should be no problem picking him up now. However, the old man is still heavily guarded in the hospital. It's Adrian that we want anyway, and tomorrow is his big day."

Later that night at the G-Spot, Adrian was on pins and needles. The doors will open in five minutes. There was a large crowd lining up for blocks outside, waiting to see the improvements. Everything was done and Adrian was satisfied with all the details that were taken care of. The staff was well rehearsed with the new equipment and their duties.

Adrian stood at the door and looked at his watch as he counted down the final seconds. He then released the rope and allowed the crowd to file in. He went to his favourite table and sat down where he already had a beer waiting for him. He lit a cigarette and watched the faces of the patrons as they looked around the bar.

The crowd looked like they approved of the renovation. Everyone was all smiles and happy. The place filled up to maximum capacity within fifteen minutes; they had to keep some patrons waiting outside until there was more room available. Adrian relished this moment. It looked like all his hard work and the money spent was worth it.

Trixie was arriving at the bar at 7:30 pm; the place was already rocking. The entertainers were in full swing and the new sound system was a hundred times better than the old one. It looked like it was a very successful grand opening. There were five minutes to go before Trixie came over. Adrian went to the door with his beer and waited for the limo.

Several minutes passed and Adrian saw the limo coming down Davis. It parked in the reserved space and Trixie came out of the car. She looked sensational with a long black gown and a string of pearls around her neck. Adrian met her at the door, gave her a kiss on the cheek and said, "Welcome to the new and approved G-Spot."

Trixie walked in and was amazed at all the work that had been done. Adrian took her on a tour of the whole place.

"Go take a look at the dressing room. There are new showers, make-up tables and lockers in there."

Adrian waited outside the room while Trixie checked it out. He was really enjoying himself. His old drinking hole was back in operation, bigger and better than ever before. The guests came up to Adrian and told him how much nicer the place looked. Adrian was constantly in conversation with guests who really approved of the new look.

About a half hour later, Trixie came out and said, "The place is gorgeous! It looks like you also won approval of our guests. I see we still have a large crowd outside still waiting to get in."

Adrian said, "We were up to legal capacity in fifteen minutes, then we had to hold them back. Let's go sit down and have a drink."

Gina came to the table and said to Trixie, "Well boss, what you think of the place? It's pretty cool, huh?"

Trixie replied, "I think it is fantastic. I love it!!"

"I'll be right back with your drinks."

"You really went full out in this place, Adrian; you even put in a new sound room.

There is absolutely nothing that is old in here; it's all brand new stuff! This must have cost a fortune."

Adrian replied, "It was very expensive indeed, but I wanted a different clientele to come here. I didn't want the perverts in ratty clothes in here. I wanted people with money and class to visit our establishment.

As you can tell, everyone is well dressed and groomed. There are no bums in here."

"Yeah...I noticed that. Good thinking. I like the line-up you picked for the shows. They are the best in the business. How did you manage to get them to share the spot-light with their competition?"

"Money!! It's all about money. They were more than willing to put on the best show ever seen in New York City. It is equal billing, and they didn't mind it for one night. After that, it is back to the back-stabbing business of entertainment."

Gina came back, put the drinks on the table and said, "Everyone I talked to says that they love the place. It's going to be a gold mine!!" She then left to serve the numerous tables waiting to be served.

ADRIAN

Trixie and Adrian raised their glasses for a toast and Adrian said, "To our success! I haven't seen you for quite a while. What have you been doing?"

Trixie said, "I spend most of my days and nights with Dad. He's pretty lonely up there and I go to help cheer him up. They got him out of bed and roaming around the halls. I don't think that he has to stay in hospital too much longer. He's stronger now, better than he ever was."

"Well, all four arteries were closed down. It was inevitable. Thank goodness it didn't kill him! He was a very lucky man. How have you been doing?"

"I'm doing ok. I'm going to be a lot better now that I have my bar back. It really sucks being off work. I was counting the days off my calendar for this day. You didn't let me down, thank-you. I'm going to chat with our guests and let them know that I'm still alive. I'll talk to you later." Trixie got up and took her drink with her; she then mingled with the crowd.

Adrian lit a cigarette and took a sip of beer. He thought that now he could sit back and enjoy the shows. He stared intensely at the women on stage and quickly his thoughts and emotions drained away from him. Soon, thoughts of passionate and relentless sex filled his mind. He was aroused and was starting to have problems controlling his urges. He grew more tense and agitated as the minutes slowly passed.

He was near his breaking point, when he got up and put his coat on. He went to the bar and bought a twelve of beer and quickly left through the front door. Adrian needed to get back to his roots.

He took the alley to the school yard and found a place to sit down. He lit a cigarette and tried to use his coping techniques to help ground him back into reality.

He was still in the immoral world of wild and hard driven sex. The veins in his neck were highly visible, his hands were shaking uncontrollably. His groin was so tight that he probably couldn't stand up even if he had wanted to. He looked around to see if there was someone to help him relieve his pulsating desires.

He got up and hid the beer behind the dumpster. He then took a walk on the strip. The ladies were out in full strength for a Friday night of partying. Adrian walked up and down the strip. He was propositioned several times, but he couldn't find anyone to his liking.

Finally, he saw a young, beautiful blonde working the corner. Adrian went over and said, "I will pay you well, if you spend some time with me."

The young lady said, "Sure, let's go."

Adrian led her to the school yard and brought out the beer. The two of them sat down and opened their beers. Adrian asked, "What's your name?"

"My name is Amber. Who are you?"

"I'm Adrian. It's very nice to meet you."

Adrian dug into his pocket and pulled out two hundred dollars and gave it to her. She smiled and accepted. She then opened her legs wide for Adrian to see the prize. He was busting with lust, his morals having subsided and he wanted to take her. He started to think about Carol and how this would hurt her. He was slowly starting to regain some thought that this was wrong. He couldn't help but imagine Carol's face with tears in her eyes.

Adrian got up and excused himself for a few minutes and raced around the corner of the school. He then exposed himself and grabbed his rod. The pleasure was exhilarating and necessary to keep Adrian in control of himself. The pent-up pleasures exploded in a burst of fury. Adrian took a sigh of relief and started to fix himself up. He waited until his breathing was under control before returning to Amber.

He went back, sat down beside her and lit a cigarette. He was finally coming down from that exotic high that he felt. He was regaining his self control and was able to continue having a few beers without any problems.

Amber asked, "Don't you want to fuck me?"

"No dear, I only wanted your company. You are free to go when you wish."

She got up and said, "I'm not going to waste my time here, when I could be making money. I'm outta here!" She stomped off in a huff.

Adrian thought it was getting a bit cold anyway, so he hid the beer and went back to the G-Spot. There was still a huge line up outside.

Once he got inside, he could see that the free buffet table and the champagne had been served. He then went back to his table, took off his coat and sat down. Gina was right behind him with his beer. She placed it on the table and continued with the numerous orders.

He lit a cigarette and took a sip of beer. He was quite relieved that he was able to refrain from having sex with Amber. His heart still belonged to Carol. It was very difficult to control such incredible urges. They were uncontrollable and harnessing the intensity was near impossible.

Adrian had lost his interest in the party and decided to go home early. He put on his coat and went and found Trixie. "I'll see you later. I'm calling it a night."

Trixie said, "What's wrong? The party is just getting warmed up."

"Nothing's wrong. I just had enough excitement for one day. I'll see ya."

Adrian arrived back at his suite and poured himself a draft. He couldn't stop thinking about Carol. He went to the phone and dialled her number. He sat down at the kitchen table. The phone rang and he heard Carol answer. "Hello."

"Hi sweetheart. I thought I would give you a call and see how you are."

"I'm fine. It sounds quiet over there. Aren't you at the party?"

"No, it looked like things were going fine, so I left early."

Carol was curious and said, "You were so excited about the opening, I thought you would be there all night. Are you alright?"

"I'm fine. I just started to think about you and all of the sudden the party didn't seem all that important anymore. I felt a little homesick and I needed to hear your voice. How is my boy?"

"Oh...he's fine. I think he is down for the night. He had a good walk after work.

We went to the park and played ball and visit all of his doggy friends. He ran and played the whole time; he really had fun today."

"That's my good boy. How was work today?"

"Same old shit, different day. I'm getting too old for their bullshit."

"It was a long day for me. I was at the bar all day and then tonight was the party. I had enough of it for one day. Maybe

I'll feel better about it tomorrow. I feel sort of blue tonight. I don't know what it is. Things are going well. I couldn't ask for anything better, but I'm still feeling a little down. I think it is because I miss you and Blackie."

"I feel like that too. Sometimes something will remind me of you and I'll look for you. Then I realize that you're not here. After a good cry, I can usually collect myself back up again."

"Do you think that being separated might be helping us?"

"I don't know. I know I love the times that we are together and that I really miss you when we are apart. I just don't think I am ready to be an Azario."

"You'll never be an Azario!"

"No, I won't be, but you will eventually be one. You're already like one now. How long do you think it will be before Azario wants you back into the family? If something happens, I am pretty damn sure that you will jump right back on that horse again. I can't remain married to a wise guy."

"I am free of his clutches," Adrian insisted. "Those days are all behind us. It's time to start fresh."

"No, it changed you too much. You will never be able to let it go. You are an Azario. You have proven that to me and to yourself. Even Mr. Azario knows that he has you by the balls. He could reel you in anytime he wants and you'll be there."

Feeling heartbroken, Adrian said, "I think I'm going to go honey. I'll see you tomorrow morning. I love you. Bye."

He hung up the phone. Carol still seemed very hurt about what had happened to Adrian. He was hoping there was something that he could do to help her to accept him again. But perhaps her mind was already made up and they would never be back together. Adrian looked at his beer mug and shed a tear.

He would always love her and the heartache was there to prove it.

Chapter Twenty-Two

The next afternoon, Adrian was in the G-Spot, drowning his sorrows. He didn't care about his promise to himself or to anyone else. He had given up hope and saw his life as being doomed. His self-esteem and self-confidence were shattered. Life didn't even feel worth living anymore. Without Carol in his life, there was no reason to continue on.

Carol and Adrian had barely talked to each other that morning. She was still upset from last night's conversation. Adrian was thinking, what else can go wrong? He signalled to Gina for another beer. He didn't know what he could do to get Carol back into his life. He had been very patient with her and was giving her some space. She was still not ready to live as husband and wife.

The beer came to the table and Adrian took a sip. There was a good afternoon crowd today. The patrons were really enjoying themselves. Trixie was back at work and she was enjoying every minute of it. She was actually going to be the headliner today. It would be her first show since her hospitalization.

From the corner of his eye, Adrian saw Matt and Mike come in through the front entrance. They were accompanied by four uniformed officers who remained at the door. The two detectives came up to Adrian and Matt asked, "Can we sit down?"

Adrian replied, "Sure, it's a free country."

Gina came back to the table and Matt ordered two coffees.

He said, "I'm sorry Adrian, but today is your unlucky day. We are putting you under arrest for conspiracy to commit murder, fifty-eight counts of murder and twenty counts of arson. We have hard evidence against you that will put you away for life."

Adrian replied, "Why not? I don't have anything else to do. I'll go with you, don't worry. Just let me order my last beer. It's much better than a foot chase or a gun battle."

Matt said, "Sure, go ahead. I'd rather do it this way myself."

Adrian signalled for another beer. "I thought you would agree with me. So, what is this hard evidence you have against me?"

Matt replied, "We will go over the details at the station. I presume that you will want your lawyer present for that."

"Yes, of course."

"I'm sorry it all turned out this way Adrian."

"You guys weren't any help keeping me out of there, were you? You didn't want my help for catching Jonathan and you didn't lift a finger against Manicotti. I was left alone. Someone had to save Trixie and it wasn't you guys. You could have done it, if you really wanted to.

I was forced to act because of the incompetence of the police department. Trixie, the two of you and Matt's wife would be all dead if it wasn't for me. This is the gratitude I get for saving your asses! You and your department are useless pieces of shit. I really needed you guys. I had serious problems and not once did you come through for me.

I had to do it; it was the only choice available. I did your fuck'n jobs for you. I asked for your help and you turned me down. Now, you're going to crucify me for doing things that you should have done in the first place."

Gina came to the table and dropped off the coffees and the beer. She quickly got out of there; she didn't want any part of what was going on.

Matt said, "We're sorry you feel that way, but the police department has rules and regulations too. We had to follow procedures just like you have to."

Adrian said, "You're both so very fuck'n lucky that I was there for you! I saved your fuck'n lives!! I hope you both burn in hell!"

Mike said, "I understand your feelings about us and the department. You might even be right about a couple of things, but you still murdered people. That is still against the law in this country and you broke it."

"I want to go to court and prove to everyone in New York City that the police department is useless and incompetent. If you really need the police and you're thinking that they will do their job, you better think again. Believe me! This is going to come up in the trial and you will look very bad in front of that

ADRIAN

jury. I am looking forward to seeing you guys sweat on that stand."

"We have nothing to worry about," Matt replied. "It is you who is going to be up against fifty-eight charges of murder. You will be the one sweating, not us. We acted accordingly. We did everything in our power to help you."

Adrian blurted out, "Bullshit!! You didn't lift a finger when I was crying on the phone to you to get me out of that mansion! You told me that there was nothing that you could do and that I had to stay alive and do what is necessary. You said that only God could help me now. Do you remember that, Matt? I sure as hell do!!"

Matt said, "Azario didn't do anything wrong at that time. We didn't have any rights to intrude on him. Besides, we would have never been allowed through those gates."

"You already knew that my life was in danger and you didn't have any rights!! That's bullshit!! You could have pulled me out if you tried, but you didn't even attempt to get me out of there. You were using me to get information for you, that's why you didn't pull me out. It was too important to you to get those fuck'n names!"

Adrian slammed down his empty mug and said, "I'm fuck'n ready! Let's do this thing."

Matt signalled the uniformed officers to make their arrest. Adrian was cuffed and read his rights. Then it was off to the station to be processed. Adrian was driven away in a patrol car and upon arrival at the station, he was read his charges. He phoned Ron Mauler and told his lawyer the situation.

Ron advised him not to say a word until he met up with him a couple of hours before the hearing. After that Adrian was thrown into the holding tank until the next morning for a bail hearing. He sat in the crowded cell all night without a wink of sleep. He was not as worried about his situation as he was about Carol. He didn't give a shit about himself. All he can think about was how Carol would react to this.

He wondered how fast he would receive divorce papers if he was convicted. There was nothing left without her in his life. He might as well rot in jail; there was nothing left to look forward to. The hours went by and the guard came and took him to a room to meet with Mr. Mauler.

They sat down at the table in the middle of the room. Mr. Mauler said, "Adrian, give me a quick run down as to what happened to you in the last two months or so. I need the whole story so that I can get you out of here on your own recognizance."

Adrian began. "I was very mentally ill at the time. I later found out that my doctor was treating me with placebos so that I would lose control. He wanted me jailed or locked away in a mental facility. Most of the time I was fighting to stay sane; sometimes I would slip out of reality and a darkness would overcome me.

I was chasing women because of my uncontrollable libido. Jonathan took advantage of those encounters and murdered the women, planting incriminating evidence against me. Soon I was on the run and went into hiding. When I was cleared of any wrong doing, Frank Azario took me off the streets and had me under his rule. If I didn't obey him, I would die.

The police anticipated that Azario would do this and made a deal to drop some minor charges, if I would help them retrieve information from the payroll. I was to get a list of names so that the police could find the real killer. I asked the police to get me out of there before something terrible happened, and they told me only God could do that.

The next day I was ordered to kill Tony Lorenzo or be killed with him. I did it.

As the other killings increased, the police were still unable to stop the murders. I had an idea that would put an end to it all and the police refused my help.

There was nothing left to do before three people were at Jonathan's mercy and the city's water system would be poisoned. The only action that was available was to kill him. I was forced by the situation to kill him and to save numerous lives.

I was forced by a mutiny towards the Azario family to kill Juan Cortez or to have a life-threatening situation erupt. I had to act fast and gain the leadership by a harsh example.

Then there was Vinny Manicotti who had the Azario family at siege. He had his men kidnap my sister and told us to surrender to extortion.

He warned us if we retaliated that they would kill her. I told the police and they said there was nothing they could do.

Manicotti destroyed five of our businesses and would have continued until somebody stopped him.

I personally killed four men, including Manicotti. I rescued my sister and stopped the carnage he had on my family. All the killings were conducted under a state of dissociation, where I lose touch with reality and enter a whole new world controlled by the environment that I am in.

I am now under counselling for that and under more counselling for alcoholism. I am also away from stressful situations and I am being properly treated and medicated for my illness. That's about it."

Mr. Mauler and Adrian continued talking. Adrian gave more precise details that Mauler could use. Mauler asked many questions. They spent two hours going over every detail and they didn't leave anything out. Now, they were ready for the court house.

Adrian was transported under shackles and chains to the court house where Mauler was waiting for him.

Mauler cautioned, "Remember, you don't have to say a thing. I will do all the talking for you."

They waited in the line up in the courtroom. After about a half hour, Adrian was called up in front of the judge.

Judge Stanley Crawford said, "Go ahead Miss Shelton. Let's hear your case."

Andréa said, "We recommended that Mr. Eisner be denied bail and stay in custody until his trial date. He is extremely dangerous.

He admitted to killing seven people, he planned and carried out the Manicotti massacre, and burnt twenty buildings to the ground. It would be a big mistake to allow Mr. Eisner to remain free on his own recognizance."

Judge Crawford said, "Mr. Mauler, what do you have to say?"

"Your honour, we ask that Mr. Eisner remain free on his own recognizance. Mr. Eisner was forced into those situations by the incompetence of the police department failing to do their duties.

With no other options open, Mr. Eisner was forced to act. He also was not treated for a series of mental illnesses and conditions at the time of these occurrences. He is now being treated to deal with those issues and is having great success.

He was insane at the time of these slayings. He pleads not guilty."

Judge Crawford replied, "Mr. Mauler, I deny your request for freedom. These crimes are numerous and heinous. I order Mr. Eisner to Bellevue for a psychiatric assessment. After that, he will return to this courtroom to review his competence to stand trial." The judge then banged his gavel and Adrian was immediately transported to Bellevue, shackled and guarded by two armed guards.

Soon after Adrian's arrival at Bellevue Psychiatric Hospital, his behaviour dramatically changed. He isolated himself from contact from the other patients. He stayed in bed all day and night.

Every time the nurse would open the blinds to let the sunshine in, he would get up and close them.

His appetite was very poor; he might only have a slight nibble at dinner time. He had a few coffees during the meal times and that was all he consumed. He never attended the group programs at the facility. Even though he was always in bed, he never seemed to feel rested.

His mood was very low and he would cry several times during the day. He avoided contact with the doctors and nurses to the best of his ability. He only spoke when it was time to answer a question. Adrian's mental health was at a diminished capacity. He was diagnosed as having a severe depressive episode. Finally, the assessment was complete and he was taken back to court after six weeks in hospital.

Mr. Mauler, along with Doctor Moss, met Adrian at the courthouse. Adrian's doctor was there to explain what had happened to Adrian while he was incarcerated. The doctor wanted to reveal what Adrian's mental condition would be like if he were to be held for a longer period of time.

It was now time for the competency hearing. Adrian was called forward by Judge Crawford.

The judge said, "The medical report states that Mr. Eisner suffers from manic depression and states of disassociation caused by a childhood trauma. His mental illness does not affect his ability to know the difference between what is right or wrong.

Mr. Eisner still has control prior to a disassociate state and therefore can avoid these episodes from happening.

It is to be known that Mr. Adrian Eisner is fit to stand trial to be set for March 15th, 2003. He is to remain incarcerated at the local correctional facility until then. Miss Shelton, do you have anything to add to this?"

Andréa said, "No, your honour. The people rest."

Judge Crawford asked, "Mr. Mauler, do you have anything to say?"

Mr. Mauler said, "I have Mr. Eisner's psychiatrist here to contest the report of those findings. They are incomplete due to the severe depression suffered by Mr. Eisner.

We have proof that Mr. Eisner loses complete control of his actions while in a depressive state, manic state or a disassociate state. His illness takes full control of his mind and removes any sense of morality.

If Mr. Eisner does not receive the medical attention of Dr. Moss, he will suffer from an irreversible effect of dissociation that can traumatize him for life. He will suffer from this incarceration to the point of going insane. He has already suffered from a severe bout of depression for being held in a hospital for six weeks. What will be the outcome if he is put into general population in prison? He will be insane and unfit to stand trial. I want to thank-you, your honour."

Judge Crawford stated, "I take the word of the medical experts that were assigned by this court. I have no reason not to believe that their report is credible and that the appropriate testing was conducted to come up with a reliable report. Nice try Mr. Mauler.

I hereby order Mr. Adrian Eisner to be held at the local correctional facility until his trial date in March of next year." The judge then banged his gavel and Adrian was on his way to general population at the prison.

Adrian was shocked to find himself going to prison to await his trial. He should have been left in the city lock up until then, not prison. The judge did not look lightly on a man who was involved with fifty-eight murders. He found himself sharing a cell with a monster of a man.

The greasy long hair and countless tattoos that covered his overly-large frame was a frightening sight on their own. His nick name was "Spaz." And Adrian didn't want to find out why they called him that. If he ever did what the name implied, Adrian could find himself in serious trouble.

After several days, Adrian was in a deep depression and incoherent of his surroundings. He just wanted to die and get it over with. It was a rough experience being in prison; life didn't mean anything in there. You could be snuffed out in a blink of an eye and no one would care.

Adrian found himself to be a target for the other prisoners. If you were not part of a gang or if you were a loner, you were as good as dead. Adrian's depression kept him isolated and in constant danger. He was sleeping in his bunk when Spaz said, "Hey!! Girly!! Do you want to be my boy?"

Adrian mumbled, "No, I'm not into that shit."

"Think carefully what you are saying, Girly. If you don't do me any favours, I'll have them have a poke at you.

I won't lift a finger to save your sorry little ass. If you're my boy, I'll give you protection. You better think long and hard before it's too late."

Adrian said, "I already told you that I'm not into that shit, now fuck off!!" He buried his head in the pillow.

"You made a really bad choice, Girly. You're almost too cute to hand over to the hounds. Now, you are going to learn prison life the hard way."

Spaz shouted out into the main foyer, "There is fresh meat in here you guys. Girly has decided to take you all on!!"

Adrian knew he was in a lot of trouble now; it was just a matter of time. He was determined that he wasn't going to be anyone's sex toy. Now, he had to try to survive somehow. He didn't have any protection or friendship to use as a defence. He was all alone in his crusade to stay alive.

Meanwhile, at Andréa Shelton's office, she was busy building her case against Adrian. Matt and Mike were giving her some details as to what Adrian had said in the bar just prior to his arrest.

Matt said, "It sounds like Adrian is going to use police incompetence, as well as insanity, as a defence. We have to gear our case to attack their position.

We have to prove that the police acted to the best of their ability in certain circumstances. Then we have to prove that Adrian knew what was right and wrong and that he made conscious decisions to carry out those crimes. Do you think we can make a good case using the evidence that we have?"

"I think we have an open and shut case," Andréa replied. "Mr. Mauler is grasping for straws to make a strong defence. We have a medical assessment from Belleview that states that Adrian's illness does not affect his knowledge of right or wrong. So, that blows the insanity plea right out of the water.

We have tons of paperwork from the police department backing up every action that was taken by the force. I don't see how Mr. Mauler can poke any holes into the case; I think we are home free."

Matt asked, "How good is Mr. Mauler?"

Andréa replied, "He is a very good lawyer. I can't take him totally for granted. He will find things within the evidence and the witnesses that may put the ball in his court. We have to anticipate every move that he may take or he will win the case. He is very observant and resourceful. Mr. Mauler has the reputation of pulling a rabbit out of the hat and winning the case."

Matt said, "I don't like the sound of that. You better make damn sure that the case is air tight. It's a big case with a lot of areas that can be scrutinized and dissected. If Mauler sinks his teeth in, we better make sure he doesn't make a hole."

"That's why we are working so closely together. I want every detail of any conversations you had with Adrian. I want dates, times and anything else you can possibly remember. We are going to put all the evidence through a strainer and make sure we don't miss any details."

The first thing I want to go over is the taped interrogation you had with Adrian. Is that the first time that you met?"

"According to my notes, the first time we met Adrian was the 21st, September, 2002. That was the interrogation that we have on tape."

"I want to set up a character profile to show the jury that he is not insane and that this taped conversation shows him in total control."

"There is a problem with that. He had two doses of medication that helped level him out."

"We can fight that point. I have a report from Belleview that those medications take up to six weeks before they start to work at full strength. Adrian was basically unaffected by those medications at the time of the interrogation. He was unmedicated and in full control of himself.

The tape proves that he was cool and calm. He remembered most details about what he did and didn't do. It shows him being unaffected by the interrogation or the questions that were asked. He just shot a man in the leg the night before and he has this unremorseful attitude about him. The tapes will demonstrate that Adrian has the character of a cold and calculated murderer.

You also have a profiler statement saying that Adrian has the character of a serial murderer and rapist. His report demonstrates that he was very capable of committing those crimes. He meets the criteria that make up a murderer. This information will be the basis of establishing his mental capacity."

Mike said, "That looks like a pretty strong establishment of character. Is there a way that Mauler can break that down?"

Andréa replied, "He will probably say that those two doses just prior to the interrogation were enough to stabilize his mood, and that they demonstrate Adrian as he would look if he had been treated. His defence would be to prove that this tape demonstrates a medicated man."

Mike asked, "Do you think there is a chance that those two doses had such a profound influence on him that it would affect him to the point of being cool and calm?

"According to the Belleview report, it would not have such a dramatic influence on him. The next thing I want to clarify is what the deal was between Adrian and the police department?"

Matt explained, "Adrian agreed to get the names of Frank Azario's employees, so that we could sift through the names and cross check them to reveal the murderer.

We would then drop the charges of illegal possession of a firearm and discharging a firearm in city limits. It was a lame deal, but he took it.

We knew that Azario would hunt him down for information about the case. Adrian would have been picked up with or without our influence. We knew that Azario wanted to know who the killer was just as badly as we did. The killings were taking a heavy toll on business on the strip, thus dropping the profit that Azario was more accustomed to."

Andréa said, "That was not very smart of you boys. You took advantage of Adrian because of the inevitable contact that would be made with Frank Azario. You knew he was going into a very dangerous situation, yet you endorsed this to happen.

You also knew that once he was on the inside, he was on his own without police protection. That was a very dumb move gentlemen. Mauler is going to have a picnic with this one."

Matt said, "It was bound to happen anyway. We couldn't protect Adrian because he wasn't a witness to a crime that would give him police protection. Azario didn't have any dirt on him, so we couldn't go in there and rip him out. There were no crimes involved, so we had no right in being there. Besides, we were out-gunned and our entrance to the compound would have been halted."

"We have to work very hard in this area of the case," Andréa said. "As it stands, Mauler can prove department incompetence. Adrian should never have been put into a dangerous situation, endorsed by the police department.

We have to prove that this was the only choice available, considering the circumstances. We have to demonstrate the urgency of getting Jonathan Azario off the street. What happened next?"

"It was 8:45 pm on the night of the 21st of September, 2002." Matt recalled. "Adrian called me on the cell phone we gave him and said that he may be forced to commit murder. He was scared and he wanted me to pull him out. I told him that he had to stay alive and that he may be forced to do some things that were against his morals.

I told him that the police could not interfere with this matter. No crime had been committed and the mansion was impenetrable.

The police do not have the resources to take on such a force; it would be too bloody."

Andréa said, "Adrian informed you prior to the murder that this was going to take place and you endorsed him to do what it takes to stay alive. Then you refused to aid him in an upcoming dangerous situation. You left him stranded to fight by himself, for his own safety! How the hell am I going to convince the jury that the police didn't endorse the murder of Tony Lorenzo? I hope you guys understand that Adrian could walk away from this a free man because of your failure to protect him! Let's move on. What happened next?"

Matt said, "6:15 am, on September 25th, 2002, Adrian called me and told me he knew how to get Jonathan. He wanted to team up with the police to bring Jonathan in. I told him that this was police business and if he interfered, I would put him in jail. He was quite determined that he knew Jonathan's every move and that he was the only one capable of getting the job done. He then hung up on me.

September 27th, 2002, Mr. Parsons, my wife and I were hostages and were at the mercy of Jonathan Azario. He had me on my knees with a gun pointed at my head when I heard a shot that was fired. When I looked up, I saw Jonathan fall to the ground with the back of his head missing.

After about fifteen minutes, I was on the way to the car to radio in for assistance.

I then saw five men with rifles get into a limo and a car that matched Adrian's Hummer. Later that same afternoon, Detective Parsons and I had a conversation with Adrian.

Upon our arrival at the mansion, I noticed the Hummer which matched the description of the car I saw at Croton Dam Road earlier on.

We talked to Adrian and I said that off the record, I knew he killed Jonathan. He replied that off the record, I was welcome. He made a point that he wasn't going to incriminate himself, but he basically did with that remark. Now, we have the tape of him admitting to killing Jonathan Azario."

Andréa stated, "Adrian came to the aid of two officers of the law and one civilian. It was suspected that he killed Jonathan Azario at the time he saved three lives from an inevitable execution. Later, you received proof that he did save your lives. He acted solely in the prevention of your death and you want me to prosecute him! You are damn lucky he was there!

Those are two murders that Adrian will walk away from! You have to do better than that. You're going to make me look like a fool in front of that jury. The only thing you did prove is that Adrian does have the capacity to kill if warranted."

Matt said, "Later that night, we received a call to the G-Spot. Adrian requested our personal appearance at the vandalism of the G-Spot. There he told us that Manicotti was after the Azario Empire in a war for power. He also said that Donna Azario was being held captive by Manicotti.

We told him if we interfered in the gang war, that Donna would certainly be killed. I also said that we don't have the resources that it would take to accomplish a rescue. Our hands were tied. There was nothing we could do without starting a war with the Manicotti Empire."

"So, the police force did nothing, but sit back and watch the carnage unfold. Adrian again asked for your assistance and you left him to fight Manicotti on his own, in order to save his sister. You left Adrian with no choice, but to take the law into his own hands!

Mauler is going to rip us apart in courtroom - I hope you understand that. We have to prove that lives were saved due to the inaction of the police force. We also have to prove that you would have exhausted all of your possible resources if the police had made a commitment."

Matt replied, "That should be easy to prove. The Manicotti and Azario families are three times as powerful as all the police departments combined."

Andréa asked, "Since you couldn't handle the job. Why didn't you call some one who could? You didn't call the State Troopers or the Governor.

The Governor could have immobilized the army to take Manicotti down. Adrian did it. Why couldn't you? We have two murders that we may be able to pin on Adrian. There is the murder of Juan Cortez; we have to prove that Adrian was in no immediate danger at the time of the killing. I'm still not sure how I am going to prove that.

Finally, there is the murder of Vinny Manicotti. The confession does reveal that Adrian couldn't handle Manicotti's big mouth, so he shot him. That might be it for the murders. We might only get him for one. The arsons are convictable for he confessed to the planning and the operation of that mission.

The other three murders were Manicotti's guards that were holding Miss Azario captive.

If you had kept Adrian safe and away from Azario, none of this would have ever happened! The police could be held accountable for Adrian's actions. It's going to be a hard case to win. I'll be honest with you; we could be in for a big disappointment.

Chapter Twenty-Three

In Judge Stanley Crawford's Chambers, Ron Mauler was trying to appeal the decision to have Adrian await trial in prison. He said, "Your honour, Mr. Eisner is a very sick man. The prison system only gave him the cheapest treatment available. They have him medicated on a cheap drug that does not work on Mr. Eisner. He is basically untreated at this time; he requires Dr. Moss's cocktail of medications to help him.

Mr. Eisner is in a deep depression and has lost forty pounds in seven weeks. He needs to be in a hospital. The prisoners have him targeted as a sex toy. Soon, he may find himself a victim of sexual abuse. He already suffered that abuse as a twelve year old. It would destroy him if it happened again.

Dr. Moss has been at the prison and has assessed Mr. Eisner. He found that Mr. Eisner is getting worse in his depressive and disassociate state. If he stays in there, it may cause irreversible damage. It is imperative that Mr. Eisner be removed from this situation as soon as possible and put into a hospital. The mental and physical health of this man is in severe jeopardy."

Judge Crawford said, "Mr. Eisner is a very dangerous man. He requires the security measures that are in place at the prison. I can't have him wandering the hallways of Belleview; he's more likely to burn it down.

I'm sorry about his predicament, but prison is the best place for a man with those types of mental conditions. They can handle him if he goes off the deep end."

Mr. Mauler pleaded, "He is only dangerous when he is not on the proper treatment plan as described by Dr. Moss. Adrian's mental and physical well being is in extreme danger because of his surroundings. That can all improve if he was in hospital and under the care of Dr. Moss. He would not be a threat to the other patients or staff of the hospital. Mr. Eisner would be a model patient. He has to be removed from his present situation immediately before he gets worse."

Judge Crawford said, "The director of Belleview put in his report that Mr. Eisner is capable of extreme violence and psychotic behaviour. He recommended a maximum security facility where, if he lost control, they would be able to control the situation more readily than a hospital.

Dr. David Ing believes that this current drug will work on Mr. Eisner, if given enough time to get into the blood stream."

"Mr. Eisner has been on this drug in the past and it had a disastrous affect on him." argued Mauler. "He needs stronger and more specialized medication to keep him under control. Dr. Ing is wrong in his observation and recommendation of Mr. Eisner. Allow Dr. Moss to take over and you will see a steady increase of good mental health."

Judge Crawford replied, "Mr. Eisner will remain where he is. That facility is equipped to handle the most dangerous situations. Mr. Eisner will remain under the care of Dr. David Ing.

If there are any other problems with his situation, I will deal with them as they come up. Until then, he is in the best suited facility in the state. Thank-you for your concern Mr. Mauler. I believe that Mr. Eisner will be able to deal with his situation as is. Have a good-day."

Ron Mauler was distraught that the judge would not listen to reason. Mr. Eisner was in severe danger and it was up to the state to protect him. A man's mental health was at risk of being damaged permanently. Ron would have to keep on bugging the judge to make him realize that prison was not the place for Adrian Eisner.

Meanwhile at the prison, Adrian was shampooing his hair in a shower booth. Most of the other booths were taken by other prisoners.

One by one, most of the other prisoners hastily left the shower room. Adrian slightly opened his eyes under the running water and saw eight hulking, tattoo-bearing slime balls, with erections, surrounding his booth.

The affirmed leader was Spaz and he said, "Its show time, Girly!"

The muscular men raced towards Adrian, plummeting him with severe blows to the body. The kicks and the fists were crushing Adrian's weakened frame.

Spaz said, "That's enough boys! We just want to weaken him enough for the main event!"

ADRIAN

The aroused men stood in line, waiting for their turn at Adrian. Suddenly, Adrian flashed back to that fateful summer day at the watering hole.

The terror and panic returned with vivid memories of a stricken child. He lost touch with all thoughts, memories and pain.

Adrian was in his peaceful world, where nothing could hurt him. His mind had blocked out the terror that surrounded him. He had a blank stare that penetrated the shower wall in front of him.

Bent over, he stood, emotionless to the ongoing brutality. He didn't even feel the pain from an obviously broken right arm. The carnage continued until all eight men had their go at him. One more brief beating erupted and he was left in the middle of the shower room, a battered man. Broken bones and bruises were the result of this brutal attack.

The guards found Adrian on the floor and took him to the infirmary for treatment. There, they taped his broken ribs and put a cast on his arm. He was treated with preventive measures against Aids. This was to be followed up by further treatment and regular testing. They allowed him to sleep overnight in the infirmary, before releasing him back to his cell the next morning.

Adrian was unaware of his surroundings and didn't feel the effects of the nurses trying to make him come out of his disassociate state. His blank stare at the ceiling was most frightening and disturbing. There was no reaction from the efforts of the nurses trying to ground him back into reality. He lay in bed, severely traumatized by the ordeal, unable to move or blink.

The head nurse remembered that Dr. Moss came in early that morning for an assessment on Adrian.

She went to the nurses' station and got him on the phone. He was furious that such an event had taken place and that Adrian's health was in severe jeopardy.

He knew he wasn't the attending psychiatrist for Adrian, but he threw diplomacy out the window and raced over to the prison. It shouldn't have taken him too long to get there, except he had to make a quick stop first. To Adrian, time was not a factor. Everything had stopped; his heart and soul were non-existent. He was emotionally destroyed inside; there was only an empty shell.

At the Azario mansion, Frank had finally returned home from the hospital. Once again, he was back in the tea room, enjoying a cup of tea. Recovery would be slow, but he had all the time in the world. Adrian had taken care of all the business for him. It was time to relax and allow his body to heal.

Steven came to the entrance of the tea room and announced, "Sir, you have an urgent call from Dr. Moss."

"Ok, I'll take it out here, thank-you."

He picked up the phone. "Hello."

"I have some bad news for you sir. Adrian was gang banged and is emotionally traumatized. He is unable to awaken from a disassociate state. I'm on my way there now. I'll keep you informed how he is doing. As for now, it doesn't look good".

"I don't care if you phone me every hour!" barked Azario. "I want to know how my son is doing around the clock! You have to wake him up!"

"I'll do my best sir. I guarantee it."

Frank sat back in his chair with a saddened look on his face.

For everything that boy had done, he was unable to help his only son in his time of need. His heart sank as he imagined that blank stare into the heavens.

He then remembered something. Julian Brinks was serving time at the correctional facility for murder. He pretty well owned the prison system. Besides that, he was over three-hundred pounds of muscles with more connections on the inside than anyone else.

Julian was a former employee of Frank's. He should be able to strike a deal with Azario and give Adrian some protection. Azario's boy needs all the help he could get. Frank got on the phone, called the switchboard at the prison and paged Julian. He waited quite some time before there was an answer. Then he heard, "Hello."

Azario said, "Julian old boy, this is Frank Azario. How are things on the inside?"

"Mr. Azario, I thought I would never hear from you again. What's up?"

"I have a business proposition for you. I will financially set up your wife and kids if you do me a favour."

"What's the favour?"

"My son is in there with you. His name is Adrian Eisner. He got pretty messed up today and he's not doing too well. Can you arrange protection for this lad? He is quite ill and is not capable of taking care of himself."

"What will you do for my family?"

"Give me their phone number and address. I will set them up for life with a new house, car, retirement plan and a college fund for the kids. It will be about a few hundred thousand dollars worth."

"I heard about the incident. They got him real good Mr. Azario. Make sure the family starts to see some of those promises tomorrow and I'll take care of your kid.

I got a few buddies who would work out just fine in these kinds of situations. But I'm not sure when your boy is coming out of the infirmary. Apparently, his mind blew a gasket and he's basically right out of it. Don't worry Mr. Azario, it won't happen again."

"Remember Julian, I'm the one on the outside. Don't screw this up!"

"I'll take care of it, sir. Just leave it up to me. My home number is 727-3146. My wife lives at #303, East 79th Street. Her name is Lisa. Just tell her who you are, I'll fill her in on the details. See ya, Mr. Azario."

Azario hung up the phone. He was feeling more relaxed, knowing that Adrian now had friends on the inside. Julian didn't take shit from anyone, so those creeps won't ever get a chance to do that again and live. He took a sip of tea and wondered what was happening to Adrian and whether he was ever going to recover.

Back at the prison, Dr. Moss arrived and was talking to the head nurse. "I stopped by Adrian's house before I got here and picked up a recent photograph of his wife. Make sure that this picture is in Adrian's line of vision all the time. I want his brain to start to focus on the present. Where are Adrian's affects? I need a necklace or something that he can put in his hand and focus on.

Pain will not snap him out of it. He already suffered a tremendous amount of that and it didn't shock him out of it.

Try feeding him things with different flavours to help stimulate his mind. Try things like different juices or fruits. I want your staff to start working on those things right away."

Dr. Moss stood by his patient and waited for any form of response. Adrian's own world was so peaceful and worry-free, that his mind would not allow him to come back to reality. He was safe where he was. Why should he return to this place where there was torment and torture around every corner?

Dr. Moss administered some medication that should help Adrian. Adrian could physically function if he was guided, but his mind was still in a zombie-like state. It was Dr. Moss's hope that if Adrian stared at the photograph of his wife, it would activate something of the present to bring him back into reality. The current treatment would never work on Adrian.

It was a good drug for millions of people, but Adrian required specialized cocktails to counter each ailment he suffered from. Everything from depression, mania, psychosis, and severe exhaustion had to be treated with a specific drug designed for that job.

Dr. Moss warned Mr. Mauler that this would happen on several occasions. The doctor that had been assigned by the court had never even met Adrian yet. His care had been neglected due to politics. Dr. Moss was breaking the rules and treating Adrian because he was a doctor first, then a politician. The mental health and well being of his patients was Dr. Moss's first priority.

The politics would be passed on to Mauler. This incident should make the judge understand now, that Adrian was no threat and needed serious medical attention. As Dr. Moss treated Adrian, he constantly talked to him and asked questions in hopes that there would soon be a response.

Adrian could hear him alright, except that his brain was not engaged with his surroundings. Dr. Moss came to the conclusion that Adrian would have to remain in the infirmary for six to eight weeks. It would take that much time before he regained enough awareness of reality to go back into the general prison population.

With careful monitoring and stimulation, Adrian should slowly come back to the real world. But he was severely damaged. It was Dr. Moss's desire that Adrian would recover, but there was a chance that it might not be very satisfactory.

An ongoing trauma counselling would have to be established, so that Adrian could lift those buried feelings into the open before he could heal properly.

This would indeed have a severe impact on him for the rest of his life. Adrian had had so much tragedy in his life that his chances of living a normal happy life were being quickly taken away from him. Dr. Moss left instructions for the nursing staff before leaving. There was nothing more he could do today. It was all a matter of time from this point forward. Dr. Moss then left the prison thinking that this could have been all avoided. The politics of this case were the main offenders in this most recent assault.

The next day, at Judge Stanley Crawford's chambers, Mr. Moss was describing the current situation. "Your honour, the red flags were up and the court did nothing to protect Mr. Eisner from this trauma that he is suffering from.

His court-ordered psychiatrist has not even met with him. He needs constant monitoring and medication to pull him out of this. Dr. Ing is not providing the care that is required by his patient.

He is neglecting his duties as a doctor. Mr. Eisner is under the care of this state. It is our responsibility to ensure that all his medical needs are taken care of.

I recommend that Dr. Moss should take over the responsibilities as the main care-giver. Secondly, Mr. Eisner requires specialized medication that is quite expensive. I need those medications approved by the state. The last request is that Mr. Eisner be transferred to a medical facility while awaiting trial.

Mr. Eisner is almost a vegetable from this ordeal; he is in no physical or mental condition to be dangerous. It will take specialized counselling to help Mr. Eisner work out his feelings. The issue has to be out in the open so that Adrian can learn to understand and accept what has happened to him. Please your honour; grant Mr. Eisner what is his right to receive under the constitution."

Judge Crawford replied, "Dr. Moss had no legal obligation to treat Mr. Eisner yesterday. Dr. Ing should have been informed of the incident in the first place. Dr. Ing is a well-respected psychiatrist in the medical profession.

I am sure that he is very competent in his field and I have no reason to withdraw him off this case.

The medical facility at the correctional institute is more than capable of ensuring that Mr. Eisner is receiving the best possible care available. You may request the state for a medical expense increase for medication. There is no guarantee that it will be approved, but it is the only chance you have of getting the medication changed. Besides, Dr. Ing is in charge of medication and he feels that the medication prescribed is adequate."

Mr. Mauler pleaded, "Your honour, Dr Ing is a lazy and non-caring son of a bitch! Mr. Eisner will die in there before that bastard ever decides to drive up there and help a patient. This drug has been proven not to work on Mr. Eisner. Dr. Ing does not care about the well being of his patients and I am putting in a formal complaint of his incompetence.

He should not be allowed to practice in this state and I will see that his license is revoked.

Your honour, I feel that the court should reverse their decision and allow Dr. Moss to take over the duties as the Mr. Eisner's personal doctor."

Judge Crawford stated, "I guess you are going to bug me every day until you get what you want. Mr. Mauler, I will grant permission for Dr. Moss to treat Mr. Eisner. He will be Mr. Eisner's personal psychiatrist and he may change the treatment as he sees fit. Dr. Ing will remain the non-biased expert in this case.

The prisoner will stay where he is at, and this is the last time I want to see you in my chambers.

And Mr. Mauler, if you ever swear in my chambers or courtroom again, I will charge you with contempt of court. Do you understand me?"

"I apologize for my behaviour, your honour. It will never happen again. I want to thank-you, for your decision. Have a good-day." Ron then left the chambers with a minor victory. Adrian would now receive the proper care as required. He left the court house with a big chip on his shoulder. Judge Crawford was a hard egg to crack. The victory was sweet.

For the next two months Adrian was on an extensive therapy designed to keep him in touch with reality. There had been great progress. He was now responsive to his surroundings and other people. He was starting to understand what had happened. He was learning coping strategies that would help stop it from reoccurring and how to use precautions against it.

He had had several meetings with Ron Mauler about how they have built up a defence. Ron felt confident that the case would go quite well, with a couple of exceptions. They may have trouble in relation to the murder of Vinny Manicotti and Juan Cortez. Ron was planning to use the disassociate state as a defence. He had to provide a reason as to why Adrian had killed those two men.

Juan Cortez's murder would be much easier to defend, since Adrian had been in a threatened position.

The Manicotti murder couldn't use self defence as a defence because ballistics proved there were six shots fired into his head from as little as two feet away. The powder burns left distinct markings from which they could judge the distance.

Adrian had not been in reality during that assault; he was under the control of the environment and the things that were happening to him at the time.

He just adapted himself into the situation; there was no thought involved. It was pure impulse. Manicotti verbally threatened him and he did have a gun in his hand. While in this condition, Adrian could have taken that as a threat and shot him.

The trial was getting close and Adrian could not wait for his chance to defend himself. He felt that he had acted in the same way that anyone else would have, if they were in the same situation.

When the meeting was over, Adrian went back to his cell for the first time in two months. Julian and his friends were close behind, keeping a good eye out for him.

Feeling very tired, Adrian climbed onto his bunk and decided to catch up on some sleep. About an hour later, Spaz came back to the cell and said, "Welcome home Girly. How was your trip?"

Adrian was out like a light and didn't hear him. Without a response, Spaz closed the door and locked it with a bicycle lock that the guards don't know about. Julian caught a glimpse as to what happened and went to the cell. He then saw the lock and knew that he had blown it.

Spaz gave Adrian a solid shake and said, "Get up Girly!"

Adrian awoke out of his deep sleep, wondering what was going on."

"Are you ready to be my boy, now? If you are, get down off of there and get on your knees."

Adrian saw the lock on the door and knew that there was no escape. There was no chance of Julian coming in to save him. He realized that this was a case of self preservation and to prevent another episode like last time, he better obey. He got off the bunk and went on his knees in front of his assailant. Spaz then exposed himself.

Adrian began to drift away. He was still aware of what was going on. It seemed that the treatment he had received for the last couple of months was working. He was not totally lost. Spaz was now starting to relax and enjoy the pleasures.

Adrian continued to drift until something snapped inside of him. His eyes widened with an evil stare. Thoughts swirled in his mind and his heart started to pump hard. The feeling that Adrian was experiencing in his heart was revenge. The darkness overcame his heart and soul. There was blackness in Adrian's world.

With the ferocity of a vicious animal, Adrian clamped down as hard as he could with his teeth.

Spaz screamed in pain and started to beat Adrian over the back with his fists. The darkness was relentless; Adrian was oblivious to the blows on his back. The animal inside of him was attacking viciously until the membrane was amputated.

The assailant had now become a victim of the dark side.

There were cheers from Julian and his men as they crowded around the cell. Deathly screams and threats could be heard throughout the facility as Spaz was squirming on the ground, clutching himself.

Adrian stood over the fallen man and stared down at him. He then meticulously ground his teeth and swallowed. There were no words or emotions, just pure revenge. Adrian's veins were pumping with excitement. His victory was sweet.

The guards heard the commotion from the cell. They could hear Spaz yell, "The bastard ate my fuck'n pecker!!"

ADRIAN

Soon the guards came running to the cell and pushed the other prisoners away from the door. They saw the lock and were unable to get in. Spaz was yelling out the combination at the top of his lungs. The guards finally got in after several tries at the lock. They rushed the man called Spaz to the infirmary to stop the bleeding to his newly created anatomy.

Other guards grabbed Adrian from the pool of blood that surrounded him and took him to the infirmary to pump his stomach. He was pumped out, but to no avail; there were no chances of repair. Mr. John Kowalski would have to pee like a girl for the rest of his life.

Adrian was then removed from the infirmary and put into solitary confinement. This is actually a good thing. He knew for a fact that Spaz or his boys would gun for him now. This was the safest place in the prison. Adrian felt good about himself for the first time since arriving here.

He sat down with his back against the wall and laughed out loud.

Chapter Twenty-Four

March 15th, 2003. 9:00 am and the court had been called in session. Adrian was sitting in the defence box with his lawyer, Mr. Ron Mauler. Adrian was wearing a new suit, but even that didn't make him look any better. He had lost seventy pounds since his incarceration. His cheek bones stuck out and his eyes were sunken. His incarceration was very cruel on him physically and emotionally.

In the DA's corner were Andréa Shelton, Thomas Brown and Charles Huntington. They were working on the behalf of the State of New York.

Judge Ryan Silverman was the presiding judge in this case. Judge Silverman said, "Miss Shelton, let us hear your opening statement."

"Thank-you, your honour. Ladies and gentlemen of the jury, what you will hear in the next few weeks is testimony and evidence proving that Mr. Adrian Eisner is a premeditated murderer. He meticulously planned a military operation that killed forty-eight people and burnt twenty buildings to the ground, thus leaving seventy-four businesses out into the street.

You will hear evidence that proves that Mr Eisner personally killed seven people in cold blood. You will hear the defence tell you that Mr. Eisner was mentally insane at the time that these horrendous crimes took place. We have the proof that he was in fact able to make a conscious decision and tell the difference between right or wrong.

The defence will try to make you believe that the police department is responsible for Mr. Eisner's actions. Only an intelligent and sane man could have devised such a precision operation like the one that happened on October 03, 2002. The strike force didn't have any casualties or suffer a single injury. Could an insane man have the capacity to carry out such a brilliant military plan? I very much doubt it. He had to know exactly what he was doing.

It was premeditated murder; it was deliberate. We will prove to you his connection to the mob and how he used it to his advantage to stop police from conducting a murder investigation. You have no choice but to find the defendant guilty of all charges. Look deep in your heart and make the right decision. Don't let a cold blooded murderer back on the streets. Thank-you ladies and gentlemen."

"Mr. Mauler, are you ready to start with you're opening statement?" asked Judge Silverman.

Mr. Mauler replied, "Yes, thank-you your honour. Ladies and gentlemen of the jury, I will prove to you that none of this would have happened, if the police hadn't taken advantage of my client's situation. They put him in direct danger and provoked the incident to take place by using a press conference to lure Frank Azario to abduct my client. My client requested police assistance on several occasions and was denied.

The dire situations were in need of being corrected. My client had no choice but to take the law into his own hands. Without police assistance, my client was forced to act alone.

Most of you would have done the same thing if you were under such circumstances.

My client has a long history of severe mental illness and emotional problems that have plagued him for decades. He suffers from a disassociate state, during which his mind loses touch with reality and enters another world. When he is in this state, he is no longer under control of his actions. The environment and the situation around him dictate what actions he will take.

He will act without any thought involved. He acts on impulse only. I will prove that when he is in this state, he does not know the difference between what is right or wrong. His morals diminish and he acts on the situation, as he understands it to be the right thing to do.

I urge the jury to put themselves in his particular situations to understand why he acted the way he did. He is innocent of all crimes that he has been accused of.

The police department is solely responsible because of its incompetence to do its job. You have no choice but to acquit Mr. Eisner of all charges. Only then, will you sleep with a clear conscience that you did the right thing. I would like to thank the jury for their time."

Mr. Mauler then sat down beside Adrian and started to thumb through his paper work.

Judge Silverman asked, "Is the state ready to call their first witness?"

Shelton said, "Yes, your honour. We call Lieutenant Matt Ruzo to the stand."

Matt came in through the court doors and swore on the Bible to tell the truth. He then sat in the witness stand.

Miss Shelton asked, "When did you first meet Mr. Adrian Eisner?"

Matt replied, "That was September 21st, 2002. Detective Parsons and I were leading the investigation into a string of rapes and murders that were happening in our city. Adrian was our number one suspect. We met him during the interrogation."

"If it would please the court. I would like to enter exhibit 1-A into the record."

Judge Silverman said, "Let it be recorded as exhibit 1-A."

Miss Shelton then played the taped interrogation in its entirety. The jury watched carefully, ensuring not to miss any details.

Miss Shelton asked, "Lieutenant, what was your impression of Mr. Eisner?"

Mr. Mauler blurted out, "I object!! This is not relevant to the case. It is hearsay."

"I'm trying to establish a character profile of Mr. Eisner," Said Miss Shelton.

Judge Silverman replied, "Objection overruled, please answer the question Mr. Ruzo."

Matt said, "I found that Mr. Eisner was very calm and relaxed. He wasn't nervous during the interrogation at all. He looked extremely composed for a man in his situation. I had heard that he was an ill man. He didn't look at all sick to me."

Miss Shelton said, "What happened on Croton Damn Road?"

"My partner, my wife, and I were at the mercy of Jonathan Azario. He had a gun to my head and then I heard a shot.

When I looked up, Jonathan fell down with the back of his brains blown out. I got my gun and I was looking for the shooter. After about fifteen minutes I went to the car to radio in for back-up. That's when I saw five men with rifles get into two cars and drive away. One car was a limo and the other car fits the description of the defendant's vehicle.

ADRIAN

Later that day, Detective Parsons and I went to the Azario mansion to see Adrian. Upon arrival, I saw a Hummer in the driveway which matched the description of the car I saw at Croton Damn. I told Adrian that off the record I knew it was him, but I couldn't prove it without gaining access to the mansion. I also thanked him for saving our lives.

Off the record, Adrian told us that we were very welcome and that he wasn't going to admit to anything that may incriminate him."

Miss Shelton asked, "What do you know about the murder of Tony Lorenzo?"

Matt replied, "The most that I know about that is from a phone call from Mr. Eisner to plea for his evacuation from the mansion. He thought that Mr. Azario would order him to kill some one and that he would die too, if he didn't obey. I told him that no crime was committed and that we couldn't storm the mansion without countless lives being lost. We deal with the mob by using our brains not our guns.

I also heard a murder in progress according to the Manicotti tapes and the taped confession by Mr. Eisner himself."

Miss Shelton said, "I would like to record into evidence article 1-B."

Judge Silverman said, "It will be so recorded."

Miss Shelton then played all of the retrieved tapes from Manicotti's safe, which had not been damaged by the fire.

After that she said, "I would like to record into evidence article 1-C."

Andréa then played the tape of Adrian confessing to all the charges that were made. Adrian couldn't believe that he was betrayed by Lori. He had trusted her and thought that she was his friend. Now, he learned that she only did it to make the biggest bust of her career! Adrian lowered his head as he heard his voice on the tape.

Judge Silverman said, "It will be then recorded."

Miss Shelton then said, "That's all I have for this witness, your honour."

Judge Silverman said, "Mr. Mauler, you can now cross examine the witness."

Mr. Mauler said, "Thank-you, your honour. Lieutenant, what was the deal that you struck up with my client prior to his release?"

Matt replied, "The deal was that we would drop two charges against Mr. Eisner if he cooperated with us."

"What were the charges?"

"It was possession of an illegal firearm and discharging a firearm in city limits."

"Those were petty charges compared to what you wanted my client to do for you. You must have been very convincing for him to accept such a raw deal, unless he was too ill to make the right decision. What did you want my client to do for the police department?"

"We told him that his father Frank Azario would have him picked up after the news was released that all the charges against Adrian were dropped. This would instigate Azario to act.

Once Mr. Eisner was on the inside, he could then gather names from the payroll and relay the information to us. We would cross reference the names and come up with the real killer's identity."

Mauler then said, "You put a civilian in a mobster's home to do your dirty work for you and you had no plan of ever helping him to get out of there? You even had a press conference to make sure that all of New York City knew that my client was innocent of those crimes. You used him as a fall guy, just so that you could get the information you wanted. Isn't that correct? A yes or no answer will be sufficient."

"Yes."

"You had a profiler named Steve Dirk go over the taped interrogation with you. What were his findings?"

"He said that Mr. Eisner's character does fit the description of a serial killer and rapist. He noted that the profile did not match while the defendant was medicated with only two doses of medication. We did find that difficult to believe. Mr. Eisner's demenour was totally different after only two doses of medication."

Then Mauler said, "Dr. Jason Freemont knew very well that the medication would have this affect on Adrian, so that it why he used it to throw you off track. These are sedative

ADRIAN

drugs. After a long period of battling a mania, those drugs gave him a solid sleep that he desperately needed.

It was the sleep that made Adrian regain his conscience; he was calmed down by the sedative affects of the medication. That is why he looked to be above normal in his behaviour. Your honour, I have three medical reports from three different doctors that support these findings. I would like these to be entered into evidence as articles 1-D, 1-E and 1-F."

"Let it so be recorded."

Mr. Mauler said, "Is it not true that Mr. Eisner pleaded for you to get him out of the mansion, for fear that he would be forced to murder someone?

"Yes."

"Why didn't you help him?

"There was no crime committed at the time; it was only speculation. We had no reason to go in. Besides, we would never be allowed through those gates without a bloody fight."

"Didn't you tell Mr. Eisner that he may have to kill in order to stay alive?"

"Yes."

"Is it not true that if Mr. Eisner didn't kill Jonathan Azario, you would not be here today?"

"Yes."

"Is it not a fact that your partner, wife and perhaps hundreds of people were saved because of that one bullet?"

"Yes."

"When Mr. Eisner found himself being extorted for money and have five businesses destroyed by Vincent Manicotti's men, you did nothing to aid him. His sister was being held hostage by Manicotti and the police department still refused to get involved.

Why didn't the police department fulfil their duties and protect these people?"

Matt explained, "This was a gang war about to erupt. The police do not have the resources it would require to get involved. These organized crime families can easily wipe out an entire police force in a gun battle. Besides, we had to think of the hostage's well being. If we got involved, Donna Azrio would have been killed."

"Since the police force wouldn't do anything, Mr. Eisner was forced to save his sister and stop the total destruction of his businesses. Why was Mr. Eisner successful in his attempt and the police force couldn't?"

"The police force is not in the killing business.

We were not going to engage in a massive battle to save one person. Scores of people died in that massacre; the police don't operate that way. We use the diplomatic method when dealing with organized crime.

Even that would not have worked this time. If we had tried to contact Mr. Manicotti, the hostage would have died. All we could have done was monitor the situation and try to keep the public safe.

We had to watch and see if there was any chance that the police may be able to get involved to save the hostage. It was all a matter of time. Mr. Eisner did not give the police a chance to act; he took it upon himself to annihilate Manicotti and his empire in one massive blow."

Mauler said, "In other words, Mr. Eisner acted in the same manner as any other desperate man trying to save his only sister. He had no choice.

Every day, Manicotti would destroy one business until the Azario family would give in to the extortion. The financial burden was in the millions and the police needed more time.

It seems reasonable that Mr. Eisner would act this way, even without being severely mentally ill. He was acting in self defence. Something had to be done and the police negligence caused this incident to occur. If they had done their job, this would never have happened. I have no further questions for this witness, your honour."

Judge Silverman said, "Lieutenant, you may step down from the stand."

Adrian looked at Ron Mauler with confidence. It looked as if the case is swaying to his side. He sat back on the bench and smiled.

The case went on for weeks. Witness after witness testified their knowledge of Adrian and his actions. There was the testimony of Doris which only proved that Adrian had planned the massacre. The rest was nothing more than circumstantial evidence.

There was Dr. Ing's testimony that was shot down by Mr. Mauler. The defence lawyer showed evidence that Dr. Ing was incompetent. He showed the jury that Dr. Ing had eight malpractice suits filed against him in the last month alone. The doctor was being brought up in front of the Medical Review Board investigating why he had lost eight patients to suicide.

Mr. Mauler had Dr. Moss contradicting Dr. Ing's methods of treating Mr. Eisner. It was backed up by testimonies of three non-biased doctors.

It was proven that the current medication was the wrong drug prescribed and that Adrian was not fit to stand trial. Those were grounds for a mistrial. Mr. Mauler did not pursue a mistrial, he wanted an acquittal.

There was the private investigator Lori Metcalfe's testimony. It backed up the tapes. However, she testified that Mr. Eisner was suffering from severe emotional problems and mental distress. This backed up the medical reports from the four doctors who had already testified.

The case was now coming to an end. Mr. Mauler had one more witness to call. He said, "Your honour, I would like to call Adrian Eisner to the stand."

Adrian got up, took his oath and sat down in the witness stand.

Mr. Mauler said, "Tell me what happens to you when you enter a disassociate state."

Adrian replied, "I lose total control of my actions; there are no thoughts involved. There are no morals or right or wrong. It is impulse that drives my body into certain situations.

My mind goes blank; the environment or situation I am in is the driving force behind any action. This was caused by a trauma I suffered as a child. I was sexually assaulted. My disassociation was very useful at the time and so was the self-mutilation.

Unfortunately, I still have that ability for my mind to shut off and lose control. I was being treated for it, until I was incarcerated. I still suffer from those effects."

"Do you know the difference between right or wrong?"

"No, there are absolutely no thoughts involved. It is purely reactions to certain situations. There have been times where I have not even remembered doing certain things."

"Are you saying that all that has happened to you were strictly automatic reactions?"

"Yes."

"What happened on the night that you killed Juan Cortez?"

"It was a formal dinner and I had just temporarily taken the leadership of the organization. There were several members banding together as a mutiny against me. They thought that my position could be better filled by someone else, like one of them.

Mr. Cortez was the ring leader. Something had to be done; I was in a very threatening position.

The leadership had to stay within the family. If I didn't do something to win over the leadership, I may have even been killed for it. I couldn't show any weakness. My dark side took over and I was no longer in control. I walked up to Mr. Cortez, aimed my gun at his head and pulled the trigger.

Instantly, the leadership position was secure and the threatening situation was over. I won the respect of the other members and I was safe once again."

"What happened between you and Vincent Manicotti?

"We were just evacuating the area after attacking the mansion. I was the last one on the ground when I heard a shot.

I hit the dirt and saw Manicotti on his hands and knees, puking his guts out. He tried to take a shot at me, but the tear gas and smoke were too much for him.

He verbally threatened me and he still had a gun in his hand. I felt that if I turned my back on him, he would shoot me.

He threatened to come back and do it all over again; I was protecting my family and my property when I shot him in the head. I was also in a disassociate state where there were no thoughts or morals involved. I was locked into the Azario world, where threats are not to be taken lightly."

"What other mental conditions do you suffer from?

"I have bi-polar depression and psychosis. I was not treated at this time; I was unknowingly taking placebos. I was very ill."

"Didn't you have a new prescription already filled prior to the Manicotti massacre?"

"Yes I did. I had to save my sister at all costs. She means everything to me. The police wouldn't help. If I took my medication, she would have been killed. I would have never been able to pull that off, if I was treated. I had to save her!"

ADRIAN

Mr. Mauler said, "I have no further questions, your honour."

Judge Silverman asked, "Miss Shelton, do you wish to cross examine the witness?"

Andréa had already lost the argument that Adrian was in good mental health but she said, "Yes, thank-you, your honour. Mr. Eisner, you were not in immediate danger when Juan Cortez confronted you about your leadership. Were you?"

Adrian replied, "I most certainly was. I had twenty or more men with guns in their holsters, wanting to take the leadership away from me. I see that as a serious threat!"

"Don't you think you could have won the leadership without killing Mr. Cortez?"

Adrian laughed and said, "Wise guys are not diplomats. All business is done with a gun. You have to remember, this is organized crime. They tend not to talk too much; action speaks louder than words."

"What about Vincent Manicotti? He was no immediate threat to you."

"He had a gun in his hand. I took that as being immediate. The hatred Manicotti had for the Azarios was unbearable; he wouldn't think twice about shooting them in the back. The threat was very real."

"He was impaired by the tear gas and smoke. He couldn't possibly aim a gun and shoot you."

"He recovered enough to do that. I was there! He could've easily have shot me. He was a real threat and I couldn't let him do it. He had to be stopped."

"Those are two murders that are considered to be cold blooded murder by you, Adrian Eisner. You are so evil that while you were in prison, you bit off and ate Mr. Kowalski's penis. You left him there to bleed to death. Luckily the guards were able to rescue the man and take him to the infirmary."

Adrian explained, "That monster and seven of his friends had beaten me and sexually assaulted me while I was taking a shower. They left me for dead. I was mentally incapacitated for two months because of that attack.

Then, after my return back to the cell, he wanted me to be his boy or they would do it again. To save my self, I agreed to give him a sexual favour. Suddenly, I went into a disassociate state, blocking out the humility that I was feeling. I then had the darkness overcome my heart and soul. The only defence I had against this abuse, was to bite the damn thing off. This was self defence and I would do it again if I had to."

"This only proves how evil you really are! You have no consideration for life. You have no morals or remorse for what you have done. You are a cold blooded murderer. I have no further questions for this witness, your honour."

Judge Silverman asked, "Mr. Mauler, do you have any more witnesses?"

"No, your honour. The defence rests."

Judge Silverman said, "Miss Shelton, you may give your closing statement."

Andréa Shelton started. "Ladies and gentlemen of the jury. In the past few weeks you have heard evidence and testimony that proves beyond a reasonable doubt that Adrian Eisner is guilty of all charges.

He planned the entire mission and we showed you the proof of that. Mr. Eisner went into that mansion with the intent to kill as many people as possible. He can control his mental condition to his advantage, allowing him to commit horrendous crimes.

He is very intelligent and calculated in his actions. He doesn't show an ounce of remorse for the people he has killed. He has no morals and will do anything to get what he wants.

Mr. Eisner is a cold blooded murderer and must remain in prison for the rest of his life. Thank-you."

Judge Silverman said, "Mr. Mauler, you may go on with your closing statement."

"Thank-you, your honour. Ladies and gentlemen of the jury, you have heard the police department admitting to gross incompetence. They actually instigated this whole thing. Mr. Eisner would have been at home with his wife at this very minute, if the police had not involved him in something that they should have done themselves.

We proved to you that Mr. Eisner should not even be in court today. The evidence proves that he was very ill at the time these incidents happened. He was clinically insane. Even today, he is ill enough to be granted a mistrial.

Every killing was either in self defence or an attempt to save someone else. This was a very sick man who was forced into unthinkable situations. A sane man would have reacted in the same manner, which is why you must acquit Adrian Eisner. He is not a killer by choice. Everything is pure circumstance. Thank-you."

Ron Mauler sat down and whispered in Adrian's ear, "Cross your fingers. Miss Shelton gave a very strong cross examination of you. She might have been able to pin two murders on you. I just hope the insanity plea worked."

The judge then gave his final instructions to the jury and sent them off into deliberation.

There was a real surprise when the jury came to a verdict in only three hours.

The courtroom was again filled and ready to hear the verdict.

Judge Silverman said, "Members of the jury have you reached a decision?"

"We have your honour.

We, the jury, find the defendant not guilty of all charges."

Adrian was ecstatic; it was finally over! He was a free man. He went to the bench behind him and hugged his father and his sister. Trixie and the old man had been there every day without fail. They gave the support he so desperately needed.

Carol had never visited Adrian in prison or come to any of the trial. She had abandoned him for nearly six months.

He needed her support more than ever and she had not been there. After the celebration in the courtroom, Adrian had been released immediately.

The first thing he did when he got to the suite was pour himself a mug of draft and light a cigarette. It felt so good! But he was nurturing his bad habits once again. It had been a long time. He had been dry for months, but he felt he just had to have a beer.

This was a private party at the mansion and Adrian was the guest of honour. After a few hours, and much more beer, he started to wonder what was going through Carol's mind. He picked up the phone and dialled. "Hello."

"Hi honey. I'm out!!"

Carol paused for a minute and said, "Before we continue, I have something to say. It's not going to work between you and me. I decided to carry on with my life and see someone else.

I am very happy now and I wish that in time that you will understand. I will have the divorce papers sent to you tomorrow morning. I'm sorry Adrian; it just has to be this way."

Adrian replied, "That's what I thought you would say. You never came to see me once. The old Carol would never have done that. She would have been there to support me through the rough times. I'm sorry too. Good-bye Carol."

Adrian hung up the phone. He then picked it up again and phoned Mr. Azario downstairs. The phone rang and Azario said, "Hello."

"Sir, can I come down to talk to you? I have something very important to discuss with you."

"Yes, please come down. I'll have a beer waiting for you."

"Thank-you sir. I'll see you in a few minutes."

Three months later in the main dining hall of the Azario mansion, all the mob bosses were gathered for a formal dinner. Tonight was a true night to celebrate. Azario had steak and lobster on the menu. The best wine that money could buy was on the table.

Adrian was seated to the right of Azario. He and the old man were both wearing their maroon sashes.

Frank clapped his hands and a parade of waiters filed out of the kitchen with the main course on huge silver trays. Soon, the guests all had their meals placed in front of them. As usual, they were waiting for Frank to eat first. Frank didn't waste time; he dug right into his favourite meal.

After about an hour, the guests were waiting for Azario's routine speech.

Frank stood up and said, "Today is the most special day of all. I have had a great time working with you, but it is time for me to retire. My heath isn't as good as it used to be and I want to spend the rest of my days travelling around the world. I would like to introduce to you, my son Adrian Azario.

That's right. He had his name changed back to what it should be. He is the new leader of the empire. Please welcome him with a roar of applause."

The two men then exchanged sashes and seats. Adrian would now sit at the head of the table for many years to come. The guests were astonished with the news, but were very pleased at the same time. They all stood up in ovation to their new leader. A lot of things had happened to Adrian in the past. Now, it was time to make things happen in the future.

Adrian stood tall and signalled the guests to sit down and be quiet. He said, "You still remember me from the last dinner we had together. Today we celebrate the long reign that my father has held for nearly sixty years. Tonight I want you to honour my father in the same way as I do.

I respect and love this man. He is a hard worker and he has a firm hand. He was very fair and generous to those whom he could trust. I will never be able to fill his shoes; I will take my own path and lead you to a bright future. Adrian Azario will never let you down."

The End

PATRICK J. SCHNERCH

About the Author

He was born in Winnipeg. Manitoba. He grew up in the farming community of Camp Morton, Manitoba. In his childhood there were obvious signs of mental illness. He suffered severe mental and emotional problems which has plagued him from his childhood right up to present time.

He was diagnosed with bi-polar depression. Mr. Schnerch is now stable and living a productive life once again. Writing has become his saving grace.

Happily married, he now resides in Victoria, British Columbia, Canada. They live in a modest home with their dog, Blackie.

He found that the writing became therapeutic and increased his well being. ADRIAN became a character that evolved from the author's own experiences with mental illness.

Printed in the United States
1479600001B/43-138